CHAOS

IN

I0668248

THE

BLINK

OF

AN

EYE

PART SEVEN:
UNDER THE ALTAR

AWARD-WINNING
END TIMES SERIES BY
PATRICK HIGGINS

CHAOS IN THE BLINK OF AN EYE: PART SEVEN – SOULS UNDER THE ALTAR COPYRIGHT © 2021 PATRICK HIGGINS

Library of Congress
Cataloging in Publication Data
Paperback ISBN: 978-0-9992355-8-4

Published by
For His Glory Production Company

Publisher's note: This is a work of fiction. All names, characters, organizations, and incidents portrayed in this novel are the product of the author's imagination or are used fictitiously. Any resemblance to actual persons, living or dead, or events is entirely coincidental.

Manufactured in the United States of America
TO ORDER PATRICK HIGGINS' BOOKS IN PAPERBACK FORMAT (AND SOON IN HARD COPY) AT DEEP DISCOUNT PRICES:

www.patrickhigginsbooks.com

All books purchased on the site will be personally signed by the author and dedicated to the readers. They make the perfect gifts for holidays, birthdays, anniversaries, Mother's Day, Father's Day, and on and on.

Order signed copies now for family members, friends and loved ones.

Prologue...

After ridding the earth of more than a million Muslims, Salvador Romanero's next target became Christ followers.

In just a few short weeks, the Antichrist of the Bible declared the Word of God illegal, cleansed the internet of all things Christian, and detained millions of dissidents in his death camps, which had been promoted as rehabilitation camps.

Billions of Bibles had already been destroyed, many at book-burning festivities. Romanero's "spiritual cleansing" campaign kept advancing on all fronts. But just knowing millions more had yet to be discovered, not to mention that countless millions of Christians were still living in hiding, felt to Salvador like acid being poured on an open wound.

Until all Bibles were ultimately located, confiscated, and later burned, and all possessors were killed for their crimes against him, the constant stabbing at his insides would continue to feel like needles piercing him everywhere, looking to destroy his wickedly corrupt soul.

The key to scrubbing all things "Jesus" from the minds and hearts of the masses was mostly intended for the youth. Salvador the Great didn't want them to ever be exposed to the Gospel of Jesus Christ. Which was why he had to keep suppressing the Truth to them at all costs!

Romanero wasn't the least bit concerned with citizens reading the Quran or any other religious books which led to nowhere in the end. The Word of God was altogether different, as it ultimately led to the salvation of the archenemy of his soul—the Lord Jesus Christ.

Once the Bible was no longer accessible to anyone, and those who believed what it taught were no longer alive, the *Miracle Maker* would be one step closer to achieving his ultimate goal of becoming godlike and, therefore, infallible in the eyes of most.

But now that Yahweh's 144,000 sealed men had been sent out on their Missions, Salvador the Great would be in for the fight of his life…

Main Characters:

<u>Clayton Holmes and Travis Hartings</u> – Co-founders of www.LASRglobal.org. Now that Salvador Romanero had been identified as the long-foretold Antichrist of the Bible, the two leaders were putting plans in motion that would hopefully counter some of Romanero's advances. Both knew if they sat back and did nothing, they would be annihilated by the enemy without even putting up a fight.

<u>Pastor Jim Simonton</u> – 51 – Lead Pastor at Southeast Michigan Evangelical Church. Left behind with everyone else, the devastated pastor, after realizing he was a false convert—and that his preaching had led many from his church to be left behind as well—quickly repented of his sins and was determined to never again preach a false or watered-down Gospel. In short: there would be no more false converts at his hands.

<u>Tom Dunleavey</u> – 65 – Catholic priest who tried consoling Brian Mulrooney the day after the disappearances. After both men had similar dreams for three straight nights, they met for a friendly debate. It ultimately led to Tom's leaving the Catholic church.

<u>Dick and Sarah Mulrooney</u> – Married for more than 30 years, the solid relationship they always had was showing small cracks in the dam, after their son Brian converted to Christianity and distanced himself from the Catholic church.

<u>Braxton Rice</u> – Chief of security and vetting for Clayton Holmes and Travis Hartings and their upstart organization the *End Times Salvation Movement*.

<u>Doctor Lee Kim</u> – Lead IT man for the website www.LASRglobal.org, and all other *End Times Salvation Movement* IT operations.

<u>Tamika Moseley</u> – 30 – NYC taxi driver. Lost her two sons, Jamal and Dante, and mother, Ruth Ferguson, on the day of the Rapture. Tamika was driving two businessmen from LaGuardia Airport to the Waldorf-Astoria Hotel when all hell broke loose, and one of her passengers vanished in the back seat of her taxicab. God ultimately used her to connect Brian Mulrooney and Charles Calloway in the days following the disappearances.

<u>Brian Mulrooney</u> – 35 – Moved from New York City to Ann Arbor, Michigan, after graduating from Notre Dame University and being recruited by the Marriott Corporation. Mulrooney was at Michigan Stadium with his childhood friend, Justin

Schroeder, to watch the Ohio State-Michigan football game, when Schroeder suddenly disappeared along with thousands of others.

Charles Calloway – 44 – Successful Florida businessman who was in New York City to teach success principles to his fellow colleagues at the time of the disappearances. Calloway was inside Tamika Moseley's cab when his colleague, Richard Figueroa, suddenly vanished in the backseat next to him. The son of a preacher, it didn't take long for Calloway to piece things together and realize it was the Rapture of the Church, and that he had been left behind.

Jacquelyn Swindell Mulrooney – 31 – Lost her husband at Michigan Stadium when he was killed by an object that fell from the sky, after a plane collided with a Goodyear blimp hovering above the stadium. Swindell also lost the child in her womb at that time. After meeting Brian Mulrooney inside the stadium, she offered to drive him home after his car was destroyed in the mayhem. As she did her best to cope in this strange new world, without her husband and unborn child, she was grateful for Brian's friendship, and agreed to join him in his quest for answers...

President Jefferson Danforth and First Lady Melissa Danforth – The First Family were at Camp David with family and friends when the disappearances happened. Many vanished at the Presidential retreat, including the President's and First Lady's daughter, their son-in-law, and all five of their grandchildren (including the unborn child). President Danforth's mother also perished that day. She suffered a fatal heart attack after seeing her grandchildren vanish into thin air.

Salvador Romanero – 33 – As the world mourned the loss of more than a billion people—either by death or disappearance—Satan raised up the young lawyer from Spain as his main agent in human form. No one knew it yet, but the young phenom was about to take the world completely by storm and become the unchallenged leader of the world...

Doctor Meera Singh – 50s – ETSM Doctor at safe house number one, in Chadds Ford, Pennsylvania. Meera was 5'5" in height and on the thin side.

Joaquim Guzman – 16 – Married to Leticia, who was the first to give birth at safe house number one, when she was only 12. Joaquim accepted the child as his own when he married Leticia. His parents were taken in the Rapture while working at the Kennett Square farm before it was turned in a safe house.

Julio and Marta Gonzalez – Julio (34) and Marta (32) were the parents of Leticia Guzman. Julio had owned a successful construction business in Providence, Rhode

5

Island, before relocating to safe house number one with his family. He was one of two construction foremen on site.

Tony Pearsall – (39) – Construction worker from Nevada. He was one of the first to be invited to safe house number one and as a construction foreman.

When he opened the fifth seal,

I saw under the altar the souls

of those who had been slain because of the word of God and the

testimony they had maintained.

They called out in a loud voice,

"How long, Sovereign Lord, holy and true, until you judge the

inhabitants of the earth and avenge our blood?"

Then each of them was given a white robe, and they were told to wait

a little longer, until the full number of their fellow servants, their

brothers and sisters, were killed just as they had been

(Revelation 6:9-11).

1

AS HUMANITY STRUGGLED TO recover from the mass tribulation bombarding the planet, on which many were feeling increasingly trapped, and with thousands of Christian dissidents being killed every day, in Salvador Romanero's death camps—labeled as rehabilitation camps—God had supernaturally sealed 144,000 Jewish men for Himself.

When Yahweh commanded the angels to hold back the winds until the 144,000 were sealed, He used that time to teach them the saving Gospel message of His son, and Israel's Messiah, Yeshua HaMaschiach, using His Two Witnesses to instruct them.

Prior to being sealed, these virgin men were well versed in the Torah. All had loving hearts and an unshakable faith in Jehovah God. In the months leading up to their sealing, the Most High used His Two Witnesses to instruct their pupils, in vivid detail, on what would transpire on Planet Earth, and which role each would play during this unprecedented time.

Just knowing they were prophesied about thousands of years ago, in the Book of Revelation, filled them all with unspeakable honor and joy.

No one heard a sound at the time of their sealing. There was no global mayhem like what had followed the disappearances, nearly two years ago.

In fact, the only proof that it took place at all was that the 144,000 suddenly appeared all over the world, a few weeks ago, preaching the infallible Word of God outside of synagogues, Catholic churches, and at all other worship houses that still preached false or mixed messages. They also preached in town squares, and on crowded street corners.

Much like the Apostle Paul, the most hostile environments the 144,000 encountered, were at these places of worship where the congregants were fully convinced that they knew the Truth, even though they really didn't.

Hoping to pluck them out of the religiosity that had kept them living in spiritual darkness, their message wasn't well received by most. They were vilified by many. But those who received the Message they preached welcomed them warmly.

But unlike Paul, whose ministry spanned more than three decades, their remaining time on earth would be extremely short before their King, Yeshua

HaMaschiach, returned to Planet Earth to usher in His thousand year Millennial Kingdom.

Even though they were spread all across the planet, by being plugged directly into the very same Source, this special, anointed, chosen group of men didn't have to resort to conference or video calls. All received their daily downloads from Yahweh God Himself.

While these young men didn't have the power to send plagues or perform supernatural miracles—like God's Two Olive Trees—what they did have was His full supernatural protection to preach the Word, without harm from the enemy. By having these special seals on their foreheads, no worldly or spiritual harm would ever befall them.

In short, whereas their two instructors would be killed at the midway point of the seven-year tribulation period—with their dead bodies being put on full display—the 144,000 would survive until the end.

Remarkably, these young men represented a precise mix of 12,000 Jewish virgin men from each of the Twelve Tribes of Israel.

The fact that God had sealed exactly 12,000 from each Tribe, was already mind-numbing enough.

For thousands of years, since the burning of their genealogy records, most Israelis had no way of tracking their ancestries. They knew they were Jews, but most didn't know which tribes they belonged to.

Even with their genealogies in tatters, it didn't pose even the slightest challenge for Jehovah God to choose exactly 12,000 men, from each tribe named after Jacob's twelve sons: Reuben, Simeon, Levi, Judah, Manasseh, Naphtali, Gad, Asher, Issachar, Zebulun, Joseph (Ephraim), and Benjamin.

Noticeably missing from the twelve tribes listed in Revelation 7:5-8, was the tribe of Dan. When Jacob (also known as Israel) had moved his family to Egypt, because of the famine in Canaan, he adopted Joseph's two sons, Manasseh and Ephraim, as his own.

The twelve tribes turned into thirteen, when Jacob gave Joseph a "double portion" blessing. This meant his two sons, Ephraim and Manasseh each became a tribe, rather than just the one tribe of Joseph.

However, the thirteen became twelve again, as the tribe of Levi was dedicated to the Lord and received no land. The Levites were given certain cities and was the tribe of the priesthood, that received tithes from the other twelve tribes who tithed from their land.

9

The fact that Levi was once again represented in Revelation, was quite symbolic, indicating that the priesthood was over. Whether Yahweh had disqualified Dan for service during the Tribulation period, due to the Danites' embrace of idolatry, or because they had declined in numbers and influence, one thing was certain, the 144,000 sealed men were Jews, not Jehovah's Witnesses, as was clearly recorded in the Book of Revelation.

Even more remarkable, the vitriolic hate speech these young men preached, that had been outlawed in the world, was being delivered in the language of the people in the countries to which they had been sent.

In short, everyone heard them speaking in their own languages. Even if they didn't know it, they were all having an Acts 2 moment, when everyone heard Jesus' Disciples preaching to them in their own languages.

And much like them, while most rejected the messages they preached, they nevertheless marveled...

"How did they do that?" was the outcry of so many.

Regardless of language, the Message they preached was that Yeshua was the Son of Yahweh God, and Israel's long-awaited Messiah, and the rightful King of the Jews to the Jew first, then the Gentile.

THOSE ON SALVADOR ROMANERO'S surveillance team, who were given the assignment to monitor every move the 144,000 made—from the *Miracle Maker* himself—knew exactly where each man had been relocated.

Using high-tech surveillance, all had been definitively identified, as they sat under the tutelage of the two whackos at the Wailing Wall in Jerusalem, before being dispersed elsewhere.

How they got to those locations was altogether different. But all were still very much on their radar screens. Then again, it's not like they were trying to hide. They wanted to be seen and heard!

Peculiarly enough, the instant they stopped preaching, it's like they became ghostlike. Even the most high-tech spying gadgets on the planet couldn't detect them. It was mind-boggling to say the least...

In a world where the Christian Bible had already been outlawed, anyone else caught speaking the words these Jewish preachers boldly spoke out in public, without a shred of fear, would have been incarcerated by now. Or killed!

It had only been a few weeks, but for the life of them, Romanero's top intel advisors—not to mention his numerous followers—couldn't comprehend why these heretics were free to keep preaching, without fear of repercussion or being harmed.

Was it because Salvador the Great still wished to extend love toward them, despite their constant rebukes of him?

Or, more ominously, was he powerless from silencing them, like they sensed was the case with the Two Men in Jerusalem?

If Romanero had the power to kill them, wouldn't they have already been wiped from the face of the earth by now? Wouldn't the *Man of Peace* have ordered them all to be executed—one by one—at the Wailing Wall, before they even had the chance to leave Israel?

Most were starting to wonder, much like the straggly Two Ancients preaching the same nonsensical messages in Jerusalem, if these men really were untouchables. How could they believe otherwise, when it seemed all Salvador the Great could do was observe in silence, completely powerless from retaliating against them?

This concerned them deeply…

2

AT 1 P.M., CLAYTON HOLMES felt his Sat-phone vibrating in his coat pocket. It was a message from Travis Hartings: *We need to meet...*
Holmes typed back: *Why's that?*
Hartings replied: *Not sure, actually, but I feel as strongly about it as I did with all past dreams we've shared.*
Clayton scratched his head. For safety reasons, the two men had agreed at the outset that they wouldn't reside at the same safe houses, and would only meet if it was an emergency. He typed: *Are you sure about this, Travis? I've had no such inclination.*
Positive!
Okay, when?
ASAP!
Clayton sighed, then typed: *I'll leave in a few minutes. See you at the usual meeting spot at 3 p.m.*
I'll do my best to be on time.
Likewise, partner. Be careful...
You too... Hartings powered down his Sat-phone and was on the road 15 minutes later.
The usual meeting spot for the two End Times Salvation Movement leaders was 80 miles north of Atlanta, in Ellijay, Georgia, nestled in the North Georgia Mountains, at the southern end of the Appalachian Mountains.
Both men arrived in Ellijay at around 3 p.m. They met in the parking lot of a restaurant they had often frequented a few miles away from the safe house, before it was forced to close its doors forever after the all-out attack on the Western Hemisphere, which caused power to be lost in the U.S. for more than half a year.
From there, Travis followed Clayton the short distance to their subterranean bunker. They parked their motorcycles behind a thicket of tall bushes in the woods, then draped a camouflage covering, which they kept hidden there, over them.
Seeing that the coast was clear, they unlocked the three locks, opened then closed the hatch leading to their subterranean hiding spot, and climbed

down into the hole as quickly as they could, praying no one had detected them, including possible squatters.

This location was among the first parcels of land the *ETSM* had purchased in the Atlanta vicinity. It was the designated location at which the two leaders would meet if contact between them was ever broken.

If one of them didn't show up, chances were good either he had been arrested and was on his way to Romanero's death camps, or he was already with Jesus—one outcome bad, the other eternally blissful.

Since they would be traveling together—the first time since their surprise visit to safe house number one last Christmas—they made sure to put a contingency plan in place, just in case, which Hartings sent to their head of cyber security, Dr. Lee Kim, before leaving for Ellijay.

For now, only Dr. Kim and Charles Calloway knew about this trip.

Unlike all other properties that were part of the initial bulk purchase, that were quickly bulldozed before subterranean hiding locations were constructed, the Ellijay location, which used to be a pumpkin and watermelon farm, was left completely intact.

The only part of the 5-acre property that had been tampered with, was a very small subterranean safe house they had built near the back of the property, farthest away from the main road.

By design, they left the five aboveground buildings to remain in their decrepit conditions. Deemed worthless, with absolutely no cash value, they figured while they might draw the attention of a few vagrants, no one else would have an interest in them, making it the perfect meeting place for Holmes and Hartings, whenever it was needed.

The small underground 10' by 12' space was basic in every sense of the word. It had no electricity, no solar panels, or any kind of technology whatsoever. There wasn't even a toilet. If they needed to relieve themselves, they had to climb up to the surface to do it.

The only things down there were two cots—which were too small for Holmes 6'5" frame to stretch out on—a small wooden table in between them with two Bibles on it, a few cases of bottled water stacked in a corner, a few fuel containers filled to the brim with gasoline, a metal cabinet full of MREs to last a couple of weeks, some toiletries and a first aid kit.

The reason for the metal cabinet was to prevent mice and all other vermin and insects from getting to them.

In short, nothing about this place comforted the two leaders in the least. To them, it was more of a safe space, not a safe house.

13

Only the select few in the organization knew this place existed. Their former chief of security, Braxton Rice, personally appointed the handful of men and women who built the simple underground hideaway for their leaders. Now that their fallen comrade had become a martyr at the hands of Antichrist—a soul under the altar—Clayton and Travis still hadn't found Rice's replacement.

Both believed it would be a mammoth challenge to be sure...

In the dozen or so times the two *ETSM* leaders had met in Ellijay, this would be only the second time they would be spending the night there.

It didn't go well for Clayton the first time. After being down in the small hole in the ground for just two hours, he felt claustrophobic and started freaking out.

When he could no longer stand the walls closing in on him, he climbed out of the hole and slept in the brush where their motorcycles were parked, silently vowing that he would never sleep there again. Yet there he was...

After consuming two MREs each, they read scripture together and prayed for nearly three hours for their organization. They also asked God to reveal to them both why they were in Ellijay in the first place.

As day turned into night, Clayton once again questioned his partner's intuition in this matter. "Sorry to keep asking, Travis, but are you sure about this?"

Travis grimaced. "Hope it wasn't my tired brain playing tricks on me!"

"You and me both!" Holmes sighed. The fact that he hadn't discerned the same thing himself only added to his mounting skepticism. "So, what do you wanna do?"

"I say we give it the night. If nothing happens come morning, I'll chalk it up as my sleep-deprived imagination running wild on me, and we can head back to our safe houses."

Clayton gulped hard at the thought. *Hope I last the night!*

Travis saw his partner's fearful reflection dimly illuminated by the battery-operated lamp on the table. He silently prayed there wouldn't be a repeat performance, and he would wake up to find Clayton sleeping in the brush again. "Still love me, brother?"

Clayton laid down on his cot. "I'll let you know in the morning."

Travis burst out in laughter. "Look at the bright side. With no one here to disturb us, we'll sleep like babies tonight. Lord knows I need it."

Clayton scratched his left thigh. "Sleep like babies? Ha! That's easy for you to say. Your feet won't be hanging off the bed all night!"

"For the record," Hartings said, his mouth stretched in a yawn, "I'm not crazy about sleeping in these confined quarters either. This place gives me the willies."

Holmes sighed. "Guess I need to keep it in perspective. Dreadful as this place is, it's like paradise compared to what our brothers and sisters are suffering in Romanero's prisons."

"Well said, partner!" Hartings replied, with another hearty yawn. "At the very least, it's good seeing you again. It's been a while..."

"Likewise, Travis..."

Travis rolled onto his side. "By the way, when's Cornelius moving into your safehouse?"

Clayton shook his head in the near darkness. "Truth be told, I thought he'd be there by now."

"So, what's the hold up?" asked Travis.

Clayton frowned. "He's having difficulty breaking away from his three rebellious sons. I love my nephews and don't want them to perish. I used to share the Word with them all the time. They always seemed receptive to it, but look at them now..."

"I pray for the four of them every day."

Clayton fought back tears. "Thanks, partner."

"Look at the bright side, one down, three to go, right?"

Holmes nodded agreement. "Just hope my nephews get saved soon, before the salvation window closes for good." He sighed. "Hopefully when I get back, my brother will already be there."

"Amen to that!" Travis reached over to turn off the lamp.

Clayton asked, "Would it be okay if I kept the light on?"

"Suit yourself! Just hope you don't see too many critters or creepy crawlies climbing the walls."

Holmes gulped at the notion.

At that, Travis drifted off to sleep, still wearing the coat he brought with him.

3

TRAVIS HARTINGS WOKE EARLIER than usual to complete darkness, after having a new dream. He powered on his Sat-phone for illumination, and saw his partner sitting on the other cot rubbing his throbbing forehead, due to total sleep deprivation.

Without looking at Travis, Clayton said, "Let me guess, you had a dream that we have to travel back to the cabin in Oak Ridge..."

Travis nodded at him. "You too?"

"Affirmative," Holmes said, still shocked that he had slept at all. "This further explains your prompting yesterday to meet here."

Travis nodded agreement. "Was thinking the same thing..."

"But couldn't we have had these dreams at our separate quarters?"

"I'm sure we could have, but that wouldn't explain my prompting to come here. Come to think of it, we've never had shared dreams apart from each other."

Clayton yawned, then stretched his arms above his head. His knees and lower back ached from sleeping on a cot that was intended for someone much smaller than himself. "True. But why the cabin in Tennessee?"

Travis shrugged his shoulders. "Beats me. Your guess is as good as mine. But it's better than remaining here!"

"I heard that! No chance I'm sleeping here tonight!"

The way he said it made Travis laugh.

The last time the two *ETSM* leaders were at the Oak Ridge cabin was when they brought Jefferson Danforth there, after whisking him out of the subterranean location 50 miles west of Washington D.C., before he was ultimately taken to Coeur d'Alene, Idaho.

They left the cabin that day with no intention of ever returning.

Apparently, God had other plans...

After consuming a quick breakfast and brushing their teeth aboveground, they filled the storage compartments on their bikes with as much food and water as they could fit inside them—just in case—then mounted their fully-fueled motorcycles for the 138-mile trek due north, to the cabin in Oak Ridge.

Thanks to secret service agent, Anthony Galiano, Daniel Sullivan—who spent much of his time in Idaho with Jefferson Danforth and Amy Wong—received daily updates from his good friend and fellow agent in Washington.

In his last briefing, Galiano warned that all license plates were being scanned looking for Christian or Muslim dissidents, and even those who were out badmouthing Romanero in public. In short, the officers didn't first need a reason, such as speeding or reckless driving.

If the search came back as an "Enemy of the Planet", that motorist would be pulled over and the appropriate action would be taken, to include killing the subject or subjects occupying the vehicle, if they became unruly or if they resisted arrest. Even if the search came back as "unknown" or "unaffiliated", the officers on the scene were nevertheless ordered to pull the motorist over, and start asking questions, at gunpoint, if necessary.

Mindful of this, Travis followed behind his partner at a healthy distance, in case they encountered law enforcement officials. Bottom line: it would be better for only one of them to get pulled over than for both of them to.

Holmes and Hartings prayed it wouldn't come to that. As an added precaution, the license plates displayed on the backs of their vehicles were partially covered with hardened putty which resembled mud.

While this infraction alone would be more than enough for law enforcement to pull them over, it was a risk they felt they had to take.

Hopefully, God would protect them from that ever happening…

Holmes and Hartings arrived at the Oak Ridge cabin just after 11 a.m. EST. They parked their motorbikes in the garage, quickly closing the door behind them. Clayton hurried out back to the storage shed for one of the gasoline cans that were kept there, to refuel their cycles in case they encountered danger and had to make a quick getaway.

If Braxton was still alive, he would already be out checking the perimeter making sure the coast was clear, then doing counter sweeps to make sure they weren't being spied on.

Clayton quickly dismissed the thought. Even if he was still alive, he wouldn't have accompanied them on this trip.

Vague as their dream had been, the one thing they both knew for certain was that they were instructed to travel to the cabin alone, meaning just the two of them and no one else, even if they didn't know who or what they might encounter there.

Clayton went back inside to find Travis lighting a few candles to combat the mustiness filling his nostrils. The two then swept the cabin and peeked out all windows looking for anything out of the ordinary. Aside from the fireplace being messy, everything looked as it did last time they were there. Nothing appeared to be missing.

Seeing nothing, no one rather, Clayton scratched his head. "Guess we wait. If we end up sleeping here tonight, it should be down in the basement where there are no windows for possible onlookers to spot us."

"Agreed." Travis blew into his hands trying to warm them. "This place still reminds me of Miss Evelyn. The meals she cooked for us!"

Clayton smiled wearily. "What I wouldn't do for her fried chicken and homemade biscuits right about now!"

"You and me both. I'm tired of eating MREs."

"Speaking of Miss Evelyn, I plan on visiting her on the way back to my safe house. Hopefully, she'll cook for me when I'm there." Holmes smiled at the thought. "Plus, it'll be good to see Charles and Deacon Stone again. It's been a while. I miss them all."

"Me too." Travis stretched his arms above his head as high as they would go, before bending down to attempt touching his toes. Not surprisingly, he fell short by a few inches. He hadn't succeeded at this task in many years. "Why don't we go out back and fire up the generator and gather some firewood?"

"Sounds like a plan, partner…"

The two men went and grabbed as many logs from the stack of firewood as their still-frozen hands could hold.

Hugging the logs in their arms, they took a moment to survey the back of the property, and the surrounding perimeter, not knowing how different the topography would look three days from now.

Satisfied that everything seemed okay, they hurried back to the front of the cabin as quickly and as quietly as they could. Upon reaching the front of the property, they were shocked to see a young man standing mere inches away from the front door they had left partially open.

Travis dropped the logs he was carrying onto the porch. His knees became wobbly, and he collapsed onto the wooden surface. Head down, he was too afraid to glance up. Terror stabbed at his insides, fearing the worst.

His mind raced back to their surprise visit to safe house number one in Chadds Ford, Pennsylvania, last Christmas Eve, and the fear in Brian's eyes upon seeing hundreds of intruders on *his* side of the wall.

Only now, *he* was on the surprise end of this unexpected encounter with this complete stranger.

After a brief stare down with the young man whom Clayton seriously doubted was older than a teenager, he fearfully scanned the front of the property. Not seeing a vehicle of any kind—not even a motorized scooter, bicycle, or skateboard—his first thought was where had he come frcm?

Had he walked there? Was he a squatter or a vagrant looking to rob them? Or worse, had he been lying in wait inside the cabin all along to ambush them once they arrived?

Holmes wasn't concerned about being overpowered physically by him. He towered over the young man by at least eight inches, and outweighed him by at least 100 pounds. But why was he here in the first place? His question was about to be answered...

"Shalom, Clayton! Shalom, Travis!"

Clayton blinked hard. "Who are you, and how do you know our names?" he demanded to know, in between heavy breaths.

"My name is Moishe. I come in peace, in the name of Yeshua HaMaschiach!"

Moishe? "Are you the reason we came here?"

A warm smile crossed the young man's face. "I am..."

Travis slowly tipped his eyes up to find the young man's eyes fully ablaze, like two lasers locked onto their targets.

Moishe extended his right hand and helped him to his feet.

Travis leaned on the natural-colored wooden fence that wrapped around the entire cabin, to collect himself. His body still quaked in terror. "How can we know for sure you are who you say you are?"

The young man smiled. "I know about your dream. The two of you were instructed to travel here alone, right?"

The two *ETSM* leaders exchanged astonished glances.

Moishe went on, "The reason I know this is that Yahweh instructed me to meet you both here. He is the One who ordained this divine appointment! So, relax, brothers, you're safe with me!"

The radiance on the young man's face rendered the two leaders speechless. His eyes sparkled like diamonds; his warmth felt like a sunbeam on their faces.

Yet, as comforting as this young man's words sounded, Travis needed more convincing. "Is there anything else you can tell us?"

"This place just happened to be the first property you purchased after the Rapture, shortly before you started the End Times Salvation Movement. Am I right?"

19

Clayton brushed off a shiver. *Is this man a friend or a foe in disguise?* He shot another desperate glance at his partner, before his eyes quickly volleyed back to their visitor. "How do you know these things?"

Travis bit his lower lip. "Since you seem to know so much about our organization, is there anything else you can tell us?"

"Alright, how about this?" Moishe cleared his throat, then declared, "Keep fighting the Good Fight. Pray for me as I pray for you. Yahweh is with us! How's that?"

Holmes and Hartings exchanged more astonished glances. The hairs on their arms stood at full attention, as if just encountering a stiff wind.

Moishe waited patiently until he knew he had their full undivided attention, to further blow their minds. "The reason I know these things is that I'm one of the one hundred and forty-four thousand!"

Clayton's eyes doubled in size. He tilted his head one way then the next. "As in the one hundred and forty-four thousand mentioned in the Book of Revelation?" As if blinders had just been removed, it made perfect sense. *Of course, a young Jewish male!*

Moishe nodded yes. "And to think I never had an interest in reading the New Testament until just recently. I had excellent instructors."

"The Two Witnesses in Jerusalem?" asked Travis.

Moishe grinned at them. "Another thing I recently discovered was that I come from the tribe of Judah. All my life I never knew this..."

Clayton's mind was completely blown. There were no trumpets announcing this man's arrival. No "Fear nots!" like the angels had done when interacting with humans in the scriptures. But Holmes also knew God often worked in humble settings. "I can't tell you what an honor it is to meet you, Moishe! I knew you'd be young, but you look like a kid to me!"

Moishe chuckled. "Why don't we head inside. I have so much to tell you."

The young man helped them reclaim the firewood that had been scattered about the front porch and followed them inside.

Holmes and Hartings were so excited they could hardly contain themselves...

4

ONCE THE FIRE WAS up to full height, and two space heaters were turned on, Travis took a quick shower then brewed coffee for himself—which he made sure to pack along with plenty of creamers and sugar.

He joined Clayton and Moishe in the living room. Both were seated on leather chairs sipping hot tea.

Clayton said, "Compared to last night in Ellijay, this is just perfect!"

"Amen to that, partner!" Travis said with a grin. "It's good to be back."

"Hear, hear..." Holmes said, raising his teacup. In a world where they were being hunted, they felt safe being with this young man, protected.

Mindful of what was about to strike the planet, Moishe was more subdued than they were. He took a few small sips of his beverage and came to the point. "The reason for this meeting of sorts is to inform you both that the two of you have been given the most wonderful blessing and responsibility by Yahweh Himself, to house many of His chosen servants."

Holmes and Hartings both sensed this might happen someday; they even announced it at the formation of the *ETSM*. But now that it *was* happening, chills raced up and down their spines.

Clayton had his chair in the reclining position with his feet propped up. He took a few deep breaths to calm himself. "That's always been our hope!"

Moishe nodded that he already knew that. "Most of my brothers will reside in Jewish households. But as more and more Jews migrate back to our beloved Israel, we'll still need places to stay until Yahweh calls us back there on that appointed day," he said, with an expectant glow on his face.

Hartings scratched the top of his head. "I need to ask; how'd you get here?"

"This was where Yahweh sent me when I left Israel. Been staying at your cabin ever since."

"Really?" Holmes was aghast. "Nice knowing it's been put to good use in our absence. But we didn't see you here when we arrived?"

"That's because I wasn't here! I was out doing Yahweh's business. I returned soon after the two of you arrived..."

21

"What was your mode of transportation? Surely you didn't walk here..." Hartings paused. "Or did you?"

Moishe leaned up in his chair and eyeballed the two men. "Haven't you ever wondered how Yahweh gathered me and my brothers all in Jerusalem, so we could be taught by the Two Witnesses before being scattered to the four corners of the earth? I assure you we didn't board charter planes..."

Holmes and Hartings looked at each other and shook their heads in disbelief. Both knew what the other was thinking, *Did he suddenly appear out of thin air?* Had the Rapture not happened nearly two years ago, the very notion would have been inconceivable.

Even with the Rapture, it was still a staggering revelation!

Moishe smiled. "Are you familiar with Acts, chapter eight, verses twenty-six to forty?"

Hartings rubbed his chin as if deep in thought. "Are you referring to when an angel of the Lord told Philip to go down from Jerusalem to Gaza, where he met an Ethiopian eunuch?"

The smile on Moishe's face widened. "Precisely! This man was an important official in charge of all the treasury of the queen of the Ethiopians. On his way home from Jerusalem, where he had gone to worship, he was sitting in his chariot reading the Book of Isaiah the prophet."

Clayton shook his head in awe. "Yeah, the Spirit told Philip to go to that chariot and heard the man reading Isaiah the prophet. When Philip asked him if he understood what he was reading, he replied, 'How can I, unless someone explains it to me?'"

Moishe nodded, then recited the following verses, "The eunuch was reading Isaiah fifty-three to be precise: 'He was led like a sheep to the slaughter and as a lamb before its shearer is silent, so he did not open his mouth. In his humiliation he was deprived of justice. Who can speak of his descendants? For his life was taken from the earth.'"

Moishe became teary-eyed. "These were the very verses Yahweh used to open my spiritual eyes..." He started weeping uncontrollably.

Clayton searched the young man's face. All he could think about was Zechariah 12:10: *And I will pour out on the house of David and the inhabitants of Jerusalem a spirit of grace and supplication. They will look on me, the one they have pierced, and they will mourn for him as one mourns for an only child, and grieve bitterly for him as one grieves for a firstborn son.* It was as if that passage had been tattooed onto his forehead.

For whatever reason, this incident forced Travis' mind back to when he and Clayton had met the Danforths for a Bible study at the White House. When the First Lady had heard enough and angrily stormed out of the room, the President started weeping right in front of them.

The two *ETSM* leaders didn't know what to do to possibly comfort him. All Travis could think was, what does one say when seated before a weeping President, despairing over his wife's spiritual blindness?

That's precisely how he felt now being in the company of one of God's 144,000 sealed servants, knowing his tears represented the mourning of the One his own people had rejected as their Messiah, even killing Him.

It was too much to take in all at once.

Moishe took a few moments to compose himself, then said, "You know the rest of the story. They came to some water and Philip baptized him. When they came up out of the water, the Spirit of the Lord suddenly took Philip away, and the eunuch did not see him again, but went on his way rejoicing, as Philip appeared at Azotus and traveled about, preaching the gospel in all the towns until he reached Caesarea."

The young man's eyes sparkled even more, after just being washed by his own tears. "We are merely continuing what Yahweh Himself had instructed Philip to do, in the brief time he roamed the earth..."

The two *ETSM* leaders nearly fell off their chairs.

"Some mode of transportation you have!" said Hartings, the former auto industry executive. "Must be nice having your own time machine. I could make a killing selling those things," he joked.

Moishe laughed, then grew more serious. "You should expect a thousand of us to arrive at your selected properties within the next three days. More will come later after things settle down a bit. Those of us who will stay in your safe houses will inhabit the locations within the closest proximities, to where we have been directed to preach the Word of God.

"The first location to be visited by one of us will be in Chadds Ford, Pennsylvania. That was your first safe house, right?"

"That would be correct." Hartings said, no longer surprised or fearful by this young man's knowledge about the *End Times Salvation Movement*.

Moishe added, "And this is important, all of them must have their own sleeping quarters."

Clayton glanced at Travis, then back to Moishe. "Done!"

Moishe nodded his thanks. "Once that happens, everyone residing at those particular safehouses will see with their own two eyes something that will further cement in their minds that we are who we say we are. Those who survive that is…"

"Survive?" Travis asked, his voice cracking.

Moishe nodded. "That's all I can tell you for now…"

Travis rubbed his chin. "Understood." What else could he say?

Clayton asked, "Is it true you'll be invincible until the Lord returns?"

Moishe nodded again. "Yahweh's supernatural covering precedes us wherever we go, which means there's nothing Antichrist can do to stop us whenever we're out winning multitudes to our beloved Messiah, Yeshua HaMaschiach…"

A surge of excitement seized Clayton. "Revelation seven-nine?"

Moishe leaned up in his chair. "Yes. Nothing will be able to silence us when we're out doing Yahweh's business, not even five-hundred pound bunker-buster bombs being dropped from the sky on our heads. This infuriates Antichrist to no end!"

Travis took a sip of coffee. "This has been a topic of debate in our organization since the outset. Some thought you would all become martyrs at some point, like the Two Witnesses. Thanks for clarifying it for me, Moishe."

The young man nodded. "What's even better is when we're not out preaching the Word, we become ghost-like, as if we've temporarily vanished from the face of the earth. So, in essence, the safe houses at which we will reside will be untraceable, invisible like, whenever we're there.

"But aside from all children residing at those locations, no one else will be guaranteed protection from what is still to come…"

Travis was astounded. "Let me get this straight, are you actually saying all children staying at those properties at which you will be residing will survive until Christ returns?"

Moishe grinned. "That's precisely what I'm saying!"

Travis sat more erectly in his chair. "This is fantastic news!"

Moishe waited until all eyes were on him to add, "So, what this means is, once we are settled on your properties, one of your immediate tasks will be to bring as many of your children to those locations as possible."

"How will we know which properties have been chosen?"

"I'll share those locations with you tomorrow, when I return from doing Yahweh's business. But for now, just know the first visitor at your Pennsylvania safe house will be a man named Jakob. He will arrive in the morning. I'll ask that you do not contact anyone within your organization regarding this matter. That will be done tomorrow."

"As you wish, Moishe," Hartings replied.

"Now, if you'll excuse me, it's time for me to pray with my brothers."

Holmes and Hartings retreated to the basement, with a million thoughts and questions racing through their minds.

Clayton scratched his head. "Will Moishe pray with his brothers on a conference call?"

Travis answered, "It seems rather implausible that there would be a communications system large enough to have so many on the same call at once."

Clayton nodded agreement. "Besides, Romanero would never allow for it. So, does it mean they'll be taken directly into the presence of the Lord? I mean, could it be?"

Travis looked up at the ceiling. "Your guess is as good as mine, partner. But what an honor we have been given to house some of God's sealed servants! I'm still trying to wrap my mind around the magnitude of it all. . ."

Clayton became teary-eyed. "You and me both, Travis!"

Once they were settled for the night, they opened their Bibles to Revelation 7—the introduction of the 144,000, which happened to be one of their favorites—and read it aloud to one another.

Now that they had just met one of them, they couldn't resist...

5

THE NEXT MORNING

SHORTLY AFTER 6 A.M., mere moments after the change of guard at safe house number one, out of nowhere, a man suddenly materialized before their very eyes. He stood ten feet or so away from the main entryway, in total silence, as if he came out of nowhere. It was eerie…

At first glance, the *ETSM* guard in charge at Chadds Ford, a man named Titus, thought his eyes were playing tricks on him. His first instinct was to reach for his gun. But since he was unarmed, his arms fell limp at his sides as if in surrender.

He shot a fearful glance over to his lifelong friend, and fellow guard out monitoring the front entryway of the property with him.

Remo's eyes remained locked on the subject, his detective eyes searching the man's body for weapons, namely bulges near the ankles, hips, or belly region. "Let me see your hands!" he barked, even though he had nothing to back up his command with. Stun guns and electric batons could only put so much fear in the potential perpetrator's eyes.

The young man obeyed the command and held out his hands, palms out, signifying that he was unarmed. If he did have a gun, they would have to find a way to overpower him and pry the weapon away from him, thus neutralizing him, before he could use it.

As a former Navy Seal, Titus still maintained a rigorous workout routine to prolong his well-toned physique. It wasn't uncommon for the tall muscular man, with military-style buzzcut and chiseled chin, to drop to the ground several times a day to do a hundred pushups at a time.

Remo was a few inches shorter and had a slight pot belly, but still maintained a hardened upper body. If this conflict ever escalated into hand to hand combat, the subject in question could never match skills with them.

Throw into the mix that all it would take was a simple push of a button, and half of the 38 other guards out patrolling safe house number one on the outside would come running, while the rest diligently maintained their posts, as they awaited reinforcements in case of a possible sneak attack.

Forty guards patrolled the outside of the property, every second of every day, as 40 more patrolled the inside. All had been well trained by Titus, and knew the plan full well, which meant if this young man was unarmed, he wouldn't stand a chance of gaining entry inside.

But if the subject in question was armed in any way, since they weren't, the advantage would quickly tilt in his favor. And what if he was a suicide bomber? After all, he did look Middle Eastern.

Why won't they let us arm ourselves? Titus thought in an angry panic.

He looked at Remo, who shrugged his shoulders not knowing how to possibly gauge the situation. They were caught completely off guard by this young man. Neither man knew that 1000 of their locations around the world would experience similar visitations over the next three days.

"Shalom, Titus!" the stranger said enthusiastically, when their eyes had settled on him again.

Shalom? The *ETSM* guard blinked hard, then shot another fearful glance at Remo, hoping his heart wouldn't give out on him. Titus easily recognized the very same fear pulsating throughout his partner's body.

Both men knew what the other was thinking. Had someone from the Cipriano administration discovered their whereabouts, and sent this man to ensnare them? Both were mindful of what was happening to their former unsaved *American Freedom Keepers* colleagues, under the direct orders of the President of the United States of America herself, Lois Cipriano.

The torture and humiliation they endured at her hands each day was unspeakable. What made it even worse was that she ordered them to be beaten to U.S. military patriotic music, for protesting what they claimed was a bogus election, and for always bad-mouthing Salvador Romanero

It was evident that President Cipriano enjoyed watching her staunch opposers cowering to the whips of their tormentors, knowing she had the power of life and death at her disposal to use in any fashion of her choosing.

These treasonous acts being committed against her own citizens were the travesty of all travesties, but what could they do to stop it? The answer to this question was glaringly obvious—nothing!

With these unhealthy thoughts running through their minds, the two *ETSM* guards couldn't help but wonder if the cavalry was looming in the background, just waiting for the order to be given to pounce on the more than 2,000 residents they were out protecting. They prayed it wouldn't happen...

Titus gulped hard, silently hoping this man was as harmless as he appeared on the surface. "Who are you?" he demanded to know. "And how do you know my name?"

"Relax, Titus, Remo," he added, shooting a quick glance at the other guard. "My name is Jakob. I come in peace, in the name of Yeshua HaMaschiach. I need you to call Brian to inform him of my arrival."

Titus' first thought was, *Who are you to bark out orders to me?* Only this man wasn't barking. He said it very calmly, peacefully, harmlessly.

He shot another quick glance at Remo, who shrugged his shoulders again, without ever taking his eyes off the target.

Comforting as his words sounded, it wasn't enough to stop his 230-pound chiseled body from quaking in terror. Until proven otherwise, they had to assume the subject was a wolf in sheep's clothing.

"Brian who?" Titus asked as softly but sternly as he could, given the circumstances.

"Mulrooney," came the reply, in his Middle Eastern accent.

The *ETSM* guard flinched. His head tilted one way then the other. "How do you know Brian?" In a world on the brink of total disaster, the fact that this man's demeanor was so peaceful, as everyone else was constantly on edge, made this encounter even more alarming.

Jakob's lips curved into an easy smile. "Just tell him I'm one of Yahweh's one hundred and forty-four thousand sealed servants."

Titus blinked hard, unable to believe what his ears were hearing. Was this man really sent by God? With trembling hands, he reached for the Sat-phone that was kept at the guard station in case of emergency. This would be the first time he would be using it to call Brian.

With so many residents occupying safe house number one, only three phones were being used for now—just to be safe.

When Romanero began his all-out assault on Christians, the *ETSM* ordered that all laptops and mobile devices—including smart watches— be confiscated from new residents at all safe houses, upon moving onto the premises, and placed in storage.

This was done to prevent lonely residents from making desperate phone calls or from sending emails or text messages to unsaved spouses, family members and friends, just to hear from them again.

This was especially true with new and expectant mothers when they felt trapped on their emotional roller coasters, and needed someone to talk to. Even Jacquelyn confessed to fighting strong constant urges to call her parents to let them know she was okay and not in prison, and that they would soon be grandparents again.

Sarah Mulrooney was even worse. She surrendered her phone long before it could be confiscated. She didn't trust herself with it. If she still had it, she would have called her husband numerous times by now, to see how he was holding up, and to assure him that she still loved him, despite their vast spiritual differences.

By no means would confiscating all mobile devices prevent outsiders from knowing people lived there; they already knew, in fact. But if hundreds or even thousands of calls and transmissions were being detected from this relatively small parcel of land, just knowing that millions of Christians were living in hiding, inquiries would surely be made.

Brian and Jacquelyn had one of three active phones. Meera Singh also had one, which she gave to Tamika when she was able to take an occasional nap. The third phone was handled by whichever guard was monitoring the main entryway to the safehouse.

When Mulrooney answered his Sat-phone, he heard heavy breathing on the other end. He knew the call had originated from the guard station, but he didn't know which guards were on duty. "Yeah?"

"Brian, it's Titus…"

Brian glanced at Jacquelyn. Of course, it was Titus! The man was like a machine. Did he ever sleep? "Hey, Titus, is everything okay?"

"Can you come to the main gate? You have a visitor."

A visitor? Brian's pulse raced in his ears, sensing bad news. Why else would he be calling? *Have they finally linked me to Brad Henriksen?*

Jacquelyn saw his change of expression. "What is it, honey?"

Brian cupped the phone and whispered to his wife, "Titus said I have a visitor. Even asked for me by name."

Jacquelyn gulped hard. Her eyes grew wide with fear, knowing exactly what her husband was thinking.

Though the couple had yet to be identified, Brad and Joan Henriksen were still among the most broadcast names on the planet. Both were international fugitives who were being charged as co-conspirators against Salvador Romanero, for triggering the mental illness within Yogesh Patel, which ultimately led to his death.

According to the *Miracle Maker* himself, the Henriksens were equally guilty of the charges, and needed to pay for it with their lives.

With exception to the eyewitness testimony coming from the postal clerk working at the main postal distribution center, in Trenton, New Jersey, plus the surveillance video they had of Joan Henriksen and her female friend—grainy as it was—their constant prayer was that Yogesh Patel was the only person on the planet who had known who they were, even if he didn't know their real names.

Now that he was dead, who else knew?

Still on edge from what had happened last Christmas, Jacquelyn's nerves were so shot that a falling acorn hitting the roof, or even hearing a squirrel running across it, could set her off. Some days it wouldn't even take that much. The sound of hammering at the front of the property or a stiff wind blowing against the side of the house would cause fear to mushroom through the expectant mother. Now this?

Brian cleared his throat. "And who might that be, Titus?"

"A man named Jakob. He proclaims to be one of the one hundred and forty-four thousand."

Mulrooney's eyes grew wide with astonishment. Chills shot up and down his spine. "Seriously?"

"Yes, sir, that's what he proclaims. He even asked for you by name. He also knew my name, Remo's, too, for that matter…"

Jacquelyn became curious and tugged on her husband's shirt sleeve. "What is it, honey?"

Brian put the speaker on so his wife could listen, then paced the bedroom floor.

Titus scratched his head in befuddlement. "What should I do?"

Brian rubbed his chin. "You know the drill, Titus. Nothing happens until the proper inquiries have been made."

"But what if he really is one of the one hundred and forty-four thousand? What if he really was sent by God?"

"Of course, it would be a tremendous blessing, Titus. But it could also be a trap. Nothing happens until I contact Clayton and Travis! Got it?"

"Roger that," Titus said, eyes darting left to right scanning the outside fence line.

Brian added, "For now, keep him out of view…"

"Remo already took him to the camouflage shed. He followed along peacefully, without the slightest hint of a struggle."

"Very good. Just don't let your guard down for even a second."

"Roger that," Titus said, his eyes surveying the area, hoping no one was surveilling them…

6

BRIAN MULROONEY SAT ON the edge of the bed, as the phone rang When it went to Clayton Holmes' voicemail, he tried Travis Hartings next. "Hey, Brian. I was just about to contact you. Have you recently had a visitor?"

Brian craned his neck so Jacquelyn could see the befuddlement on his face. "Yeah, a man named Jakob. That's why I'm calling, actually. Titus called me warning of his arrival. He caught us completely off guard. And get this, he proclaims to be one of the one hundred and forty-four thousand mentioned in the Book of Revelation."

"Hallelujah!" Hartings shouted, joyfully. "I'm in the process of blast emailing all property managers informing you all on what's going on."

Brian looked confused. "What *is* going on?"

"Our prayers are being answered, Brian! Clayton and I both had identical dreams, which led to what's happening now."

Not wanting to miss a single word, Jacquelyn scooted up a bit, which took a little longer due to the extra weight she was carrying from being eight and a half months pregnant. She pressed her hands onto the mattress behind her, palms down, and asked, "What dreams?"

"Hi Jacquelyn. In short, we were summoned to go back to the main cabin at once." Hartings felt no need to mention the night they had spent in Ellijay. "Shortly after we arrived, we met with another one of the one hundred and forty-four thousand, a man named Moishe from the tribe of Judah. It's been an amazing encounter, to say the least."

Travis took a deep breath. Even though he anticipated this call from Brian, he was so excited he could hardly contain himself. "Moishe told us Yahweh had dispatched a thousand of His chosen servants to reside at our safehouses. And that's only for starters!"

"That's fantastic news!" Mulrooney shouted. Then, "What about the rest of them?"

"When we asked, Moishe told us we're not the only large Christian group on the planet that Yahweh's been preparing for them since the Rapture, to include the use of our facilities. But he did say more than half of them would reside within the Jewish communities of the world."

"Is Moishe with you now?"

31

"No. He's out doing His Father's business, as he likes to say. But he told us the reason God's blessing us with some of His servants is to reward us for the ten percent we've faithfully put aside for their full use."

Hartings became emotional. "As you know, we always thought this could become a possibility at some point, but now that it's happening, it seems so surreal. No matter how hard I try, I can't wrap my mind around how one of God's own chosen servants knew us by name. I always knew we were doing the will of our Father, but to hear Moishe call me by my name is too wonderful to tell!"

Brian stared at Jacquelyn. "So, just to confirm, the man presently standing outside our safe house, named Jakob, is one of the one hundred and forty-four thousand from the Book of Revelation?"

Travis dabbed at his eyes with a tissue. "He most definitely is! As the first ETSM safe house, Moishe told us yours would be the first one visited. He even mentioned you and Jacquelyn by name! How cool is that?"

Brian and Jacquelyn became teary-eyed. After everything they had endured the past few months, this came as a most welcomed surprise for the couple. "What can I say, Travis? We're speechless!"

"What an incredible honor that God would use our safe houses for some of His sealed servants!" Travis exclaimed joyously.

Relief flooded Jacquelyn's soul, comforting her greatly. "I don't believe I've ever heard you so happy, Travis! It's invigorating!"

"Yeah, well, this may be the last reason to rejoice, until we meet Jesus face to face. I'm gonna ride this feeling out for as long as it lasts."

Chills shot all throughout Mulrooney's body. "I'll call Titus and tell him to let him in…"

"No. You must go there and do it yourself. But don't let him enter the property until you hear him say, 'Shalom! I come in peace, in the name of Yeshua HaMaschiach.' That will be your final confirmation."

"Got it! I should go now. Don't want to keep our special guest waiting a second longer. I can't wait to meet him!"

Travis yawned into the phone. He didn't sleep much the night before. "Oh, and one more thing, Brian, just like Clayton had alluded to way back when, now that Jakob's been revealed to you, whatever he needs, he gets—no questions asked!"

"Of course!"

Travis added, "And don't let his youthfulness fool you. Not only is he wise beyond his years, but he's being supernaturally protected…"

"Understood…"

"Please call me back after you've been properly introduced."

"Yes, sir…"

At that, the call ended.

Jacquelyn kissed her husband on the lips. "Well, what are you waiting for? You'd better get going! Will you be bringing him back here?"

"Like Travis said, sweetie, whatever he wants he gets. I'll leave that decision to him."

Jacquelyn nodded. "Understood…"

Mulrooney got dressed, kissed his wife on the lips, and raced down the stairs as quickly as he could.

He ran the entire distance to the front gate, and was completely winded. He took a puff from his asthma inhaler. "Bring him in at once!"

Titus stiffened, then shot him a sideways look. "Sir?"

Mulrooney raised his hands, palms out. "At ease, Titus! Jakob is who he proclaims to be. His identification's been confirmed from above." Brian smiled at his words. They were true on more than one level.

"Roger that." The *ETSM* guard sighed relief, then signaled with his right hand for Remo, who was peeking through a tiny slit in the camouflage shed, to bring Jakob to him immediately.

When Jakob entered onto the property, Titus quickly closed the gate behind them. For added seclusion, 50 large canvasses were stitched together and placed on top of the camouflage netting, which stretched from the front wall to some of the 100-foot oak trees.

Brian smiled when Jakob said, "Shalom, Brian! I come in peace, in the name of Yeshua HaMaschiach."

Mulrooney mouthed the words as Jakob recited them. Every hair on the back of his neck, arms, and legs, stood at full attention. "Hello, Jakob! I just spoke to Travis Hartings. He told me to expect you. I can't tell you how honored I am to meet you!"

Jakob smiled warmly. "Likewise, Brian!"

Brian greeted his visitor with a hug. "Please make yourself comfortable. Our safe house is your safe house."

The way he said it made Jakob laugh. "Thanks in advance for your kind hospitality. But you must know that wherever I stay on the property, no one else can stay under the same roof as me. I must always be alone. If I ever need anything, I'll come to you. Are we clear?"

"Sure, whatever you want!" Brian wanted to further inquire, but he didn't know what to say. "This property is yours to do whatever you want."

33

Jakob smiled warmly. "I look forward to meeting Jacquelyn."

Even though he was warned in advance that Jakob knew their names, just hearing this man utter his wife's name nearly took his breath away. "So, what next?"

"Follow me."

Without saying a word, Brian did as he was instructed.

The way the young man moved about the grounds; one might think he had been there before. Jakob led Brian to the cottage situated directly behind the church pavilion, at the center of the property on a bit of an uphill slope from the back of the sanctuary.

"This is where I will stay…"

"Good choice, since it's currently vacant," Brian said, in reply, already sensing Jakob already knew that.

"Thank you, Brian. Now let's go meet Jacquelyn and some of the others…"

Brian beamed. "Follow me…"

Once they were seated in the living room of the main house, Jakob told the Mulrooneys, Tom Dunleavey and Tamika Moseley, many of the things Moishe had shared with Clayton and Travis, including how his presence would offer protection to all children residing at his safe house.

As the brief meeting came to a close, Brian asked, "Will you have any particular role here at safe house number one, like preaching, for example?"

Jakob shook his head. "Me and my sealed brothers are here to win souls to Yeshua, not preach to those who are already saved!"

The way he said it comforted everyone, putting smiles on their faces…

"Most of the time, you won't even know I'm here. So, feel free to go about your business without being concerned for me. I am in perfect hands. Now, if you'll excuse me, I must be alone so I can pray with my brothers. It was a pleasure meeting you all."

"Pleasure meeting you too, Jakob…" Tom Dunleavey said, still trying to wrap his mind around how one of God's sealed servants would be staying with them at safe house number one.

7

TWO DAYS LATER

TAMIKA MOSELEY DESCENDED THE stairs, to find Brian in the living room with Tom Dunleavey, Donald Johnson, Manuel Jiminez, Julio Gonzalez, and his son-in-law, Joaquim Guzman, having a Bible study.

She just finished having one of her own in her bedroom with Jacquelyn, Brian's mother, Sarah, and her new bunkmates.

As the safe house kept swelling with new residents, the third upstairs bedroom that Tamika had all to herself for more than a year and a half, was now shared with three other women. Two bunk beds took up most of the space of the moderately-sized room.

It took some adjusting to, but the head nurse at safe house number one knew way in advance that this time would eventually come.

One of her bunkmates was Lila Choharjo, the 44-year-old former Hollywood actress who was among the first 77 expectant mothers invited to Chadds Ford, before losing her baby to miscarriage.

Lila's first job was on the cafeteria crew, until she was recently promoted as one of the nursing assistants at the subterranean hospital. She had left the house a few minutes ago for the cafeteria, before beginning her shift.

"Evening, gents," Tamika said. "Enjoying the Bible study?"

Brian looked up from his notes. "We're just about to start. How was yours?" Having one of God's 144,000 sealed servants living among them had caused them all to hunger and thirst even more for the Word of God.

As much as they wanted to invite Jakob to join them, everyone knew he wasn't to be disturbed. If he wanted something, he would ask for it.

"Well, we were studying Matthew twenty-four until we got to verse nineteen, and Jacquelyn started feeling discomfort."

Brian didn't need Tamika to recite that verse for him. The closer his wife came to giving birth, the more Christ's words about how dreadful it would be in these days for pregnant women and nursing mothers tormented her. "Is she okay?"

Nurse Moseley nodded yes. "I just examined her up in your bedroom. Won't be long now...," she said, not knowing how prophetic her words would be. "Your mother's with her now."

35

With hundreds of deliveries already under her belt since becoming the head nurse, Brian trusted her estimation. "Thanks for the update. I'll check on her soon."

Tamika nodded that it would be a good idea. "As much as I'd love to chitchat, it's time to head off to the cafeteria for a bite to eat, before going down into the dungeon," she said, with a chuckle.

"The tilapia was delicious tonight. Whoever prepared it deserves a raise," Miguel Jiminez said, with a laugh. The Mexican native who'd lived in Los Angeles before coming to Chadds Ford, Pennsylvania was still hoping to go to Mexico to manage a safe house just outside of Guadalajara.

Tamika rubbed her belly. "M-m-m, yummy."

Donald Johnson said, "Hope it's not too busy for you at work."

"With only two women in labor, it shouldn't be too crazy," Tamika said, not knowing how wrong her comment would prove to be.

Nor did she know there would be more than just two deliveries this night at safe house number one, or how drastically life was about to be changed for all of them. None of them did for that matter.

"Stay safe out there," said Tom Dunleavey.

Tamika shot him a warm smile. "I will. Enjoy the Bible study, boys…"

When Tamika left, Brian excused himself to check on his wife. As expected, he found her on her emotional roller coaster for being pregnant at the worst time in human history. "Tamika said it won't be long now."

Jacquelyn could only sigh.

When Sarah left them, Brian sat on the bed and stroked his wife's hair. "Still can't believe we're gonna be parents soon." When she didn't reply, he asked, "Remember the first time we said we loved each other?"

Jacquelyn looked up at her husband. "How could I forget? It was the day we settled on the property…"

"Just a shame Rhonda Kimmel died in the Universal Children's Day explosions. She turned out to be a good real estate agent, after all."

Jacquelyn nodded softly. "Seems like so long ago…"

"Sure does." Brian kissed his wife on the back of the head, then rubbed her belly. "So much has changed since then. But what hasn't changed is my love for you. I'm so blessed to have you as my wife. You're the best thing that's ever happened to me. I know you're scared, but we'll get through this together, okay?"

After a while, Jacquelyn smiled wearily. "I'm fine now, promise."

"Rest well, my love. I'll be up as soon as we're finished."

"Take your time, sweetie."

Brian kissed her on the lips and rejoined the men downstairs in the living room. In what could be best described as the irony of all ironies, just as Tom Dunleavey finished reading Revelation 6:12-17, and was expounding on the sixth seal which was next to strike, the whole house shook. "Whoa!" Tom shouted; his nerves jolted. "Did you feel that?"

Before anyone could answer him, it happened again, only worse, much worse. There was loud rumbling all around them. Like a throttle turned on full speed, the deep grinding, rumbling sound intensified and kept intensifying, throwing drinks off tables, and pictures off walls.

Each man was momentarily lifted off their seats, when the floor shifted beneath them, giving them the sensation of butterflies thrill seekers felt in their bellies while riding on a roller coaster speeding downhill at top speed.

Only this wasn't a thrill ride! That mild sensation was quickly escalated to full-blown terror, knowing Revelation 6:12-17 was materializing before their very eyes!

The last thing Mulrooney saw before the lights went out was the unbridled fear etched onto his brothers' faces. It was something he knew he would never forget, especially since they were just reading about what was now happening all around them, knowing it was occurring globally.

Like most East Coasters, this was his first time experiencing an earthquake. While they did register in this part of the world, humans seldom felt them. Then again, not even those living in earthquake-prone areas had ever felt anything close to this!

Brian's first thought was to check on his wife and mother upstairs. As his brothers clung to whatever their hands could find in the darkness, he began the tedious process of climbing the stairs, his phone screen providing the only illumination. He found it impossible at times to navigate the moving floor beneath his feet. He was sometimes forced to take several steps sideways before he could take a single step forward.

It felt like he was riding on a locomotive train that kept banking unexpectedly. He couldn't remember feeling any more helpless.

His fear intensified when the railing he was gripping with his left hand snapped off and fell to the living room floor below. A small piece of wood had splintered and got stuck in his fingernail. The pain was excruciating but he blocked it out for now, fully determined to get to his wife.

Slowly inching his way to the top of the stairs, he heard Jacquelyn screaming at the top of her lungs. "Help me, Brian!"

"Hold on, honey, I'm coming," he shouted, hoping she could hear him above the deafening noise. Before he could take another step, the quake intensified, slamming Brian to the hallway floor with a hard thud. His left cheek took the worst of it. It was the least of his concerns.

Mulrooney remained frozen in fear, his body prostrate on the carpeted floor for what seemed an eternity. It felt as if God, who had the whole world in His hands, as the song said, was presently using it as a saltshaker.

The constant rumbling had caused the dust in the carpet to take flight, quickly filling Brian's lungs. He started wheezing heavily. On his last doctor's visit, Meera Singh discovered three small holes in his lungs, which she believed was the result of the Universal Children's Day fiasco.

The *ETSM* doctor suspected that microscopic particles of the deadly agents used on that day had gone undetected, and had slowly trickled down into the atmosphere, gradually attacking those with weaker immune systems. Either that, or it may have come from a vapor cloud as an added attempt to decrease the human population. Whatever the cause, Brian's lungs were permanently damaged as a result.

The more Jacquelyn yelled and screamed, the more panicked he became. He felt powerless to protect his wife and unborn child, helpless, really. About the only good thing was that she couldn't see the terrified expression on his face. "I'm coming! I'm coming!"

Brian aimed his cell phone at the door leading to his bedroom. Even through the thick cloud of dust, he could see that it had been rocked off its hinges. The doorframe had slanted at a 15-degree angle. The door itself must have been slightly ajar before the quake struck.

Brian aimed his cell phone toward the bed, and saw Jacquelyn cradling her belly, terror etched on her face, as her body shifted awkwardly on the mattress, bouncing up and down and side to side, in rhythm to the bed's constant movements, as small parts of the ceiling rained down on her.

Brian noticed the ceiling fan above the bed had been jarred loose and was hanging by its electrical wires. He prayed that it wouldn't fall on her.

He slowly lifted himself up off the floor and tried diving on the bed. With the mattress constantly moving in all directions, he aimed for the center but still missed the target, falling hard to the floor.

Gathering his phone with one hand, he used his free hand to grip the bed and slowly hoisted himself up, then positioned himself behind his wife, and held her as tightly as he could. There wasn't a chance he would let go of her until the house stopped shaking.

"Are you okay, sweetie?" he shouted above the ear-splitting rumbling noise, sensing the roof above them might collapse at any second, or even the floor beneath them.

Jacquelyn wept and waited for the rumbling to stop before saying, "My water just broke! I'm in labor…"

Brian's eyes widened in the darkness. He started hyperventilating. Hearing his mother screaming for dear life in the bedroom next to theirs, only made it worse. "Stay right here, sweetie. I'll go for help…"

"No," she screamed. "Please don't leave me, Brian!"

The fear in her voice cut through him deeply. "I need to look for Tamika or Meera. Don't worry, I'll bring Mom here to stay with you…"

Mulrooney's wheezing intensified. He pointed his cell phone screen at the table on his side of the bed, looking for his asthma inhaler, but the table was flipped onto its side. Scanning the floor, he breathed a sigh of relief seeing it in the corner of the room. But the nebulizer machine he used twice a day had been totally destroyed. *Can't worry about it now!*

He took a hit from his inhaler and went to check on his mother. The door frame leading to her bedroom had also shifted, causing the door to be jammed. Try as he might, he couldn't open it. It took kicking it a few times as hard as he could before it finally opened, but only slightly.

Brian squeezed past the small opening to find his mother laying on her bed trembling so much, it was as if the quake had somehow materialized inside her frail body. A cold wind invaded the room, from every window being blown out. "Are you okay, Mom?"

"I, I, I think so…," Sarah said, stuttering. She had just dozed off when the quake roused her from her sleep. The battery-operated lantern she kept by her bed, in case of emergency, went flying through the air and nearly hit her in the head. The plastic covering was cracked after hitting the wall, but the light was still working. She clung to it looking completely terrified.

"Jacquelyn's in labor, Ma! I think the quake prompted it. I need to go for help. Can you sit with her and prepare her for giving birth?"

"I'll do my best, son…" Sarah knew her daughter-in-law was feeling discomfort during the Bible study, but when she laid her head on the pillow to sleep, she never expected that this would be the night.

Then again, she never thought her bedroom windows would be blown out, and who knew what else? She was having difficulty processing it all.

Brian grabbed his mother's robe, which thankfully was still hanging on a nail on the door, took her by the hand, and slowly led her into his bedroom, using his phone screen to illuminate the dusty path, thankful he had charged it before the Bible study.

They tiptoed every step of the way on the suddenly lopsided floor, silently praying it wouldn't give out on them.

Brian sat on the bed and kissed his wife several times on the lips, cheeks, and forehead, hoping to calm her down. "Hold tight, my love. I'll be back as quickly as I can."

"I'm scared, Brian. What if the house comes tumbling down?"

Brian was thinking the same thing. First earthquake or not, after what they'd just experienced, it was a miracle the house hadn't been turned into a heaping pile of destruction by now. "Just keep praying for God's protection."

Jacquelyn closed her eyes, then nodded. "Please hurry! I think the baby's coming out."

Brian kissed his wife on the lips again. "I'll be back as quickly as I can. I don't want to miss it…"

"Be careful, son."

Brian kissed his mother's forehead. "You too, Mom…"

As Sarah helped her daughter-in-law get undressed, Brian carefully maneuvered his way down the stairs, his phone screen leading the way, not knowing what to expect...

8

BRIAN DID A QUICK search of the house, and wasn't surprised to find no one down there. He gulped in fear seeing how part of the kitchen had been damaged when the ceiling collapsed on top of it. Part of the wall had also collapsed, leaving a gaping view to the outside. Sparks flew from the exposed wiring, illuminating the darkness, frightening him even more.

Brian prayed, "Lord, please don't let the house burn down with my pregnant wife and mother upstairs. Protect them as only You can..."

He was never more thankful that both his and his mother's bedroom were on the opposite side of the house, away from the kitchen.

Mulrooney grabbed as many military-strength flashlights as his hands could hold, which were purposely kept in the closet by the front door for situations like this, and went outside to find his Bible-study brothers bloodied and bruised with minor cuts all over their bodies.

They were badly shaken, but grateful for having survived the mayhem.

Tom said to Brian, "Thank God you're okay! I thought for certain that the house would collapse on us, burying us all alive. I was just headed inside to check on you all."

"Jacquelyn's in labor! My mother's with her now. I need to find Tamika or Lila or Meera immediately." Brian's voice was panicked.

"I want to congratulate you, but I don't think now's the appropriate time." Tom removed his dust-filled eyeglasses and cleaned them with a tissue from his pocket, still shocked that his heart didn't attack him again like it did last Christmas Eve.

As he clung to the living room couch during the quake, he thought for sure it would happen. *I guess you still have things for me to do down here, Lord!* The dream he'd had about Brian's father came to mind. It was a dream he'd yet to share with anyone, not even Brian...*That must be it...*

Brian handed each man a flashlight. "Start checking on the others." He looked up at his bedroom window, feeling guilty for leaving his wife and mother up there, but what choice did he have? Jacquelyn was in labor. "Stay safe, fellas. There may be aftershocks..."

Tom glanced at Donald. "Why don't we check the nursery?"

Johnson nodded his reply, still trying to catch his breath.

41

As a Mormon missionary living in the Philippines for so many years, Donald Johnson had experienced his fair share of quakes, but nothing he ever encountered could compare to this!

Convinced that this was the quake described in Revelation six, he feared for his family and friends over there, for having led so many of them spiritually astray. His constant prayer was that God would let him return there someday to preach the true Gospel this time, but with tragedy after tragedy striking the planet, he wasn't sure if it would ever happen.

Manuel Jiminez also experienced several earthquakes growing up in Mexico, before migrating to Los Angeles, only to experience much of the same.

As he banged on cottage doors with Julio Gonzalez, Joaquim Guzman, and a handful of others, looking for survivors or dead bodies, his mind was focused on his family and friends back home—saved and unsaved alike—knowing the entire planet was the epicenter of this quake.

If no one answered they did their best to enter inside, but most cottages were too badly damaged. Many survivors walked around in a daze; fear clearly etched on their faces.

With so much broken glass everywhere, once contact was made with someone, the first command they were given was, "Put your shoes on!"

On his way to the subterranean hospital, Brian prayed no one was trapped down below. His heartrate was through the roof.

Flashlight on, he gasped loudly seeing so many cracks in the ground and on the grassy surface. Some stretched as far as his flashlight would allow him to see. But what frightened him even more were the massive crevices in the ground, where some of the cottages used to be.

There was an explosion at the rear of the property opposite the house Brian lived in. One of the massive oak trees fell on the fuel tanker that was parked there. Thankfully, it was only 10 percent full of fuel.

After the large trucks and other large equipment was shipped off to other *ETSM* properties, at the outset, most of the fuel was placed in barrels, and spread out across the property, or shared with other *ETSM* safehouses, in case something like this ever happened.

Even so, it was a big loss. No doubt everyone within a five-mile radius heard it. *Not good!* But if this was the sixth Seal Judgment, which Brian had no doubt it was—no one would come offering help anytime soon.

It wasn't the only fire burning at safe house number one. Flames, smoke, and clouds of dust billowed up in the air everywhere. He would worry about it later. For now, he was on a mission.

It didn't take long for Brian's worst fear to be realized—dozens of lifeless bodies scattered along the way. As the property manager, part of him wished the flashlight wasn't working.

Safe House Number One looked like a bomb had been dropped on it. *I'll never again refer to this place as a Pocket of Peace!*

Meanwhile, Tom Dunleavey and Donald Johnson arrived at one of the military-style bunkers that was constructed where one of the seven burned out cottages once stood. With so many children being born at safe house number one, this bunker had become the new nursery.

The two men didn't need to use a door to get inside. They walked through a hole in one of the side walls, to find most children crawling on the floor in the darkness, weeping hysterically for their mothers.

According to one of the distraught women on the nightshift, most of the infants and small children were sound asleep when the ground started shaking all around them. Yet, despite that most of the little ones had bumps and bruises on their bodies, they all seemed okay.

But two daycare workers were killed.

In the adjoining military-style bunker, Tony Pearsall was sleeping when the cot he was on started bouncing up and down like a giant pogo stick in all directions. "Whoa! What's happening?!" He rolled onto his belly and hugged the cot shouting above the loud rumbling, "Brace yourself, everyone! I think Revelation six, twelve's happening!"

Someone yelled, "What should we do?"

It was a valid question, since they never had fire drills let alone earthquake drills at safe house number one.

"Press your faces into the mattresses, and cling to your cots for dear life!" The fear in Pearsall's voice frightened everyone even more.

Tony's fear was taken to unimaginable heights when his cot flipped onto its side. His knees hit the hardened floor, bruising his right kneecap. His face slammed into his cot on the way down, costing him four of his upper front teeth and two of his lowers. The pain was excruciating.

Every cot in the bunker flipped over, causing many men who were hugging them to dislocate shoulders and fracture bones. Some ended up with head injuries and concussions. But when the roof and two of the walls suddenly collapsed, many were killed.

Even though the military-style bunkers were more sturdily built than the cottages, all had sustained massive structural damage.

A hundred yards away, Mulrooney finally arrived at the subterranean hospital. What would normally take three minutes at most, even with his weakened lungs, took fifteen this time. He had to jump over a few large cracks in the ground—one even required a running start—just to make it.

He found Meera Singh outside with Lila Choharjo and Mary Johnson, holding three shivering, hungry babies in their trembling arms. Two were newborns and one was born 10 days ago, prematurely, and was being kept underground for further observation.

All three women looked completely disheveled. Meera was already exhausted and was waiting for Tamika to arrive, so she could take a much-needed nap after a 16-hour shift, when the subterranean hospital started shaking ever so violently.

"Jacquelyn's in labor…" Brian shouted, through panicked breathing.

Meera gasped. It was the last thing she wanted to hear. "We can't bring her underground. It can't be trusted at this time. As it is, I need to transport all surviving patients above ground pronto!" Guilty expression splashed on her face, she added, "Usually, I would never leave a patient behind, but I had to make sure the newborns were safe."

Brian punched his palm with his right fist out of frustration. The clock was ticking, and he didn't know the first thing about delivering babies.

With her free hand, Meera scooped the crying newborn from Lila's arms. "Go and be with Jacquelyn. If I can join you later, I will. If not, you're more than capable of doing it yourself."

Lila nodded and raced off to the house.

Brian sighed relief, then shouted to Lila who was already 20 feet away, "Watch your step. The ground has been split in many places. Some of the holes are massive." Even as the words came out of his mouth, he couldn't believe it. "Tell my wife I'll be there as soon as I can…"

Mary asked Brian, "Where's my husband?"

"Don's fine. He went to the nursery to check on the babies with Tom."

Face quaked in anguish; Mary nodded her thanks.

Mulrooney could tell just by looking at Meera that she wanted to scream at the top of her lungs, or burst out in tears. Holding two wailing babies in her arms only made it worse. "I'll take them…"

"It's okay. What I really need is for you to gather anyone you can and bring them back here immediately," she said, bouncing the infants in her arms. "We haven't a moment to waste!"

Brian said, "Where's Tamika?"

Meera frowned. "I was going to ask you that…"

Brian shrugged a shoulder. "She left the house for the cafeteria shortly before the quake." He gasped. "Let me grab as many people as I can and send them your way, then I'll go to the cafeteria looking for her."

"Please hurry..." The newborns sobbed more loudly as the seconds passed, adding to the mountain of stress Dr. Singh kept trying to suppress.

"I'll do my best." He lowered his head. "Not to further stress you out, Doctor, but I saw many dead bodies on the way here. And some of the cottages were swallowed whole."

Meera gulped, knowing it would be a long night. *There goes my nap!* She glanced at Mary Johnson. The joy on her face after it was confirmed mere moments before the quake that she was pregnant, was gone.

After so many years of constant letdowns, heartaches, and constant disappointments, the adopted woman who never felt like she belonged anywhere prior to joining the End Times Salvation Movement, was finally about to start a family of her own, short lived as it would be.

Even though Meera had warned that at her age—Mary was in her mid-forties—she was potentially at high-risk for giving birth, Mary still couldn't wait to go back to her cottage and tell her husband the good news.

It was the last thing on her mind now.

Brian said to Mary, "If I see Donald, I'll tell him you're okay!"

"Thank you," Mary mumbled, shivering in the cold.

At that, Mulrooney went in search of helpers to send to the hospital.

Waiting for reinforcements, all Dr. Singh could think about was the dire warning one of the engineers had given at the outset, before leaving safe house number one for another *ETSM* property.

He was emphatic that even though the subterranean location had passed the bare-minimum compression tests, since it was so shoddily built, if the soil ever shifted near or below the underground holes, the structures could easily collapse under their own weight.

As she clung to her desk chair in the darkness, face pressed into the cushion, with the ground shaking violently beneath her, she vividly remembered him saying that even without an earthquake, by not allowing the cement to properly settle, all three floors would surely collapse within ten years. His words now haunted her.

Meera couldn't help but wonder during the quake if they would end up being buried alive. Having inhaled copious amounts of dirt and dust underground, it was hard to think otherwise. Each new inhale had tasted earthy in her mouth.

She was painfully mindful that all it would take was a downed tree to cover the hatch, thus trapping them until their oxygen supply was exhausted and they were suffocated to death. There was more than enough oxygen for a night or two—nothing more.

It was the most frightening sensation being underground knowing if this really was the quake described in Revelation, chapter six, every mountain would be moved and uprooted in the process, followed by volcanic eruptions the world over, all simultaneously.

The instant the quake had subsided, Meera, Lila, and Mary snatched the three newborns in their arms and climbed aboveground, fearing strong aftershocks. Their mothers, covered in more than a foot of dirt like all other patients, begged them not to leave them down there without their babies.

Dr. Singh still heard their emotional pleas ringing in her eardrums.

Julio Gonzalez and Manuel Jiminez were the first ones to arrive, snapping Dr. Singh out of her fog. They wasted no time lowering themselves down in the hole with the two women, to begin the tedious process of transferring the dozen or so patients up to the surface.

As much as Meera didn't want to bring the infants back down in the hole, there was no one there to take them. And at least it was a little warmer down there.

It didn't take long to discover that two patients had perished...

9

MEANWHILE, ON THE WAY back to the main house, Lila Choharjo spotted Joaquim Guzman with his flashlight on, looking to help someone, anyone.

Through deep breaths, and with a panicked expression on her face— knowing she might have to deliver the baby alone—she said, "I need you to go to the underground hospital and bring me one of the labor kits. Jacquelyn's about to give birth. It's urgent that you find one. But be careful, there are gaping holes in the ground everywhere."

Joaquim saw the desperation in Lila's eyes and nodded that he understood, then went on his way. Since his wife, Leticia, had helped assemble the birth kits at home, he knew what he would be looking for.

Lila raced up the stairs and tried opening her bedroom door to check on her bunkmates. It was jammed and wouldn't open.

She pounded on the door with both fists, shouting their names at the top of her lungs, "Are you okay in there? Say something! Anything!"

There was no answer from either of them. As much as she wanted to believe they had somehow escaped, the fact that she couldn't open the door didn't leave her feeling hopeful.

The sound of Jacquelyn screaming in the bedroom next to hers forced the former Hollywood actress to refocus on why she was there. Cruel as it sounded, she needed to block her bunkmates out of her mind for now, and focus on the immediate task at hand.

When she entered Jacquelyn's bedroom, she found Sarah rubbing her daughter-in-law's lower back. Having given birth twice herself, if help didn't arrive soon, she believed she could manage on her own.

Even so, Sarah sighed relief upon seeing Lila.

In between loud groans, Jacquelyn asked, "Where's Brian?"

"He'll be here as soon as he can. It's bad out there!"

Jacquelyn and Sarah both gulped at Lila's words. They dared not ask her to further speculate on just how bad it really was!

Lila turned on the flashlight to check Jacquelyn's cervix. "I can see the baby's head. It's time to start pushing. Are you ready?"

Jacquelyn took a deep breath and nodded at her…

BY THE TIME BRIAN arrived at the cafeteria, a handful of men and women were moving debris out of the way, after hearing Tamika's cries for help.

Before she could even take a bite of the fish on her fork, the ground started shaking furiously. The bench she was seated on was lifted off the floor, sending her airborne, slamming her into a wall.

Tamika fell hard onto the floor just as the wall came crumbling down on top of her, trapping her beneath a pile of debris. She wouldn't need Meera to confirm that her left wrist was broken in many places, or that her hip had been fractured, she already knew.

Mulrooney ignored the lifeless bodies he saw on the cafeteria floor, and joined in on the rescue. "We'll have you out in no time, Tamika!"

"Hurry, Brian! I'm in agony!"

Brian thought to ask her where it hurt, but what would be the point? He got busy helping the others removing parts of the roof and wall as quickly as he could. Twenty minutes later, they finally cleared the way so Tamika could be freed.

Brian knew he couldn't take her to the underground hospital. He scooped her into his arms and left for home, praying the house they had shared would still be standing when they got there.

"Can you hold this flashlight, and keep it steadied downward, so I can see where I'm going? The ground's unstable in so many places. Last thing we need is to fall into a hole or crevice along the way!"

Tamika groaned in agony. "I'll do my best."

"Thanks. By the way, Jacquelyn's in labor!"

"Congratulations, I think," Tamika grunted, wincing, and groaning in pain with every step Brian took, especially in the hip region.

At about the halfway point, Mulrooney's lungs started burning with each step he took. As much as he needed a break, he was determined to be with Jacquelyn.

They arrived at the safe house the same time Joaquim returned with the birthing kit. "Could you give this to Lila. She needs it for Jacquelyn. I need to get back to the hospital where I'm needed."

"You'll have to grab it, Tamika, I have no free hands."

"Just lay it on top of me, Joaquim…" Tamika said, groaning in agony again.

Joaquim did as he was told and quickly left them.

When they entered the house, Brian was about to set her down on the couch with one of its legs broken off, but Tamika objected. "Take me upstairs. I need to check on my bunkmates…"

Brian didn't argue with her. There wasn't time for that. He took his time walking up the uneven steps, feeling guilty for not checking on the two women earlier. It never even crossed his panicked mind!

When they arrived, Jacquelyn was still pushing. "I'm back, sweetie!"

Jacquelyn squinted in the darkness, barely seeing her husband's grime-stained face behind the glare of his phone screen. She sighed relief. "Thank God! It's almost time…"

Brian gently placed Tamika on the opposite side of the bed, away from his wife. "Joaquim asked me to give this to you…"

Lila looked up at the damaged ceiling. "Thank you, Lord!"

After a few more minutes of intense pushing, at 1:16 a.m., Jacquelyn gave birth to a baby girl. If the constant body trembling did any good, the baby came out rather quickly, which was a minor miracle to be sure, since Dr. Singh had warned that with this being her first time giving birth, it could take many hours. No doubt it was stress and quake induced.

Sarah cried tears of joy upon seeing her granddaughter entering the world. Or were they fearful tears? It was a combination of both.

"Time of birth," Lila asked, pulling scissors out of the labor kit to cut the umbilical cord.

Brian glanced at his phone screen. "One-sixteen a.m."

As Lila began the stitching process, Sarah wrapped her granddaughter in a towel and placed her on Jacquelyn's chest to keep her body warm.

Brian became teary-eyed seeing his daughter laying on her mother's chest. "You've never looked more beautiful than right now, my love…"

Even amid the tears of joy streaming down her cheeks, there was no glow on her face. She was still too traumatized.

Brian kissed his daughter on the forehead. "Welcome to the planet, Sarah Eleanor Mulrooney!" He knew the timing couldn't have been any worse to make such a joyous remark, but he couldn't resist. *What's left of it, that is!*

Had the newborn known what she was being born into, if she could speak, she would have begged her parents to send her back from where she came.

Brian pointed his phone screen at his mother. "We wanted to surprise you, Ma, by naming her after you..."

Some of Sarah's tears were joyous ones. The rest came from not having her husband by her side. Their son had just fulfilled a desire they both had for so many years, by finally making them grandparents.

Dick had no idea. Without even inquiring, Sarah knew this was the sixth seal judgment. She wondered if her husband was still alive...

When Lila was finished stitching her patient, she wiped her hands with a towel that was inside the birthing kit, doused her hands in hand sanitizer, then hugged Brian. "Congratulations to you all."

"Thanks for everything, Lila," Brian said, teary-eyed.

"My pleasure. Can I ask for your help now?"

"What do you need?"

"Help me kick down our bedroom door so I can check on my two bunkmates. I tried earlier but couldn't open it...."

"Sure." It took several attempts using his right foot, but Brian finally succeeded in breaching the bedroom door with his right foot.

Tamika wanted to join them, but she was too banged up to offer much assistance. She remained with Jacquelyn and Sarah, silently praying for her two sisters, already sensing they had become souls under the altar...

When Lila opened the door, her lungs were filled with a moldy dust. She turned on the flashlight and saw huge chunks of the roof and thick insulation covering the floor and beds.

One of the bunk bed legs had partially fallen through the sizable hole in the floor. She gulped hard, seeing sparks flying down in the kitchen below.

Heart pierced within her, Lila walked awkwardly toward the bunk beds, head down, body bent over. With a lump in her throat, her worst fears were confirmed. Both women were dead, crushed by the fallen roof.

Tears flooded Tamika's eyes when she heard Lila say, "Enjoy Paradise, my dear sisters! I'll see ya when I see ya..."

NINETY MINUTES AFTER SARAH was born, Dr. Singh came to check on Jacquelyn and the baby. Dirt was still caked in her hair, which was pulled back in a ponytail, and all over her clothes. It wasn't the most sanitary of conditions, but what choice did she have?

After checking the newborn's vitals, it didn't take her long to diagnose that the child had been born with Down Syndrome...

Jacquelyn's heart sunk in her chest.

With sadness in his voice, Brian asked Meera, "Thanks to Jakob being here, we know our daughter will survive the Tribulation period. But will Jesus heal her in the Millennial Kingdom?"

Meera sighed. "That's a question I cannot answer for you. But why would you want to change her? When I was living in Seattle, my neighbors had a child with Down Syndrome. He was the most precious child.

"I jokingly told his parents I would love to adopt him. They said there wasn't enough money in the world to ever entice them to part ways with the most perfect child on the planet. He really was special."

Meera let her tired eyes settle on the new parents. "I've always believed it takes special parents to raise special needs children. Seeing how God is trusting you both—all of us, in fact—with this precious child only reinforces to me just how blessed the two of you really are. I believe in time you will agree with me on this..."

Jacquelyn wanted to smile, but she couldn't. Her mind was too cluttered with many fearful thoughts. At the top of her mental list was whether or not the house would still be standing in the morning, or would it come crumbling down with everyone still in it, including her newborn child...

She blinked away the thought before it consumed her from within.

WITH EXCEPTION TO THE newborns and small children, who'd drifted merrily off to sleep, as if nothing had befallen their world, no one else at safe house number one, or at any other safe house on the planet, would sleep a wink this night. How could they?

10

FOR THE FIRST TIME in recorded history, a single earthquake had struck the entire planet. Simultaneously, the whole earth started rocking on all seven continents, and didn't stop for the better part of five minutes.

When the shaking finally stopped, every mountain and island had been uprooted and moved out of place, and every continent had been realigned, making what happened after the Rapture look like child's play.

The ensuing volcanic eruptions only made it worse for everyone affected by them.

Once-sprawling cities were instantly reduced to massive piles of rubble. Many of the metal and glass skyscrapers that were iconic fixtures in most cities, came crumbling down one after the other.

Those who had paid millions of dollars to live in penthouses on the top floors of those skyscrapers, so they could be high above everyone else, went down with them.

With so many buildings flattened like pancakes, many city streets no longer looked recognizable or canyon-like. Some tall buildings dubbed as "earthquake proof" had survived the initial quake. But with their foundations so badly damaged, they eventually came tumbling down under their own weight a few hours later.

So much of the planet was covered in broken glass, concrete, brick and mortar, sheet metal, mangled steel, drywall, wrecked vehicles, dead bodies, and a myriad of other things.

There was so much broken glass, in fact, that it looked like it had rained down from outer space for many days on end.

Death and carnage were visible as far as the eye could see.

Some of the cracks in the streets and even in fields and backyards were so deep and wide, they could have been mistaken for new zoning for state or county lines. Many who had spent small fortunes on subterranean shelters, and were assured they would be earthquake proof, were destroyed.

The millions of miles of gas and water lines that were repaired after the disappearances had ruptured again. Power lines were down as far as the eye could see, causing countless fires and explosions. Flames rose high into the sky. Smoke billowed up, further darkening the skies everywhere.

The numerous roads, highways, and bridges dotting the planet, that were badly damaged after the Rapture, and later repaired, were severely damaged again. Many bridges were destroyed. They would never be repaired.

Citizens of the world who had miraculously survived the mayhem, watched in total disbelief as their cities, suburbs, towns, and villages fell like weightless decks of cards.

Hundreds of thousands of women were in delivery rooms worldwide when the quake struck. Many of them were killed along with their children.

Most farms on the planet were completely devastated by the quake and ensuing volcanoes. Since it was late Spring, all crops that were recently planted were destroyed before they could ever be harvested.

Whereas the quakes the *Miracle Maker* had claimed to send more than a year ago were targeted and had borders, this quake was global, singular, impacting every country on earth, making the quakes that had devastated the nations upon which Yahweh God Himself had recently rendered judgment—not Salvador Romanero—look like a mere training exercise, when compared to this one.

BEFORE TOP MEMBERS OF the scientific communities of the world could even warn anyone, multiple volcanoes started erupting one after the other. The friction generated from so many tectonic plates grinding and scraping against each other in so many places, all at once, caused massive waves of energy to travel through the earth at blinding speeds, looking to escape somewhere.

The enormous seismic waves created by the global quake had weakened the tops of numerous magma chambers—large underground pools of liquid rock found beneath the surface of the earth—disturbing the gases inside, causing volcanic eruptions in so many places.

Tens of thousands of fissures were opened planet wide. Toxic steam pumped out of these dangerous cracks in the ground, spitting out carbon dioxide, with no sign of letting up anywhere.

Initially, 87 of the 452 volcanoes that were part of the "Ring of Fire", which accounted for 80 percent of the world's volcanoes, were part of the first round of eruptions. But as the seconds passed, more and more of them roared to life, angrily belching out lava from the bowels of the earth.

Cannon-like explosions could be heard from many miles away, sending volcanic gases, ash, and rocks as high as 50 miles in the air, filling the atmosphere with this dangerous toxic smoke.

Millions of tons of debris were being ejected every second, darkening the skies, and blocking out the sun and moon. They looked like dirty cloud makers, angrily pumping toxic smoke high into the atmosphere.

As the pyroclastic flows raced downhill at speeds greater than 100 miles per hour, with temperatures easily reaching anywhere from five hundred to a thousand degrees Fahrenheit, they completely transformed the landscape, destroying everything in their pathway, leaving behind a deep layer of solidified lava and thick ash in their wake.

These scorching rivers of fiery lava quickly engulfed homes and buildings, destroyed roads, highways, power lines, and devoured everything else that hadn't been destroyed by the global quake.

They flattened forests, scorched rich farmland, leaving behind thick layers of toxic debris everywhere. Trees that were left standing were stripped completely bare. All grass was completely burned up.

Some of these pyroclastic flows had mixed with melted snow and icebergs, creating dangerous liquid landslides of hot ash and toxic gases, known as lahars. They flowed down into the surrounding river valleys at remarkable speeds, destroying everything in their way, completely changing the topography wherever they flowed.

It didn't take long before volcanic ash started falling on towns and cities the world over, like powdery snow, covering sidewalks, grass, cars, rooftops in a gray toxic shroud. Several feet of it fell in some areas, quickly suffocating plants, animals, and even some humans.

It looked like a nuclear winter had just seized the entire planet...

Many who had survived the quake in those areas, were now trapped in the volcanic pathway with no time to evacuate. Knowing they were doomed, most were resigned to remain where they were, hoping it would end quickly for them, and that someone would eventually discover their burned, contorted, mummified bodies and give them a proper burial...

Most of these victims were burned alive by the pyroclastic flow. Others ended up dying of asphyxiation from inhaling too much ash.

Others were killed by the falling rock—some the sizes of basketballs— as some were killed by the mudflows which were caused by the resulting tsunamis.

Some who foolishly tried escaping in their vehicles were burned to death trying to evacuate. The roadways were already too badly damaged by the earthquake to even consider navigating them.

Once the lava from the volcanoes reached the roadways, they became instantly unrecognizable, never to be driven on again.

In most areas, the destruction went on for many miles.

Strangely enough, no aftershocks followed the global quake. Apparently, once was enough for God to fulfill this long-foretold prophecy...

11

WHEREAS AMERICA WAS SPARED the first round of earthquakes, the once-sovereign nation wasn't spared this time. More than 200,000 miles of railroad track—roughly 80%—in the United States of America was uprooted in the great quake. Mangled piles of worthless crumpled up steel now lay in ruins, thus crippling the locomotive industry.

Every town and city in California, Oregon and Washington situated to the west of the San Andreas fault, which cut clear through the state of California, now lay in ruins. What the earthquakes and volcanoes didn't obliterate, the ensuing tsunamis took care of…

Much of Washington D.C.—including the White House, Pentagon, the National Monument, and many other power structures scattered about the Capitol City had been leveled. At first glance, it was as if America's enemies had strategically taken out key targets in warfare, not a quake.

President Cipriano and Vice President Whitmore were both killed in the quake, along with a handful of secret service agents and White House staff.

The two women clung to each other in bed, for dear life, only to discover they would be eternally separated from this point forward, as both awaited God's full fury. There would be no more cuddling or holding each other in bed.

The last official order President Cipriano gave before she was killed, was to remove all crosses from church edifices, in all 50 states, so the buildings could be put to better use in serving their communities. Even the many wooden crosses that had stood for many years on the sides of highways were ordered to be taken down and burned.

It was only one of numerous decisions she had made in life that would haunt her for all eternity. With her soul now quaking infinitely more than the quake that the Most High God had used to end her life, she didn't need anyone to inform her about her spiritual fate—every core of her being trembled in fear knowing what was to come.

EVEN MORE PRECARIOUS, MUCH like when the Church had reached its fullness, which triggered the Rapture, it was at that precise moment when Romanero's death camps had all reached their full capacities, and there wasn't room for even one more detainee at any location, that God sent the global quake.

All prisons detaining His precious children were quickly obliterated. Some prisoners were crushed to death by falling objects—prison walls, roofs, or metal bunk beds. Some were swallowed whole like open graves, when the grounds upon which they had rested suddenly gave way.

But not a single prisoner belonging to the Most High God survived. All went to be with Jesus.

All on-duty guards and employees who took great pleasure in raping, torturing, and dismembering their detainees, were also killed in the quake.

Now that they had slipped into eternity, they were mindful that the God they always mocked and ridiculed had just fulfilled Revelation 6:9-11. *When he opened the fifth seal, I saw under the altar the souls of those who had been slain because of the word of God and the testimony they had maintained. They called out in a loud voice, 'How long, Sovereign Lord, holy and true, until you judge the inhabitants of the earth and avenge our blood?' Then each of them was given a white robe, and they were told to wait a little longer, until the full number of their fellow servants, their brothers and sisters, were killed just as they had been.*

What began with Ajit Laghari when he became the first martyr in Romanero's death camps, for not denying his Lord and Savior to the point of death, had just resulted in millions of more souls under the altar.

Now eternally doomed, their tormentors would all be forced to relive the countless atrocities they had committed on God's chosen children, knowing they would be held fully accountable for each one come Judgment Day—along with their former colleagues—as the Most High God they had always rejected would most assuredly avenge the blood of His precious saints, by condemning their souls to hell for all eternity.

YET, IN WHAT COULD only be described as a miracle from God Almighty Himself, with the entire world rocked off its axis, the cottage at which Jakob had resided just up the slope from the church pavilion at safe house number one, had been perfectly preserved.

Not a single pane of glass had been shattered. None of the walls had stress fractures on them. The same was true with his 143,999 sealed brothers. Supernaturally protected by Yahweh Himself, all were unharmed in the global quake, and everything that followed it.

There wasn't a single scratch on any of them.

Those situated in areas halfway around the world who were preaching when the quake struck, were taken back to the locations at which Yahweh had sent them to reside. Some were in mid-sentence when they suddenly vanished into thin air.

As the world shook ever so violently, mindful that they would be completely free from harm, the 144,000 sealed servants praised their Maker in unison, in perfect peace, harmony, and safety.

The instant the earth stopped quaking, much like how Philip had vanished from the presence of the Ethiopian eunuch before reappearing elsewhere, in the blink of an eye, they reappeared at the same locations they were preaching at a few moments ago, and resumed with great boldness, amid the total devastation all around them, to include numerous dead bodies.

Their voices rose high above the landscape, as they boldly proclaimed what had been prophesied 2,000 years ago by the Disciple John, in Revelation 6:12-17: "'I watched as he opened the sixth seal. There was a great earthquake. The sun turned black like sackcloth made of goat hair, the whole moon turned blood red, and the stars in the sky fell to earth, as figs drop from a fig tree when shaken by a strong wind. The heavens receded like a scroll being rolled up, and every mountain and island was removed from its place.

"'Then the kings of the earth, the princes, the generals, the rich, the mighty, and everyone else, both slave and free, hid in caves and among the rocks of the mountains. They called to the mountains and the rocks, 'Fall on us and hide us from the face of him who sits on the throne and from the wrath of the Lamb! For the great day of their wrath has come, and who can withstand it?'"

For the many kings, princes and generals who were hunkered down in their subterranean locations, the first part of their wish had been granted, only to discover that they had just gone from bad to worse, as there would be no escaping the wrath of the living God for all eternity!

Whereas the Two Witnesses had forewarned humanity for three straight days on what would happen, as recorded in God's Holy Word, now that Revelation 6:12-17 had come to pass, the 144,000 boldly declared what the Two Ancients had prophesied, with remarkable clarity.

But the greatest miracle that took place was, as the globe shook ever so violently, the one country that was immune to it all was Yahweh's beloved Israel...

Much like His 144,000 sealed servants, as was written in Deuteronomy 32:10, God had shielded, cared for, and guarded Jacob (Israel). As the rest of the world lie in a barren and howling waste, the apple of Yahweh's eye remained perfectly intact, without having sustained even a single tremor.

12

THE FOLLOWING DAY

AT SAFE HOUSE NUMBER one, the breaches in the 12-foot wall circling the property, encompassing it, were even worse than originally feared in the darkness. Many sections came crumbling down, leaving gaping holes all throughout. They would have to be repaired pronto.

Another thing that left residents feeling increasingly vulnerable was that the canvasses fronting the property, which took many months to stitch together, were shredded like paper.

Even the canopies covering most walkways so *ETSM* members could walk or jog and get fresh air, were shredded like sheets of paper.

What was left of them dangled helplessly from still-remaining trees, or blew wildly in the wind, completely helpless from protecting anyone.

Of the 263 cottages that were scattered about the property, more than half were completely leveled, or swallowed whole. Dozens more that weren't finished off by the quake itself, were severely damaged when massive 100-foot oak trees came crashing down on them, killing many inside.

Equally devastating, hundreds of more trees were uprooted on the outside of the wall, making them feel even more visible and vulnerable to the outside world.

At the church pavilion, some of the overhead trusses had snapped in half or were badly splintered. Every overhead light had been shattered. Every ceiling fan had been disjointed, and five of the six speakers that were mounted to the beams had come crashing down onto the pews below.

The stained-glass window behind the stage that had comforted so many, was blown out. The cement floor was badly cracked in so many places. Every bench was tipped over. Some had been splintered in many places.

What came as no surprise to anyone was that the entire foundation of the subterranean hospital had shifted. Putting it on the bottom floor was poor decision-making on their part. Then again, who were they to think that the outdated measly cottages they were living in could withstand what they all knew was headed their way?

With all patients safely relocated to the military-style bunker that had sustained the least amount of damage, and with the two deceased patients buried, they brought whatever medical equipment and hospital beds they could salvage to the new hospital location, where patients and infants were wrapped in many blankets to help keep them warm.

Gasoline-powered generators were used to power the space heaters, but with so much damage done to the building, only those closest to them benefitted from the warmth they generated. Much of the heat floated skyward, before ultimately escaping the building.

The cafeteria was also severely damaged. Parts of the roof came crashing down, injuring many who were eating at the time before starting the midnight shift. More than a dozen workers were killed. It was too soon to know for sure if the stoves and ovens could ever be used again.

The underground jail that was situated on the middle floor of the other subterranean location also sustained a substantial amount of damage. The rooms no longer looked rectangular. The LED screens that had hung on the walls in each room, projecting pleasant sceneries and Bible quotations for all who were sent there, fell to the floor completely covered in dirt.

But what had caused their greatest fears to surface was the damage sustained on the top floor of the second subterranean hole, where the underground hatcheries and plant beds took up the entire space.

Two-thirds of the fish tanks that were filled to the brim with catfish and tilapia had shattered in the quake. Tragically, some workers were crushed to death when the heavy tanks came crashing down on top of them.

Those who survived turned on battery-operated lamps and scooped as much of the fresh mounds of dirt and drywall out of the remaining tanks as they could, as the others did their best to gather as many of the flopping fish that hadn't fallen through the cracks in the floor, before placing them in the still-remaining tanks, and in buckets and waste baskets.

After what they had experienced, they were surprised that even one glass tank was left standing. For that, they were grateful.

Equally devastating was the aquaponics technology that had been working like clockwork producing bumper crops at safehouse number one. Much of it now lay on the floor in various growth stages, covered in dirt, which was rather ironic considering that soil hadn't been used to grow them.

They still had plenty of seed to start over but, knowing even greater calamities were still to come, what they didn't have was absolute assurance that they would survive long enough to consume it all.

One unexpected blessing was when Joaquim Guzman took a handful of teenagers to survey the damage outside the safehouse. They discovered a water main break along the way, just off U.S. 202, and made three trips back and forth, on 4-wheelers, filling 50-gallon barrels full of water each time. The water that was collected on the first two trips was used to help put out some of the smaller cottage fires. Many still smoldered.

When they went back a third time, the township was in the process of shutting off the water. They squeezed every-last drop they could get into the barrels, which were then used as temporary fish-tank replacements until more could be obtained later.

Had the roads not been so badly damaged, they would have been able to make several more trips. But what would normally take five minutes at most took 45 each way. Had they not been riding on 4-wheelers, it would have been an impossible endeavor!

It took a while, but the fire caused by the fuel tanker explosion was finally extinguished. Three men sprayed fire retardant, as seven others shoveled heaping mounds of dirt on the flames. They also managed to extinguish some of the cottage fires the same way.

Some of the multi-station workout machines, treadmills, and elliptical bikes in the newly renovated exercise room, were damaged or destroyed.

More than half of the washers and dryers were crushed and were beyond repair, when the old general store that had been recently transformed into the new laundry room, came crashing down on them, killing five members working on the late shift.

With exception to Jakob's cottage, all other structures on the premises looked entirely different...

Another mounting fear was that the large steel safes and industrial-size walk-in refrigerators on the bottom floor of the second subterranean hole, storing cash, medicine, and thousands of pints of blood, would have to be dug up ASAP. They would also have to do their best to recover the many backup generators and Level A hazmat suits that were buried under mounds of dirt and other debris.

Whatever foods and medicines could be recovered would be stored in refrigerated trucks, which would be brought in from the Kennett Square farm/safehouse for the time being, along with whatever food could be salvaged, before it spoiled and would have to be tossed out.

As the clean-up process began, Julio Gonzalez assembled a crew and ordered half of them to start cutting the massive trees that had toppled over on the inside of the property, as the other half did the same on the outside, so they could start the rebuilding process immediately.

The 35-year-old former construction business owner from Providence, Rhode Island, ordered that the largest downed trees be sectioned into telephone-pole style beams, which would be used to hold ceilings in place until they could be fixed or reconstructed, log cabin style.

The branches would be used for firewood and kindling.

Tony Pearsall assembled another team of men and women to measure the gaps in the 12-foot wall, so it could be patched up immediately. For now, whatever wood was salvaged from the destroyed cottages would be used to cover the holes, until the wall could be replaced in the coming days.

The wood would also be used to patch holes in damaged roofs and walls, and as planks for crossing the three major fault lines on the property.

They reclaimed anything they could from the destroyed structures— copper-fittings, nails and screws, bricks and wood, air and water filtration units, and everything in between.

With the nursery floors being so badly cracked and damaged, mattresses that weren't shredded to pieces were taken there to cover the floor, to protect the many babies who were already crawling.

Since they still had leftover bricks, cement mix, steel, and lumber from the massive shipment Jefferson Danforth sent before the Islamic jihad attack on the Western Hemisphere, they would begin rebuilding at once.

"What I wouldn't do for a bricklaying machine now!" Tony Pearsall said to Julio Gonzalez, three hours into the rebuilding process.

"I heard that!" came the weary reply.

Motivated by fear, though bloodied with numerous cuts and bruises all over their bodies, they would work all day and night fixing whatever they could, wherever they could.

But, without a doubt, the most staggering loss suffered at safe house number one was the human death toll, which had just eclipsed 500 and was steadily rising. Thirty-three of them were safe house guards.

Remo was among them. Titus watched in horror, as his best friend was swallowed whole and buried alive. Other guards were killed after being thrown into the wall or trees, as if being flung out of slingshots. Blood splatters could be seen wherever impact was made.

Titus wept many tears of joy and sadness for his fallen brothers.

One man solemnly drove a flatbed truck from the back of the property as far as it would go, before a large crevice prevented it from going any farther, then waited for more facemask-wearing residents pushing wheelbarrows full of dead bodies to reach him. Once they were loaded onto the truck, he took them off property for burial.

They just hoped the 20-foot burial ditch would be wide and deep enough for the mass casualties. If not, they would have to be burned. The fact that they couldn't seek outside advice or assistance with the grim task of burying so many dead bodies, only elevated the angst everyone felt...

Seeing the mass carnage and annihilation all around them, those who had somehow survived the insanity marveled that they were still alive. They mourned the loss of their fellow safe house residents, whom they felt closer to than their unsaved friends and loved ones, silently wishing that they, too, had been killed, so they could finally be at rest.

THE KENNETT SQUARE SAFEHOUSE had also suffered numerous losses. One hundred and twenty of the 300 residents living there had perished in the quake. All were essential workers, most of whom were in charge of secretly stashing food for their brothers and sisters at surrounding *ETSM* safe houses.

Equally devastating was that more than half of the livestock, chickens, planted crops, silos full of grain, and farming equipment were wiped out.

This would make it even more difficult to supply *ETSM* residents in the Northeast with a steady supply of food shipments in the coming months...

13

MEANWHILE, TRAVIS EARTINGS WOKE before Clayton, totally unaware of what had just befallen the planet. He went upstairs to brew a pot of coffee. The first thing he noticed was the kitchen sink faucet wasn't working.

He looked outside the cabin windows and couldn't believe what his eyes were seeing. The sky was ominously dark and hazy. But that's not what had caused his eyes to grow as wide as silver-dollar pancakes. It was what he saw *under* the sky.

Through panicked breaths, he yelled down the stairs, "Clayton, come quickly!"

Clayton heard the urgency in his partner's voice and raced up the stairs. *What in the world?* He rubbed his eyes with two fingers to make sure his mind wasn't playing tricks on him. It wasn't. *Could it be?*

What terrified him most weren't the hundreds of downed trees or wooden fences he saw, but the foothill mountains in the near distance that were practically split in half, not to mention the fault-line crevices in the ground that were deep and wide enough to easily absorb 18-wheeler tractor trailers. His mouth became dry as cotton. *This is bad!*

For the life in him, Holmes couldn't fathom how the cabin they were in had survived with such unspeakable devastation all around them. Even more mind-numbing was that he and Travis had slept through it all. "How come we didn't feel anything?"

Travis was too blown away to utter a reply, which was fine, because Clayton was asking himself more than he was his lifelong friend.

They went to check on Moishe, but he was gone. This wasn't unexpected. He was always out preaching during daylight hours. But if this was Revelation 6:9-17, who would be out listening to him?

Not knowing if it would be safe to leave the cabin, they decided to wait until he returned before taking the next step. If anyone could confirm what both were thinking, it would be him.

Moishe's dire warning when they first met, about survivors seeing with their own two eyes something that would cement in their minds that they were who they said they were, now loomed large in their minds.

Like most East Coasters, this was the two *ETSM* leaders' first earthquake encounter. Though they frequently registered on the Richter scale in this neck-of-the-woods, they were very seldom felt by humans.

Holmes and Hartings knew this day was coming. Even so, it was impossible to properly explain how helpless they felt, powerless really.

Clayton tried calling Charles Calloway. He had been staying at the same safe house as Deacon Stone and Miss Evelyn.

Whereas cell phones relied on cellular towers to make calls, send text messages, or access the internet—which Holmes already sensed were destroyed—Sat-phones bypassed all that by connecting directly to stationary or orbiting satellites overhead.

The satellites that were being used by the *ETSM* were sent into space by Jefferson Danforth when he was still President. They ran through a secure network that only the counter shadow government knew about.

The problem was, they were designed to work in clear skies. The technology had advanced to where calls could still be made in cloudy conditions, but the cloudier it was, the spottier the signal was.

Even with a satellite signal to draw from, he couldn't get through to him. He tried Dr. Lee Kim, Pastor Jim Simonton, and Brian Mulrooney next, to warn them about the global volcanic eruptions that were no doubt engulfing much of the planet in flames by now, but he kept getting the same result.

Holmes sighed, then powered down his phone to save the battery. "Lord, please protect them as only You can..."

Moishe returned to the cabin at dusk, just before the sun set. With the skies so darkened, one might think it had set hours ago. "You should see it out there! Total devastation as far as the eye can see. Far worse than what followed the Rapture."

"Was it the sixth seal judgment?" Travis asked, already knowing it was.

Moishe nodded at him. "But, praise Yahweh," he said, his eyes surveying the cabin, "just like this location, every place at which my brothers are residing were perfectly preserved, including those who were in the pathways of the rivers of lava. Everything else was destroyed...

"Much like Shadrach, Meshach and Abednego, who were bound and thrown into the blazing furnace for refusing to serve King Nebuchadnezzar's gods, and for not worshiping the image of gold he had set up, they never felt the scorching heat from the lava.

"In similar fashion, Yahweh once again performed the mind-bending miracle of preserving His servants from what seemed impossible in human terms. We all appeared at the places of duty right on time without ever losing stride. Guess you could say it was business as usual for us."

Clayton blinked hard. "I'm confused, if it was global, and everyone was affected by it, who did you possibly preach to?"

"If you're asking if I had an audience to preach to, the answer is no. But with power out everywhere, no one within the sound of my voice could escape the message I preached!"

The three men sat down for a meal together.

After Moishe blessed the food, Travis said, "I can't believe we slept through it all…"

"Since you were here with me, the two of you were never in danger. Consider it a blessing of sorts from Yahweh Himself for your faithfulness to Him. But this is a one-time occurrence."

Even if Holmes and Hartings had been awake when Moishe was praising his Maker along with his 143,999 sealed brothers, during the quake and volcanic eruptions—with full-throated voices—they still wouldn't have seen or heard a thing. This was their special time with Yahweh, and no one else was invited, including the two *ETSM* leaders.

Moishe added, "As we had already discussed, we cannot stay under the same roof together. You'll have to leave come sunrise."

Travis glanced at Clayton then at Moishe. "We understand. It's not like it's our cabin anyway. It's God's cabin, to use as He sees fit."

Moishe added, "Precisely. Another thing you will hear about in the coming days, when communications slowly come back to life in some areas, is that Yahweh had spared all of Israel from the trumpet judgment."

Clayton was incredulous. "Seriously?"

Moishe nodded. "Don't get me wrong, I'm sure some of my fellow Israelis died in my homeland from sickness and disease, auto accidents, and on and on, but none died as a result of the global quake. How could they when the ground never shook over there?"

The young man paused. "Unless, of course, they suffered heart attacks watching the global destruction all around them."

Travis Hartings shook his head in wonderment. "Simply fascinating."

"Indeed," Moishe agreed. He grew more somber. "When you return to your safehouses, you will find numerous casualties. Those who survived will be shocked to see you both. Your sleeping quarters were destroyed. Had you not been here with me, the two of you surely would have been killed."

Holmes and Hartings exchanged shocked glances.

67

"That explains your urgent text message the other day," Clayton said, scratching his suddenly throbbing head. "It was a true life saver."

Travis nodded agreement.

Jakob put the last spoonful of soup in his mouth, then rose from his seat. "Now, if you'll excuse me, gentlemen, it's time to pray with my brothers. I won't be here in the morning, so kindly let yourselves out. The two of you will be included in my prayers."

At that, Moishe excused himself from the table, and went to the bedroom that had become his prayer room.

Clayton wanted to ask the young man a million questions, but now wasn't the time. His mind raced back to the prophecy website he had launched before the Rapture. *How wrong I was on so many levels!*

Travis broke him from this dreadful thought. "I think we should record a message for everyone. Even if it takes many days before they can listen to it, at least they'll know we're still alive. With so much volcanic ash filling the atmosphere, the clouds will eventually reach here too."

"Agreed." Holmes powered on his Sat-phone again. "Not sure when any of you will hear this. I'll keep it short to save the battery. But for now, just know your leaders are safe. It'll take some time before we can know what's what, but no doubt we've suffered numerous casualties this day.

"But we can rejoice knowing all of our brothers and sisters are in Glory now, with Braxton Rice and Nigel Jones, Hallelujah! As we begin the rebuilding process, let us be ever mindful that we win in the end!

"We'll do our best to keep you updated in the coming days. Until then, keep fighting the Good fight. Pray for us as we pray for you. God is with us. Out!"

Holmes felt like an army general giving desperate orders to a greatly outnumbered battalion. Even though he knew they would win in the end, it didn't feel that way now.

14

THREE DAYS LATER

WHAT HAD TAKEN CLAYTON and Travis 2.5 hours to travel from Ellijay, Georgia to the cabin in Oak Ridge, Tennessee, before the global quake, took three bewildering days before they could finally make it back there.

When the two men left the cabin at 8 a.m., the plan was to go to the safehouse on the Georgia-Tennessee border at which Charles Calloway, Miss Evelyn, Deacon Stone, Santana Jiles, Purnima Rushi, and Dylan had all resided, along with a handful of others.

But after traveling in that direction for nearly four hours, the back road they were on became impassable, and they were forced to backtrack looking for new routes to take without the use of GPS to guide them.

It wasn't the only time they had to backtrack, but the eight-hour loss that time was gruelingly deflating.

With the skies steadily darkening from the dust caused by the quakes, and from the plumes of ash already reaching this part of the globe, blocking out the sun in so many places, it looked more like it was 8 p.m., not 8 a.m.

It was as if they were driving in Tromsø, Norway, in the dead of winter, not Tennessee in late-Spring!

Despite Moishe's warning of the total devastation, as far as the eye could see, they weren't prepared for what their eyes drank in.

It looked every bit as apocalyptic as all those sci-fi flicks they used to watch before the Rapture. But now that it had suddenly materialized before their very eyes, it was infinitely more horrifying!

There were no unaffected areas—destruction was everywhere! With so many upturned and twisted parcels of road, and with so many uprooted trees, downed streetlights, wires, crashed vehicles of all types, and large mounds of dirt, concrete, and boulders from the many landslides littering the roadways, there were numerous casualties. It was staggering.

While Holmes and Hartings may not have seen these cars being shot up off roads as if bombs had been detonated underneath them, they clearly saw the aftereffects of it all. Some of the now mangled vehicles landed on guardrails before rolling over many times down into ravines below.

69

Even worse, large chunks of roads and highways broke apart, leaving gaping holes in so many places. Some were so wide and so deep that they looked like miniature canyons.

Most stretches of road were so badly damaged or full of debris, they could never support 4-wheel vehicles of any sort, let alone big rigs. This would further paralyze the already-decimated supply chains which delivered goods and services from manufacturer to consumer.

Instead of following from a safe distance, Clayton and Travis rode side by side this time. Senses on full alert, they were determined to stick together at all times, in case one of them crashed into something or fell into one of the gaping holes along the way.

They were forced to pull their vehicles to the side of the road, every few miles, then push them around whatever damage they encountered at that particular time—sometimes a mile at a time—before they dared trust the road for driving again. Had they not been riding on motorcycles; it would have been an impossible endeavor.

They had no plans of driving at night. It was already difficult enough during the daylight hours, when the sun was still up there somewhere. If the roads couldn't be trusted during daylight hours—darkened as they were—how could they expect them to be better at night?

Even the LED headlights on their motorbikes wouldn't be bright enough to illuminate what their eyes were forced to horrifically drink in during the darkened daylight hours. If they tried, they wouldn't make it five miles!

After passing numerous closed gas stations on day one, they finally saw one that appeared to be open.

A handmade sign was posted on the badly damaged brick wall:

GAS FOR SALE
$55 PER GALLON!

Holmes and Hartings were exhausted, hungry, and stressed from the grueling trip. They were also low on fuel. They offered to pay the station owner $500 in cash to fill their tanks, feed them and let them rest their bleary eyes indoors for a few hours.

Thankfully, the kind man had accepted their generous offer. He manually filled their fuel tanks, fed them franks and beans and offered them a small room at the back of the station which, remarkably, was still intact.

In normal circumstances, seeing the vast damage the building had sustained in the quake, they would have never stepped foot inside.

They slept inside old, dirty sleeping bags on the floor, using their arms as pillows. Remarkably, they both woke feeling refreshed.

As much as they would have loved to shower, with no water or electricity, they couldn't even wash their hands. After helping themselves to leftover franks and beans, they thanked the owner again for his hospitality, and went on their way.

Six hours into the trip, even driving at relatively slow speeds, Travis' eyes were so strained and bloodshot from staring at the road too long, that he couldn't avoid hitting an eight-inch pothole that had snuck up on him.

Hartings went airborne before falling hard onto the road, dislocating his right shoulder in the process. Clayton helped him pop it back into place. Thankfully, his motorcycle had only sustained minimal damage.

But it was extremely difficult navigating it mostly with one hand.

Every bump in the road or sharp turn he was forced to make, to avoid being swallowed up by one of the gaping holes they encountered along the way, had caused a throbbing pain to rip through him.

Both men had microphones on their helmets. Every few minutes, Clayton would ask, "How ya holding up, partner?"

And each time, Travis would wince in excruciating pain. "Not so good, but we must keep going!"

"Roger that," was Clayton's most common reply.

Later that day, they silently rejoiced, upon seeing another gas station open for business. A sign was taped to one of its broken gas pumps:

GAS FOR SALE
$75 PER GALLON!

Much like the night before, the *ETSM* leaders offered to pay the station owner $500 in cash to fill their tanks, feed them and let them rest indoors, so they wouldn't freeze to death.

He even threw in a container of extra-strength Tylenol for Travis' throbbing shoulder. It didn't help much. The pain was so severe at times, he tried keeping his groans to a low decibel level so Clayton wouldn't hear him.

It was an impossible task. Needless to say, he hardly slept a wink.

They had fully expected to encounter delays along the way, especially since all 12 roads and highways on which they'd traveled were badly damaged, and might never be repaired, but three days?

What made the journey even worse was that they had to push their motorcycles at least 25 of the grueling 138 miles!

They coasted into Ellijay on fumes. With electricity out everywhere, once the sun set, it's like the darkness was taken to a whole new level. It went from dark to pitch black. It was horrifying. And with the sun being blocked out worldwide for going on three days now, it felt 50 degrees colder than it did when they left the Oak Ridge cabin. At least that much!

Clayton turned on the flashlight he kept in the rear storage compartment on his bike. "Wait here, Travis."

Holmes wasn't overly surprised to discover the secret latch securing the subterranean space below had broken off its hinges. He climbed down below to find a foot of dirt covering the floor. Large chunks of plywood and drywall had fallen onto their mattresses, easily breaking the small wooden table separating the two beds into many pieces.

And one of the gasoline cans had flipped over, leaking its contents into the soil. Just one whiff and Clayton knew all it would take was a tiny spark to potentially blow them both to kingdom come, which, right now, sounded just peachy to him.

He yelled up to Travis, "No way we're sleeping down here tonight! One of the gas cans spilled over. The fumes are overpowering…"

Travis gasped. He was tired and still in excruciating pain. Now that they had no place to sleep, he could no longer control his emotions. Tears streamed down his cheeks one after the next.

Clayton detached the mattresses from the cots and dragged them up to the surface. Ignoring his friend's tears for the moment—Holmes felt like crying himself—he said, "I know you're injured, partner, but we need to light a fire. Can you gather a few twigs and branches with your good arm, while I go back down in the hole for gas, matches, blankets and pillows?"

Hartings sniffled softly, "I'll do my best…"

When Clayton returned to the surface, he shook the dirt off the mattresses and blankets and prepared Travis' bed for him. "I'll take it from here. Take more Tylenol and rest. We'll have a fire in no time."

Travis could only nod his thanks. He buried himself beneath the blankets, praying they wouldn't freeze to death or be spotted by someone, whichever came first.

Clayton piled a heaping amount of wood on top of the twigs and branches that Travis had gathered, doused them all in gasoline and struck a match, instantly killing the chill in the air.

Even with a blazing fire, both men still felt the eerie darkness pressing in on them. The heat from the fire was enough to warm their bodies, but both men shivered uncontrollably, as their minds tried catching up to what

72

had just befallen their world. No doubt their organization had suffered numerous casualties this day. Time would tell just how many had perished.

Clayton stared at the flames licking the pitch-black sky, and thought about the endless streams of lava that had no doubt wiped out countless cities and villages by now, killing everyone in their destructive pathways.

He could only assume that some of their safe houses were destroyed in the global quake, or had been buried under fiery-hot lava, or the pyroclastic mudflows. *Are the animals as terrified as we humans?*

He blinked away the thought and glanced over at Travis. Despite the constant pain, having not slept the night before, he was out cold.

Holmes silently gasped. What had started with a simple text message from Travis 72 hours ago, ended up saving their lives. As it turned out, had they not met, both would have been killed in the quake. It was as if God had given them a heads-up warning of sorts. Travis, anyway.

Usually, their shared dreams came in threes. But in this case, it was a single dream producing three separate realities—they were together which meant they wouldn't lose contact, they would have been killed had they not gone to the cabin, and they got to meet Moishe.

Clayton pulled the blanket up to his neck and rolled onto his side. After what they had encountered the past three days, he didn't know if he would have the strength to face whatever would come their way in the morning. He felt completely overwhelmed, hopeless even.

The tears he had held back for his partner's sake now flowed freely down his cold cheeks, one after the next. He uttered a soft but desperate prayer skyward, "Help me, Lord, I can't continue without You!", already sensing that even more tragic news would mercilessly greet them in the morning...

15

CLAYTON HOLMES WOKE EARLY the next morning, mildly shocked that he had slept at all. The sun had already risen but with so much volcanic ash in the atmosphere, the skies were even darker than the previous two mornings had been. But there was enough light above to see the ash falling ever so softly in Ellijay like gray powdery snow, that was being generated from the volcanic eruptions thousands of miles away.

Holmes surveyed the five-acre-property they had purchased way back when. The dilapidated buildings scattered about had been reduced to piles of rubble. *Had there been vagrants living in them, I hope they survived!*

Clayton glanced over at Travis. "How ya feeling, partner?"

Travis rubbed his lower back with his good hand. "Well, I'm still alive."

"Are you at all surprised that we didn't see one of the hundred and forty four thousand at this dump?" Clayton said, hoping to elicit laughter from Travis. "Perhaps if we stay here a few hours more, he'll show up."

Travis wanted to laugh, but it would hurt too much. "Not gonna lie, I'm terrified just thinking about traveling these roads alone with my injuries. Do you mind if we stick together?"

Clayton stretched his arms above his head. After what he experienced the past three days, he was just as frightened himself. "Sure, so long as you don't mind going to Miss Evelyn's safe house with me. I need to know if they're okay. I won't rest until I know one way or the other…"

Travis sighed relief. "I don't mind at all."

Before leaving for the safehouse on the Georgia-Tennessee border, they filled their fuel tanks full of gas, prayed for God's protection, then left, not sure what they would encounter…

What would usually take 45 minutes at most, in normal times, took five hours this time. Compared to the three days it took to travel from Oak Ridge to Ellijay, it was more than a fair trade off.

When they were roughly a quarter mile away from the safehouse, they smelled smoke. The closer they got to the property, the more pungent the aroma became. Mindful that the nearest property was several miles away, both men knew in their hearts the smell was coming from their location.

To their dismay, they found the safehouse burned to the ground, still smoldering in some places.

They saw Charles Calloway sitting on a wooden rocking chair that had somehow survived the mayhem, 50 feet away from the charred remains. He had cuts, bruises and burn marks all over his body, and the clothing he had on was blackened and bloodied.

When he heard the motorcycles approaching, he never bothered looking up. He sensed it was his two friends. After all, he knew the mode of transportation they had taken to the Oak Ridge cabin before the quake.

The way he felt now, if it wasn't them, oh well, so be it…

Travis removed his helmet. "Charles, are you okay?"

Without looking up, Calloway said, "They're all gone, fellas. There was nothing I could do to rescue them…"

Pain stabbed at Clayton's heart. "What happened?"

"I went outside to reply to a text message I received from Jonathan Steinberg, president of the company I was involved with before the Rapture. He warned me to cease and desist immediately from sending outlawed messages in my online newsletter, even though I hadn't done that since before Romanero outlawed Christianity…"

Calloway stared out in the distance with no emotion whatsoever. "You'd think he'd have better things to do with his time than read my past newsletters. After reminding me that I hadn't placed an order with them in months, he then warned me that he couldn't allow me to keep using his company platform to spread my mumbo-jumbo hate speech!

"He told me he empathized with my mental illness, but he wouldn't be held responsible for my illegal actions! Can't help but wonder if he knows about the warrant out for my arrest? Probably…"

Holmes and Hartings stared at each other. Clearly, Charles was still in shock.

He went on, "Anyway, just as I was about to reply, the ground started shaking all around me. I wanted to race inside to rescue everyone, but before I could move, I was slammed to the ground a few inches away from that crevice over there," he said, pointing in that direction.

"It only took a few seconds for the roof to collapse. At first, I thought they had a chance to escape." He closed his eyes. "But when the entire house was quickly engulfed in flames, from the fireplace that was at full height at the time, there was nothing I could do to rescue them."

Calloway hadn't felt this broken since the day he returned to Florida after the Rapture, to find clothing scattered all throughout the house that had been worn by his wife and five children, when they were taken to Heaven with the rest of his family.

He shook his head sadly, then started bawling like a baby. "I found Deacon Stone's and Miss Evelyn's charred bodies in their bed. They clung to each other until the very end." His sobs intensified. "I was supposed to protect them..."

Travis placed a hand on his shoulder. "It's not your fault, Charles."

"Everyone inside was killed, even Dylan and Purnima whom you recently married. Santana's also gone," Calloway lamented, referring to his lifelong friend, Santana Jiles.

Clayton's heart burned within him. "Where are their bodies?"

Through soft sniffling, Charles said, "It took two days for the fire to finally burn itself out, before I could go inside. I used that wheelbarrow over there to collect the bodies." he said, pointing at it. "Not knowing what else to do, I found a tarp in the shed and cut it into five sections to wrap them in, before dumping them in that crevice. I feel so dirty..."

Clayton placed his right hand on Charles' shoulder. "You need to keep reminding yourself that they're in a better place now. I know it'll be difficult for you to shake off how they left this planet. But they look nothing like that now, brother. I know Deacon Stone was a close family friend, especially to your father. And you know how much I loved Miss Evelyn. But we must cling to the promise that we will see them again soon. As we suffer, they are being comforted..."

When Charles remained silent, Travis asked, "Have you slept?"

Calloway sniffled again. "I took a short nap in the storage shed, after I finished burying everyone..."

"Have you eaten anything?"

Calloway shook his head. "I'm not hungry, Travis..."

"I understand, but you need to eat something." Travis pulled three MREs out of the motorcycle storage compartment, and three bottles of filtered water. Clayton started a fire a few feet away from the shed where he knew they would sleep, before leaving in the morning. "Let's all eat."

Charles ate his meal very slowly, as his two friends shared their mind-twisting encounter over the past few days with him. He already knew about their meeting with Moishe. He had been so encouraged by the things God's sealed servant had told his two mentors, that he could hardly contain himself.

The young man had given them all a new sense of direction.

Then came the quake...

Before sleeping that night, Holmes and Hartings laid hands on Charles and prayed aloud knowing the God they served was listening, even if all three felt like their Maker was far away from them now.

And to think that this was one of their smaller safehouses. How much worse would it be when they arrived back at the other properties?

THE NEXT MORNING, THE three men left for the safe house at which Clayton had been residing before the global quake, silently praying that it wouldn't be as traumatic as this encounter had been.

Charles wanted to follow behind them in his car. Clayton warned that if he tried, he wouldn't get two miles before he was forced to turn back.

As Charles drove Travis' bike, with Travis riding shotgun, it didn't take long for Clayton's words to be proven true. What he saw was unbelievable!

The three men arrived at the safehouse just before sunset, to find widespread damage. Sure enough, just as Moishe had proclaimed, Clayton's sleeping quarters had been leveled in the quake.

Of the 200 residents living there, 83 of them had perished. Those who had survived were thankful to see their leaders again.

One of them was Dr. Lee Kim. Among those who had perished was their newest resident, Cornelius Holmes. He arrived the day before it happened.

Lee Kim said to Clayton, "When I searched the property after the quake, I found your brother sleeping in your bed. He wanted to surprise you when you came back from your trip. Sorry, Clayton…" he said somberly.

Overwhelmed by the news, Clayton lowered his head and wept, as everyone stood silent, not knowing what to say or do.

As if returning a favor from the day before, it was Charles' turn to comfort Clayton with these words, "Your brother was never tortured in Romanero's death camps, but since he fled his former life, to include leaving his three unsaved sons, you can rejoice knowing he's a soul under the altar. As we suffer, he is being comforted…"

"Amen," Holmes said softly, drying his eyes. He looked skyward. "Thank you, Lord, for saving my brother before his death, and for saving Miss Evelyn after the Rapture. I can't wait to see my departed brothers and sisters again, whenever that day will be. But mostly, Father, I am even more eager to live with You now than ever before. Even so, come Lord Jesus…"

"Amen!" came the reply from everyone within earshot.

16

HANA PATEL WAS COMPLETELY beside herself. Still mourning her husband's death, she didn't know if she was coming or going. She was doing all she could to remain strong for her daughter, but as the days passed, she felt her strength leaving her body like a helium balloon being emptied of its contents.

How could she feel otherwise when each day was like dangling on the precipice of a full-blown nervous breakdown, with the whole world seemingly watching? The constant juggling act kept robbing her of what little strength she still had left in her malnourished body, due to the fact that she hadn't had an appetite in weeks.

Like most others on the planet, the way her body trembled in fear most days, Hana looked like someone who had recently developed Parkinson's.

A lack of nourishment only made it worse, especially since she was still breastfeeding her daughter.

If for only that reason, she needed to remain healthy, even if it meant forcing herself to eat, just to achieve that objective.

In truth, the body tremors started long before the global quake shook the planet. The first jolt to her body struck at the precise moment when life seemed most perfect to her, that is, until her late husband accused Salvador Romanero of being the Antichrist of the Bible, as she sat next to him up on stage to receive her million-dollar monetary card.

The timing couldn't have been any worse! Hana was already angry with Yogesh before he foolishly did that, incensed even. Anger quickly turned to shame, embarrassment, and humiliation after he accused the man of something she thought so heinous at the time, before walking off the stage and doing his best to flee his captors.

The second jolt came when she received the anonymous call in her hotel suite the following morning, from a woman who threatened her life if she dared publicly confess her secret, that she was already pregnant before Salvador Romanero announced the contest.

This made Hana feel entirely insignificant, like she didn't matter to the *Miracle Maker*, whom she was convinced had put the woman up to it.

The third jolt came mere moments after the nerve-shredding call, as she watched in horror as the airplane on which her fugitive husband was traveling was destroyed by a missile ordered by the *Man of Peace* himself.

The global quake only made her trembling grow worse!

The house itself had sustained massive damage during the quake. Part of the roof had collapsed, every window was blown out, and there were measurable cracks in the floors and on most walls. Most alarming was that it had caused a sizable shift in its foundation.

Hana was grateful that all windows had since been replaced, but the roof wouldn't be fixed for quite some time. Most roofers were still awaiting aftershocks before assessing damage that had already been done.

But they did cover the roof with a few tarps, which made Hana harken back to her days living in a shack whenever she looked up at it, which was frequently throughout the day.

Now that her daughter was taking her first steps, what concerned her the most were the sizable cracks in the floor in so many places. The larger ones had since been filled with sand, then covered with throw rugs, but it wasn't enough to prevent her child from potentially hurting herself.

Monitoring children in normal conditions was already difficult enough. Hana needed to be twice as vigilant now. The very thought overwhelmed her.

She sighed and glanced outside the massive windows. With or without curtains covering them, the view she once loved so much no longer appealed to her. It wasn't the view itself, but the many debilitating thoughts that ran through her head each time she peeked outside, wondering what percentage of the many people in her city now hated her, or at the very least thought she was an enemy in disguise?

Whereas all past visitors to the residence were there to sing her praises, and all but worship her daughter, before taking her ill-fated trip to the Middle East, it was anything but that now.

What once represented a microcosm of what had quickly mushroomed into a global adoring public, had quickly changed for the worse.

Even before the global quake, the number of visitors had been on the steady decline. It started the day she returned from Dubai.

There were some among the scoffers who still sympathized with her situation. Chennai locals chanted to their gods on her behalf—along with travelers stranded there after the quake—hoping to catch a glimpse of Hana and the baby, knowing the child, especially, had nothing whatsoever to do

79

with her father's meanspirited actions, which led to his much-deserving death at the hands of the *Miracle Maker*.

They just hoped the mental illness that had befallen him hadn't been passed on to her...Yogesh had already brought more than enough shame down upon their city to last a lifetime.

Thanks to him, the very house that had become a mecca of sorts to so many was anything but that now.

To make matters worse, her relationship with the homeowners kept steadily declining. The way Hana felt now, with all those disturbing thoughts constantly assaulting her mind, and with so many mixed emotions linked to this house, she wasn't sure if she wanted to remain there much longer.

Then again, even if she wanted to stay, she didn't know how much longer the owners of the house would let her remain there. With the constant criticism they received online from so many around the world, accusing them of harboring the enemy, Hana was mildly surprised they hadn't kicked her to the curb by now. She knew the reason—her daughter...

Perhaps another reason why they hadn't evicted her by now was that the residence had sustained so much damage, to include a sizable shift in its foundation. Who in their right mind would want to rent it now?

With so much uncertainty circling her life, Hana took a preemptive step the other day by relieving the entire staff of their duties. The reason she gave for letting everyone go was that it was only her and the baby, and she was quite capable of taking care of her daughter on her own.

But after hearing the many negative slurs and rumors being spread about her online, her staff of more than 20 workers sensed it ran deeper than that.

In truth, Hana no longer wanted to be pampered by anyone. Why be treated with special care when she felt nothing close to special?

The only staff she kept on was her security detail. With so many angry people out to get her, she couldn't imagine how her life would be without their protection.

At any rate, with the entire staff gone, the house looked dreadfully larger with only two occupants living there—one of them a child—than when they first moved in.

Hana felt trapped in her own home. What made her feel even more trapped was, thanks to social media, she went from near-invisibility before giving birth to her daughter, to suddenly living in a giant fishbowl for the whole world to see.

When she emerged as the contest winner by 97 seconds, it resulted in a free home, free cars, free electronics, free wardrobes, free everything! It all happened at warp speed, as if in the blink of an eye.

Suddenly the darling of the media, the whole world was interested in her opinions on virtually any topic. Just liking someone's social media post would cause it to trend even more.

It mattered not that she had no formal education, or that her life experience before giving birth was as the wife of a peasant fisherman, if Hana Patel liked it, it must have been newsworthy!

In a million lifetimes, she would never be able to outwit her elitist friends on any level. Yet, until just recently, each time she had spoken or posted something online, her words became a gospel of sorts to so many.

It was as if she had been temporarily transformed into a trendsetter...

With the tide of public opinion now steadily swimming against her, going online as a possible distraction was entirely out of the question. The very notion now terrified her to no end!

With the walls steadily crumbling all around her, both physically and metaphorically, life seemed more fake to her than real, more fleeting than it was before she became famous.

Who was she to think that a poor, unknown peasant woman could rise to the societal status she had achieved in so little time? And for what, giving birth to a child? It was enough to make anyone's head spin...

She went from being quiet and shy to sociable and prideful, in just a few short months. The world had truly become her oyster, as the saying went.

One of the biggest regrets she had about her brief trip to the Middle East, was that she had allowed herself to get so caught up in the constant adulation she had received from so many. So much so that she even contemplated life beyond marriage.

The more erratic Yogesh's behavior became, the more she started feeling this certain sense of empowerment that she could handle life on her own with the baby, but without her husband.

A tear escaped Hana's left eye. *How wrong I was!* She felt anything like that now. The very things that used to thrill her beyond measure now seemed utterly ridiculous to her.

Then again, with the role of fathers and husbands having been so massively downplayed—as if they no longer mattered in Romanero's new society—because Yogesh professed faith in Jesus, had he still been alive, life would have been increasingly difficult for the married couple.

81

As the days and weeks passed, a growing percentage of women were also starting to feel less safe with the *Miracle Maker* in charge.

This included Hana, and scores of other new mothers. Even though these women of all ages had been practically worshiped since becoming pregnant and giving birth, they were starting to sense just how superficially shallow, and temporal, the adulation they received from Romanero really was...

They silently sensed that one false move on their part would result in disaster, much like it had for so many others in the world, male and female alike.

It was becoming more and more evident that the universal worship which Salvador the Great constantly craved, demanded, was something he would never share with anyone else; not the Pope, not women, no one!

With so much death and devastation in the world since he became leader, they also questioned how anyone could rightly call him a *Man of Peace*?

All these thoughts left Hana feeling extremely vulnerable, for having to go through this unrelenting storm alone. More than anything, she wanted Yogesh by her side now. But that wasn't possible...

The expression, "Be careful what you wish for" was coming back to bite her in a very big way.

CHAOS IN THE BLINK OF AN EYE PART SEVEN: SOULS UNDER THE ALTAR

17

ONE WEEK AFTER THE GREAT QUAKE

SALVADOR ROMANERO HAD PLENTY of reasons to feel enraged. The peace he exuded when he first rose high above the landscape to become the undisputed, unchallenged leader of the world, soon after the disappearances, was all but gone.

His behavior kept worsening as the days passed; he was edgy, erratic, and short-tempered. And for good reason...

For starters, the instant he signed the peace treaty with Israel, the Two Men at the Wailing Wall hadn't stopped tormenting him since. They went from judging him with their mouths to now sending devastating plagues!

On top of that, he was forced to observe in silence, as Yahweh's Two Lampstands instructed the 144,000 young Jewish preachers on the Gospel of Jesus Christ, before their King scattered them to the far corners of the globe to preach a message that he himself had outlawed, without fear of repercussion.

Now, just when his rehabilitation camps were running at full capacity, and the vermin-like inhabitants were being slaughtered in record numbers, by way of guillotine, the Two Witnesses at the Wailing Wall had successfully predicted the global quake, shortly before it happened.

It took all week to confirm that every last Christian in his deathcamps had indeed perished. Instead of rejoicing like he did when countless millions of Muslims were exterminated, Romanero felt anything but comforted upon being informed of their demise!

While it clearly fit his narrative, and he would surely take credit for their deaths; just knowing they were being eternally comforted by their God stripped him of any peace he would have otherwise felt.

Romanero knew there was nothing he could do to pluck them out of Yahweh's hands. The fact that not a single prisoner had renounced Christ up to this point indicated that much.

What Salvador the Great kept insisting was "mental illness", starting with Ajit Laghari and Yogesh Patel simply wasn't so. Even those living with

83

PATRICK HIGGINS

real mental disabilities openly confessed that if they were imprisoned at those places, they would have said or done anything to avoid the extreme torture Christ followers endured on a daily basis.

Yet, all had remained loyal to their King...

The only pleasure Romanero derived was having these dissidents forever silenced on his command. The sensation of feeling drunk with their blood was intoxicating, short lived as it was. Just when his vats were overflowing, the two lunatics who were always blaspheming his name, took it away from him. *They were mine to kill!*

Another thing that gnawed on him was, when he first rose to power and rightly predicted three days after the disappearances that no rain would fall during the global vigil, that he himself had orchestrated, he no longer felt he had that same unyielding power at his sole discretion like the Two in Jerusalem possessed.

He also felt that same unbridled power coursing through his being, a few months later, when he proclaimed to have sent the "targeted" quakes to punish enemy countries, who had temporarily disrupted the peace treaty signing with the failed sneak attack on the Holy Land.

The sensation of feeling godlike at that precise moment wasn't something which could be properly explained to mere humans, except to say it was, without a doubt, the ultimate of highs.

There was nothing in the universe the *Miracle Maker* craved more than possessing this limitless power on a "sustained" basis.

Another thing that infuriated him to no end was that the Two Men at the Wailing Wall could breathe fire out of their mouths, much like dragons did in fairytales. While the other powers they harnessed could be explained away, sort of, anyway, there was no explaining away this one.

Why can't I do that? was something Salvador had thought about continually since he first watched the Two consume their enemies with the whole world watching. It was something he still couldn't accept.

What the Antichrist of the Bible didn't understand was that the fire from Heaven coming from the mouths of Yahweh's Two Lampstands in Jerusalem, didn't refer only to a literal consuming fire burning its victims, but also to the Word of God being preached with full authority.

Jeremiah five, verse fourteen made this explicitly clear: *Therefore this is what the LORD God Almighty says: 'Because the people have spoken these words, I will make my words in your mouth a fire and these people the wood it consumes.* Essentially, all who reject the testimony of their preaching would become subject to the eternal fires of hell, not only Messiah-rejecting Israel, but peoples of all nations, tribes, and tongues.

But what feasted most on Romanero's insides was knowing his ruler—the devil—wouldn't let him do as he pleased, as evidenced by the fact that many of his requests to Satan had been denied. On many levels, as the days passed, he felt more and more restrained by the one he served.

Salvador wanted more power, needed it! Yet, much to his dismay, he hadn't felt it since on those two occasions when he stopped the rain from falling and when he sent the targeted quakes…

About the only assurance he took away from his last meeting with the Prince of Darkness, reassurance rather, was that he would one day overpower the Two Witnesses and kill them. Yet, despite his constant inquiring, he had no such assurance with the 144,000 Jews whom he despised just as much as God's Two Lampstands.

Knowing he was powerless from stopping them from slandering him or from preaching salvation through Yeshua HaMashiach, at least for the time being, had caused many verbal tirades to echo throughout his palatial residence in Spain, which paled in comparison to the opulent palace he was having built in the Middle East—New Babylon to be precise—before it was destroyed in the global quake.

Ironically, Romanero was in his personal chopper getting a bird's-eye view of the progress that was being made to his palace and the new city as a whole, when the quake struck. The Pope was on board the chopper with him, along with Jurgen Staat and Li Ping, former secretaries-general to NATO and the UN.

Watching from above, as building after building came tumbling down, their eyes pleaded with him, "Why don't you do something?"

Shortly before they had lifted off, all four of them heard the Two Witnesses proclaiming what would soon transpire on the planet. As usual, they rolled their eyes and brushed off their words as nonsensical.

When it happened, precisely as they had said it would, Staat and Ping, especially, became more stressed by their prediction than they had with the calamity itself. They silently wondered if the Two Men at the Wailing Wall were more powerful than the man that they had pledged their lives to…

85

With all of Israel's surrounding countries so badly decimated, they were forced to land in Jerusalem. When Israel's prime minister received confirmation that his country had been spared, the expression on his face conveyed to whoever could see him of just how truly blessed he felt to lead the only country that hadn't been directly affected by the quake.

This alone was enough to totally enrage Romanero. His rage was taken to even greater heights when word leaked out that his palace had been destroyed. He erupted like a spoiled entitled teenager.

What came as a surprise to no one was the person who broke the story was later killed for his insubordination.

Salvador Romanero was in serious damage control mode. His scores of followers needed assurance from him that he really was who he proclaimed to be, and that he really would lead them into a better future, as he had promised time and again.

He was quite mindful that his reputation as a godlike being was coming more and more into question, as the days and weeks passed.

The world was in shambles, and he had to find a way to stop the bleeding.

18

IN SALVADOR ROMANERO'S FIRST address—post-quake—he tried to remain calm, but the devilish spirit inside wouldn't allow for it.

The shell-shocked expression on his face was put there by the Two Witnesses, after their successful prediction that the whole world would be shaken and that every mountain and island would be removed from their places. Try as he might, nothing could quell his anger and rage.

For that reason, the *Miracle Maker* didn't allow cameras for his speech. The last thing he needed was for speculation to abound that he had been totally humiliated by the God of Israel's Two Lampstands.

Romanero took a deep breath, and spoke into the microphone on his desk, "Greetings, fellow citizens of Planet Earth! I know this isn't an easy time for any of us, after the staggering blow that recently struck our planet. Many of you have sustained massive property damage, or have lost your homes altogether in the global quake and volcanic eruptions. Even more tragic, many of our precious friends and loved ones were also lost.

"Much time will have to pass before our world can once again be rebuilt. While my heart certainly goes out to all of you, despite the mind-bending devastation, two good things came as a result of the global quake. The first thing has to do with the nation of Israel.

"While the two troublemakers in Jerusalem may have predicted what happened," Salvador the Great admitted sarcastically, to those he was determined to rule over, "despite the widespread devastation, as a further proof of my ongoing commitment to honor the covenant that was signed between myself and the nation of Israel, that country was the only one on the planet to not be affected by it."

Romanero paused to let his statement hang thick in the air.

Swallowing back venomous hatred for that tiny nation, he went on, "Temple construction commenced the very next day. The progress has been so great that what was projected to take seven years to finish, will be completed in half that time. It's quite miraculous, I know…

"Mindful in advance that there would be widespread devastation, as much as I wanted my palace to be completed before the Temple was finished

87

in Jerusalem, which still is the goal, I realized with everyone else suffering, I was being a little selfish."

Somber expression on his face, not that anyone could see it, Romanero tried to sound compassionate. "To put things into perspective, while I spared Israel, I didn't spare even my own palace or even Vatican City! Both were destroyed in the quake, so we could all rebuild together. So, in that light, when I say I feel your pain, I really do!

"Now, if you're wondering why my palace is being built in a location that I had ordered destroyed in the quake I sent two years ago, before I could build the future city of all cities, all past evils had to first be cleansed and swept away, before a pure foundation could be put in place.

"As if rising up from the ashes like a phoenix, New Babylon will soon become the center of the universe. All global currency will be managed from there. And since Vatican City was also leveled in the quake, the Pope will have a palace of his own constructed in New Babylon, where he will head up the new world religion from there."

Romanero gritted his teeth but remained calm. "With so much widespread damage, those plans have been temporarily put on hold. But the reasoning for it is quite simple; if we suffer, we suffer together."

In truth, he wanted to unveil the new city upon completion, as if performing a mighty miracle. The global quake changed everything...

"The second good thing that resulted was that all dissidents detained in my prisons were killed in the global quake. None were spared. It was the next obvious step to take after I recently banned all things Christian.

"I can't tell you how many complaints were received from prison workers, prior to the quake, that they had outgrown their facilities, and that it was greatly hampering all progress. Believe me when I say, the prisons were so full, you couldn't squeeze another person inside any of them.

"In that regard, the timing had been perfect, especially since we were already in the process of building new prisons. If the global quake did any good, it forced me to reimagine the facilities we will use to detain Christians and all other dissidents in the future..."

Romanero paused a moment and rubbed his chin, as if deep in thought. "Here's what I've concluded. These animals don't deserve to be housed in concrete buildings, but in barn-like structures in open fields with no heat or running water, surrounded by electrical fences to keep them caged in.

"The only concrete facilities that will be constructed at these prisons will be used to harvest their organs, eyes, and various other body parts, before they are slaughtered like sheep. The good news is, not only can these detention centers be constructed very quickly, we will end up saving billions of dollars in the process.

"So, in that regard, this was the right time to destroy them all, and start over with prisons that will be more conducive to our needs. By predicting the quake and causing the deaths of all dissidents in my prisons, the Two Men at the Wailing Wall were merely doing my bidding for me..."

Romanero shifted his weight again. "To the large groups of Christ followers out there still inhabiting this planet in hiding, if you think the recent events have changed anything, do not be deceived, your days are numbered—we will root you out! And when we find you, much like your now-condemned misguided 'brothers and sisters,'" he scoffed, using his fingers in quotation marks, "you will be detained!"

There was no time for diplomacy, fake as it always had been in the past. "But unlike those who were incarcerated before you, we won't waste a single moment trying to rehabilitate you. That grace period has come and gone. Once we harvest your organs for the betterment of humanity, we will execute you on the spot.

"The toxic energy you evildoers have plagued humanity with over the centuries, has left a morbidly dangerous stain on our world!" *My world!* "Mark my words, I will not cease until the earth has been ridded of your warped thinking and from your wickedly evil atrocities, in the soonest possible fashion!

"Once the deep, dark stain of your wicked religion has been removed, the tapestry upon which the future resides will finally be cleansed, once and for all! Only then can a proper foundation be set in place, so all who are with me will finally get to experience the utopia I am in the process of creating!"

Romanero wanted to add, "This will conclude the second step toward achieving my ultimate goal." But since the third step was to exterminate the Jews, he left it alone. "I just wish there hadn't been so much collateral damage as a result of achieving this most necessary objective," he said, feigning sympathy. "For that, I send my deepest condolences to all who were affected by the quake.

"At any rate, now that the damage has been done, for those of you who have lost your homes, and I know it's many of you, shelters are open in all cities and towns that haven't been destroyed, to assist all who need it, to include cots to sleep in, three rationed meals a day, medical care and counseling.

89

"With the population reduced by more than half over the past year and a half, you should have little trouble securing a place to sleep at those places, once you confirm your identity.

"As much as I don't want to, with so many crops destroyed, before they could ever be harvested, I will be forced to access many of our polar seed vaults which store millions of different pristine seeds from around the world in impenetrable vaults, so we can start replanting as soon as possible. These seeds have been fully pressurized and preserved at zero degrees in arctic America.

"To those of you who relocated before I sent the first round of quakes, and have already received extensions, if the residence at which you've been staying is still habitable, remain where you are for now."

The expression on his face became even more determined. "But in order to receive assistance of any kind, your loyalty to the greater good must once again be proven to GC officials in your regions."

It was time to delve into the crux of his speech. Much like the Rapture had greatly accelerated the plans of a cashless system, this next round of global chaos opened the door all the way.

"One industry that will never fully recover is banking and finance. Even if your banking institution survived the mayhem, the tragic truth is that most won't recover.

"The ten trillion dollars that were pumped into the world's system, a while back, did nothing to improve the economy. Had those funds been more centralized, I'm convinced they would have gone a lot further.

"As we are forced again to push the financial reset button, the time to centralize all things monetary is now! In order for this to happen, all cash assets you have in your possession must be forfeited to local GC officials in your communities, within the coming months, to include all banking and all other financial statements. Whatever amount can be verified will be instantly credited to your new monetary card, dollar for dollar."

He paused, then added, "For your loyalty and obedience to the new world that will soon be ushered in, a five-thousand-dollar disbursement will be added to your cards upon activation, to give all who qualify a little more breathing room, until things settle down a bit.

"In case you're wondering, these are the same monetary cards that were recently awarded to the first one-hundred new mothers to give birth. After the awarding ceremony, government employees in most countries were the next to receive them.

"Once you have them in your possession, you'll be able to use them immediately for your weekly food, fuel, and medicine rations. This reset of sorts means that all past debts you may owe, to include tax liens you may have, are hereby canceled out, forgiven if you will.

"As most of you already know, there has been much talk over the years about creating a cashless society. Many have opposed it at every turn. With many of those backward thinkers no longer alive, and with the rest of them living in hiding—totally voiceless—the time to implement this no-cash system is now.

"It is with that in mind that I hereby decree that six months from now, cash will no longer be accepted anywhere on the planet! I wanted to enforce it sooner but have decided that it would be prudent to wait until we recover from the global quake. This will give you plenty of time to get your affairs in order.

"Now, in order to use your cards, fingerprint and ocular facial recognition confirmation will be required. Let me be clear, these monetary cards will be but a temporary solution until a more permanent one is in place, which is already in the works and will be announced in the near future. But I feel it's a step in the right direction.

"The next step will be a mark or tattoo on your bodies which will allow you to keep your handbags and wallets at home. Imagine going shopping or eating at a restaurant or paying your utility bills, and leaving your handbags and wallets at home! Unless, of course, you want to accessorize. All you'll have to do is scan yourself! Yes, indeed, the future is bright…"

It sounded ridiculous to be saying such things in a world on the brink of total collapse, but Romanero was trying to help them look beyond the tragedy by focusing on what was still to come for them.

He ended with, "If you choose not to forfeit your assets, you will only be hurting yourself. When I sign this decree into law six months from now, everything you keep will become worthless items with zero cash value. So consider this fair notice.

"That's all I have to say for now. I will update you all in the coming days. Until then, stay safe out there. May all who are truly with me be blessed in my name."

19

HANA PATEL LISTENED TO Salvador Romanero's address. For someone who always spoke of peace, prosperity and love, his actions didn't mirror his words. It was becoming more and more evident that if you weren't completely for the man—as in all in—you were deemed to be against him.

Then again, if he really was looking out for his followers, why did everyone have to suffer if it was intended for Christ followers only? What sense did that make that millions of ordinary citizens also had to perish?

Blessed in his name? Seriously? After all this?

Hana still hadn't put her daughter in her crib since the global quake. Usually when her daughter fell asleep while still on her breast, chances were good she wasn't yet finished, and it wouldn't be long before she woke up again wanting more milk. So, in that regard, it was best to keep her close to her...

Another reason was that her daughter was asleep in her crib on the night of the quake. The house shook so violently that Hana couldn't get to her frightened daughter until the rumbling stopped. Seeing her infant body being thrust up and down, crying hysterically for her mother, yet not being able to rescue her, made her feel entirely helpless.

At one point, Hana despaired that her daughter would hit the ceiling, or be thrown into a wall or even out of one of the broken glass windows. It was the most frighteningly powerless experience of her life.

She felt certain that night that the house would come crumbling down on top of them. Thankfully, it never did...

Now widowed, as a single parent, the one thought that kept invading her mind was, how could she fully trust Salvador Romanero as godlike, as he often proclaimed, when he couldn't even protect the first child to be born since the disappearances, as he had promised to on numerous occasions?

As the days passed, he appeared more and more imperfect in her eyes.

As of yet, no one had a reason to question her loyalty to Salvador Romanero. Her constant proclamations on TV and online leading up to the awards ceremony, confirmed that much.

But the fact that she never publicly denounced her late husband's actions as vile, not even a peep, caused some to now question her motives.

The Domino effect started when a group of celebrities said in interviews that they wished they could forward all cash and gifts that had already been given to Hana to the Gomes family in Brazil. As more and more celebrities joined the protest, it ultimately became a reality.

The steady flow of gifts Hana had received on a daily basis, had been redirected to Paula Gomes in São Paulo, Brazil.

The way her husband Thiago praised the *Miracle Maker* after Yogesh accused him of being the Antichrist, with the whole world watching, made him an endearing figure to so many, including Salvador Romanero, as Yogesh became more and more vilified!

The Gomes family quickly catapulted over the Patels as the new "first family" so to speak. Sadly, for them, the movie that was set to be made about Hana Patel's life, which was later awarded to the Gomes family had since been scrapped. Filming was set to begin in the fall.

The global quake changed all that.

Though totally innocent of her husband's wrongdoings, Hana's numbers of followers on social media kept tanking, along with her finances.

Hana knew to expect blowback from his vile actions, but she never envisioned it would be something of this magnitude!

Many of her elitist friends stopped following her on social media.

Even common folks who had all but praised Hana a few short months ago, and spent money on gifts for baby Salvadora that should have been used to pay bills, now felt gypped by her.

She even read somewhere that due to the constant public outcry from scores of well-known individuals, many who'd sent Hana gift cards—to the tune of tens of millions of dollars—were refunded their money and the cards were ultimately voided.

Mostly out of fear on her part, Hana still hadn't tried using the million-dollar international monetary card that she alone was awarded, for being the first woman to give birth post-disappearances.

She was tempted to use it after the quake to purchase new windows for the house. But in the back of her mind, she couldn't help but wonder if Romanero had also voided it? The thought of trying, only to have the merchant say it was declined, or worse, frozen, mortified her.

This unnerving thought wasn't without foundation. Whereas there had been constant contact between herself and Romanero's underlings *before* the ceremony, there had been no communication between them since she returned to India. It was as if she no longer mattered…

When Yogesh's death was first broadcast on live TV, the Global Community reached out to her in droves, assuring Hana that the world had her back, baby Salvadora's too. Such assurance didn't last.

Hana shook her head in befuddlement. Stories like this just didn't happen in the real world, especially to someone who should have been automatically disqualified from the contest at the outset, because of her firm belief that she was already pregnant before Romanero ever announced it.

Now that they knew her secret, instead of disqualifying her, they ominously forbade her from telling anyone else about it.

What was Romanero trying to hide? Hana knew the answer. He didn't want the masses to be exposed to what was starting to become "glaring" fallibilities on his part, infrequent as they were.

If they knew, it would completely nullify their belief in his god-like powers.

The completely shattered woman brushed aside tears, suddenly ashamed for allowing herself to be totally caught up in her "instant" notoriety, long before her mind could catch up to it all. It was like giving a minimum-wage earner a $10M bonus, before he/she had ample time to grow and settle into such affluence.

Without the proper financial experts guiding them, chances were better than good that most who went from rags to riches would ultimately end up in financial ruin, without the proper professionals teaching them how to best manage their wealth.

This was something the countless thousands of lottery winners and once-famous world-class athletes who ended up destitute in the end would all agree upon.

Much like them, Hana was now paying a heavy price financially, mentally, physically, relationally, and spiritually, especially since it had caused the most important aspect in her life to be destroyed, her marriage.

As much as she silently blamed Romanero for it all, overwhelming guilt took hold of her soul for the way she had treated her husband—mistreated him rather—before his death. She was too caught up in the moment, too blinded to see what really was going on.

She felt this unquenchable shame from knowing she had placed a mountain of material things above the genuine love she'd always received from Yogesh. With everything quickly deteriorating, the last place she wanted to be standing right now was on top of a crumbling mountain, for her many haters to witness...

94

Selfish as it sounded, this personal quake to invade her life easily rivaled the global quake that had moved the mountains from their very foundations.

It was like a knife that kept twisting in her heart. Worse, she was doing all the twisting. She feared this dreadful feeling would never leave her.

The only remaining joy in her life was her daughter. Without a doubt, she was the only thing preventing a full-blown meltdown from happening. Much like Yogesh had vowed on live television, Hana had recently taken the same vow herself, to never call her child baby Salvadora again.

For now, she called her, "Daughter", until another name came to mind.

20

IN DUBAI, UNITED ARAB Emirates, Abraham—one of the 144,000—declared to the open air, "Salvador Romanero likes taking credit for things for which he had no involvement. He didn't send the global quake! He didn't spare Israel! He doesn't have the power to do those things!"

What made Abraham's declarations even more chilling was that no one was outside listening to him. With devastation as far as the eye could see, including many of the world-renowned iconic skyscrapers dotting the city, most were too afraid to step outside of what was left of their homes.

But with power out, and no TVs or speakers to drown out his voice, everyone heard his booming voice rising into the air, loud and clear!

His 143,999 sealed brothers were preaching the very same message in their locations. "Ask Romanero to breathe human life into existence! He can't! Ask him to create a fish or a tree with the world watching! He can't! Ask him to create a planet or even a single star! He can't. Ask him to perform miracles like Yeshua, the only true Messiah, did on countless occasions when He walked the earth raising the dead, giving sight to the blind, sound to the deaf, healing the lame and crippled and cleansing lepers. He can't.

"The reason he can't do these things is because he is not a creator or a savior, he's nothing but a destroyer of souls! He is no miracle maker, he is merely a man, created in the image of the same living God as everyone else, only he doesn't belong to Yahweh. The god he bows down to is the devil himself! But make no mistake, he is every bit as human as you and me!

"Amos eight, verses eleven and twelve declare, 'The days are coming,' declares the Sovereign LORD, 'when I will send a famine through the land—not a famine of food or a thirst for water, but a famine of hearing the words of the LORD. People will stagger from sea to sea and wander from north to east, searching for the word of the LORD, but they will not find it.'

"Antichrist may have succeeded in removing the Word of God from most places on the planet, but he cannot remove it from the hearts and minds of Yahweh's true children!"

Yasamin Dabiri glanced down from her penthouse, not at all surprised to see the loudmouth Jewish preacher again, standing across the street from her high-rise condominium, speaking judgment over Salvador Romanero. This was something he had done for two straight weeks now.

With all her windows blown out, she heard every word he spoke, with perfect clarity, in her native tongue.

The one thing the 28-year-old Iranian woman, who had the distinct honor of gaining full custody of the child birthed by the "no-longer-alive" Nigerian woman, couldn't understand was how the man who called himself Abraham was still allowed to preach his globally outlawed messages of derision? Why hadn't they dragged him off to jail by now? Why was he still drawing breath in his lungs? It made no sense to her.

What perplexed Dabiri even more was every time she took baby Salvador for his daily walk in his stroller, in the days leading up to the quake, Abraham would stare at her very intently.

His preaching was intended for everyone in the area, yet it seemed his eyes were always locked on her until she was out of his sight.

It was as if he was peering into her soul. *Doesn't he know I was raised a Muslim?* If he did, he wasn't holding it against her.

Equally spine tingling, was that Muslims were taught to hate the Jew first, then the Christian, yet representatives of both those religions were attacking her in real life and in her dream world...

These were things she wanted to share with her best friend, Hana Patel.

But how? The two women in their 20s had first met at each of the many galas at which they were being honored as among the first 100 mothers to give birth, leading up to the highly anticipated *Day of New Beginnings* awards ceremony, which was the first of three new holidays the Antichrist of the Bible had recently decreed.

Hana and Yasamin hit it off immediately, as the expression went. Their friendship deepened considerably after the plane her husband was on was blown out of the sky over Manila, Philippines shortly after takeoff, killing everyone on board.

Yasamin saw Hana looking ever so distraught in the hotel lobby the next morning, as she waited for the limo to take her to the airport for her flight back home to India, she did all she could to console her new friend.

But Hana was inconsolable. Her body shook so violently that she could barely hold her daughter on her lap.

Yasamin still knew nothing about the threatening call Hana had received in her suite, mere moments before her husband was killed.

Before leaving for the airport on that solemn day, Hana hugged Yasamin and whispered in her ears, "Be careful what you say or do. They're watching and listening…"

Yasamin gulped hard, then nodded that she understood.

The two women had maintained constant contact ever since. Without even asking (How could she?), Yasamin sensed that Hana was also having second thoughts about Salvador Romanero.

But knowing that global authorities were monitoring them both very closely, to possibly include bugging their residences, instead of sharing their true thoughts online, or in text messages, they exchanged general pleasantries only, nothing more.

Both were mindful that their deepening friendship presented a potential problem, partly due to the fact that they were widows of men who had trusted in Jesus Christ for their salvation—one during the disappearances, the other after all hell had broken loose on Planet Earth, which was why they mostly spoke in general terms.

What they didn't have in common, however, was whereas Hana had skated through the entire vetting process with relative ease, Yasamin's experience was intensely stressful from start to finish.

Prior to being awarded the child born to the woman from Africa, the biggest red flag to go up with GC interviewers was her late husband's deep faith in Christ. The fact that he was among the disappearances confirmed that much.

Yasamin pleaded with her interviewers that she had no involvement, whatsoever, with the religion that had caused her husband to vanish before her eyes on that fateful day.

They then shifted their focus onto her Muslim faith. She admitted to being raised in a Muslim home, but quietly identified as a closet atheist to her many online friends.

When they asked her to elaborate on why she wanted nothing to do with the Islamic religion her family had clung to with all their might, she vainly confessed it was the natural beauty God had blessed her with at birth.

Yasamin believed her radiant face and light-skinned body were too beautiful, too inviting, too sexy, to be covered from head to toe. How could anyone admire her succulent features if they could only see her eyes?

To her, it was a ridiculous notion. The eyes may have been the windows to the soul, but she wanted to be admired for her overall beauty, not just her eyes!

And since Dabiri never spent a single second in the delivery room, her figure hadn't changed a bit. If anything, the daily workouts at the world-class gym in her unit only enhanced her already-impressive physique.

They ultimately concluded that she was being truthful, and became convinced that Salvador Romanero was her true religion, as she openly proclaimed. Had she made this confession to her fellow countrymen and women *before* Romanero became the most powerful man in human history, it very well would have meant prison for her, or even death.

It was then that Yasamin was treated as a full-fledged mother of one of the first 100 children to repopulate the earth, and given all the benefits the biological mother would have received, had she only played her cards right, beginning with naming her son, Salvador.

Thanks to the *Miracle Maker*, after trying unsuccessfully to conceive with her husband, Navid, for many years before the disappearances, as far as Yasamin was concerned, that woman's loss was her gain.

She went from deeply grieving the loss of her husband, to living in the lap of luxury, in her very own high-rise luxury condominium.

How could she not be full of hope for a bright and prosperous future?

Then came the dreams…

21

EVER SINCE THE AWARD ceremony, Dabiri hadn't had a good night sleep since. It had gotten so bad that her model-quality looks now needed an extra application of makeup before leaving the condo for anything.

How could she sleep when her dreams kept frightening her to the very core of her being? Equally troubling was the timing of it all. Why did she start having them on the very night she achieved celebrity status, when she was awarded $100,000 at the gala ceremony?

Her dream world was rocked nearly as much as the high-rise condominium she lived in, which swayed back and forth during the global quake—causing mass casualties and 90% of the building's windows to be blown out—further shaking her confidence that life would keep improving, as the *Miracle Maker* had always promised it would.

It had gotten to where she was terrified to fall asleep each night. Hence, the increasing dark circles beneath her eyes.

When she first relocated to Dubai, all dreams leading up to the awards ceremony were nearly as pleasant as her newfound reality had become.

So why the nightmares immediately after?

Yasamin did not know. Nor did she know the man who kept invading her dreams. All she knew was that Aarush was a fellow Iranian who proclaimed to be good friends with her late husband, Navid. He had apparently worshiped the God of Israel underground—just outside Tehran—with him for many years, before Navid was taken in the Rapture.

Yasamin knew all along that her husband had met with a group of men each week; it was quite common for Muslim men to do that. She just never knew at that time that they weren't worshiping Allah, but the God of the country that was their country's chief nemesis—Israel.

Since Aarush was clearly Iranian, she knew he wasn't one of the 144,000 Jews preaching an outlawed message, as the rest of the world hid in fear.

Though it was only a dream, the conversation they had was so real, so lifelike, it was impossible to push it out of her mind. Even against her strongest mental protests, it constantly replayed in her mind during her waking hours, from start to finish. She did all she could to delete this man from her mind, but it was impossible.

If this man was to be believed, millions of Iranians had trusted in Christ Jesus before the Rapture. He told her there were so many at his location that they had to meet in shifts.

Aarush told her that on the day of the disappearances, everyone had suddenly vanished into thin air on that Saturday evening, except for him. The only things left were their personal belongings.

He said he was terrified and didn't know what to do. As much as he wanted to flee from that place, he was too afraid to leave, for fear that someone might arrest him.

At first, he thought the Iranian government had somehow exposed them and had found a way to vaporize everyone…everyone but him, that is.

He said in the dream that he camped out overnight hoping that someone from the church would arrive. When no one did, he finally mustered the courage to leave the following morning.

He left a handwritten note behind begging anyone finding it to contact him immediately. He said it was the most frightening walk home of his life, and he kept looking over his shoulders praying no one was following him.

When Aarush made it home, it was then that he learned that it happened globally. Scared out of his wits, he went back to the underground meeting location every day for a week or so, hoping to see someone he might recognize. But no one ever came.

According to him, that was when it dawned on him that Jesus came back for His church, taking everyone except for him. He was forced to admit the main reason he went there in the first place was that he was terribly lonely and desperate for fellowship, male fellowship to be precise.

He also confessed in the dream that he found her husband attractive. Even though he knew he had no chance with Navid, he was the main reason Aarush went there each week.

Another thing he confessed to Yasamin in the dream was the reason he never married, was that he had battled homosexual tendencies all his life. He even engaged sexually with two men, one of whom was later imprisoned then killed for being caught in the act with another man.

When he turned 30 years of age, his parents started pressuring him to get married. His siblings too, for that matter. He said he had done a good job of hiding his secret from them, but he also sensed they were slowly catching on, especially when he turned 40 and still hadn't courted a single woman in his life.

He told her the day he repented before the God of Israel, truly repented, was the day God saved his soul, and delivered him from the sin of homosexuality.

Up until that point, he said he always knew deep down inside he was a false convert. He was merely honoring God with his lips in that subterranean gathering place.

He would often lay in bed at night wondering why he would subject himself to possible punishment, or even death, if caught worshiping the God of the Jews, especially since his faith in Christ had been lukewarm at best.

But he always insisted that Navid was a true follower of Jesus in every sense of the word. He was even one of the underground leaders.

One thing Yasamin could still hear ringing in her ears were his words, "Your husband longed to share the Gospel with you, Yasamin, but his fear was that you would share it with your family whom, according to him, were totally committed to their Muslim faith.

"But there wasn't a time when I was underground that he didn't ask us to join him in praying for you. His constant prayer was that you would one day come to know for yourself that Jesus is the Way, Truth, and the Life, and that no one came to the Father, but through Him.

"Then came the Rapture and he never had the chance…I know you're a big fan of Salvador Romanero, but you must know his power comes from the very darkest of places. The man is being supernaturally empowered by Satan himself. If you accept Romanero's mark in the coming months, there will be no hope for you or your son. You will both be doomed…"

And that was when Yasamin would wake up in a cold sweat, her senses tingling on full alert.

And that was only the first round of dreams she had had about Aarush.

Each new round was more terrifying than the last round!

Even though Aarush did all the talking in the dream, the fact that she was listening, she felt like she had committed a crime, because he kept talking about the name of her late husband's Savior who was forbidden from being uttered in society.

As ridiculously farfetched as it sounded, she couldn't help but wonder if Romanero had the ability to eavesdrop on her dreams?

If he could, how would she possibly defend herself?

First to have one of her fellow countrymen tell her about Jesus in dreams, then to hear it echoed out of the mouth of the young Jewish male across the street. It was too much to absorb.

Yasamin was desperate to tell someone about her dream. Perhaps it was because both women had lost their husbands to Christianity, but the one face that kept popping into her mind was Hana Patel.

But how could she share these troubling thoughts with her? Not having an answer to her desperate question, all Yasamin could do was sigh...

22

WHILE EXPOSING SALVADOR ROMANERO as the Antichrist of the Bible—in the man's presence—was what had sealed Yogesh Patel's fate, the tailspin had started for the married couple a few weeks before they went to the Middle East, when Yogesh started reading the Bible that Brad and Joan Henriksen had sent to him. That so-called gift ended up costing him his life, leaving Hana feeling completely gutted inside, numb.

What had started so euphorically for the young family ended in total devastation. When Hana arrived back to India—without her husband—she was so infuriated with the Henriksens, she contributed $100K to an online campaign to help track the evildoers down. She was painfully mindful that that was the only thing global netizens had praised her for since her return.

Yes, being introduced to the American couple was where Yogesh had slipped. His fall came when he humiliated the *Miracle Maker* in front of the whole world, which ended up costing him his life, which in turn started Hana's own personal tailspin…

For reasons she couldn't fully explain—let alone understand—she never removed from the house the Bible the Henriksens had sent to Yogesh, even though Salvador the Great had already outlawed all things Christian.

If someone ever discovered it, it would surely bring a new world of trouble down upon her.

Another thing she never removed from her house was the scripture that had caused constant quarreling between the married couple, especially after Yogesh had handwritten it on a sheet of paper, before posting it on the wall on his side of the bed, shortly before they ventured to the United Emirates.

He had told her he didn't do it to spite her, but as a constant reminder to himself during these difficult times. But when he quoted it on stage on what turned out to be his last night on earth, Hana fumed in anger.

Upon returning from the trip, she was so humiliated, so mortified, and so furious with her husband that she tore the piece of paper off the wall with such a vengeance, it caused one of her beautifully manicured fingernails to be badly chipped in the process.

But instead of shredding it into a million pieces, like she had threatened to do prior to taking the trip—claiming it had totally brainwashed her late husband—she folded it and placed it inside the 10-foot safe in her bedroom closet.

Opening one of the drawers inside the massive safe, she found a one-page letter written to her from Yogesh. It read:

Hi, my darling! By the time you read this, you will have returned home from the Middle East without me. As for me, either I'm living in hiding or I'm dead. Sorry for all the trouble I have surely caused you for what I did in Dubai. But you must understand that every word I spoke that day about Romanero was true. He really is the Antichrist of the Bible. If you keep following that man, it will lead to eternal destruction.

Only Jesus is to be worshiped. Only He is King of kings and Lord of lords. No one has the power to save souls from hell—only Christ alone!

I'm not sure if you checked the secret wall you had built into the safe. Shortly before we left for that trip, I hid the Bible that Brad and Joan Henriksen had sent in there. My prayer is that you will read it and be transformed by the Message it tells. Only then can you have freedom, my dearest Hana!

Sure enough, when Hana checked inside the secret wall, where she kept her passport and all other legal documents, expensive jewelry, and all other valuables, she found the Bible and letter the Henriksen's had sent to him.

Hana placed the scripture written on paper inside the Bible. That scripture was Mark 8:36: *What shall it profit a man to gain the whole world yet lose his soul?*

After everything that had happened, it should have been the first thing she removed from her house. But it wasn't...

The reason? In a strange way, even though Yogesh's conversion to Christianity had ruined what was quickly becoming a near-perfect life for them—at least by her estimation—just knowing the Book that was now outlawed had so consumed him at the end of his life, brought a strange level of curiosity to her.

Gazing out at the destruction all around her, the one thing Hana still couldn't understand was why the Americans had addressed the package to her husband only? How did they know he would be receptive to the Message, but that she wouldn't be? It was mind boggling, to say the least.

At any rate, with her fortune dwindling a little more each day, Hana thought, *Who would want to gain this world?* Since she had always referred to Yogesh as her whole world before winning the contest, she couldn't help

105

but wonder if she had lost both the world and her soul within a matter of weeks…

This left her feeling gutted and guilt-ridden. So much so that she stopped blaming Yogesh for her present dilemma, and took a good, hard look in the mirror. She didn't like the glamorous woman she saw staring back at her.

Perhaps the reason she kept the Bible and letter the Henriksens had included with the gifts that were intended for their daughter, was to spite the *Miracle Maker* for publicly killing her husband like he did to all his enemies, including the former Prince of Spain.

And who could forget how Romanero had allowed the many atrocities to happen to Ajit Laghari to be shown on live TV, the internet and on every smartphone on the planet? It was cruel, heartless, and inhumane.

One thing had become glaringly certain to Hana: He was no man of peace. If anything, he was a cold and calculating monster!

Hana scoffed at the thought of referring to Romanero as a miracle maker any longer. How could she call him by that name when he left a trail of destruction in his wake, to include destroying her marriage?

And how could she ever forget the great evil pouring out of him like sweat, when she sat next to him on stage, on that soul-shredding day?

If there was one other constant in Hana's life, it was the man who showed up every morning among the stragglers, as one of his daily stops each day, to preach the Gospel of Jesus Christ to everyone within earshot.

Even when everyone else ran for cover after the global quake, Yitzhak never missed a day. The young man's voice was so loud and commanding that everyone within a quarter mile of the house easily heard him.

After a while, as people slowly started trickling back, many became so intrigued by Yitzhak's captivating messages, that they kept coming back for more. But to avoid repercussions from law enforcement, they faced the house as if they were there for Hana and her daughter when, in reality, they wanted to hear more of what he had to say in the brief time he was there.

The proof was that when Yitzhak left, many in the crowd also dispersed.

Hana was listening too! She had no choice—his strong powerful voice had all but demanded her attention!

She could only assume he was the one Yogesh saw in his dreams standing outside their house in the middle of the night, before the Patels met the *Miracle Maker* in Dubai.

One thing was certain: he was clearly one of the 144,000 Jewish men that her late husband had spoken about—as the whole world watched and listened—as being recently sealed by God Himself.

It was becoming more and more evident to Hana that this man, along with the Two Witnesses at the Wailing Wall, had their God's full supernatural protection. Nothing could shut them up, not even Salvador Romanero!

Hana still vividly remembered Yogesh saying anyone having dreams about these men were truly blessed. That was the part she was struggling the most with. How could they be "blessed" when so many of them were tortured mercilessly in prison, before their lives were snuffed out in the global quake, because of their faith in the God the 144,000 always preached about, with their messages all pointing to their God's crucified Son?

She couldn't imagine having her daughter being ripped out of her arms while she was thrown in prison and treated worse than an abused animal, like she had witnessed with many Christian mothers on TV. Her heart ached for each one of them.

Blessed? How could that be considered as "blessed" on any level?

At any rate, as the days passed, Hana felt herself withdrawing more and more from the lifestyle she had loved so much.

Perhaps it was because of the young man outside preaching the Word of God, or because she was increasingly curious to know more about what had totally transformed her husband before his death.

Whatever the reason—it was probably a combination of both factors— it drove Hana to start reading the Book her husband had left behind for her, whenever her daughter was sleeping.

She always read it in her bedroom closet out of fear that spy cams and listening devices had been planted all throughout the house. If they had eavesdropped on her in her hotel suite, why should she think for a second that they weren't doing it at her house as well?

If it was bugged, surely even faint whispers could be detected and recorded. But even that troubling thought didn't stop her from reading the Word of God each chance she got...

She was still unaware that the prompting she felt was a direct result of the prayers of millions of Christians, who had been praying for her every day since her husband was killed, asking the Most High to change her heart and open her spiritual eyes and ears.

23

AFTER SPENDING TWO WEEKS at Clayton Holmes' safehouse, Clayton, Travis and Charles Calloway left to check on the location at which Hartings had been residing, in western South Carolina.

When they arrived, they weren't the least bit surprised to discover that more than a hundred residents had perished in the quake. Partly for selfish reasons, the dozens of survivors all rejoiced upon seeing their leaders again.

At any rate, with the volcanic ash in the atmosphere slowly dissipating in some areas, Sat-phone connections were greatly improved. The signal was still spotty in most areas, but it was better than nothing.

Clayton silently rejoiced when Jefferson Danforth answered his call. "So nice to hear from you, Clayton. We pray for you and Travis every day."

"Likewise, sir," Clayton said. "We've tried calling you many times, but couldn't get through. Who's there with you?"

"It's only me, Amy Wong, and Agent Sullivan. Physically, we're fine. Just a few bumps and bruises. The way this place shook, I wasn't so sure we'd make it. We felt and heard the mountains crumbling all around us. I thought for certain we'd be buried alive!"

Clayton sighed. "We just arrived at our third safe house since the quake. All three suffered massive casualties. But Charles Calloway survived. He's with us now."

"Praise God for that," said Jefferson. "Tell him I said hello."

"I will, sir. Do you think it's safe to remain where you are?"

Jefferson bit his lower lip. "I think so. At least for the time being…"

"How's Amy?" asked Travis, about the former White House chef, who was residing at the subterranean safehouse in Idaho with him.

"She's a mess. Never saw her so out of sorts. Not sure how much longer she can remain underground. She looks like someone who wants to give up."

"We'll keep praying for you both."

Clayton asked, "Did you know President Cipriano's dead?"

Jefferson crossed one leg over the next. "I know. Agent Galiano told Agent Sullivan who then told me."

"We weren't sure if you knew or not. We also want to let you know about another development, only this one's good."

"Sure could use some good news right about now. What is it?"

"I'll give you the short version, in case we lose contact. Travis and I had dreams that we had to go to the cabin in Tennessee. Remember the one you stayed at before being transferred to your current location?"

"How could I forget?"

"Well, it turned out God sent us there to meet a man named Moishe. He's one of the hundred and forty four thousand sealed servants."

Jefferson raised an eyebrow. "From the book of Revelation?"

"Yes. He told us God would be blessing our faithfulness to Him, by sending one thousand of His sealed servants to live in our safe houses."

Jefferson rubbed his chin. "That's quite a development!"

"I'll say," remarked Clayton. "The name of the young man sent to safe house number one, in Pennsylvania, is Jakob. I spoke to Brian earlier. The property sustained massive damage like all other properties. But Jakob's cottage was perfectly preserved. Moishe informed us after the quake that this was the case with each location they inhabited, so Travis and I weren't surprised to hear Brian tell us that."

Danforth shook his head in amazement. "Simply miraculous..."

Clayton nodded agreement. "And here's the best part. Moishe told us all children living at those locations would live into the Millennial Kingdom. I haven't been able to confirm it yet, but I have every confidence that not a single child at any of the safehouses at which they are residing was killed. These children represent all nations, tribes, and tongues."

"What was Moishe like?"

Travis answered, "Well, sir, he's quite young and full of wisdom. And better protected than you ever were, as President, with all due respect."

Jefferson cringed. The last thing he wanted to think about was his time in office. "I don't doubt that for a second. By the way, I have something to share with you as well, that I think God brought to my attention to forward on to you and Travis."

"What is it, sir?" asked Clayton.

"When the White House and Pentagon were destroyed, Agent Galiano did a little sniffing around looking to obtain any information that might help us. One thing he discovered was despite Romanero's promise to protect all children, he secretly ordered the killing of newborns with deformities or with physical disabilities, privately claiming they had no redeeming qualities, and didn't fit the profile of a perfect society.

"We already knew he stopped providing hospital beds, medications, and even food ration allotments to seniors and special needs patients. In his diabolical mind, the sooner they're put out to pasture, the better." Danforth sighed. "Now he's doing it to special needs children."

Travis could only shake his head. "Your timing couldn't be more perfect, sir. Do you remember Brian Mulrooney's wife, Jacquelyn?"

"Vaguely. What about her?"

"She went into labor during the quake and gave birth to a baby girl with Down Syndrome."

Danforth felt a cool shiver shooting down his back. "Now I know why the Lord put it so strongly on my heart to share with the two of you. Brian and Jacquelyn should be thankful that monster doesn't know about their daughter. If he did, the child surely would be killed."

Holmes grimaced. "She isn't the only special needs child living at our safe houses. There are many others. But now that you've brought this to my attention, we must find a way to bring more of these children our way. The question is how…"

"Your guess is as good as mine, Clayton. But I'll certainly join you in praying for that…"

Travis asked, "Speaking of that monster, did you hear Romanero's address?"

"No. It's difficult to secure any sort of signal down here. What did I miss?"

"We heard it on a battery-powered radio. It keeps replaying on all radio frequencies. While he conceded that the Two Witnesses in Jerusalem had indeed predicted the global quake, he followed it up by saying they were merely doing his bidding for him. What arrogance!

"But since the masses can't confirm for themselves what we wholeheartedly believe in the Word of God, they have no other source than Romanero himself. But there was one thing he said that will affect us…"

"What is it, Travis?"

"He declared that cash will be illegal six months from now."

Jefferson leaned back on the couch. "Well, we all knew this day was coming."

"True. It's not the Mark of the Beast yet, but it's the final step to be sure. At any rate, we now have six months and counting to spend all of our cash reserves, before they become worthless."

Travis added, "We already know how difficult it'll be to purchase food, water, and various medicines. Not impossible, but extremely difficult. Some of the things we desperately need are glass and fiberglass windows, plywood, tarps, and all other construction materials.

"After spending a few days on the road, and seeing how bad the roadways are, we're going to need more motorcycles, motorized bicycles, scooters, and even motorless bicycles. Four-wheel vehicles simply cannot traverse the roads at this time."

Clayton said, "In a way, the damage done to most roads actually helps us now. If the enemy knows where we're hiding, they can't get to us, not by foot or vehicle anyway. Another blessing is that many of the checkpoints and scanners that were set up all over the world were no doubt destroyed in the quake. It's like God gave us a temporary buffer of sorts."

"Yeah, but for how long?" Jefferson asked.

Travis answered the question. "Time will tell, sir. Another thing we need to rethink is how we will generate power to our safe houses. We did our best to reconstruct the properties with what little we had. Roughly seventy percent of our safe houses were powered by solar panels. I wouldn't be surprised if most of them were damaged or destroyed altogether in the quake.

"Even if not, with so little sunlight to draw from, how can they possibly be effective? Clayton often reminded me that the sun would often be blocked out as time marched on, ultimately rendering solar energy iffy at best. We need to look no further to see that he was spot on. It's time to rethink everything…"

"Where do you plan on obtaining these things, Travis?"

"The good news, sir, is that many are trying to sell and barter these things, but with only few buyers. One advantage we have over everyone else is that we should have little trouble purchasing the high-ticket items most need but can't afford, especially at such highly inflated prices.

"Since we have lots of cash to spend, I'm sure there will always be someone out there willing to strike a deal with us, especially since Romanero has forgiven all past debts and liens. He's even offering to credit the cash they receive onto their cards, no questions asked."

"How nice of him," Jefferson said sarcastically, stretching out on the couch.

Travis snorted. "I know, right! At any rate, we must use this blessing of sorts to our advantage. The important thing is that we spend the billions in cash we still have before it becomes worthless.

"I believe the closer it gets to the six-month deadline, the more difficult it will be for us to spend it. I'm about to send a recorded message to all our safe house managers, advising them to get ready to spend every last dollar they have stored in their safes, in the soonest possible fashion."

Jefferson Danforth sighed. "I appreciate the update, gentlemen, but I'm not sure if I can be of much assistance to you in this regard..."

"We know, sir, and we understand. You've already done enough for us. Now it's our turn to do our best to protect you."

Clayton's words brought tears to his eyes. "Thank you..."

"You're welcome, sir. Call if you need us for anything..."

"Likewise, gentlemen..." At that, the call ended.

24

SIX WEEKS AFTER THE GLOBAL QUAKE

DICK MULROONEY WAS DRIVING south on the New Jersey turnpike. He left the house just after 10 p.m. This was his third attempt, after chickening out the first two times. The damage he saw on his street alone told him it would be a treacherous trip, one that could be deadly.

Add to that, he didn't even know if Sarah was still alive. So, why chance it all for nothing? In the end, the not knowing if his wife had survived the quake or not would constantly eat away at him, until he knew one way or the other. Yes, that was the ultimate deciding factor.

Or was it from the dreams he had before the global quake that suddenly visited his dream world again just recently? He honestly didn't know.

All Dick knew, and what the past few months had reinforced to him, was that his life made no sense without his wife in it. He knew he was taking a significant risk just by getting behind the wheel of his vehicle. But if he miraculously found Sarah, it would be well worth the risk.

If he needed more proof that he was living in apocalyptic times, he spent ten minutes clearing three inches of fallen ash off his car, from the many volcanic eruptions thousands of miles away. Having not driven his automobile for so long, he was just thankful it had started.

With most streets, roads, highways, tunnels, overpasses, and bridges severely damaged in the global quake, what normally should have taken 90 minutes at most to travel, post-Rapture, had already taken four hours, and that was just leaving Manhattan!

The Holland Tunnel was the only way in or out of the city for passengers in New Jersey, but only one lane was being used.

With more than 40 percent of its buildings having been utterly destroyed, the city was unrecognizable!

Dick fully anticipated being stuck in traffic along the way, due to the widespread road damage. As an added precaution, he filled his hybrid fuel tank with gasoline, in case he needed it.

It was a car Renate McCallister had talked him into purchasing way back when, so he could do his part to help save the environment. "A lot of good it did!" he scoffed to himself, sarcastically.

113

According to Google maps, when he finally reached the New Jersey turnpike, he was 112 miles away from the apartment that Megan McCallister and Rachel Stein were renting in Concordville, Pennsylvania.

Yet the projected remaining time was 6 hours and 45 minutes. Just ten minutes ago, the projected arrival time was 5 hours and 37 minutes. A short while before that, it was 9 hours and 12 minutes. It kept fluctuating.

At 4 a.m., even though Megan and Rachel were both night owls, and were probably still awake, Dick stopped updating them with estimations. The constant changes would only make their heads spin like his was.

Scores of engineers and programmers worked day and night, trying to create new routes for travelers to take. Despite their best efforts, the satellites up in space kept recalculating, which in turn caused the voice on the GPS to do the same. Too much damage had been done.

Most feared many months would pass before their collective task could be deemed as anything close to successful. And since most experts feared more "delayed" aftershocks, the green light had yet to be given for reconstruction and repaving to commence, only a few patch-up jobs were being done here and there.

Dick glanced out his window and saw what was left of Newark International Airport off to the right. All runways were destroyed in the quake, as well as the tower and a sizable portion of the terminal.

This was merely par for the course with most airports in the world. All had sustained massive damage, far worse than after the disappearances, which many still refused to believe was the Rapture of Christ's Church.

As much as Dick would have preferred traveling by bus or train, those modes of public transportation weren't available to him.

In New York City alone, more than 500 of the 850 miles of subway and train tracks scattered about its five boroughs, had been displaced and were now in total disrepair. The damage was so severe that the city was forced to shut down all routes indefinitely. No one knew for sure, if ever at all, when rail service would be available to the many in the Northeast who had relied on it for their daily mode of transportation.

New York City was home to more than 2,000 bridges, which helped connect its five boroughs. Most had sustained severe damage, including the city's suspension bridges, which were used by trains and subways, and scores of motorists each day. Six were deemed beyond repair.

Whereas all modes of public transportation were severely disrupted in the *Big Apple*, after the disappearances, it took some time but the bridges and roadways were ultimately brought back up to speed. Unlike now...

114

It was becoming more and more apparent, as the days passed, that their city would never again become even a shadow of what it had once been, let alone the envy of the world. The defiant belief that most New Yorkers had mustered after 9/11, and subsequently after the disappearances, that they could ultimately rebuild was gone.

Now they felt trapped, claustrophobic even, and wanted to flee from the city they once loved. But where could they go? There wasn't a city on earth they could escape to that wasn't under constant siege!

And even if there was, how would they get there?

Even at this hour, though there were far fewer vehicles on the road now than what had followed the disappearances, the constant slow flow of traffic—to include several standstills—not to mention the many checkpoints in place, made it feel like a rush hour traffic jam.

This had nothing to do with roadway overcrowding, but due to the fact that only one lane was open most of the way. But Dick wasn't overly concerned about what time he arrived, so long as he arrived there safely.

At any rate, it was a little unnerving seeing how so many had resorted to traveling on the highways and byways of America on bicycles, 4-wheelers, mopeds, and motorcycles, so they could maneuver in between severely damaged roads, and squeeze in and out of traffic with relative ease.

Though it was both dangerous and illegal operating motorless vehicles on major highways and interstates, what would be the point in ticketing them when they were the smart ones?

It was never a consideration for law enforcement...

Dick was mindful up front that the roads would be treacherous to travel on. But if Rachel Stein drove 600 miles just to find his son, while in her third trimester, how could he, as Brian's father, not travel one-sixth that distance to hopefully fulfill their joint mission?

Granted, her road trip came before the great quake shook the whole earth off its axis. But that wasn't the point. The point was that she did it.

Ever since his last phone conversation with Renate's sister, followed by three nights of dreams, the relatively small suburb town in the Keystone State suddenly became the most important place on earth to him.

Was Sarah really living there? Was she still alive?

Dick hoped to find out soon enough...

One thing was certain, if his dream was true, it meant Tom Dunleavey was hiding in Pennsylvania with Brian and Sarah. While Tamika Moseley and Charles Calloway weren't part of the dream, he had to assume those two other lunatics with warrants out for their arrests were there as well, undoubtedly fearing for their lives along with the rest of the false converts.

The question was, where was this diabolical safehouse of sorts? Was Sarah living on a compound with thousands of others? Or was it a small number of runaways shacking up in one big house? Had it been damaged in the quake? If Sarah was still alive, had she been displaced?

Dick hated not having answers to his many questions. He tried imagining the place a million times in his mind, but with no point of reference, his thoughts always wandered from one extreme to the next.

But the prospect of knowing that he might be closing in on Sarah was so overwhelming—both in a good way and bad—he would be hard pressed if asked to properly describe it.

The biggest question Dick still had no answer to was why was the former Catholic priest the focus of his dreams instead of his own wife?

As of yet, he still had no clue...

At any rate, for the first time since Chelsea's suicide and Sarah's equally devastating departure, Dick was properly groomed. He wanted to look presentable in case he miraculously bumped into his wife somewhere in Concordville.

Shaving the four-month-old gray, straggly beard off his face was a good first step. Instead of looking 20 years older than his actual age, removing the facial hair slashed that number in half. He looked recognizable again.

Also, for the first time in his life, Dick cut his own hair. Going to his barber of more than three decades wasn't an option. He had to assume at this point that Angelo knew about Brian's criminal misgivings, not to mention Chelsea's suicide.

The last thing Dick wanted was to be peppered with embarrassing questions for which he had no logical answers. He wondered if Angelo's barber shop had been leveled by the quake. Probably.

But even if his shop had been spared, and he was still miraculously open for business, how could his customers possibly get to him?

Heartless as it sounded, Dick had too many catastrophes of his own to deal with, to even consider thinking about taking on anyone else's problems.

If there was one thing on which he could hang his hat, he was mildly impressed with his new haircut. It was nowhere near in the same league as his skilled barber had consistently performed over the years, but even Angelo might agree he looked presentable. *Goal achieved!* Then again, having so little hair to cut made it a rather easy accomplishment.

116

It was the only positive task he had achieved since Sarah left him, in what seemed like an eternity ago. His only other daily endeavor was trying to combat the sinister thoughts constantly swimming in his head, which always proved to be an impossible task.

For the life in him, Dick never thought something like this could happen to his family. Prior to last November, everyone described the Mulrooneys as a good family, a tight family. Most neighbors looked up to and respected them. Then came the disappearances…

Without a doubt, the downward spiral started when Brian left the Catholic Church. While the disappearances didn't result from a choice Brian had made—it was suddenly thrust upon all of humanity—leaving the church *was* his decision. The instant he did, it was as if Satan had entered inside him, causing his criminal nature to surface practically overnight.

When his son's face appeared on the news for helping Tamika Moseley escape capture—even paying for her lodging for two weeks, and who knew what else—it led to detectives banging on their door looking for him.

The only good thing was that the media stopped camping outside the house day and night, waiting for Brian to hopefully emerge, so they, too, could bombard him with questions as he was carted off to jail.

But when paramedics removed Chelsea's lifeless body from the house not too long after that, that was when Dick could no longer make eye contact with anyone. Her actions served to take the family devastation to a whole new level.

He still couldn't comprehend how his own flesh and blood could be capable of doing such things. As the man of the house, did his neighbors of so many years think it was all his fault?

At the very least, did they think he wasn't strong enough to prevent it from happening? How could they think otherwise? If there was one good thing, with so much tragedy inundating his neighbors' lives as well, they became much less nosy after the quake than they were beforehand.

Dick blinked those dreadful memories away. He had too many other thoughts to wrestle with, namely what he would say to Sarah *if* he found her. He wanted to be more optimistic about his chances, but after several weeks of searching for her, Megan and Rachel still hadn't made any significant advances on that front.

If he did miraculously find his wife, would he drop to his knees and beg for her forgiveness, even though she was the one who had left him?

He sighed. Sarah wasn't the only guilty one. There was plenty of blame to be laid at his own feet as well—more than he cared to admit.

The one regret he still couldn't shake off was how poorly he had acted on the day he tore Sarah's Bible to pieces in front of his daughter. What he saw on his wife's face, conveyed to him that he was shredding part of her heart and soul as well.

It was no family secret that when it came to faith in God, Chelsea was always the weakest link in the family. Dick sensed his lack of spiritual maturity on that day, had served to push her even farther away from God.

I would've left me too! he thought, pounding the steering wheel, his car once again forced to a near standstill, as construction cones on the turnpike forced all vehicles to switch lanes from the far right over to the far left.

Dick removed his eyeglasses and wiped his eyes with his coat sleeve, before they became steamed from this new round of remorseful tears.

Was reconciliation even possible at this point? After this lengthy tumultuous passage of time, would they be able to talk things out and salvage what had been a thriving marriage for three and a half decades?

Or was it true that Sarah really was suffering from mental illness like Romanero constantly proclaimed? Had her brain been reprogrammed to the point of no return? Had the disappearances caused some sort of magnetic shift in her brain, like it had for the unfortunate many?

Dick didn't know. All he knew was that the separation wasn't caused by infidelity on either one's part. Nor was it due to spousal abuse, or from an ongoing addiction. It all came down to a difference of religion, leaving him feeling lonely, desperate, and totally dejected.

What jolted his pride even more from a spiritual standpoint, was when Sarah abandoned ship and joined Brian, it was impossible to accept being outwitted by his own son, cruelly checkmated by him in the name of religion. This feeling easily paralleled the anger and betrayal he felt at Sarah's hands for leaving him.

Like a buzz saw turned on full power, Brian's madness had cruelly and mercilessly severed the family in half, placing himself and Sarah on one side, and Dick and Chelsea on the other.

With his daughter now gone, it was suddenly two against one.

All because of Brian...

25

DICK ARRIVED AT THE apartment in just under 18 hours. Not surprisingly, the apartment complex looked like a warzone. The gaps in the parking lot asphalt were so wide they resembled miniature fault lines.

And the sidewalks were severely chipped in most places or completely damaged. Four of the six buildings looked almost uninhabitable. Caution signs were posted everywhere. It looked like a tornado, hurricane and earthquake had struck the region all at once.

When Dick got out of the car, his body was so stressed and fatigued, it felt like the ground was trembling beneath his feet. He needed sleep.

He opened his car trunk and retrieved his suitcase, which was stuffed with enough clothing to last for weeks, and two bags full of canned foods for Megan and Rachel.

He spotted the two women waiting for him at the front door, waving at him. Both were happy to see him, but they easily recognized the troubled expression on his skeletal-like face.

After this latest round of judgments to rock the planet, they understood. Megan said, "Welcome to what's left of our humble abode! Glad you made it in one piece!"

Dick glanced up at the building he was about to enter. *Is it safe to even step foot inside?* "Thank you. Nice to finally meet you both in person."

Megan sighed. "Yeah, my father and I just missed you at your son's ridiculous wedding. You left shortly before we arrived."

Dick snorted. Just thinking back to that day forced so many unhealthy emotions to resurface. "I could no longer stand being there. How much worse would I have felt had I stayed?"

"I know what you mean..." Megan replied.

"Anyway, I brought you some canned soups and vegetables that haven't expired yet. I figured you could use them more than me."

Both women smiled their thanks. Even with Romanero's assistance, with extreme food rationings in effect, it was like gold in their hands.

Rachel said, "We had hoped you could join us for breakfast. But at least you made it in time for lunch. Since we still have leftover bacon from breakfast, hope you don't mind BLTs and tomato soup."

119

The only reason they had bacon at all was that pregnant women always got first dibs when certain foods became available, especially meats, fruits, and vegetables. This was the first time they had been able to obtain bacon since the global quake.

"Sounds good!" Dick glanced down at her midsection. "Looks like someone's close to giving birth."

"Won't be long now. A little more than a month and I'll be a mommy." There was this dreamy expression on her face. "Still hard to fathom…"

"Congratulations in advance." Dick wondered how she did it. Despite the constant chaos in the world, Rachel still managed to display that special glow first time mothers were known for, even if momentarily. The constant madness hadn't yet robbed her of all her joy.

"Thanks, Mister Mulrooney," she said, rubbing her tummy. The child inside her womb was her meal ticket, her legacy, making him worthy of protecting at all costs, which was quite a peculiar thought coming from someone who was openly pro-choice all her adult life, before Salvador Romanero came to power.

Rachel even fundraised for *Planned Parenthood* on occasion, before the disappearances. She wasn't alone in her rethinking of sorts. Millions of other women who were pro-choice before the Rapture, were fully determined to protect the child in their wombs with every ounce of strength they possessed.

"Call me Dick." He glanced up at the building again. The damage was quite severe. Had he not been living in similar conditions this past month and a half, he would never dare step foot inside this place.

The two women followed his eyes upward. Megan said, "Sadly, the people living above us were killed in the quake. I think thirty were killed all throughout the complex."

Dick lowered his head. "Sorry to hear that…"

"Yeah, well, it's not like we knew them all that well. Everyone pretty much kept to themselves. Still, it was an eye opener for us…"

Rachel hugged her belly. "We're just lucky to be on the first floor. Our walls are cracked in so many places. In fact, until a maintenance man applied a few steel clamps and a boatload of caulk to the many cracks last week, we could see clear outside."

Dick raised an eyebrow. "Clamps only?"

"I know, right?" said Rachel, in astonishment. In normal times, this place would have been condemned, and we would have been ordered to leave as well. So, in that sense, we're lucky to still have a place to live in."

Megan interjected, "You should have seen this place before the quake. It was so beautiful. We used to stroll to the pond behind our building each day, to feed the ducks and Canadian geese. It was our number one stress reliever. Now they're gone..."

Rachel sighed. "That's why we always keep the curtains shut. Why look outside when it's so depressing?"

Megan shot a quick glance at Rachel before her eyes volleyed back to their visitor. "It's also done for protection. Lots of robberies here lately, most of them vagrants out looking for food, water, and medicine."

Rachel added, "We're actually thinking about getting a gun." She shook her head, unable to fathom how much their lives had been severely altered. "This would have been unthinkable before the disappearances..."

Dick could only shake his head. "It's like this everywhere."

"I'm sure you're right, Mister Mulrooney, but since all solar panels were destroyed there hasn't been much sun to draw upon. We have sporadic power and limited access to the outside world. Even when the TV's working, why watch it when it's nothing but constant doom and gloom? We prefer listening to music instead."

Dick couldn't argue Rachel's logic.

There was a brief pause in the conversation, until Megan said, "That'll be your bedroom. Feel free to put your things in there before lunch. Since the bacon's already cooked, it'll be ready in a jiffy."

"Thank you, Megan." Dick took his things into the bedroom and sat on the bed. Eyes surveying the room, what they saw wasn't encouraging. *Caulk and clamps only?*

With the dining room table set, Megan told them it was time to eat.

Dick said a silent prayer at the table then blessed himself, performing the sign of the cross, to which neither woman objected. He took a bite of his rather skimpy bacon, lettuce, and tomato sandwich and took his time chewing it. Swallowing, he said, "Did you find a good doctor here?"

Rachel nodded yes. "I was required to notify the local hospital when I arrived in Pennsylvania. All pregnant women traveling are required to, in case of emergency. I have my next appointment next Wednesday."

The expectant mother grimaced. "Looks like I'll be giving birth in Pennsylvania. The plan was to have the baby in Michigan, so I could be close to my family. My parents are chomping at the bit to meet their grandson.

121

"Looks like it ain't happening anytime soon," she said, with a weighty sigh. "Once my son's born, I'll need to remain under quarantine for a minimum of six months for the baby's sake. So, if my parents want to see their grandchild anytime soon, they'll have to come here."

Megan smiled at Rachel, before her eyes volleyed to Dick. "When Rachel told GC officials why we were here, they were eager to help us locate Brian and Jacquelyn." She sighed. "Then came the quake..."

Rachel rubbed her belly. "Even without their help, we're determined to remain here until we find Brian and justice is served."

Megan added, "Then we can all finally move on. Just hope it's soon, so we don't go broke first..."

Dick nodded his understanding, not realizing she was trying to subliminally remind him of the promise he had made to fund them.

Rachel smiled wearily when their guest didn't take the bait. "In a perfect world, we'll find Brian before the six-month quarantine expires once my son is born. If we don't find him by then, I'll have no choice but to apply to the GC for a housing extension here in Pennsylvania, until we do."

Dick couldn't contain his astonishment. *Perfect world? How could she think such wildly absurd thoughts when I'm barely hanging on?*

Rachel took a large bite of her sandwich, which was twice as thick as Dick's and Megan's sandwiches, and a spoonful of tomato soup. "More than anything, I'm eager to move into my condo back home, compliments of Salvador the Great. That is, if it wasn't destroyed in the quake."

Dick gulped hard. Even though both women had promised that nothing would happen to Brian until after he plucked Sarah away from the evildoers, he was suddenly unsure.

Megan noticed his change of expression. "Why don't you tell us about your earthquake encounter."

Dick took a sip of water. "I was lying on the living room couch when I felt this strong rumbling. The only thing I could think to do was roll onto my belly and cling to the sofa I was laying on, for dear life.

"You should have seen me. The way my right arm clutched the bottom of the couch, six inches off the floor, as my left arm clung to the top of the couch, it felt like I was hugging an awkwardly shaped mattress."

Dick looked down at the table. "Truth be told, I was okay with being killed that night. I wanted to die, in fact. Now, I'm not so sure..."

There were no audible gasps or astonished glances following his comment. These were different times, and this was a different world, and Megan and Rachel both knew exactly where he was coming from...

Dick took the final bite of his sandwich. "Where have you been searching for Brian?"

Megan answered, "Mostly at supermarkets, fast food restaurants, convenience stores, and gas stations. The one place we never stake out is the local hospital. There's no chance those evildoers would ever step foot in that place! If they did, they would be taken into custody immediately."

Rachel added, "The fact that so many businesses have closed down since the disappearances really helps us. With so much heat on them, I seriously doubt they'd be foolish enough to go to a restaurant."

Dick nodded. "Makes sense to me..." He couldn't stop yawning. "Sorry. It was a long drive. Not sure how many more of these grueling eighteen-hour trips I can take."

Rachel stretched her hands above her head. "No need to apologize. I could use a nap myself."

Megan said, "Why don't we all relax and resume our search for Brian tomorrow?" Seeing Dick grimace, Megan added, "Sarah, rather."

"Thanks for lunch and for the hospitality. I appreciate it so much."

Rachel smiled. "We're honored to have you..."

Megan thought to herself, *You'll be more welcome after you give us the money you promised!* "Enjoy your nap..."

Dick showered then went straight to bed hoping, praying, that the building wouldn't collapse on him in his sleep.

But if he discovered that Sarah never survived the quake, he would utter the same prayer skyward, only in reverse...

26

THE FOLLOWING DAY – DAY 2 IN PENNSYLVANIA

DICK MULROONEY WOKE THE next morning amazed that he had slept so long, 14 hours to be exact. It was the first real sleep he had had in too long to remember. The instant his head hit the pillow after lunch, he felt the room spinning mostly from sheer exhaustion.

Grateful as he was for the extended sleep, he also woke up feeling panicked, not only from fear of the building collapsing on him, but because his dream world had suddenly gone rogue on him. It had flip-flopped, to the extent that this dream was at odds with his real-world plans, as if trying to take him in a new direction.

Unlike all other past dreams about Brian, this one was full of fond memories of days spent with his son, from his early childhood days leading all the way up to when he received his degree from the university of Notre Dame, followed by his quick hire at the Marriott corporation.

There were too many good moments to count...

Dick felt his chest swelling within him like when it happened for real. He dried his moist eyes, wondering about its meaning. Brian's impressive accomplishments before the disappearances had crossed his mind numerous times since the world was forever changed, but always with Dick shaking his head in disgust.

Brian had a top-notch education, a flourishing career, a good woman to love—before Renate killed herself—and a stable family. *Those were good things, weren't they?*

Yes, they were, Dick concluded for the hundredth time.

So, why this dream now, when the anger and disappointment he felt for his son was so well founded? Why was he shown Brian's vast accomplishments, when his life had turned out so disastrously after his so-called conversion to Christianity?

Anyone close to the situation would concur the instant he left the Catholic church, everything quickly spiraled downward for the Mulrooneys. Dick sneered to himself. *Anyone close to the situation? I'm the only one left!* Mostly out of sheer humiliation, Brian forced him to self-isolate from the rest of the world all this time.

124

Dick wanted to cry his eyes out. Couldn't Sarah and Brian see God was severely judging them both for what they had done? Wasn't it as obvious to them that converting to that false religion was what had led to Chelsea taking her life, as it was to him?

Couldn't they see his anger toward them was the same righteous indignation that Jesus had shown toward the Pharisees and Sadducees, for turning His Father's house into a den of thieves?

Yes, Dick was utterly convinced that the downward spiral for his family had little to do with the disappearances, and mostly to do with his son's total disassociation with all things Catholic.

When they met Brian at Penn Station a few days after what Brian had claimed was the Rapture of Christ's true Church—a theory that stood diametrically opposed to the Pope's findings, and therefore against the Catholic Church's conclusions—the family was still very much intact, even with chaos and turmoil creeping in all around them.

Then Brian met Charles Calloway at the Waldorf-Astoria Hotel, who proclaimed to know what happened to the planet on that fateful day.

Without consulting a Roman Catholic priest, Brian bought the Florida businessman's bogus story hook, line, and sinker, which led to his sudden departure from the Church, despite the many years he spent in their system studying religion.

The next sign of Brian's mental illness was when he asked Charles to be the best man at his wedding! He then put his illness on full display by having Tom Dunleavey as one of his groomsmen, and Tamika Moseley, of all people, as one of his wife's bridesmaids! It was pure insanity! Who did such things? Only those who had been brainwashed into a cult!

What hurt most was, had his son not suddenly changed religions, Dick was convinced Chelsea would still be alive. Renate too for that matter! And the family would still be intact. Then again, he refused to call Brian's spiritual experience a "conversion to Christianity" in any way.

As a Catholic, Dick firmly believed he was the only "true" Christian left in the family. He didn't need Brian or Sarah to remind him that salvation came through Jesus, or that He was the only begotten Son of God, and He was born of the Virgin Mary.

These were things he had believed all his life, from hearing it preached at Sunday mass. These truths were deeply instilled in him. He even recited those very words when saying the "Our Father" and "Hail Mary" prayers.

Unlike Brian and Sarah, Dick had tradition on his side.

125

Yet, despite all that, because of his recent dreams, he felt a deep yearning for his son he hadn't felt in a very long time...

Dick sat up in bed and saw his disheveled image staring back at him in the badly cracked mirror hanging on the wall. He couldn't understand why his dream world had been so disrupted on the first night he slept at Megan's and Rachel's apartment.

He got dressed and joined Megan and Rachel in the kitchen for a cup of instant coffee. With so much faulty wiring all throughout the apartment complex from the quake, many of the outlets weren't working properly, if at all. On two separate occasions, they tried brewing fresh coffee, but when power was lost, it stopped brewing at the halfway point.

Not wanting to burn the place to the ground, they switched from fresh brewed to instant coffee, when they could obtain it, that is.

After a quick breakfast, consisting of powdered eggs, Spam, white toast, and powdered milk, they resumed their search for Brian Mulrooney.

Driving on U.S. 202, as Dick dodged in between sections of road that weren't passable, the two women pointed out some of the supermarkets and convenience stores/gas stations places they had frequently staked out since arriving in Pennsylvania.

They parked outside a local supermarket situated in a shopping center which, for the most part, had been completely leveled. The supermarket also sustained massive damage, which meant those going there for their rationed groceries had to wait outside, as their orders were filled for them. There were no refrigerated or frozen foods to offer to anyone.

With strict rations in effect, shoppers had to make appointments days in advance, due to mass shortages. Megan's and Rachel's next scheduled appointment was still three days away.

For the next few hours, they parked at one location for a few minutes before driving to another, without ever spotting Brian, Jacquelyn, or Sarah.

Rachel was laying on the back seat. "I need a nap."

Megan glanced back at her best friend. "Can you sleep in the car?"

"I'd rather go home. I have an upset stomach."

Dick looked in the rearview mirror. "I'll take you back..."

Rachel looked relieved. "Thank you..."

Driving north on U.S. 202, on the way back to the apartment, Dick couldn't believe his eyes. *The convenience store in my dreams!* He slowed the car to a near stop and did a doubletake to make sure his eyes weren't playing tricks on him. They weren't. His breathing became irregular, erratic even.

126

Megan said, "What is it, Mister Mulrooney? You look like you just saw a ghost!"

Dick's eyes narrowed, as he surveyed the convenience store parking lot. He didn't see Tom Dunleavey—a man Megan or Rachel knew nothing about—but he was certain this was the place in his dream. "Uh, nothing. Thought I saw something."

"Brian?"

"I wish!" *Think!* "Sorry if I startled you, Megan. Ever since Sarah left, I've been a bundle of nerves. The stress I encountered yesterday, from driving here isn't helping."

"I think we can all relate to that! Right, Rachel?" Megan glanced back at her friend, to find her snoring ever so softly in the backseat. "All the more reason to find your wife as soon as possible."

Dick nodded. When the light turned green, he was finally able to calm his nerves enough to resume driving.

When they reached U.S. 322, Megan pointed out Dick's side window. "That's the hotel Brian stayed at!"

"The one Renate found on Brian's credit card statements?" asked Dick.

Megan teared up at the mention of her sister's name. She hesitated, then nodded sadly.

There was no need to stake that place out. Had Brian tried checking into the Concordville Inn, or at any other local establishment, he would be arrested on the spot.

When they arrived back at the apartment, the nonstop Brian bashing continued. Even though Dick was in total agreement with most of what they said, after 24 hours of constant berating, he quickly grew tired of it and kept trying to change the topic. He was starting to take it personally, if only for his name's sake. *I thought I was mad at him!*

As much as he dreaded being alone, the comfort he felt when he first arrived was slowly dissipating. He excused himself from their company, showered, then climbed into bed hoping his dream world wouldn't go rogue on him again...

27

DICK WOKE TO ANOTHER dream. This one was more in line with the one he'd had about Tom Dunleavey at the convenience store they drove past the day before. Only it was a continuation of sorts...

Instead of it ending with the former Catholic priest lowering his head and leaving the store as quickly as he could, after Dick threatened to call the police on him, Dick followed him this time as he made his getaway.

That was when he woke from the dream. He sat up in bed and, like the morning before, saw his disheveled image staring back at him in the mirror hanging on the wall. He rubbed his sweaty hair, totally confused about the dream. It was so real he felt every emotion.

And why did his dream suddenly revert back to his original one?

Dick suddenly felt bi-polar in that dimension. He got dressed, and joined Megan and Rachel in the dining room for breakfast. "Perhaps it might be good if we split up, so we can monitor two locations at a time. I don't mind going it alone. Not sure how long I'll be staying, so time is of the essence."

Megan sipped her coffee, wondering why he was acting so strangely, distant. She chalked it up to the paranoia he felt sleeping at this mangled place. "See, the building survived to see another day," she joked.

Dick smirked nervously. She was only partly correct—his mind was already parked at the convenience store in his dreams. "Thankfully!"

Rachel asked, "Which location will you be staking out?"

"Not sure. Think I'll find a place to charge my car, then drive around a while and see where it leads me." There was no way he was about to tell them he wouldn't be out looking for Sarah, or Brian either, but for the disgraced Catholic priest neither woman knew anything about.

Megan shrugged her shoulders. "Sure, if that's what you want..."

"If I see them, I'll call you immediately. Please do the same."

"Of course," remarked Rachel. "We'll leave the key under the door mat when we leave, in case you get back before us."

Dick nodded his thanks, took the final bite of his powdered eggs breakfast, and put his dish in the sink.

Megan said, "Just leave it there, Dick. I'll take care of it."

"I don't mind washing it..."

Megan glanced at Rachel before her eyes settled on Dick again. "It's okay. I insist..."

"Okay, as you wish. I'll see you both a little later then..."

Rachel said, "Good luck!"

"You too..."

Dick left the complex. A few minutes later, he parked his car in one of the charging station stalls at the convenience store and turned his engine off. He still had enough battery power to follow the man if he showed up

After waiting just 45 minutes, Dick's eyes doubled in size when he spotted Tom Dunleavey heading inside the convenience store, looking to his left and right, as if anticipating something or someone.

Dick stopped charging his vehicle, and went inside the convenience store, to find Tom waiting in line. Now that his dream was materializing before his very eyes, his heartbeat was jacked to the max!

ETSM residents were required to wear disguises whenever they were out in public, but if Tom did that, how would Dick notice him? Not having it on left him feeling even more exposed.

He had no idea why he was even waiting in line; he wasn't there to purchase anything. He was there to meet Brian's father.

When he spotted Dick Mulrooney entering the store a few moments later, all thoughts of what to purchase went out the window. He panicked and left the store empty-handed.

Dick followed the disgraced former Catholic priest outside then hurried to his car. In no way would this be a spying mission. He wanted him to know he was being pursued, like a cop chasing a bad guy, minus the flashing lights and siren.

Dick zigged when Tom zigged on the mansion-lined country backroads, and zagged when he zagged—which was frequently, due to the damage sustained by the quake.

Tom kept nervously peering into the rearview mirror, mildly shocked that his pursuant hadn't struck the back of his car by now. As someone who'd always prided himself on being a safe driver, few things rattled his nerves before the Rapture more than aggressive, erratic drivers the likes of the man presently tailing him, even if it was a slow car chase.

Tom wasn't skilled enough to outmaneuver a New York City driver, especially on these winding roads. He finally gave up the chase and pulled his vehicle to the side of the road.

129

Dick approached his car to find him trembling even worse than when their eyes first met back at the convenience store. His breathing was labored, as if he'd been running, not driving a vehicle.

If it was sympathy induced, Dick was having none of it. Further, if this man expected him to bow down in reverence—something Dick was known to do with Catholic priests, cardinals, and bishops in the past—he had another thing coming!

He glared angrily at Tom. "Take me to my wife this very instant, or I'm calling the cops!"

Tom gasped, then lowered his head.

Dick pulled his cellphone out from his coat pocket and entered 911 on his phone screen. With his finger practically touching the SEND button, he pointed his phone screen at Tom. "I'm not kidding!"

Tom glanced up fearfully at Dick and clutched at his chest, hoping he wouldn't suffer another heart attack. Then again, having his heart fail him seemed like a comforting proposition right about now. He took a few deep breaths. "I can't do that. Sorry."

Dick's face reddened. "Wrong answer, *Father*!"

Ignoring the sarcastic reply, Tom pleaded with him, "Please, if you'll just let me go, I promise to inform Brian of our meeting."

"Brian?! Did I say Brian? I don't want Brian, only Sarah!"

Dick's loud, angry voice caused Tom's body to quake even more. "Sarah too!"

She's still alive! "When?!" Dick barked.

"Soon as I get back."

"What if I keep following you?"

Tom lowered his head again, shaking it from side to side. He had not only his own life to think about, but his surviving co-inhabitants as well. This compounded his fear all the more.

Finally, he said, "Sorry, but I cannot and will not take you there. I've been sworn to secrecy. I'd rather be arrested and tortured by the enemy, than reveal our hiding place to you, or to anyone else for that matter."

Dick took a moment to consider his options. If he let Tom go, he might never see him again. If he followed the man, it would lead to nowhere. If he called the police, Tom would be arrested, and Sarah would remain in hiding until authorities finally discovered their location.

Mindful of the intense torture false converts were being subjected to before they were killed in the quake, he sensed Tom wouldn't last five minutes before he sung like a canary. If so, what would happen to his wife?

130

Once he rescued Sarah from their evil clutches, he wouldn't give a hoot about what happened to them after that.

Tom looked up at his pursuer again; his eyes pleaded for understanding. "If you'll give me a little time to inform your family that you're here in Pennsylvania, we can take the next step. Fair enough?"

Dick sighed and shrugged his shoulders. "When?"

"I don't know. I'm not in charge."

Dick was growing more impatient. "Who is?!" he snapped.

A deeper sense of desperation filled Tom's face. His eyes projected sheer terror. "Can't share that with you, sorry."

Dick pounded the roof of Tom's car in frustration, startling him again. "I'm sick and tired of all this secrecy nonsense!"

Tom didn't need further convincing of just how determined Dick was to find his wife. Now that he was potentially closing in on their hiding place, there wasn't a chance he would give up the search and simply go away.

In between erratic breaths, he said, "It'll take a little time to organize a meeting, but I promise someone will eventually contact you."

"When?" This was said more softly.

Tom took a deep breath and exhaled very slowly. His head throbbed. He was certain it was due to his blood pressure being through the roof. "Can't say off the top of my head. Perhaps a few days."

Dick's eyes narrowed. "Why do you act as if you're holding all the cards, when I have the clear advantage? I'm not the one living in hiding. All it would take is one phone call to bring a whole world of hurt down upon you all…"

Tom clutched at his chest again. In his fragile condition, it wouldn't take much to go into cardiac arrest. He raised his hands from the steering wheel, as if in surrender. "Like I said, I'm not the one in charge…"

Dick lowered himself a little more so that his head was practically invading Tom's space. "Let's say I go along with it. How will I know who to look for?"

"You won't. It might begin with a text message with instructions to follow. They're quite thorough…" Tom looked up at Dick and squinted in the bright sunshine. "By the way, I know about your dream…"

Dick flinched. "What dream?"

"About me." Before Dick could reply, Tom said, "The reason I know is that I had the same dream myself. Why do you think I was at the convenience store in the first place? I assure you it wasn't to purchase milk

131

or gas." He wasn't about to tell him that his dream led them into a spiritual debate.

Dick couldn't believe what he was hearing. "Okay, genius, since you proclaim to be the great interpreter of dreams, why don't you tell me how it ends?"

"This isn't the time or place. I'm not even supposed to be out in public without wearing a disguise."

Dick paused, then said, "You better not be leading me on!"

"I'm not, Dick. But you'll need to remain patient until I contact the right people..."

After a three second stare down, Dick backed off. He had to protect Sarah. "If I don't hear from *someone* soon, it could get ugly for you and everyone else hiding with you!"

"I understand. Someone *will* contact you, Dick..."

Dick glared at him one last time, then walked back to his car. Without hesitating, he made a U-turn and drove away.

Instead of feeling relieved, Tom's trembling only increased...

28

FORTY-FIVE MINUTES LATER, Tom was back at safehouse number one. He was amazed that he'd actually found the strength to drive back to the compound. Normally an encounter like this would have frozen the old Tom Dunleavey dead in his tracks until he pulled himself together enough to venture back home.

He didn't have the option of remaining parked on the side of the road until his nerves were calm enough to resume driving. The last thing he needed was for authorities on any level to see him.

As far as he knew, there wasn't a warrant out for his arrest yet, but the fact that he was among the first to be added to the "Catholic defector" database meant even without a warrant, he was a wanted man.

Upon clearing various checkpoints and reaching the back entryway, the guards monitoring it from the outside couldn't ignore what they saw on Tom's face. Nor could they overlook his trembling hands. They quickly waved him inside.

"Are you okay, Tom?" Titus asked. "You don't look so good."

Dunleavey frowned. "I just saw Brian Mulrooney's father…"

The *ETSM* guard stiffened. "Where?"

"At a convenience store on 202."

Titus searched the perimeter, his steely eyes looking for possible company. Thankfully, he saw nothing. "Did he see you?"

Tom took a few deep breaths and nodded yes.

"Where's your disguise?"

"I didn't bring it with me. I needed him to see me."

"What?!" the buff former navy seal barked. "Are you actually telling me he saw you without it?"

Tom closed his eyes and nodded in the affirmative again.

Titus grunted frustration, and glanced over at Ingrid, his female counterpart who was trained as an ETSM guard after so many were killed in the global quake. "Why would you do that and possibly endanger us all?" he barked again.

Tom held his hands up, as if in surrender. "Sorry, Titus, but it was part of a dream God sent to me. Dick confessed to having the very same dream himself. Sort of, anyway…"

Ingrid inched in closer. "I'm confused. What dream?"

Tom took his time explaining the dream to Titus and Ingrid, even stuttering at times. "Frightened as I was with the prospect of bumping into him, why else had God sent the dream?"

Tom gasped. "What a coward I turned out to be! Instead of talking to him, like I vividly saw in my dream, I got scared and fled the store seeking safety.

"In the end, my cowardice and lack of obedience proved once again just how weak my faith is at times." Tom's breathing became more erratic as he briefly relived the traumatic experience.

"Calm down," said Titus. "Take a few breaths. Relax…"

Tom took a moment to collect himself. "But God wasn't about to let me off the hook so easily. I'm convinced He wanted Dick to follow me out of the convenience store parking lot, before chasing me through many backroads. I couldn't shake him despite my best efforts, so I finally pulled the car to the side of the road."

Ingrid glanced at Titus and shrugged her shoulders. "God does work in mysterious ways. Think he's on to us?"

Tom shook his head up and down several times. "Most definitely. He even threatened to call the cops if I didn't bring him here immediately."

Titus's eyes widened. "He knows our location?"

Tom shook his head. "As far as I could tell, all he wants is Sarah back. But that could quickly change if we don't get back to him soon. Talk about a relentless individual!"

Titus ignored the last part. "So, what do you suggest we do, Tom?"

"Naturally, I told him I couldn't bring him here under any circumstances, but if he let me go, I would inform his family that he's in Pennsylvania looking for them."

Tom waited for one of them to reply. When both remained silent, he added, "There was no time to rehearse a better excuse. I never expected him to follow me. I was caught completely by surprise."

Titus paused a moment to think things through. "Park over by the pool and stay there until I know what to do next."

"You got it." Tom drove his car the short distance to the swimming pool area that was badly damaged in the quake, extremely grateful that he'd made it back.

He wasn't so sure he would ever see this place again. He breathed a sigh of relief seeing that his blood pressure, which had reached as high as 220/110 during his brief encounter, had lowered considerably.

Since he no longer had access to his smart watch, and with his blood pressure meds cut in half, post-quake, he made sure to take his BP monitor with him earlier when he left the residence.

Titus called Travis Hartings' Sat-phone. After explaining what Tom had just told him, he added, "I must say, even though it ended favorably, if he was followed here, I feel powerless from protecting everyone. Why can't we be armed, even if only for show?"

Hartings breathed heavily into the phone. "Once again, I understand your concern, Titus, I really do. But we must be ever mindful that some of God's children are destined for imprisonment or worse. The last thing we need is for reports to surface that Christians are participating in the killing of others. The guard dogs will have to do…"

"But…"

"I'm sorry, Titus, but we cannot and will not allow for lethal force to be used by our guards. Consider the matter finished…"

Titus approached Tom's car. "Okay, here's the deal. For now, no one can know about it. Not even Brian. Got it? Travis' orders!"

Tom sensed his agitation and nodded his head nervously. "As you say…"

"Good. You can go to your cottage now. Go take a nap or something."

Tom sighed wearily. "That's precisely what I need right now…"

29

IT TOOK THREE DAYS before the green light was given for the next step with Brian's father to be taken. The reason for the lengthy delay—three days was like an eternity in this present climate—was that while Tom Dunleavey and Dick Mulrooney both had common dreams, Dick wasn't saved.

If he had truly been born again, he surely would have mentioned it to Tom the other day—with great joy in his heart—but he didn't...

Travis Hartings and Clayton Holmes both knew the late Braxton Rice would never have considered allowing a meeting like this to move forward, under any circumstances.

The two *ETSM* leaders were fully mindful that they were breaking a rule that was essential to their overall survival. Just meeting with Dick could bring a world of hurt down on them all. They got to see with their own two eyes just how angry he was at Brian's and Jacquelyn's wedding. And that was *before* he learned about Sarah's conversion to Christianity!

Tom also felt the force of his fury when he followed him the other day. His overall mannerisms didn't reflect a recent conversion of any kind.

If by chance, Dick remained spiritually blinded to the Truth in the end, it would be all for naught. On the other hand, if God was using them to rescue Brian's father, it would be well worth the risk they were about to take. Had it not been for their shared dreams, it wouldn't be happening.

The three Mulrooney residents still had no idea what was going on. Why get their hopes up for nothing? If nothing came of it, they would never know the meeting happened at all...

Dick woke at 5 a.m., after receiving a text message from a restricted number. He was given simple instructions and ordered not to reply to the message, under any circumstances.

He got dressed then quietly tiptoed out of the bedroom, into the living room and out the front door, trying not to wake Megan or Rachel. Then again, at this hour, even if he paraded himself all throughout the apartment, chances were good they wouldn't hear him. Both were night owls, which meant they probably weren't even at the halfway point of their sleep yet.

After three more days of being subjected to their constant Brian bashing, Dick didn't know how much more he could take.

It was slowly devouring him from within.

As instructed via text message—sent from only God knew who—Dick parked his car in the badly-damaged shopping center parking lot across the street from the convenience store, at precisely 6 a.m., and waited.

Then waited some more...

In normal times, with every store leveled, and with dozens of destroyed vehicles littering the parking lot, there wasn't a chance he would park his car there. But as the days passed, the widespread destruction had become so commonplace, everyone was desensitized to it, including him.

Meanwhile, Tony Pearsall and Joaquim Guzman monitored him from a short distance away. After sweeping for counter surveillance devices, they detected nothing to cause concern.

They already knew the cameras in the shopping center their target had just pulled into weren't working, making monitoring him even less risky.

Dick didn't know, but wouldn't be surprised to know, he was being monitored. Another thing he didn't know was that they had no intention of meeting him this day. This was a test of sorts, to see how he would react after they had wasted his time by making him wait for someone to show up, so he could take the next step toward getting his wife back.

Both knew they were taking a massive risk by standing him up. Would he feel so betrayed by them that he would go straight to the police, or even to the local media? Soon, they would know...

The strongest card they held was that they had his wife. But would that be enough to prevent him from contacting local authorities on them?

After waiting nearly three uneventful hours, hoping and praying the entire time that this would be the day he would see Sarah again, Dick drove back to the apartment feeling like he had just wasted his time.

He walked through the front door; disappointment was written all over his face. He also looked aggravated.

Megan asked, "Are you okay, Mister Mulrooney?"

No, I'm not! I've just been flimflammed! "I made no progress whatsoever. I feel like I'm looking for a needle in a haystack..."

Megan glanced at Rachel. "Welcome to our world..."

Dick sighed. He felt bad for not being transparent with them, but the more they kept bashing Brian, the more his gut told him to keep Tom Dunleavey a secret from them for now.

He was completely unaware that Miguel Jiminez—someone else he didn't know—had followed him back to the condo development, to hopefully take photographs of whoever he was staying with.

137

Even though Dick had passed the test on day one, they decided to stand him up again on day two, just to make sure.

Jiminez remained camped out at the apartment after Dick left, waiting for whoever else was in there to show themselves.

Finally, just before 7 a.m., two women emerged. Miguel captured their images, then followed them to see where they would go. It turned out to be the supermarket. From there, they went straight home.

Jiminez went back to the safe house and quickly identified them as Megan McCallister and Rachel Stein, using facial recognition technology and their social media accounts.

Meanwhile, after waiting 90 minutes at a different location this time, Dick was greatly disappointed. He seriously contemplated going home. He wasn't in the mood to be toyed with by whoever was behind this charade of sorts.

In anger, Dick disobeyed their order by sending a text message to the restricted number, asking if they had sent him to the wrong location.

They didn't reply to his message. But the fact that he had made no threats was a good sign. All he did was ask for clarification.

Now convinced Brian's father was acting alone, without Megan's or Rachel's help, or without the local police, once Dick was settled at his third different location in three days, Tony gave Joaquim the green light to call his cell phone at 6:15 a.m.

Dick looked at his phone screen: *Restricted number.* "Hello?" He sounded agitated, which was fully expected.

Joaquim's voice was digitized, making the 16-year-old sound like he was 60. "Proceed north on 202, until you reach Dunkin' Donuts a few miles up on your right."

"Who is this?" Dick demanded to know.

"Don't talk. Just listen," the voice barked. "When you get there, stay in your car until you receive further instructions."

Before Dick could reply, the call abruptly ended. His eyes darted this way and that looking out all six of his car windows, wondering if he should go through with it or not? But what other options did he have at his disposal?

He started the car and drove off, constantly looking in his rearview mirror to see if he was being followed. "See how far I'm willing to go to preserve this family, Sarah?" he told his reflection in the rearview mirror.

He missed his wife so much and felt so lonely, it was impossible to feel anger toward her now.

With very few cars and trucks on the road, Dick arrived there in no time. He pulled into the lot and eased his car into a parking space, then waited 20 minutes before his phone rang. It was a restricted number again. "Yes?"

"Now I want you to proceed south on 202 until you get to U.S. 1. Take U.S. 1 south for roughly ten miles. I'll call back to give you further instructions once you've cleared the next checkpoint."

Dick stared at his phone screen. *Next checkpoint? What in the world?* Before he could further inquire, the call ended. He started his car and drove back in the direction from which he had just come.

Nearly a half hour later, while traveling south on a badly damaged U.S. 1, he received the next call. "Pull to the side of the road." Dick raised an eyebrow.

"Now, Dick!" the voice barked.

Are they following me? Dick was startled. He fumbled his cell phone, but he was able to hold on without it falling to the floor. He followed the gruff digitized command and pulled his car to the side of the road, at the bottom of the hill, 20 feet behind one of the many piles of broken up cement and tar, which had been removed from the hilly road.

Dick smirked. They looked like piles of plowed dirty snow.

Almost immediately, the tow truck Dick saw in his rearview mirror the past mile and a half or so, pulled directly behind him on the shoulder of the road.

Tony Pearsall got out and limped very slowly toward Dick's car, wearing mechanic's clothing and a facemask.

Without asking permission and without apology, the construction foreman slashed one of Dick's rear tires with a pocketknife.

Pearsall looked skyward. "That's for you, Braxton!" he said, remembering what the late Braxton Rice had done to Charles Calloway's rental car, after smuggling Tamika to safety.

Pearsall said, "If anyone, namely law enforcement inquires, you have a flat and no spare tire. I'm here to tow your car to the closest station. Got it?"

Dick nodded yes.

Tony held out his hand. "Car keys and cell phone."

In normal times, this would only happen during a carjacking. Without hesitation, Dick handed them over to him.

Tony powered down Dick's phone and tucked it into his overalls with his keys. "Wait in the truck! This won't take long."

139

Dick had no choice but to do as he was told. Tony had the clear advantage over him. Whereas Dick knew nothing about this man, Tony probably knew everything about him, the important details, anyway.

Once the car was hooked to the back of the tow truck, Pearsall climbed behind the wheel, placed Dick's phone in a copper-fitted box to avoid detection, and left for the auto mechanic garage two exits away, in total silence.

Upon arriving at the garage that was secretly owned by the *ETSM* farmers in Kennett Square, Dick was escorted to the back office, and frisked and swept for mobile or recording devices.

He was then blindfolded and escorted to the back of a 22-foot delivery truck—also owned by the *ETSM*—that had just been serviced, and would be taken back to the farm/safehouse.

Tony and Dick both rode in the back of the truck, once again in total silence, rocking and bouncing to the commands of the damaged roads, until they reached the Kennett Square safehouse. The truck pulled to the back of the farm, out of sight of everyone else.

What should have taken 10 minutes at most took roughly an hour. The driver made many frequent turns along the way. After the maze Tom Dunleavey had already led him through, Dick sort of expected it.

But at least last time, he wasn't blindfolded, and he was wearing a seatbelt. He felt discombobulated, queasy, nauseous. But if it led him back to Sarah, it would all be worth it. "I'm doing all of this for you, my love."

140

30

UPON ARRIVING AT THE safehouse in Kennett Square, Dick was led from the truck that was parked in the barn that had sustained the least amount of damage, and escorted to the back office. The window blinds were closed, and thick curtains added another layer of protection.

In a world in shambles, and with most businesses still closed, they decided to risk allowing Dick onto one of their properties.

The fact that so many trucks were always coming and going made Kennett Square the right choice to host this meeting of sorts.

Tony helped him get settled onto a wooden folding chair. Now that the moment was finally upon him, Dick gulped in anticipation. *Was Sarah here?* When the blindfold was removed, it took a few seconds for his eyes to adjust to the dim light coming from a small floor lamp.

Dick silently gasped seeing Tom Dunleavey seated on a wooden chair opposite him. *What in the world?* With the hope of seeing his beloved again quickly squashed, his hands became sweaty, his throat dry and his breathing erratic. He blinked hard a couple times. "Where's Sarah?"

"Thirsty?"

"Water would be fine." There was no anger in Dick's voice this time. Part of the reason was that he was at a complete disadvantage. For one thing, he had no idea where he was. Then there was Tony to consider.

Though he never felt threatened by the man, per se, even with a severe limp, he was quite an imposing figure. With so many missing teeth, he looked like he used to be a professional hockey player.

"Hungry? Food's really good here. And plentiful for now…"

Dick shook his head. His stomach was still doing backflips. He felt like vomiting. With all that driving on winding country roads—mixed in with frequent stops and detours, he had no way of knowing he was only 12 miles away from Megan's and Rachel's apartment. It felt more like 50. "Just water's fine."

Tom got up and poured his visitor a glass of filtered water.

Taking the glass, Dick said, "I want to see Sarah…"

Tom stared at him cautiously. "In truth, she still doesn't know you're in Pennsylvania…"

Dick's eyes widened. "But you said…"

Tom extended his hands, palms out. "Everything I promised I would do, I have done. Only I wasn't given permission from those at the top of the organization to tell your wife. At least for now…"

Dick snorted frustration at the man who was one of his son's groomsmen. "Does Brian know I'm here?"

"No."

Dick panicked. *Is this some sort of attempt to brainwash me too?* "Are they even here?"

Tom hesitated, then shot a quick glance at Tony, who answered for Tom. "No," he said, gruffly, "but they're not too far from here."

Dick craned his neck back and gulped hard at the man who had slashed his car tire. His palms became even more sweaty. Not knowing where he was, and with no phone to call for help—spotty as the signal was—he was in no position to make threats or negotiate a favorable ending.

Instead of being demanding, he said, "May I please see my wife? I'm desperate." *Looks like they're holding all the cards after all…*

"Perhaps soon," said Tom. "But first we need to have a serious discussion."

Perhaps soon? "About what?"

"Namely, the Catholic Church."

Dick grew fidgety in his chair. "Hmm, what about it?"

"Let me put it this way, if our meeting is successful, you'll come to realize your problem's not with Brian or Sarah, but with the Church itself."

Seriously? Dick raised a skeptical eyebrow. "In what way?"

Tom paused to take a sip of water. "Not too long after the Rapture, Brian and I both had dreams about the Catholic Church. In fact, it's what had brought us together…"

Dick grimaced hearing Tom refer to what happened way back when as the Rapture. He wasn't at all surprised. He took a sip of water. "Go on, I'm listening…"

"The first time I spoke to your son, he was just as lost and confused as everyone else, myself included. He peppered me with many questions which I confess I had no answers to, although I must say I had my suspicions."

Dick rubbed his chin; confusion was stenciled onto his face.

"When we reconnected a few weeks later, Brian sounded nothing like he did the first time we spoke. By that time, he had already left the Catholic Church. He invited me over to his apartment for a friendly spiritual debate.

"Believe me when I say, I went there that day with every intention of persuading him to come back to the Church, through rigorous debate if need be." Tom frowned. "Needless to say, it didn't go well for me…"

Dick raised an eyebrow. "Why's that?"

"Every time I tried gaining control of the conversation, it was like God had sealed my mouth shut, so all I could do was listen." Tom shook his head as if he still couldn't believe it. "I've never experienced anything like it before. As much as I wanted to defend the Church, I couldn't, especially after Brian told me about a dream he had.

"As I listened, my mind was completely blown. The reason for this was that I had the very same dream he had. Only mine ended much differently than his. Did Brian ever tell you about his dream?"

"He tried to," Dick scoffed, "but I wouldn't let him finish…"

Tom sighed. His facial expression dimmed. "Did you know I was the priest he saw in his dream?"

Dick shook his head.

"It's true. Like Brian, I saw myself saying mass to a congregation that was suddenly set on fire. It was as if I could smell the smoke and feel the flames. Peering through the smoke above me, I saw the Catholic Church hierarchy. I also saw Two Men at the back of the sanctuary preaching a condemning message to the Church I'd dedicated my entire life to.

"As a priest for more than thirty years, their words shot straight into my soul. I assure you not in a good way. The more I tried out-preaching them, the louder they spoke, easily drowning out my voice."

Dick silently scoffed. He was there to see Sarah, not engage in a religious debate with someone who had defected from the Church he had totally dedicated his life to.

Tom noticed his change of expression and took a small sip of water. "Suddenly, the strangest thing happened. Some of the parishioners were plucked out of the fire, without a single burn mark on any of them, as everyone else screamed in agony begging to be rescued, including many whom I considered to be the most religious in the church…"

Tom shook his head sadly. "Religious or not, since their hearts remained hardened to the true Gospel of Jesus Christ, they were ultimately consumed by fire, and were without hope or excuse."

Dick winced at Tom's words. *Is this evidence of mental illness like with Brian? Is Sarah having similar thoughts?* With his heart still hardened to the true Gospel message, it sounded utterly ridiculous to him.

143

Tom noticed but felt no need to defend himself. He was right where Dick was not too long ago. "Like Brian, I saw demons fleeing the many focal points of worship I'd prayed to all my life and urged my flock to as well, just before the church was blown to smithereens.

"In Brian's dream, once the smoke cleared, all things pertaining to the Catholic Church were gone, completely incinerated in the flames, replaced by a serene field full of fertile soil where the church once stood.

"Brian told me he saw Jesus standing in the center of the harvest field saying, 'I am the Way, the Truth and the Life. No one comes to the Father except through Me. Everything else is merely chasing after hell.'"

Tom paused, waiting for Dick to make eye contact with him again. "Brian was emphatic that no one else was with Him. No Popes, cardinals, bishops, priests, statues, or Mary. Only Jesus!

"One thing that really struck me about your son's dream was how God had revealed to him that Catholics represented extremely fertile ground. Brian told me many would be part of the plentiful end-times harvest, but only those who distanced themselves from the religiosity of the Church— clergyman and parishioner alike."

Tom grew more somber. "I wish I could say my dream ended that way, but it didn't. Instead of seeing Jesus where the church once stood, I saw myself standing before a just and holy God, totally naked and ashamed, after being found guilty of preaching a false message all those years."

Tom momentarily looked down at his feet. "What had roused me from my dream was this feeling of falling into a dark abyss, with an eternal lake of fire at the bottom just waiting to receive me. I'll never forget that horrifying sensation as long as I live. I woke all three nights shivering uncontrollably, terrified for my life...

"Mostly out of shame and embarrassment, I never told Brian we had similar dreams. In that light, only he was being transparent that day. You must understand, as a former priest and educator, I always prided myself on knowing I was part of the One true Church."

Tom frowned. "I learned the hard way that day that I was so caught up in church doctrine and tradition that I became blinded to the simplicity of God's salvation message in the Holy Scriptures.

"I left his apartment that day licking my wounds, knowing he had clearly won the debate. After more than three decades of service, I feared I never really knew the God of the Bible."

Dick became incredulous. "Come on, Tom," he snickered, "are you actually suggesting the Catholic Church isn't the one true church?"

144

Tom nodded at Dick. "That's precisely what I'm saying. I understand where your zeal comes from, Dick. Imagine mine as one of her priests for so many years? Yet, after carefully comparing the Scriptures to the Catholic Church, it became crystal clear to me that your son was in a very good place, spiritually speaking, and I wasn't..."

Tom leaned up in his chair. "Later that day, when Romanero announced the contest granting young girls and women of all ages permission to get pregnant for the betterment of humanity, with the Pope's full blessing, no less, it was as if blinders had been removed from my eyes, and I realized I had been preaching a false gospel all my life." He frowned. "I felt this strong conviction in my spirit, and I cried out to God begging for His forgiveness, asking if I was worthy of another chance with Him.

"There was nothing I wanted more, Dick. I asked Him to strip away all things man-made, so I could be part of the end times harvest Brian told me he saw in his dream. I told my Maker I would forsake all other things, including the church I'd dedicated my entire life to.

"I'm aware that Catholics utter similar prayers to God. But for me it felt different. I was completely changed. And to prove it, when I finished praying, just as I was about to perform the sign of the cross, something deep inside told me this was one of the many man-made gestures I'd just begged to be delivered from."

Tom lowered his head wearily. "For the first time ever, I felt led by God's Holy Spirit, and not the religiosity of the Catholic Church. I must say receiving Christ as Lord and Savior for real was quite freeing. It was then that Jesus was no longer my religion, but my personal Savior.

"It's no big secret, Dick, that the Catholic Church is shrinking in size. But what's not being reported is many of the deserters have fled the church after having similar dreams like your son and I both had, which ultimately led them to the true Gospel message..."

Dick shook his head in disbelief. "I've always believed in salvation through Christ Jesus."

"Do you know how many times I've preached on the need of faith through Christ, Dick? Thousands upon thousands of times! Yet here I was, left behind with all the other false converts, including many whom I had falsely shepherded over the years...

"For the most part, the words out of my mouth were right, but my understanding of God's salvation had been so diluted that I was merely a false convert preaching those words. I had profession without possession."

145

When the confused expression on Dick's face deepened, Tom said, "What I'm trying to say, Dick, is while you are right to believe the Church preaches salvation through Christ Jesus, if you asked most Catholics why they'll go to Heaven, their answers will vary—either they will be works-based or Jesus plus Mary and a whole slew of other things.

"So many other components have been added that most Catholics don't have a true understanding of the Gospel message..."

Dick was clearly confused. *Just one more proof!*

"The point I'm trying to make is thanks to people like me," Tom said remorsefully, "many Catholics have been so inundated with false doctrine that they do not have a clear knowledge of the Gospel.

"Most aren't even sure if they'll go to Heaven when they die. They fail to understand that being baptized into the Catholic Church or going to mass can't save them. The simple truth is, as sinners, there's nothing they can do in and of themselves that can bring them any closer to God.

"It all comes down to God's grace and forgiveness. Merely agreeing with the Gospel and being transformed by it are two very different things. They must be born again!"

Dick became fidgety again. "I need to use the restroom..."

"Sure. Tony will show you the way. But you'll have to be blindfolded again. Sorry for the inconvenience..."

"It's okay..." What else could he say?

As Tony led Dick to the restroom, Tom chuckled softly to himself, remembering his past encounter with Brian. How the tables had been turned! It's as if he had jumped into Dick's skin, or vice versa. *Open his eyes, Lord, as only You can!*

31

WHEN DICK RETURNED A few minutes later, he tried shifting the focus back on to why he was there. "When will I get to see my wife?"

Tom looked down at his feet. "It probably won't be today. Sorry."

Dick's heart sank in his chest. He shifted his weight on the chair. He felt deceived by Tom. "When will I see her?"

"I wish I could answer that for you, Dick, I really do, but until we know for sure we're on the same page spiritually, it has to remain this way. I'd love nothing more than to see you reunited with your wife someday. That's been my prayer for you for many months now. It's been the heartfelt prayer of so many, in fact.

"You now know the only thing preventing it from happening, is a difference in religion. Since you're already here, can we at least finish our discussion? I haven't come full circle yet."

Dick's brow furrowed. He didn't want to hear anymore, but what choice did he have? "You may proceed."

Tom stretched his arms above his head. "One thing your son told me that really stung was, had the Rapture not occurred, he never would have broken away from the Catholic Church. He never would have felt the need to. And he'd still be living in spiritual bondage as a result.

"He told me he shuddered to think how many Catholics who thought they were going to Heaven were now in hell, simply because they were deceived into believing that being Catholic was their ticket to Heaven. And if they didn't make the first cut, so to speak, they could work it off in a place known to Catholics as 'purgatory'".

Dick thought about Chelsea. In the back of his mind, he kept hoping she was in purgatory serving her sentence for committing that most grievous sin, before she was ultimately elevated to Heavenly status.

That had become his prayer to Jesus and Mary each day, on his daughter's behalf.

Tom leaned forward in his seat. "Listen to me carefully, Dick. There is no such place. I assure you the multitudes of Catholics who believed the purgatory lie and are now in hell, eternally separated from God, no longer believe in such a place.

147

"They know better than anyone still alive that the moment a soul leaves a body, it's either A or B—Heaven or hell, forevermore! What pains me most is knowing many are there because of my teachings.

"Another thing that saddens me is knowing how many Catholics believe Mary has the ability to save souls, thanks to preachers like me. At the very least, they believe she's a key component to obtaining salvation.

"While Mary's certainly highly favored for having been chosen by God to give birth to Jesus, God's Word is crystal clear that salvation comes through Christ alone, and no one else.

"Because Catholics have been taught to trust in Mary as much as Jesus, sometimes even more than Christ, not to mention the many other saints Catholics pray to, it's easy to see why most always take the Pope at his word, without ever giving it a second thought."

Dick flinched. *Does this man know my thoughts?*

Tom noticed his change of expression, and kept going, "I assure you, Dick, the pope is not the 'vicar of Christ' as he proclaims himself to be. Only Jesus is the Bridge to God. Can you look me in the eye and tell me you agree with his decision to allow young girls to get pregnant for the betterment of humanity?"

Dick slumped his shoulders. He thought about the dream he had shared with the late Renate McCallister, about her giving birth to Brian's son. At that time, he was in total agreement with the Pope's edict for girls and women of all ages to get pregnant in the soonest possible time.

Even though it went against everything he believed leading up to that point, he was thrilled to say the least. It suddenly sounded evil to him.

Tom pressed on, "I'm not sure what you think about Salvador Romanero, but he's no man of peace. He's the Antichrist of the Bible. And the Pope's his right-hand man. Together they will usher in the One World Religion that's being set up in New Babylon. Everyone who follows their false religion will end up in hell with them.

"Which leads to the crux of the issue. The reason Romanero wants to kill all born-again Christians, is because we will never bow down to him. You need look no further than the millions of my brothers and sisters who have already been killed in his prisons, without ever renouncing Christ, for proof of this. This infuriates him!

"Conversely, the reason he leaves practicing Catholics alone is because he knows they're being spiritually blinded to the Truth. I praise God for using your son to make me realize by being part of that false system, my teaching wasn't bringing others closer to Heaven, only closer to hell. It literally saved my soul from destruction."

Ignoring his "false system" comment—it jolted his ego too much—Dick asked, "How can that be? My son never attended seminary like you! He's a hotel man..." He sighed. "Used to be, anyway. I don't know what he is anymore."

Tom scratched his forehead. "I'll tell you what he is, he's a servant of the Most High God. Nothing more. Nor does he wish to be anything more. Why would he when there is no greater title a person can have in life?

"Everything I'm telling you can be verified in the Bible, Dick, word for word. The reason so many Catholics never bat an eye when hearing such outrageous statements being made by the Pope, is that they don't read their Bibles enough, if at all. Nor do they study church history.

"If they did, they would be mindful of the many gross errors that have been perpetrated by the Catholic Church over the centuries." Sadness filled Tom's face. "I can't say it enough, mostly because of priests and educators like me, so many Catholics are on God's bad side, eternally speaking."

Dick gasped. "It's almost too much to absorb."

"Try absorbing this, Dick. I had a heart attack on Christmas Eve and nearly died. Truth be told, I thought I would suffer another one when you followed me the other day. My BP was two twenty over one-ten.

"But here's what I want you to consider: Had I died without being born again, this former Catholic priest would be in hell right now suffering unspeakable anguish with many of my peers, including cardinals, bishops and even popes."

Dick shifted uncomfortably in his chair again. He had the saddest expression on his face.

Tom Dunleavey momentarily looked away. If he kept staring at him, he would burst out in tears. His heart ached for him.

Finally, Dick said, "Can you pray for me, Father, before I go?"

Chills raced up and down Tom's spine. *Thank you, Lord!* "It'll be my pleasure. But please don't call me 'Father'. Call me, Tom. I'm just a servant of the Most High God, just like Brian, Sarah too for that matter."

Dick looked deep into Tom's eyes. There wasn't the slightest detection of pride or arrogance, only humility and meekness. He wasn't trying to rub his face in it. It stirred him in the deepest chambers of his heart. He felt broken inside. *Perhaps they're right after all...*

After the two men prayed together, Tom said, "All I ask in the meantime is that you don't tell anyone about our meeting, especially those whose company you now keep."

Dick looked flabbergasted. "You know who I'm staying with?"

Tom nodded that he did. "I'm sure they seem friendly enough, but I assure you, their actions could end up endangering your life. Your wife's, too, for that matter…"

Dick's eyes narrowed. "How'd you find out?"

"Perhaps another time, Dick. Tony will take you back to your car now. And don't worry, you'll find a new tire on it…"

Dick was so engrossed in the conversation that he had totally forgot about the tire. He glanced back at the man he now knew as Tony. "Do I have you to thank for it?"

"Don't mention it…" The way he said it, it was as if Dick had slashed his tire, not the other way around.

Tony blindfolded him and led him out of the building, before going through the same process, only in reverse, until they reached his car.

As Dick left for Megan's and Rachel's apartment, he had no idea that the mechanic who replaced the slashed tire had also disabled the GPS in his car...

150

32

DICK ARRIVED BACK AT the apartment to find Megan sitting on the living room loveseat, scantily dressed in a black nightie. Nothing more.

The reason he knew this was because the way her right leg was thrown over the arm of the chair, it left her rather exposed, as the soft candlelight illuminated her silky-smooth fair skin.

Dick's face turned pink. His head was already spinning thanks to his soul-stirring encounter with Tom Dunleavey. Now this?

"Welcome home," Megan said, rather sweetly. "How was your day?"

"Uneventful," he said, looking down at his feet, so she wouldn't catch on that he was lying. "And yours?"

"We had a false alarm while you were out. Rachel thought she was in labor. Turns out, her doctor thinks she still has three weeks to go. Just got back from the hospital an hour ago."

After the week Dick was having, he wasn't overly surprised to hear this. "Did they keep her for observation?"

"No. If you saw the hospital, you'd understand why. They said she'd be much safer here at home than she would be there. Not only because of the structural damage but because of the outbreak of various diseases due to the power outages and sewage backup everywhere. So many are sick."

"I see. Where is she then?"

"She's in the bedroom sleeping. At least I hope she is. It was a stressful day for her."

"I can imagine." Dick had difficulty reaching for his next breath. His cheeks turned a deeper shade of pink. "Uh, would you like me to get you a robe or a blanket or something?"

Megan burst out in laughter. *Adorable!* "Don't be shy, Mister Mulrooney, we're adults, right?"

Perhaps it was because she was Renate's sister, but seeing the half full glass of wine on the table next to her forced Dick's mind back to her sister's suicide video. Only Renate drank whiskey on what turned out to be her last day on earth. Dick cleared his throat. "Yes, but…"

"I know this is going to sound forward, but…"

Dick gulped hard, unsure if he wanted her to continue. "Yeah?"

151

"I'd like you to get me pregnant."

Dick blinked his eyes hard a few times. "Come again?"

Megan stretched her hands behind her back and slid them upward, lifting her just-washed long sandy-blonde hair through her fingers. "It seems everyone else on the planet is pregnant except for me."

Perspiration formed on Dick's forehead. "I'm a married man, Megan. I've been married longer than you've been alive."

"I respect that, Mister Mulrooney. I really do."

"In thirty-six years, I've never been unfaithful to my wife."

"Come on, it's not like I'm looking for a romantic encounter or anything like that. I mean, you're older than my father." What she didn't tell him was that his receding cul-de-sac hairline made him look fifteen years older than her father, instead of only two.

Her comment made him flinch. He felt guilty even being part of this absurd conversation. "Then why are you dressed like that?"

Megan smirked. *Isn't it obvious?* "To help set the mood! What else?"

Dick scratched his head. "You can't be serious!" This didn't feel anything close to romantic. It felt like a full-blown seduction! It felt evil!

Megan twitched her nose ever so cutely. "Are you saying you don't find me attractive? Or sexy?"

Dick's mouth was so dry he had to swoosh his tongue around several times to make sure it still worked. "That's not it. You're very attractive, Megan. I just never looked at you that way."

Now 32, Megan McCallister could still turn heads. Much like her late sister, she was long-legged with a very shapely body, wavy long hair, and near-perfect teeth. While she looked just as beaten down as everyone else on the planet, she was still strikingly attractive.

Megan stared deep into his eyes. "How do you look at me then?"

Dick gulped hard again and fumbled with his fingers. His eyes couldn't remain steadied on her. Before he could answer, she said, "We can either do it here or in your bedroom. It's up to you. If we're quiet, Rachel will never know."

I'm sure she already knows! Dick cleared his throat. "I don't know, Megan. Even with no feelings attached to it, it feels wrong. I'm here to rescue my wife, not impregnate another woman…"

Megan was fiercely determined to have her way with him. "I know, but consider it a business transaction with no future obligations connected to it; you know, like a sperm donation. How could that be considered as cheating?"

Dick hesitated. Despite how pretty a bow and ribbon Megan tried putting on this conversation gift, it very much felt like cheating to him! Like his meeting earlier, this was something else he never expected to encounter in Pennsylvania.

He was already frustrated. Now this? Her seducing spirit made him think of Tom's warning that these women could endanger not only his own life, but Sarah's too. Dick grimaced. "Sorry, Megan, I can't do this."

Megan became teary-eyed. "Please, Mr. Mulrooney, I'm desperate!" As if on cue, she leaned up on the loveseat causing one of the black spaghetti straps on her lingerie to fall off her shoulder, exposing another part of her body he should have never seen—her left breast.

Dick's eyes widened; he turned his head away from her as quickly as he could. He knew it was intentional, calculated. His hands were clammy, and his breathing became even more labored. Regaining eye contact with her, he held out his hands, palms out. "Megan, please!"

Even though he was doing his best to refuse her advances, Megan was pleased by his reaction. In truth, she wasn't physically or emotionally attracted to the man. But she found his vulnerability to her advances adorable. It made her want him for real.

In a soft voice, she said, "I never told Rachel but, ever since we came here, I've been jealous that she's pregnant and I'm not. At the very least, I could really use the help of the GC. I haven't worked in months. I'm flat broke."

Tears welled up in her eyes. "As you know, had it not been for our few sponsors, we wouldn't even be here now. Most who promised us ongoing support before the quake, have since changed their minds. Everyone's hurting financially.

"Rachel and I won't remain roommates forever. Eventually, I'll have to move on. But if you get me pregnant, it'll be my ticket to living in a safe place of my own, with all expenses paid by the Global Community. Then I'll finally be able to breathe easily."

Dick signaled for Megan to cover herself then studied her face very carefully. The tears were genuine. But the intent was wrong. "You're an attractive woman. I'm sure you would have little trouble finding someone to impregnate you."

Megan sighed. "It's not as simple as you might think. Attractive or not, most men are sick and tired of being sperm donors only. They figure, why get someone pregnant only to be discarded like trash afterwards?"

153

Dick couldn't argue their logic. "I understand your situation and your willingness to want a child in these uncertain times, I really do, but…"

Megan panicked. "I want this for you, too, you know."

"How's that?"

"I know about your dream…"

What?! "What dream?" *First Tom, now Megan?*

"You know, where Renate gave birth to your grandson. Am I right?"

Dick winced. "Who told you?"

"Renate, after she heard Rachel was pregnant. Truth is, after my sister's death…" Megan paused and silently gasped. It was still painful saying it. "…I had a similar dream, too, only instead of Brian getting my sister pregnant, it was you and me.

"Not only would this be the perfect revenge on Brian, it might also help with the grieving process from losing cherished loved ones at the hands of your son."

"I don't know, Megan. Nothing about this feels right…"

Megan sensed that despite his protests, he was slowly caving into her advances. "We can also honor Renate's wishes to give birth to a Mulrooney child. But this will be even better for you. Instead of giving you a grandson, you'll have another son to raise. You know, sort of like replacing Brian. Talk about a legacy!"

Dick jerked his head not knowing he was already a grandfather. *Is this really happening?* "How? You live in Michigan; I live in New York."

Megan twirled her hair through her fingers. "I'm sure we can iron out all the details later. No need to discuss it until after I'm pregnant. But just know I would never prevent you from seeing your son."

Every time Dick tipped his eyes up at her, he felt himself burning with more desire for the young woman that he had no business engaging with in the first place. The fact that he was racked with loneliness wasn't helping his decision making. He felt needy for the affection he had lost from Sarah.

His breathing became more accelerated. "The way you're dressed, you're making it difficult for me to say no…"

Megan smiled cutely again. "Why say no when saying yes would feel so much better for us both."

Dick rubbed his forehead. A seductive spirit filled the apartment that nearly knocked him over. "I don't know, Megan…"

Megan sat more erectly on the chair. "We both know Brian will get caught at some point, it's just a matter of time. When it happens, if Brian and Jacquelyn ever have a child, they will never see their kid again. Neither will you, for that matter. Someone deemed trustworthy in the GC will be given parental rights to raise him or her. But if you get me pregnant, you can start over again with another son. Problem solved..."

Dick swallowed back fear. "How? First off, if I decide to go through with it, how could you guarantee it would be a boy?"

"From my dream..."

"Have you forgotten how my shared dream with Renate ended? In total disaster—nothing close to what I saw!"

It was time for a distraction. "I'm willing to have sex with you every night you're here, to increase the chances. Twice a day if you want. For your contribution, my body is yours for your sole pleasure—do with it whatever you want."

Dick lowered his head. "I'm flattered, Megan, I really am, but can we discuss it later? It's too much to take in all at once. I have a headache..."

"Isn't that the excuse we women are supposed to use?" Megan asked, with a chuckle.

Dick chuckled back at her without humor. "Sorry, but it's true."

Finally, Megan backed off. "Sure. We still have time."

Dick went to his bedroom. *Not as much time as you think!*

DICK WOKE VERY EARLY in the morning, like he did the past few days. Only he took his belongings with him this time.

The only thing he left behind in his room was a letter to Megan:

I'm sorry, but I can't impregnate you. To prevent from falling into temptation again, I'm going back to New York City.

If you find any significant clues, let me know and I'll come back. Sorry for disappointing you. Stay safe...

155

33

TWO WEEKS LATER

HANA PATEL LAY IN bed, her mind racing a mile a minute. The only comfort she could draw upon was watching her daughter's chest gently rising and falling, as she slept next to her on the bed after her morning feeding, totally unaware of the constant danger humanity kept facing on a daily basis.

Even after all this time, her daughter still slept with her, mostly because she dreaded the empty feeling of being all alone in the world.

Hana still found it impossible to believe that Yogesh was gone. She missed her late husband more and more as the days passed, and would give anything to bring him back, including her newfound riches. Even if it meant living in an old shack again, she would do it in a heartbeat.

But it was too late... She felt consumed by his absence.

Hana sighed in the darkness. Prior to winning the contest, Yogesh was constantly racked with uncertainty over how he could provide for a child, when he could barely feed the two of them. Stress often ate away at him, as the couple lay in bed each night.

Hana always tried comforting her best friend in life by reminding him that she didn't need much to live on, and that she was perfectly contented being his wife. Together, they could overcome any obstacle—big or small.

Then Romanero announced the contest. Upon learning that she was one of the frontrunners, suddenly, she was the greedy one as Yogesh slowly transitioned into the one possessing a contented soul. It was as if their personalities had flip flopped.

The more contented he became, the more he distanced himself from the many material items they had received from so many fans and well-wishers the world over. Not counting Brad and Joan Henriksen—a couple Hana had contemplated contacting more than once—and a few other believers he had recently met, he gradually distanced himself from society as a whole.

Hana burst out in tears. Having chosen the world over her best friend; she was now paying the piper. *My best friend in life. How could I treat him with such disrespect?*

She glanced over at her daughter. Still totally unaware that millions of Christians were praying for her, out of nowhere, her daughter spoke her very first word, "Dada."

Hana's eyes widened. She turned on the light and saw the most amazing expression on her daughter's face. "What did you say, sweetie?"

Even though it was early morning, the light was needed due to the darkened skies plus the fact that all windows were covered with bed sheets, for added privacy. It very much looked like evening.

When she heard her mother's voice, her arms and legs flailed wildly, as only an infant could do. Bright toothless smile on her face, she cooed sweetly, before out of her mouth came that word again, "Dada!"

Tears filled Hana's eyes. She took her daughter's word as a sign.

With trembling hands and through blurred vision, she kissed her daughter softly on the lips, powered on her late husband's mobile device and typed a text message to Brad and Joan Henricksen...

BRIAN MULROONEY WAS AWAKENED in the middle of the night when his cellphone vibrated, informing that he had a new text message notification. He rubbed sleep from his eyes and grabbed his Sat-phone off the old wooden crate on his side of the bed, that replaced the table that was destroyed in the quake. *Yogesh Patel? What in the world?*

He rubbed his eyes again to make sure they weren't playing tricks on him. He gulped in air; a chill raced through him. Consumed by anxiety, he started wheezing heavily and took a puff from his inhaler.

Just when he was starting to think the "shock factor" couldn't be raised any higher, he was wrong.

Brian opened the text message, then extended his arms a good 12 inches from his face, so he could read the small print: *Hi Brad. This is the wife of the man whom you and your wife Joan had sent a book a few months ago. I hope the fact that I'm using my late husband's phone to contact you will be enough to validate to you that I really am who I proclaim to be.*

I've wanted to contact you and Joan for quite some time, but I was too angry at first, then too scared. But now that I've been reading the book you sent to him, and starting to believe what Yogesh believed before his death, I don't know what to do or how to escape my present situation.

I don't know if you or Joan survived the quake. But if you did, can you help bring us to safety? I'm frightened for my life and feel so helpless being here with only me and my daughter. Please, Brad, I'm desperate!

157

Brian bolted up in bed and scratched his head. He nudged Jacquelyn's right arm. Not wanting to wake the baby, in a whisper, he said, "Honey, wake up! You have to read this text message…"

Jacquelyn was laying on her side facing away from him, cuddling their daughter. She brushed off her husband's nudge, signifying that she wanted to sleep a little longer. In this insane climate, motherhood had already taken a huge toll on her.

Brian nudged her again.

"Okay, okay…" She slowly rolled onto her back and sat up. Mouth stretched in a yawn, she lifted her arms above her head.

As her vision adjusted to the text, her eyes widened. The first two words nearly caused her heart to explode in her chest. She gasped. *Hi Brad…* She glared at Brian, suddenly fearful for her life, not knowing who had sent the text message, or if she even wanted to read it.

"It's from Hana Patel. At least that's who she proclaims to be. She sent it from Yogesh's phone. Keep reading…"

In the brief amount of time it took to read the message, a wave of emotions crashed over Jacquelyn's body. Her chest heaved up and down, as she struggled to reach for her next breath. She was tempted to use Brian's asthma inhaler. If someone in India had tracked them down—sort of anyway—how long before authorities finally unmasked them as the Henriksens, and stormed the front gate to capture them both?

The very thought seized her with even more uncertainty, adding to the already mountain-sized fear she was doing her best to cope with. Now, suddenly out of the blue, Brian receives a text message from the dead man's phone addressing him by that name?

Jacquelyn took a few more deep breaths and handed Brian his phone. "How can we be sure it's from her? Maybe it was sent by a Romanero operative, in a desperate attempt to ping our location."

Brian stared at the curtain that now covered the door that was still off kilter. "All I can say is I hope not. The only thing we know for sure is that Yogesh didn't send it. Just glad he never knew our real names. If so, it would be game over for us."

Jacquelyn glanced over at her husband. His face was dimly illuminated by his phone screen. She saw his countenance change, as ominous thoughts swam through his head. "So, who sent it then?"

Brian took another deep, exasperated breath. "Do you think a trap is being set for us to fall into?"

Another chill shot through Jacquelyn. She sat up in bed and folded her knees up to her chest, something she often did to help calm her nerves. This was something she couldn't do in her third trimester. Her tummy would have been in the way. "I dunno, Brian. How can we know for sure?"

"Beats me." Brian stroked his chin with two fingers. "All I can say is we better think everything through first, and pray about it before we even think about replying to the message."

Jacquelyn was incredulous, "Don't you mean, *if* we reply back?"

Brian kissed his wife's forehead. "Of course, sweetie. We won't make a move until it goes up the chain of command." He searched his wife's eyes, hoping his words would calm her spirit. They didn't.

There was a moment of silence as the couple mulled everything over in their heads.

Finally, Jacquelyn said, "Okay, for argument's sake, let's say it really is her. How on earth can we, as two of the most wanted fugitives on the planet, help one of the most recognized women on the planet escape to safety?"

Brian rubbed his wife's back. "Good question, my love…"

Jacquelyn shook her head in fear. "I mean, didn't we have a good escape plan for Yogesh? Yet in the end, our plan failed, and it cost him his life, not to mention Braxton, Nigel Jones, and his personal pilot…"

Seeing his wife so distraught filled Brian with overwhelming guilt. *It could have waited until morning.* "Try not to think about it, honey…"

Jacquelyn sighed. *Try not to think about it?* Now that she had a child of her own to care for, how could she not think about it! She empathized with Hana Patel's situation, but her focus had to remain on Sarah for now.

She frowned in the darkness. "The global community is already scouring the planet searching for the Henriksens. You know, *us*! The global quake changed nothing. They're still out looking for us."

The couple were silent as baby Sarah was roused from her sleep at the sound of their voices. It didn't take long before she dozed off again.

Brian kissed the back of his wife's head. "I know, sweetie. I haven't forgotten about it. I don't want to be caught by the enemy, either. With my gradually worsening lung condition, if we ever had to escape, I don't think I'd make it off the property."

Jacquelyn laid back down on the bed and stared at where the ceiling fan used to be, wishing it was still there. It was one luxury she sorely missed. The constant breeze it would generate would often offset the hot flashes running through her body during the pregnancy.

159

The couple remained quiet as they tried piecing things together in their minds. While they both considered it a great honor and blessing to be part of Yogesh Patel's immense spiritual growth, since it had ended so horrifically, with exception to the fact that they were in Glory, it wasn't the most pleasant of sensations.

For that reason, the Mulrooneys did their best not to talk about the Patels. Each time they thought about them, they were reminded that they were wanted fugitives!

The thought of being separated from her daughter was too much for Jacquelyn's heart and mind to absorb. Selfish as it sounded, she wanted to keep that brief part of their history buried as deep as it would go into her subconscious.

She reached for Brian's hand and kissed it. "The more I think about it, honey, the more I think it may be a trick. My heart goes out to the poor woman, it really does, but I say we leave it alone."

Brian understood the fear he saw in his wife's eyes, but it wasn't enough for him to stop protesting on Hana's behalf. "We can't just leave her out to dry. We must do something to help them, sweetie. I mean, what if I was killed and it was just you and Sarah?"

Jacquelyn rolled onto her side without answering the question.

Brian pressed on, "If God opens a door for us, we must walk through it, right?"

When she remained silent again, Brian decided to let it go for now.

As he held his wife, a man he had never communicated with and had no idea what he even looked like, came to his mind—Ahmed.

The only thing Brian knew about the man was that he and Yogesh had met along with a handful of others, after they all had the very same dreams about a man named Yitzhak, whom Yogesh had referenced in his speech in Dubai, who proclaimed to be one of the 144,000.

Before venturing to the Middle East, Yogesh had insisted to Brian that Ahmed was trustworthy, to the extent that he secretly gave him a sizable amount of money, without Hana's knowledge, to build an underground shelter in India for everyone within their group of believers to live in, when the time came.

Mulrooney sensed that if they had any shot at rescuing Hana, Ahmed would have to play the leading role. Yes, he would be the link.

But first things first. Brian sent a desperate text message to Charles Calloway, informing him of what had just happened.

160

As he had promised to Jacquelyn, Brian wouldn't take a single step until it first went up the chain of command, and he heard back from his spiritual big brother in this regard.

Before going back to sleep, Brian silently prayed for Pastor Jim Simonton, the man who'd married Brian and Jacquelyn in Michigan before the Mulrooneys relocated to Chadds Ford.

No one had heard a word from the Michigan pastor since the global quake. After so much time had passed, Brian sensed more and more that his good friend had become a soul under the altar. The fact that he hadn't heard from him only escalated his concern.

Perhaps the safe house he managed in upper Michigan was destroyed in the quake, and everyone living there had perished. Until this was confirmed, he would keep praying for Jim on a daily basis…

34

A WEEK LATER

CHARLES CALLOWAY TEXTED BRIAN Mulrooney, informing that the military-strength encrypted virtual private network that Dr. Lee Kim had designed for Hana Patel's use was ready to be downloaded, which meant it was time to reply to her text message.

Now that Kim's name was out there, thanks to the Henriksen story which led to the death of his former boss—billionaire Nigel Jones—he worked tirelessly to make sure the connections were as secure as he had hoped. The VPN had the strongest firewalls known to man, and were used by most governments and militaries.

Brian wasted no time ramming keys on his phone to whom he hoped was Hana Patel. It read: *This is the man you messaged the other day seeking my help. If this is who I think it is, to say I was shocked to hear from you last week would be an understatement.*

Hana saw the "restricted" number appear on her late husband's phone screen, which she made sure to check several times a day hoping for Brad's reply. She quickly replied: *Brad?*

Yes. Can I call you?

Can you wait a few minutes? I'm feeding my daughter. After I change her diaper and put her to sleep, I will have a little free time to myself.

Jacquelyn whispered to Brian, "Could be a delay tactic..."

He nodded agreement, then typed. *Sure. In the meantime, I'll need you to download this app. It's a secure VPN that will allow us to talk in private. Text me after you've done this.*

The Mulrooneys waited nearly 30 minutes before Hana replied that she had successfully downloaded the encrypted app, and they could now safely call her.

"Hi Brad. Thank you for calling me," she said softly.

Brian glanced over at Jacquelyn. Whoever was on the other end was clearly female, and Indian. Mulrooney waited a few seconds until he received a text from Dr. Lee Kim that the line was indeed secure, but he needed her to keep talking in general terms, so he could confirm it really was her, using voice recognition.

Brian said, "Sorry for the lengthy delay in getting back to you, but we can never be too sure these days." He waited a few seconds for her to say something. She didn't. "Before we can proceed, as much as we'd like to take you at your word, we need more proof, more convincing, that you are who you proclaim to be. For starters, how did you gain access to the phone you messaged me on?"

Hana sighed. "Yogesh left it in our hotel suite before accusing Romanero of being the Antichrist of the Bible. After receiving a threatening call later that night, I put his phone in an unused diaper then threw it away with the rest of the soiled diapers, hoping investigators wouldn't find it. Thankfully, they didn't. I wasn't quite sure why I did it at the time, Now I know."

"I see," Brian replied evenly. "What else can you tell us?"

Hana rubbed her throbbing forehead. "I confess that I provided the GC with your names. I was furious and blamed you both for my husband's death. I wanted you both to pay a steep price for sending the package. Had it not been for that, I'm convinced he would still be alive, which was why I donated the large sum of money to aid in your capture."

Brian glanced over at Jacquelyn. She still wasn't convinced. The woman's answer was too vague. "Could be a trick," she whispered.

Brian said, "We need more..."

Hana could only assume the "we" was himself and his wife, Joan. "I don't know what else you want me to tell you, Brad..."

Brian received another text from Dr. Kim. *It's her! Proceed with caution.* He didn't need him, or anyone else at the top of the organization telling him that. Jacquelyn was paranoid enough for the both of them.

It seemed to get worse with each new sunrise.

Lee Kim had assured the Mulrooneys that any possible eavesdroppers would have their location pegged at Helsinki, Finland, and Hana Patel's at Brisbane, Australia. And those locations would change every minute.

As an added precaution, Kim programmed viruses into it that would cause the connection to self-destruct with a simple push of a button.

With or without those safeguards in place, the instant Jacquelyn sensed something wasn't right, she was prepared to end the call.

Brian went on, "Can you tell me something that only you would know about my relationship with Yogesh?"

Hana looked at the ceiling and searched her memory thinking of what to tell him. "Okay, I remember one night when Yogesh was out on the

163

balcony talking to you on the phone. I knew it was you because, as far as I know, you were the only person he spoke to on the phone.

"He wanted nothing to do with my friends or the many things we received for being the first parents on the planet again. Yogesh was always paranoid that people were listening to our conversations."

Hana sniffled. "I learned too late that he was right." She paused. "Anyway, when the call ended, he gazed skyward, apparently a million miles away. Whatever you had told him, you gave him so much to think about. This concerned me very deeply at the time..." Her voice trailed off.

Brian shrugged his shoulders. Her answer was still too vague. "I remember that call very well. Even so, we still need more convincing. What can you tell us about the package we sent to your husband?"

"GC investigators demanded to know what was inside the box. I told them it was mostly gifts for the baby. They wanted the box the gifts came in, so they could obtain fingerprints or perform a forensics investigation looking for hair or tiny droplets of blood or sweat secretions. I told them I no longer had it, which was true."

Hana paused to take a few deep breaths. "What wasn't true was what I told them about the Bible you included..."

Brian and Jacquelyn braced themselves. "And that was?"

"I told them I burned it. You know what will happen if they ever discover I still have it. I even kept the letter you sent. The reason I'm hated by so many now is that I never publicly condemned my husband's actions in Dubai. How can I when I'm starting to believe the same things he did?"

Hana started weeping. "I feel so cursed for having won that stupid contest. My life has been a living hell ever since the awards ceremony. I want my husband back..." Her sobbing intensified.

Brian glanced at Jacquelyn. She nodded. "I admit that's convincing, but the only way to know for sure is to have a video chat with you. But for our own safety, my wife and I will both wear ski masks. It's not important that you see us, but that we see you."

Hana paused a moment, then said, "We can try, but it will be hard for you to see me."

"Hmm, why's that?" asked Brian.

"I'm in my bedroom closet talking to you, just in case...I believe the house is wired, and all conversations are being recorded."

Jacquelyn interjected, "We appreciate the effort, but we'll need to see your surroundings just to be sure no one is coercing you behind the scenes. Don't be offended. We just want to make sure this is a safe conversation."

"Okay," Hana said, with a nervous sigh, "but I won't speak. And I'll ask that you don't either, just in case." She came out of the closet and turned the video on. She looked completely lost, dejected. And frightened for her life.

After giving them a quick tour of the house, she let them see her face, before retreating to her bedroom closet again, and sitting on a chair she had placed in there.

Jacquelyn said, "Was that your daughter on the bed?"

"Yes. Her new name is Cristiana." Hana whispered in reply.

The Mulrooneys both raised curious eyebrows. *Interesting!* Now convinced that she was alone, and being truthful with them, it was time to share their greatest concern with her.

Brian asked, "What makes us hesitant to take the next step with you, Hana, is something you had said in your initial text…"

Hana raised an eyebrow. "What did I say, Brad?"

"You said you were starting to believe what you were reading in the Book we sent to Yogesh. Can you be more specific?"

Hana hesitated, not knowing how to answer the question. "I don't know what to believe, Brad. I really don't…"

Jacquelyn asked, "Are you still reading it?"

Hana sighed. "Yes. This is where I go to read the Bible when my daughter is sleeping."

"Do you read it every day?"

"I try to. Sometimes it comforts me. Other times the words frighten me to no end. That is, when I can understand what I'm reading. It's difficult to think straight these days, let alone read something that's so deep and confusing…and terrifying!"

"I know what you mean, Hana," said Jacquelyn. "Unfortunately, until we know for sure you're a tried and true Christ follower, like your husband was, we can't take the next step with you…"

Hana started weeping.

Jacquelyn said, "We want to help you, Hana, we really do. But until we know for certain you're a believer, we simply cannot take your word for it. The stakes are just too high. Everyone who is part of our organization has been confirmed from above."

"In what way?"

"I'm afraid we can't share that with you at this time, sorry…"

Hana's weeping intensified. "How will I know if I'm a believer?"

PATRICK HIGGINS

Jacquelyn explained, "Believe me, you'll know. Just like your husband did. Ask the Creator of Heaven and earth and everything in them to give you the wisdom to understand His Holy Word.

"Keep seeking Him with all your heart, mind, and soul. If you'll only do that, you *will* find Him. Then you'll get to experience what having God's eternal assurance is all about."

Hana's shoulders slumped; her face cringed with sadness. "I don't feel anything close to having this eternal assurance you speak of..."

Jacquelyn nodded thoughtfully. "All we can do for now is pray that God will open your spiritual eyes and ears to the Gospel message..."

When Hana remained silent, Brian said, "So many have been praying for you and your daughter. I'm talking millions of believers!"

Hana smiled wearily, not realizing the power behind the prayers that were being offered up on her behalf from millions of Christians the world over. All she knew was Brad and Joan Henriksen weren't monsters, as they were portrayed in the media. They seemed infinitely more genuine than the so-called friends she had made since giving birth to her daughter.

She sniffled. "Thank you..."

Brian shifted gears. "Are you familiar with a friend Yogesh had made after converting to Christianity, a man named Ahmed?"

Hana shook her head sadly. "I knew he had Christian friends here in Chennai. But, in truth, I wasn't interested in meeting them."

"I understand. But I was wondering if you could find a way to help connect me to him. I would be most grateful if you could do that..."

Hana shrugged her shoulders. "I wouldn't even begin to know where to look, Brad, especially with Christians living in hiding. How can you know for sure he's still alive?"

"I don't know. But if the day comes that we can help you escape, I feel he might be the person to help us."

Brian received another text message from Dr. Kim. It was time to end the call. "We have to go now, but let me end by saying, in the short time I knew Yogesh, I felt so blessed to call him my friend and brother in Christ. His spiritual transformation has inspired millions around the globe. Are you aware that God's still using his testimony as seed-planting for the great end times harvest, to include Jews, Muslims, Hindus, and Buddhists?"

Hana hung her head. How could she know this, when she purposely ignored that part of her husband's life, thinking they all were a little screwy.

Brian went on, "In that regard, he's still a fisherman. And the rewards he'll keep receiving are geometrical, meaning every life he touches on earth, whether directly or indirectly, will result in eternal rewards for himself on the other end."

Hana sighed. *Unlike me...* "Other end?"

Jacquelyn said, "Your husband's very much alive, Hana, in the most awesome of Places. Even though Yogesh is gone from the physical world, he's still winning souls for his King, even in absentia. This is his eternal legacy. How amazing is that?"

Hana didn't know how to answer the question. It may have been amazing for her late husband, but how could it benefit herself or her daughter? "I need to leave this house. I can feel the walls closing in on me a little more each day."

"Believe me, I know that feeling," Jacquelyn said.

Hana grimaced. "I no longer want the things I have. I'll gladly trade it all just to have a place to escape to for me and my daughter..."

Brian twisted his lips in confusion. "I need to ask, is it safety you seek or the salvation of your soul?"

"How can I know, Brad?"

"No one can offer you safety in this world, not even us. Those days are long gone. But what we can offer is God's eternal assurance that Christ spoke of in the Book you now have in your possession...

"Once we're convinced that you're a true Christian, we'll do everything in our power to help you escape into a new life. But until then, all we can do is pray for you and your daughter. Stay safe over there..."

At that, the call ended...

167

35

THREE MONTHS LATER

HANA PATEL GULPED HARD upon seeing that the owners of the house she had been living in since winning the contest, had sent her a text message. When she read the first four words, *You have ten days*, her first thought was that this was an eviction notice.

But after reading the entire message, it turned out being a ten-day notice to remove the pod that was dropped there the day the Patels moved in, storing the many gifts that were received at the hospital, so the driveway could be repaved, after being badly damaged in the quake.

The house owners always thought the pod was a hideous eyesore. But like everyone else in the world, they were so caught up in the Hana Patel hype and felt so honored to have her staying in one of their homes, that they left it alone.

But after being frequently vilified by friends and family members, and scores of netizens online, for housing the wife of the man who had humiliated the *Miracle Maker*, they started looking for anything to complain about which might lead to Hana's eviction.

Since there strangely hadn't been any aftershocks following the global quake, the house owners finally agreed that they would start fixing up the property before putting it on the market.

Like so many wealthy individuals before the disappearances, their finances took a drastic hit when all global business markets were forced into a complete standstill. The two financial resets Romanero had introduced to hopefully jump start the economy did nothing to help them.

The millions of dollars they had lost were never recouped. Then, after the global quake, the banking industry totally collapsed, and they lost most of their fortune. It was time to liquidate.

They didn't share these morbid truths with Hana in the message. It was none of her concern.

With trembling hands, Hana replied: *Okay.*

She took a moment to let it sink in, then contacted her late husband's friend, Ahmed, informing him of the message.

After she started seeking the Lord with all her heart, mind, and soul, as Joan Henriksen had challenged her to, it led to her being connected to him.

Disguised as a repairman, he was able to enter her residence without ever arousing the suspicion of others. It was during these times that Ahmed got to share the Gospel of Jesus Christ with her, which led to Hana's conversion. They started praying and fasting for hours on end, that God would provide a way for her to escape this life. Popular as she was, she couldn't just suddenly leave without many noticing it.

Hana and Ahmed both sensed the text message from her landlords was God's way of answering their prayers.

In that light, it really was an eviction notice of sorts, only she would be evicting herself from the premises, not the other way around.

On the day before the pod was scheduled to be picked up, Hana hired Ahmed and a handful of others to empty it before it was hauled away.

Since the things inside the pod were mostly diapers and baby clothing, everything would be taken to the safe house then distributed to children born of *ETSM* parents in Chennai and beyond.

As all that was going on, Dr. Jameel Khan, also dressed in ragged clothing like the other movers, scanned Cristiana's body looking for the GPS tracker that all newborns were injected with at birth, to prevent from possible kidnappings. The former family physician to Ahmed's family for many years—before he and Ahmed were excommunicated by their families for converting to Christianity—found it rather easily.

He froze the area where he would dig it out using a scalpel. "I'm sorry, Baby Cristiana, but this is going to hurt."

The instant he dug the scalpel into the child's left arm, she screamed in agony. "It's okay, precious child..." the doctor said softly, removing the GPS locator.

Knowing it was both motion and heat sensitive, he placed it in a plastic baggie in a bowl of hot water, to hopefully maintain the child's body temperature. "This will buy us a little time, nothing more."

Since all mothers giving birth in Romanero's hospitals were also injected with these GPS implants—Hana was next. Dr. Khan easily located it and froze the area where he would dig it out. "Ready?"

Hana said, "This is nothing compared to giving birth to my daughter."

Dr. Khan chuckled politely, quickly removed it, and placed it in a plastic baggie in the same bowl of hot water, thus starting the clock ticking for Hana and Cristiana.

They only had so much time before authorities stormed the residence to detain them all. Every second had to be wisely spent...

169

Hana sent a voice text message to the Henriksens: "I don't know if you have internet access, but if you do, go to any of my social media platforms. But please hurry, I'm not sure how long it will remain online before it's taken down."

Jacquelyn quickly replied: *Okay...*

For whatever reason, Hana also sent a message to Yasamin Dabiri, asking her to do the same.

Hana was quite mindful that any post or video referencing the Word of God, or Jesus, would be instantly removed. But thanks to her dream, she knew exactly how to take full advantage of the few seconds she would be given.

When the livestream began, instead of speaking, she held up white placards one at a time, each with a few words written on them in black marker.

The first card read: *"For I am not...*

The second card read: *"...ashamed of the gospel...*

The third card read: *"...because it is the power of God...*

The fourth card read: *"...that brings salvation...*

The fifth card read: *"...to EVERYONE who believes...*

The sixth card read: *"...first to the Jew...*

The seventh card read: *"...then to the Gentile..."*

Hana smiled wearily, then lowered the camera enough for her many viewers to see the white T-shirt she had on, with Romans 1:16 handwritten on it in black marker.

She lifted her daughter up off her lap so her 377,000 livestream viewers—ever curious to see what she was up to after many months of total silence—could read the red letters on the white bib she had on. *Hello, my name is Cristiana Patel. I can't wait to see my Daddy again. And Jesus!*

Before the livestream ended, Hana held up four more placards.

The first card read: *"Trust in Christ alone for your salvation...*

The second card read: *"...Only He can deliver on His promise of a better future...*

The third card read: *"...Salvador Romanero cannot do this...*

The fourth card read: *"...Seek Jesus while you still can!"*

At that, the livestream ended.

As expected, it was red flagged and quickly taken offline.

Now that Hana had just burned her last bridge, there was no turning back. Just as Ahmed was about to smash her mobile phone into many pieces with a hammer, it started vibrating. She saw Yasamin Dabiri's name appear on her phone screen. "Wait!" She answered it.

"Hi Hana, I saw your livestream…"

Through deep, heavy breaths, Hana said, "Sorry, Yasamin, I can't talk right now."

Yasamin sounded desperate. "Please hear me out! I've been having dreams ever since the awards ceremony about a man I'd never met, who told me he used to worship Jesus with my husband before the Rapture.

"I've wanted to tell you for the longest time, but didn't know how. Then, when I saw your livestream, it was if the Spirit of the living God opened my eyes. I want to know Jesus like you know Him, Hana! Can you help me?"

Hana said, "Praise God! Yes, I can help you, but not now. I'll contact you when I can. For now, seek the Lord Jesus Christ with all your heart and soul. If you'll only do that, you will find Him, Yasamin. Believe me, I know! I must go now. Love you."

Hana jotted Yasamin's number onto a small piece of paper, and handed her phone back to Ahmed, who quickly smashed it with three heavy blows from the hammer.

At that, she changed into the same baggy work clothes the others had on, threw on a baseball cap, hid Cristiana beneath the baggy coat she had on, and left the house never to return.

She now understood how her late husband felt. After witnessing the sheer brutality that Romanero had ordered on everyone connected to her late husband's failed escape, how could she not be concerned for her own life as well? She was terrified and wanted out of India as quickly as possible. The only things she took with her were diapers for her daughter and whatever she could fit into the duffel bag she brought with her.

Everything about the house reminded her of Salvador Romanero, which meant it was stained in evil. She was glad to leave it all behind.

A few kilometers away from the safehouse at which the Patels would temporarily reside, the driver of the truck, also a believer, pulled to the side of the road where a waiting windowless cargo van that Ahmed had purchased with some of the funds provided by the late Yogesh Patel, was waiting to take Hana and Cristiana to relative safety.

When they arrived at the subterranean location, which she had unknowingly helped fund, thanks to her late husband, the Patels were welcomed warmly.

The location itself was roughly 1500 square-foot of sectioned-off space. The section Hana and Cristiana would occupy would be shared with three other mothers and their children, which was a blessing. They would help keep her daughter occupied until the next step was taken, whenever and whatever that step would be.

As Hana was being introduced to her new housemates, police stormed her residence to find the two GPS locators submerged in a bowl of water, thus confirming their suspicions that something had gone wrong at the Patel residence.

Within minutes, Hana's monetary cards were all frozen, and a warrant was issued for her arrest.

As Cristiana play on the floor with her three new friends—one boy and two girls—she knew nothing of the danger her mother's actions had just created for them, or that the world was on the lookout for them...

THE MULROONEYS WATCHED AND were moved to tears by Hana's online sermon of sorts. Knowing it would be immediately taken offline, Brian made sure to record it on his phone so he could share it with the others.

Jacquelyn couldn't stop the tears from flowing down her cheeks. She cupped Brian's hands in hers, now fully convinced that Hana was a believer. "We must do all we can to help her..."

Brian wiped tears from his wife's eyes, then kissed both of her cheeks. There was no need to say, "I told you so..."

He sent the video they recorded to Clayton and Travis and would wait to hear back from their two leaders before making a move...

36

ONE MONTH LATER

AFTER HANA PATEL, AHMED, and everyone else living at that safe house were warmly welcomed by Brad and Joan Henriksen as new *ETSM* members, Hana initially wanted to remain there, so she could find a way to share the Gospel with her unsaved family members and in laws, hoping that they too would repent and trust in Christ for their salvation.

But knowing that the global search for the two Patel females had started off locally, meant there wasn't a chance she could remain in India.

Even though Brad and Joan Henriksen weren't successful in their daring attempt to bring Yogesh to their *ETSM* safe house in America, Hana nevertheless felt a special kinship with the blessed couple who were instrumental to her having the eternal assurance she now had.

In that light, she was adamant that she wanted to be with them. More than anything else, if she didn't survive the final few years of the Tribulation, she wanted Cristiana to be placed in their care in America.

No one had to tell her she would be taking the risk of a lifetime by traveling halfway around the world, as a wanted fugitive. Romanero would leave no stone unturned until she was ultimately captured.

After her dangerous request was granted, Brian had told her that with cash no longer being accepted anywhere on the planet, their options with the outside world had just become infinitely more limited.

This meant Hana would need to remain underground in India longer than originally was anticipated. Once all the details could be finalized, she would travel by cargo ship to Singapore, before ultimately sailing on another cargo ship to America. Lord willing...

Until then, Brian encouraged her to redeem the time by drawing even closer to the Lord Jesus Christ...

When Hana told the Henriksens about Yasamin Dabiri and the dreams she'd had, and that she, too, was a believer looking to escape out from underneath Salvador Romanero's evil clutches, Brian offered to set up a VPN conference with the two women, as he and others listened in...

Much like he had done for Hana earlier, Dr. Lee Kim set up a military-strength VPN account for Yasamin Dabiri to have a secure chat with Hana.

173

And just like last time, all possible eavesdroppers would be sent on a digital wild goose chase which would span the globe, before even the best hackers on the planet could possibly come close to tracking their real locations.

After brief introductions were made, Brian—posing as Brad Henriksen—asked Yasamin, "Tell us about your dreams…"

Yasamin sighed. "In my first dream, which came on the night of the award ceremony, a man named Aarush told me he used to worship underground with my late husband, Navid, every Saturday night, just outside Teheran. Only they weren't worshiping Allah. It was the Lord Jesus Christ in the Christian Bible. Of course, I didn't know this at the time.

"When Aarush told me that millions of Iranians had trusted in Christ Jesus before the Rapture, I admit I was shocked. Before Romanero rose to power, only one god was openly worshiped in Iran. Many who foolishly tried worshiping other gods were incarcerated, which was why they always met underground in secret.

"Aarush told me he was there on the night Navid vanished into thin air, along with everyone else except for himself. When it dawned on him that Jesus came back for His church, he was forced to admit the main reason he went there was that he was lonely and desperate for fellowship, male fellowship to be precise. He told me he was a homosexual until he got saved after the Rapture, and he found his new identity in Christ."

Yasamin grimaced. "Another thing Aarush told me in the dream was that my husband longed to share the Gospel with me. The reason he didn't was his fear that I would share it with my family who were totally committed to their Muslim faith. He didn't want police storming their meeting location to arrest them all if my family ever notified the authorities, which I'm sure they would have done, had they only known…

"After Aarush told me my husband was in a real place called Heaven, with Jesus, he then told me Salvador Romanero's power came from the very darkest of places. He said the man I had pledged my loyalty to was being supernaturally empowered by Satan himself.

"That's when I woke from the dream. I knew my husband had vanished on that nightmarish day, but that's the only thing I knew. If Aarush did one thing, he gave me a certain sense of closure. Anyway, when I first got word of his detainment, I thought it would finally put an end to the nightmares."

Yasamin gasped. "I was wrong. Even when Aarush was in prison, I still had dreams about him. I saw the prison guards torturing him. It was so real and lifelike that I almost felt the intense pain myself.

174

"What I found most difficult to shake off each time, was this man's faith in Jesus. Despite being tortured mercilessly, he declared to me in the dream, 'This is how much I believe Jesus is the Way, Truth, and the Life, and that no one can come to the Father, but through Him. I'm willing to suffer and die for Him, because He did the same for me. How about you, Yasamin?'

"I woke from that dream each time asking myself, 'Why would I want to die for someone I don't even believe in? What sense would that make?'

"Anyway, when I heard all Christians in Romanero's prisons were killed in the quakes, I was relieved knowing they couldn't torture Aarush anymore. I was equally relieved that I would no longer have dreams about him. I did my best to forget about the man, but I couldn't.

"Perhaps it was because we both lost our husbands to Christianity, but I've always wanted to tell Hana about my dreams. But since I believe we're both being spied on; I didn't know how to tell her...

"When I watched Hana's livestream, it's hard to explain but I suddenly wanted to know Christ like she did. Thanks to Ahmed, who later shared the Gospel with me, at Hana's insistence, I'm a Christ follower now."

"Praise the Lord!" Mulrooney declared.

"Amen!" Yasamin wiped tears from her eyes. "I don't know what I ever saw in Salvador Romanero. He's nothing but a murderer! So many of my friends and loved ones met their demise at his hands, just for being Muslims. Even though I never believed in Islam, what he did was evil! I'll never again call my son Salvador. I now call him Navid, to honor my late husband."

Yasamin shook her head sadly. "What still consumes me with guilt to this day is, as I selfishly got to live in the lap of luxury, many Muslims who were solid, law-abiding citizens in every sense of the word, were killed after the *Miracle Maker* declared all-out war on them.

"I was quite mindful of his hatred toward Muslims when I received my monetary card, but I was too blinded by my newfound good fortune to lament it. Besides, I never imagined that monster would take it so far. How blinded I was...," she said sadly.

Brian said, "I understand how you feel, Yasamin, but don't expect the hatred to stop. He hates Christians even more than Muslims..."

A new batch of tears rushed to Yasamin's eyes. "Despite what he will do to me if I get caught, I love the Lord with all my heart and will not turn my back on my Savior. How could I when He saved my soul from hell?

"I honestly believe God sent me the dreams about Aarush to strengthen me in advance of what may come to me as well..."

175

"Amen to that!" Brian said joyfully.

Yasamin smiled wearily. "Growing up, my father used to tell me about the many miracles Allah had supposedly performed. But I never had an interest in searching the Quran to prove my father right or wrong.

"Even without having access to the Bible, now that I'm a Christ follower, there's too much evidence pointing to the God of Israel as being the one true God to ignore. Not only did He cause my husband to vanish into thin air, what about how Israel's God protected His people when Jerusalem fell under attack?

"I still remember the day the Dome of the Rock was destroyed, and what the Muslim pilot said during his interview before he was hung on live TV, about the God of Israel deflecting the missile that he himself had fired at a Jewish target, and sending it straight into their own holy site!"

Yasamin frowned. "I was with my parents that day. I'll never forget hearing my father lamenting that it was the beginning of the end for Islam. Turns out he was right.

"And what about the Two Men breathing fire out of their mouths? As much as the world hates them, no one can deny the special powers they have. And what about the young Jewish preachers out there preaching, with no repercussions whatsoever?

"Surely, they are being supernaturally protected. There's no doubt in my mind now that all things point to the God of Israel. What really amazes me is how only a few can see it…"

Brian and Jacquelyn were blown away by Yasamin's testimony. Both were convinced beyond a shadow of a doubt that she was a true believer.

Jacquelyn said, "Since everyone in our organization has been connected by dreams, we're taking it as a good sign. But we still need to talk to our higher-ups to see how we can best help you."

"I understand, Joan. But if you can help me, may I make one request?"

Jacquelyn paused. "Sure, what is it?"

"Hana is my best friend in life. Wherever she ends up going, I'd like to join her there. My dream is to have our kids play together someday before Christ returns. Besides, I don't want to go through this crazy time alone."

Jacquelyn answered, "We'll see what we can do. For now, you need to leave your residence as quickly as possible. But we cannot relocate you to one of our safehouses over there until the GPS locators have been removed from your bodies, by one of our contacts in Dubai."

Yasamin nodded gratefully. "I understand, Joan."

Jacquelyn smiled at her new sister in Christ. "The good news is once you are relocated, you'll have access to your very own Bible, until the next steps can be taken…"

A relieved smile crossed Yasamin's face. "Thank you, Joan. I appreciate it so much. I will do everything you ask of me. God be with you both…"

"God bless you too, Yasamin. Hope we get to meet you and Hana in person someday."

Hana interjected, "That will be my daily prayer…"

"Mine too!" said Yasamin.

At that, the call ended…

37

LOOKING UP WITH THE naked eye, it could have been any one of the millions, if not billions, of bright, glimmering stars illuminating the skies above. Initially, most people were still trying to pick up the pieces from past tragedies to strike the planet to give it much notice, except to say that it appeared to be getting a little brighter each day.

Upon discovering that the object racing toward their planet, at fifty thousand miles per hour, was actually a meteor the size of a huge burning mountain, the world became panic-stricken yet again.

Global Community scientists had been monitoring it for weeks, hoping it would change its course and miss the earth altogether. Many kept warning that if it wasn't somehow diverted, it would hit somewhere in the Pacific Ocean, thus causing another round of unspeakable global destruction.

Top scientists practically begged the *Miracle Maker* to work his magic again, by stopping the meteor dead in its tracks. If he could send targeted quakes to strike only the countries of his choice, surely, he could prevent this lethal object from striking their planet.

But as the days passed, when it didn't veer off course, it seemed more and more likely that not even he could stop or redirect it.

If he couldn't, the end result would be that many coastal cities on the planet would be completely decimated from the massive tidal waves alone, causing numerous more casualties. Some countries would cease to exist.

Everyone living at those places would already be dead before the next round of earthquakes and volcanic activity followed, once again darkening the skies, and greatly affecting weather patterns, for many months on end.

In short, there wasn't a place on earth where a meteor this size could strike without having serious cataclysmic results planetwide.

When the meteor was just three days away from making impact, as a last line of defense, Romanero ordered all "space defense" nuclear weapons fully operational.

Once launched, if they couldn't change the meteor's trajectory, or break it apart so the earth's atmosphere could burn up the smaller particles, or destroy it altogether, the devastation they would suffer would be far worse than anything else they had already endured and barely survived.

Romanero waited until the very last minute before placing the entire planet on the highest state of alert and warned everyone within its trajectory to evacuate to higher grounds. The reason for this was that he wasn't overly concerned about it causing a loss of life on a massive scale. His only hope was that casualties among the children would be minimal.

When the meteor entered the strike zone, the command was given to fire at will. Thousands of nuclear-tipped missiles raced toward the burning mass, at Mach speed, hoping to destroy or redirect it.

They succeeded in breaking off bits and pieces of the meteor, but it wasn't nearly enough to save the planet from impact. What was left of it—the core—penetrated the earth's atmosphere without the slightest resistance.

The deafening sound it made entering the earth's orbit, pierced eardrums causing instant deafness to tens of thousands of humans and animals. The heat radiating from the massive-sized ball of fire was so extreme, it incinerated plants and crops hundreds of miles away, that had been replanted after the global quake with seed from the polar vaults

When the meteor slammed into the Pacific Ocean, 300 miles east of China's coastline, the entire planet pulsated.

Massive waves instantly rose hundreds of feet in the air, rolling out in all directions, at 500 miles per hour, flash-boiling fish, and all other underwater life, turning the ocean blood red.

As the waves came dangerously closer to land—carrying with them dead sea life of all varieties, and numerous boats and ships—the rumbling became louder and more terrifying.

Everyone situated in those places knew it was coming for them...

It took less than 15 minutes for the first waves to hit the Japanese, Chinese and Philippine coastlines. All were submerged beneath hundreds of feet of seawater, which quickly moved inland devouring everything and everyone in their pathway.

Many of the buildings that had miraculously escaped the global quake and ensuing volcanoes, weren't as fortunate this time. They quickly gave way to the massive walls of seawater like defenseless tumbleweeds blowing in the wind. Vehicles of all types, even helicopters and airplanes, were swept away to their watery graves, as easily as Matchbox cars being swept away in a flash flood.

The only thing that broke the waves' momentum were mountain ranges. If anyone survived the first round, which was highly unlikely, the next rounds of smaller waves dashed out all hopes of survival.

179

By being island nations, much of Japan, the Philippines, Indonesia, Taiwan, Singapore, Thailand, Malaysia, Vietnam, Cambodia, and Hong Kong were completely decimated by the massive flood waters.

All Pacific islands, to include Hawaii, Fiji, and Guam were wiped out. Coastal Australia and New Zealand were wiped out. The east coast of India was wiped out.

It didn't take long for the destructive waves to reach the Western Hemisphere. Once they did, the western parts of North, Central and South America were wiped out. Many living in those locations were able to evacuate in time, to seek higher ground. But many weren't so fortunate.

Others, who probably could have escaped, figured if they ended up miraculously surviving this tragedy, what catastrophe would befall them next? After weighing their limited options, many concluded that they were too tired and drained to keep fighting, and resigned themselves to remaining where they were and let come what may.

About the only good thing was that it happened so quickly…

WITH CHENNAI, INDIA BEING in the impending strike zone, everyone residing at the safe house that Ahmed was in charge of, left the night before for another subterranean location just outside Tirupati Andhra Pradesh, India, 83 miles northwest of Chennai.

It was risky, to be sure, but the reason they waited until the last minute before making their move was their fear of their caravan being pulled over by law enforcement. Had that happened, the instant they recognized Hana Patel, it would be all over for them.

The closer the meteor came to making impact, the more panicked everyone else became, as they sought out safe places for themselves and their families. This included law enforcement officials. The last thing they had on their frightened minds was pulling someone over!

Thankfully, God had protected them…

As it turned out, had they not relocated, they all would have drowned in the underground safe house from which they had barely escaped.

Even the house that Hana and Cristiana Patel had recently vacated—a house that had all but consumed Hana prior to her conversion—was destroyed by a hundred-foot wave…

With the port of Singapore completely obliterated, and with limited connections to the outside world, Hana and Cristiana Patel would need to remain in India much longer than they had previously anticipated, before attempting to relocate to the States.

The same was true for Yasamin Dabiri. But she didn't mind. Now that she had been safely relocated to an *ETSM* safe house in Dubai, and had direct access to the Word of God, she knew Revelation 8:8-9 had just been fulfilled: "The second angel sounded his trumpet, and something like a huge mountain, all ablaze, was thrown into the sea. A third of the sea turned into blood, a third of the living creatures in the sea died, and a third of the ships were destroyed."

Though frightened by what had happened, knowing it was prophesied thousands of years ago, gave her all the confidence she needed that the Book she now read day and night was indeed the inspired Word of the Living God, which meant it could be fully trusted in good times and in bad.

With that truth settled in her mind, she was fully determined to keep reading it and growing in her faith, until God opened the next door for herself and her son, Navid, to relocate elsewhere...

38

THREE MONTHS LATER

BRIAN MULROONEY WALKED FROM the main house to the cafeteria, looking for Tamika. He was bundled up in a thick maroon parka jacket, with a maroon and white striped pom-pom hat covering his head. A matching scarf circled his neck, that was neatly tucked into his coat for added warmth.

Normally, he wouldn't dress like this to walk the fairly short distance, especially at this time of the year. But with his lungs and immune system steadily worsening, in addition to the severe temperature drop, it seemed every few weeks he caught another cold. Each one took a little longer before his lungs could recover.

All it took was a few hours outdoors and he was forced to spend the next day in bed. Most times it wasn't the flu; there was no fever. But his lungs had become so weakened from dust, mold, fallen ash, and from the toxicity in the air caused by the explosions last fall, that he oftentimes had difficulty breathing.

Dr. Singh was doing all she could to properly treat him. During his last check-up, she told him it was possible that he could survive the next few years, but his lungs and immune system had reached the point that they would never recuperate.

In short, the long-term prognosis wasn't good. Having Cocoa in the house wasn't helping his breathing difficulties. Unlike when he first met the feline in Tamika's mother's car, he steered clear away from her now, and from her new friend, Revelation, the stray cat Tamika found strolling the property after the quake.

Brian reached the cafeteria. All things considered he was impressed with the many improvements that had been made since the global quake.

The large tarps covering the new roof and walls may have looked like eyesores, but they were necessary, not to protect from precipitation—there hadn't been any rain or snow since last Christmas Eve—but as buffers to prevent the howling winds from invading.

Even with space heaters spread sporadically throughout the cafeteria, it was always drafty inside.

Thankfully, they were able to salvage some of the stoves from destroyed cottages and bring them to the cafeteria, to replace the three commercial-size stoves that were destroyed in the quake.

Most of the replacements were badly mangled, but all that mattered was that they still worked. Brian lowered his facemask. "Good morning, sis, you have a phone call."

Tamika was finishing her breakfast in the cafeteria, before beginning her work shift. She shot Brian a confused glance. "Who is it?"

"Brother Amos."

Tamika raised an eyebrow. "Nyarwarta?"

Mulrooney nodded yes.

Even though the expression on Brian's face indicated otherwise, she glanced at him suspiciously, hoping it wouldn't be more devastating news. "Why is he calling me?"

Brian looked to his left then to his right. Not that it mattered—he was among friends and fellow believers. "I'll let him tell you…"

Tamika grabbed Brian's Sat-phone. "Hello, brother Amos!" She silently wondered if he was still in Georgia, but she knew better than to ask him.

"Greetings, my dear sister!" Nyarwarta said robustly, with what sounded to Tamika like an unafraid laugh. "God's grace and peace be with you!" The big-boned, fleshy man was more energized than usual, after just consuming his daily jolt of caffeine. He seldom drank coffee before the Rapture.

Tamika scratched her head in amazement. He was so upbeat, despite that the walls were constantly closing in on them. *Are we living in the same world?* "Same to you. What can I do for you? I'm about to start my shift."

"I know they're keeping you busy, but do you have a minute to spare?" Amos paused, then added, "It's about a dream I had."

Tamika sat more erectly on the cafeteria bench. "Does it involve me?"

"I think so…"

Tamika mouthed the words, "He thinks so?" softly to Brian.

Amos overheard her and chuckled softly. "May I ask, what's your husband's name?"

Tamika winced, then shot another glance at Brian who was standing beside her listening, with a look on his face that said, "See, told you you'd be interested!" *What in the world?* "His name's Isaac Moseley."

"And his Muslim name?"

"Abdul Mohammed. Why do you ask?"

183

"Praise God!" Nyarwarta said more to himself than to Tamika. "I'm certain I had a dream about him the past three nights."

A chill shot through Tamika. She flinched. "What makes you think that?"

"Well, for starters, the man in my dream, whose name just happened to be Abdul Mohammed, was living in fear for his life. He lives in New York City, right?"

Tamika scratched her scalp. "Yeah. But I'm sure there are many Muslims in New York with that name."

"You may be right. But the man in my dream was pleading with an angry mob of Muslims to stop calling him Abdul Mohammed. He told them he no longer identified by that name, or as a Muslim for that matter, and wanted to be called by his birth name instead, Isaac Moseley."

Tamika's eyes widened. Her heart rate accelerated. "What happened next?"

"That's all I can remember, except to say his Muslim brethren felt completely betrayed by him. They were furious! Whereas Christians pray for those who depart from the faith, Muslims punish them, even to death."

Nyarwarta sighed. "I can relate. That used to be me before Jesus saved me! Anyway, Isaac looked frightened for his life. When the men from his mosque asked if he was leaving the Muslim faith to follow Romanero, Isaac sneered at them and said, 'No way! I will never follow the Antichrist of the Bible!'"

Tamika gasped into the receiver. Her heart pounded wildly in her chest. "Then?"

"That was pretty much it. Though he made no mention about forsaking Islam to convert to Christianity, I think the Lord is calling him to salvation. Otherwise, why would I be having dreams about him? And why would he say, he will never follow the Antichrist of the Bible?"

There was a pause as tears flooded Tamika's eyes. She didn't quite know how to feel. After so many years of trying to work him out of her heart, now this? Like a tidal wave, a new rush of emotions nearly knocked her off the cafeteria bench she was seated on. It was impossible to think about Isaac, without Jamal and Dante flooding her mind.

But from a spiritual standpoint, if true, the fact that she had prayed for him every day, without fail, her soul would rejoice for Isaac. She started sniffling. "I don't know what to say, Amos…"

Amos sighed into the phone. "It's a lot to digest, my sister. I don't know where it will all lead, but even though it was only a dream, I think God wants

184

me to travel to New York City to meet with your husband. I'll keep praying about it, but I wanted to give you a heads up, just in case…"

Tamika stiffened again. "I appreciate it, Amos."

"My pleasure. Until we talk again, stay safe, my dear sister. Keep fighting the Good fight. Pray for me as I pray for you. God is with us…"

"Amen." The call ended. Even among the constant chaos striking the planet, Amos sounded optimistically upbeat as usual, without a hint of fear. It was impressive. *Did he ever have a bad day?*

With trembling hands, Tamika handed the phone back to one of her best friends in life. "What do you make of it all, Brian?"

Mulrooney scratched his forehead. "Personally, seeing how God's been connecting believers through dreams, how could we not take it seriously? I mean, it's not like Amos ever met Isaac before. So I'd be shocked if his dream wasn't credible."

Tamika stared at the cafeteria wall behind Brian. "Speaking of New York City, I've been having dreams about two people in particular…"

"Who are they?"

"Believe it or not, one of them is a New York City cop. I met him the day after the Rapture, when I went to the police station to file a missing person's report on my two sons and my mother. He didn't exactly treat me good…"

Brian shot Tamika a sideways glance.

"I know, crazy, right?" she scoffed at herself. "His name's John Reitz. I totally forgot all about him. Had it not been for my dream, I wouldn't even know his name. I think God wants me to contact him…"

Brian grimaced. "But how?"

Tamika shrugged her shoulders. "Good question. All I know is I can't go there! The instant he recognized me, I'd be put in handcuffs…"

"That makes two of us!" Brian gulped at the thought, almost wishing he had never asked. "And the other person?"

"Nila Mirano, someone I went to nursing school with. Came close to driving to the hospital she worked at, on the night of the graveyard incident, and having her to tend to my injured leg. The guard dog tore it up real bad."

Brian nodded agreement. "I can only imagine the pain you were in…"

"Oh, it hurt, alright. But I was more concerned about the infection than with the actual wounds!" Tamika sighed. "Funny thing is, pride and shame always kept me from calling Nila to say hi, or from visiting her at the

185

hospital before the Rapture. I was embarrassed with how we both had started at the same place, yet our careers turned out so differently."

Tamika shook her head sadly. "But after the Graveyard Incident, those things had nothing to do with it. It was the fear of being incarcerated. Had I gone there, who knows where I'd be now?"

Brian shot Tamika a quizzical look wondering where the conversation was headed.

"Unlike me," she went on, "Nila earned a nursing degree and was hired at Presbyterian Hospital. As I drove a taxicab all throughout the city for a living, she kept rising through the ranks until she became the hospital's general nurse practitioner."

Brian patted Tamika a few times on the right shoulder. "Well, at least you can rejoice knowing you have the same position here."

Tamika smiled wearily. "Just wished Nila knew it too…"

Brian moved the conversation forward before Tamika burst out in tears. "If they still have their jobs, both should be easy to locate."

"If my dream was accurate, Officer Reitz still works at the same precinct." Tamika scratched her scalp. "This concerns me very much…"

Brian gulped air into his lungs. "I heard that!"

"Do you think God's calling them both to salvation, Brian?"

"If I had to guess, I'd say chances are good. Otherwise, why would you be dreaming about them, right?" It dawned on Brian. "Why didn't you tell Amos about your dream?"

"In truth, I didn't take it seriously until just now. I thought I was having paranoid dreams because of my situation back home."

"That's understandable," Brian remarked, glancing at the line of somber-looking residents waiting in the chow line. "I'm hungry. Think I'll join them. To be continued, sis…"

Tamika nodded agreement. "You're scheduled for a check-up today, right?"

"That would be correct. Ten thirty, to be exact. Meera wants to check my lungs again. I can't get rid of this cough. It's been three weeks now."

Tamika already knew that. As she slept down in the living room, with no bedroom door upstairs, she easily heard Brian coughing most nights. "See you at ten thirty, brother…"

"Okay…"

Tamika took the last sip of tea in her cup. *Isaac, huh?*

39

FIFTEEN MONTHS AFTER THE GREAT QUAKE

DICK MULROONEY STOOD OUTSIDE the police precinct and took a few deep panicked breaths. Even though he had never committed a crime in his life, every limb in his body trembled in fear.

What would have taken less than 15 minutes in normal times, even in moderate traffic, took 90 minutes this time. With the population cut in half in just three years, vehicle congestion had nothing to do with it.

Even after all this time, mountains of twisted steel, drywall, splintered wood, concrete, bricks, and glass, still littered much of the city. Much of it had been swept or bulldozed into massive piles, but they had no way of removing it from the city.

The reason Dick was even there in the first place, was that he received a text message early this morning, presumably from the same restricted number that was used when he met with Tom Dunleavey in Pennsylvania, instructing him to go to this police precinct looking for Officer John Reitz, as a favor to his wife, Sarah, on behalf of Tamika Moseley.

Dick had to read it three times to make sure his eyes weren't playing tricks on him. He kept coming to the same conclusion: do a favor for the woman who had caused his family so much grief after the *Graveyard Incident* story gripped the entire city for many weeks on end? Seriously?

He could only shake his head...

What had caused him to loathe the woman so vehemently wasn't what she had done to her decorated grandfather's gravesite—despicable as it was—but that she had coerced his son into helping her escape capture, by bringing her to Michigan, only to end up being one of his wife's bridesmaids of all things! Now they were asking him to do this for her, as a favor to Sarah?

It was too much to fathom, insane really. If his wife was involved, which he seriously doubted—after all, they pulled this antic on him last month, and it never led him to her—why didn't she contact him herself?

It was a question he had asked himself a hundred times already. *They won't let me see my wife, but it's okay to ask me to do favors for her...*

187

Tony and Joaquim would have used Brian's name in the text message, instead of Sarah's, but if pressure was ever brought to bear by the NYPD, would Dick ultimately break? They were uncertain.

But what they did know was that he would *never* provide them with information that could lead to his wife's capture. He had already proven that much by keeping his dealings with them from Megan and Rachel.

This would be another big test...Brian, Jacquelyn, and Sarah were still being kept out of the loop for their own good.

Dick paced the sidewalk trying to talk himself out of it. The very thought of walking through those doors caused an uneasy energy to rip through his body. While the *Graveyard Incident* story was ultimately carried away in the dust clouds of unceasing tragedy and devastation, New Yorkers hadn't forgotten about it; they were merely too caught up in their own personal tragedies to give a hoot about what happened to the two fugitives, if they ever got caught.

One thing he knew for certain: the police database inside the building hadn't forgotten about it. All it would take was a simple click of a mouse for the story to once again be staring them square in the eye.

Finally mustering the courage to go through with it, Dick went inside. "I'm doing this for you, Sarah", he muttered, under his breath. *Truly, I'm not in my right mind! Help me, Mother Mary!*

Officer Lupe Santos had been watching the subject pacing outside on one of the monitor screens, before finally coming inside. She stared at him suspiciously, wondering why he was so nervous. Was he there to report a crime or even turn himself in?

Her training had taught her to be prepared for anything. "Yeah?" came the gruff question.

"I'm looking for Officer John Reitz," Dick said, his voice trembling.

"He's not here." The female officer stiffened in her chair, her detective eyes crawling all over the man's face and body. "Is there something I can help you with?"

Dick glanced down at the floor. "I'm afraid it's a personal matter."

Officer Santos wasn't about to tell this stranger that her colleague was badly injured in the quake, or that he hadn't been back to work since. John's roof collapsed along with one of his bedroom walls, breaking his collarbone, a few ribs and his left arm and leg. But that was none of this man's business.

She asked him, "Are you in any sort of trouble?"

Dick removed his eyeglasses and massaged the bridge of his nose. His eyes projected anything but confidence. "Like I said, it's a personal matter."

The surveillance cameras inside the building quickly captured Dick's image. Using facial recognition technology, if no match was found, he would be temporarily detained until a positive identification could ultimately be made.

It became a moot point when the first round of information popped up on Officer Santos' computer screen, confirming that the man standing before her—Richard "Dick" Mulrooney—was a lifelong Catholic in good standing, who wasn't affiliated with any of those rogue religious groups.

But what caused her demeanor to change was that this man was Brian Mulrooney's father. Was he there to provide information that would lead to his or Tamika Moseley's capture?

She shifted on her chair then sat more erectly, when another red flag popped up on her screen. On a recent trip to the state of Pennsylvania, the man standing before her had apparently disabled the GPS on his car.

The question was, why did he do it? And why did he do it in the Keystone State? She glanced up from the computer screen; her steely eyes locked on him again. *This could get interesting*, she thought.

Without even inquiring, Dick knew what had caused the woman's face to crumple in skepticism—his son. *Does she know Sarah left me and is living with Brian in hiding?* Perspiration covered his forehead.

A million questions flooded Officer Santos' mind, as she waited for the "warrant" search to be completed in the National Crime Information Center database (NCIC). Not that it mattered all that much. In a world on the brink of utter destruction, she seriously doubted if there would be grounds to detain Tamika Moseley or Brian Mulrooney for that matter.

Even before the quake, facilities detaining the worst of the worst that society had to offer, were setting prisoners free.

The unspoken rule among law enforcement was that the only subjects they could arrest were those who received or performed abortions, committed indecent acts on children, or those who were labeled as "dissidents", namely cultist extremists who were living in hiding.

Aside from Moseley's known involvement with that rogue, outlawed religious cult, the New York City police department had no further interest in pursuing the fugitive, for the crimes she had committed during the *Graveyard Incident*, and had already been convicted of in absentia.

It angered Officer Santos knowing if she saw a serious crime being committed in the streets of her city—robbery, carjacking, physical or sexual assault—she had to look the other way and pretend that nothing happened.

189

Then again, even if she tried making an arrest, the criminals would laugh at her or spit in her face or even worse, leaving her with no recourse. It was pure insanity! *Can't wait to retire and live happily ever after with my wife!*

But if Tamika had accompanied Dick Mulrooney to the precinct, the female law enforcement officer would have taken great pleasure in arresting her on the spot for being a Christian.

The many years of harassment she had received from Muslims and rogue Christians, for denouncing the lifestyle she and her wife had enjoyed together, had caused her to burn with anger all her adult life.

Which was why she would have zero hesitation arresting Moseley and charging her as a criminal. In her mind, this was her "get-even" time.

Officer Santos snapped out of it when the search came back with no outstanding warrants on the man. "I think he'll be back tomorrow morning."

Dick fidgeted with his fingers, then looked at his wristwatch. "It can wait until then. Thanks for your help, Officer."

Intense scorn on her face, she asked, "Does this have anything to do with your son or Tamika Moseley?" *How I would love to be the one to slap the cuffs on them both for being part of that religious cult!*

Dick flinched, then gulped hard. "Nothing at all, actually. Far as I'm concerned, the day my son helped *that* woman was the day he no longer was my son."

This was said with zero conviction. Had he uttered those words before taking his trip to Pennsylvania, the woman would have believed every word out of his mouth. But not now...

For one thing, when Megan McCallister and Rachel Stein had contacted the Philadelphia and Wilmington police departments, informing that they had good reason to believe Brian Mulrooney was hiding in the *Keystone State* with Tamika Moseley, according to Brian's credit cards statements, New York City eventually got word of it.

And since his father's last GPS reading before being disabled was in the southeastern part of the state, in Delaware County, Officer Santos had reason to believe this man was keeping something from her.

Dick could tell she knew his being there had *everything* to do with it!

She scratched her chin with an ink pen, aiming her withering gaze at him. "So, what is it then?"

The expression Dick saw on this woman's face turned his legs into jelly. His eyes drifted down to the floor, suddenly feeling like a criminal himself. "Could you kindly have Officer Reitz contact me?"

Officer Santos' eyes narrowed. "Phone number?"

As Dick told her, she entered it into the police database, nodding her head very slowly with a growing suspicion on her face. "I'll tell 'im."

Dick cleared his throat. "Thank you, Officer..." He left the precinct, feeling like he was a breath or two away from experiencing a full-blown hyperventilation. He kept looking over his shoulders, already knowing he would never step foot inside that place again.

Officer Lupe Santos wasted no time calling John Reitz on his cellphone. "Yeah?" he said, in a pained grunt.

"Sorry to bother you, John..."

Officer Reitz scratched his head in confusion. "Yes, I'll be in tomorrow. I know you're overworked and need a break, but there's no need to confirm it again!" He sounded angry, frustrated. This was the third time she had called him this week alone.

"Actually, that's not why I'm calling this time..." Santos said.

"That's a relief. So, what is it then?"

"Someone stopped in to see you. He just left."

This wasn't unusual in his line of work. "Open case?"

"That's what I'm trying to figure out, John. I tried pressing him on it, but he only wants to speak to you."

John leaned up on the couch and winced in pain. Even after all this time, his injuries hadn't healed to the extent that he felt he could put in a full day at work. Many of them would never heal. As it was, he could barely walk to the bathroom—but they nevertheless kept pressuring him to come back. "Okay, so who was it then?"

"Dick Mulrooney."

Reitz paused a moment to search his clouded memory. The name sounded vaguely familiar to him, but he couldn't connect the dots, so to speak, perhaps due to the many meds he was taking. Usually, his mind was like a steel trap. "Okay, I give up. Who is he?"

"Brian Mulrooney's father. You know, the man who helped Tamika Moseley escape to safety after the Graveyard Incident. Is there any reason he would come here asking for you?"

Well, I'll be... John's eyes grew wide with astonishment. "Not that I know of," he lied, potentially, anyway. "What did he say?"

Officer Santos stared at the monitors before her. "Basically, that it was a personal matter and he only wanted to speak to you. I tried getting him to talk to me, but he wouldn't budge. I told him you'd be in tomorrow..."

191

John Reitz's heart raced. *What in the world?* "Guess we'll find out then. Are you working tomorrow, Lupe?"

"Sadly, yes, but since you're coming back, it'll only be a half day. My last day off was sixteen days ago," Officer Santos scoffed. "My next scheduled day off isn't until next Sunday. My wife's running out of patience. I don't need to remind you again that she was badly injured in the quake herself. She's starting to take out her frustrations on me," the female officer lamented. "I need to be there for her more…"

John ignored her blabbering and guilt-shaming. He wanted to tell her, "At least you still have a wife!" Instead, he said, "See you tomorrow then…"

The call ended. John Reitz shook his head in confusion. The fact that Tamika Moseley and Brian Mulrooney were listed as "dissidents", much like his wife and son, was what had piqued his curiosity more than anything else.

With so much free time on his hands, as the city desperately tried rebuilding, and filling shifts in all municipal departments, to hopefully maintain what most now believed was unattainable—stability in their once mighty city—John used this time to read the Word of God, on a daily basis.

It took 60 years to finally read and study the one Book he should have been reading all along. Yet, not counting the time he fingered through the Bible as part of a murder investigation, a decade or so before the disappearances, it never occurred to him to open it for the sole purpose of reading the Message inside, like his wife and only son had regularly done the past few months before their deaths.

With his soul now starved for the Truth, he read it day and night. He couldn't get enough of it!

As much as he didn't want to return to work, thanks to his visitor, he finally felt enticed to go back, if only to see where it might lead…

40

THE NEXT DAY

OFFICER JOHN REITZ WAITED all day for Dick Mulrooney to show up during his shift. It was the only thing the 38-year veteran had looked forward to on his first day back at work, in nearly a year and a half.

As much as he hated desk duty, having sustained so many injuries in the global quake, there wasn't much else he could do. The bumps and bruises were gone, but inwardly, he still had a long way to go before he would feel anything close to how he was before the quake.

And even that was wishful thinking!

When the man who drove through streets of chaos, just to see him the day before, never showed up, instead of calling him, Officer Reitz searched the database for Dick Mulrooney's home address. Thanks to his son's recent malfeasance, he found it rather easily. With a strong conviction in his spirit that the two of them had to meet, the sooner the better, Reitz decided that he would pay the man a visit later that evening.

At 10:27 p.m., Dick heard loud banging on the front door, and nearly hit the roof. He was buried under a mountain of blankets on the couch, and had almost drifted off to sleep, something he hadn't done much—at least not for prolonged periods of time—since Sarah left and Chelsea took her life.

He glanced fearfully at the kitchen wall where two windows used to be. When the police and media were camped outside the house for weeks on end, waiting to pounce on Brian the instant he appeared, a few pesky, story-obsessed photographers had shamelessly hoisted themselves up the black metal ladder out back, just enough to peek through the kitchen window to take snapshots of him and Sarah, violating what little privacy they still had left.

Dick was grateful that the damaged back kitchen wall was now covered with a huge tarp.

When the banging persisted, Dick finally lifted himself up off the couch. He tiptoed to the front door which, thankfully, hadn't been damaged in the quake. He peeked through the peephole and saw someone from the New York City police department standing on his stoop leaning on a cane.

193

Fear gripped him, to the point that he thought he might faint. *Is that Officer Reitz?* Having never met the man, he had no way of knowing.

As a longtime veteran of the police force, John Reitz knew exactly what to look for. Even with dimmed vision, he saw the peephole circle darken and knew someone was inside peeking out of it.

He was exhausted after a long shift, and in a considerable amount of pain from sitting on an uncomfortable chair all day.

The prescription meds he was taking, post-surgery, weren't working nearly as well as he had hoped they would. He shot a confused look at the peephole. "Mister Mulrooney, it's Officer Reitz from NYPD."

When Dick remained hesitant, the New York City cop glanced up at the residence silently evaluating whose house had sustained more damage. At first glance, this house appeared to have fared slightly better than his.

So many houses in New York City were sadly beyond repair, and needed to be bulldozed, forcing homeowners to seek shelter elsewhere, either with friends or family members who were more fortunate than they were, or in local homeless shelters, which hadn't been too badly damaged.

Under normal circumstances, Reitz would never dare step foot inside this house. "Come on, Mister Mulrooney, I know you're in there. Open the door before someone sees me standing out here." *Geez, you contacted me first!*

This man's voice wasn't angry or edgy, like with past intruders out looking for Brian, but Dick still felt panicked. How could he not when the only time someone banged on his front door these days was to share tragic news? How he wished he could blink his eyes and return to normal life— pre disappearances—and open the door to find a neighbor dropping by to say hello, or even a girl scout out selling cookies. "Are you alone, officer?"

"Yes…" Reitz said, softly.

"May I see some identification?"

With every muscle in his body hurting, it took a while, but Officer Reitz finally held his badge up close enough to the peephole so Dick could see it in the near darkness. Even shaving was difficult for him.

Satisfied that this man was who he said he was, Dick unlocked the door and waved him inside.

John Reitz limped very gingerly, using his cane to lead the way.

Before closing the door, Dick stuck his head outside and looked up and down the block. He breathed a sigh of relief seeing no one in either direction. The fact that nearly 40 percent of the houses on his block were destroyed no longer shocked him. "Can I get you something to drink?"

John wiped his sweaty brow with the sleeve of his coat. "Bottled water, if you have it."

"Have a seat," Dick said, pointing toward a chair in the living room. "Be right back with your drink."

Officer Reitz slowly lowered himself down onto the chair. A rather unpleasant odor assaulted his nostrils. It smelled like a combination of stale body odor, dust, residual smoke, and who knew what else! One thing was sure, this house hadn't been cleaned in quite some time.

He covered his face with a mask.

When Dick returned, he stopped dead in his tracks. *Is it really that bad in here?* "Here you go…"

Nodding his thanks, Officer Reitz lowered his facemask and took a long swig from the bottle. "Don't mind the facemask. I smell a faint trace of smoke in here. My lungs were badly damaged in the quake. These days, even a lit candle can cause my asthma to flare up."

Dick sensed that it went beyond the man's damaged lungs. "It's residual smoke from the explosions that rocked the city way back when. I can't seem to get rid of it." he said, reclaiming his position on the sofa which became his bed the day Sarah left him. He covered himself with the blankets he had stripped off the three beds upstairs, long before the quake.

Even with the space heater on he was always cold.

Officer Reitz remembered that day all too well. He worked three days straight without going home. It seemed like an eternity ago.

The New York City cop leaned back on the chair hoping to relieve the pressure he felt on his lower back. Finding the most tolerable position, he said, "Ever think you'd see the day when an earthquake would level so much of our city. New York City, seriously?!"

Dick could only shake his head at his question.

John Reitz was unmistakably a New Yorker. His accent and mannerisms indicated that much. He had NYC police officer written all over him. Yet, there was a softness in his eyes that was downright comforting.

He took another swig from the bottle. "So, what was so important, Mister Mulrooney, that you felt the need to travel down many dangerous streets just to tell me? Officer Santos said you were nervous as all get out."

Dick hesitated. "Well…"

"It's okay," he said cautiously, "you can speak freely. My hope is that we can find a way to help each other…"

195

Dick fought off a strong shiver and covered himself with another blanket. He sighed. "I was asked to contact you..."

"By whom?" Reitz was fairly certain it was either A or B—Tamika Moseley or this man's son, Brian.

Dick took a few deep breaths. *Oh, why not?* "Tamika Moseley. I knew the instant I told her my name; she would know who I was. I kept praying to Mother Mary, asking for her protection."

Reitz jerked his head. *Mother Mary? If he isn't a believer, why am I even here? Is this a set up?* "Go on..."

Dick gulped hard again and extended his hands, palms out. "Let me be perfectly clear, I haven't seen her since my son's wedding in Michigan. Haven't seen my son either, for that matter..."

The way his visitor nodded his understanding, so thoughtfully, relaxed Dick a little more. He went on, "This may sound a little strange to you, officer, but she claims to have had dreams about you."

Reitz raised a curious eyebrow, before the detective in him asked, "What kind of dreams?"

"That's just it, I don't know. Truth be told, I'm sort of flying blind here."

"Uh-huh. But how would you know she's having dreams about me, if you haven't seen her?"

Dick's shoulders slumped. "She's living in hiding with my son..."

Reitz wasn't surprised to hear that. Taking a moment to cross his right leg over his left until his ankle was resting on his left leg, he very calmly asked, "And where might that be?"

Dick's pulse raced in his ears. "I'm afraid I can't tell you." He thought it rather ironic how he sounded just like Tom Dunleavey now...

"Is it because it may endanger your son as a result?"

Dick sighed. *Here goes nothing.* "My wife, actually..."

The look on Officer Reitz's face told Dick that he had caught him off guard. "Why your wife?"

Sadness filled Dick's face. "She left me to join Brian and the others." He gasped just loud enough for John to hear it. "It happened not too long after we returned from our son's wedding, but just before our daughter committed suicide..."

Dick braced himself, not sure what would happen next. Would this man pressure him into giving them up, or handcuff him and drag him down to the station for questioning, under the suspicion that he was aiding and abetting two wanted criminals?

The calm demeanor on his face led him to think it was the last thing on Officer Reitz's mind. If anything, his voice was empathetic. "Sorry to hear about your wife and daughter. I didn't know."

"Thank you, officer..."

Reitz shook his head sadly. "In a way, I can relate. My wife Valerie and son John junior were both killed in the quake. Valerie and I were still awake when it happened. I tried reaching for her, but the roof collapsed on top of us. She never had a chance..." His voice trailed off...

"Had it not been for the soft mattress beneath me, the roof would have crushed me to death too. My son died from head trauma in the other room, after being struck by one of the heavy wooden drawers that went airborne.

"John junior was a New York City firefighter. His wife Ling was from China. The reason he was staying with us was that they had separated a few months before the quake.

"One thing I had prided myself on after the disappearances was that we were able to keep our family together all that time. If anything, the chaos brought us closer together. Everything quickly changed when Valerie and John junior got saved after listening to one of the Jewish men openly preaching the Word of God, no less."

Reitz shook his head. "I can't tell you how many arguments this caused between us. Even though I vehemently disagreed with the radical Message the hundred and forty four thousand men were preaching, I couldn't deny they were being supernaturally protected from above.

"Despite all that, my heart remained hardened toward God. The more my wife and son embraced their teachings, the more angered I became, especially after they refused to destroy their Bibles."

Reitz grimaced. "And get this, my wife told me one day that she would rather be arrested by me or even killed than destroy the Word of God. This caused even more tension between us! It's like we became arch enemies overnight! At times, I felt like I was sleeping with the enemy."

Dick pulled the blanket up to his neck. This man was hitting too close to home!

"Ling wanted nothing to do with his new religion. Her greatest fear was that it could put them all in prison someday..."

Dick brushed off a shiver. Not knowing what else to say, he asked his visitor, "So, how do you know Tamika Moseley?"

Reitz stared at the damaged wall behind Dick, as if recalling a memory in midair. "She entered the precinct the day after the Rapture looking all distraught, demanding assistance regarding her missing kids. By that time, I was aware that all small children were among the disappearances.

"She knew it too, but she refused to believe it. All I could do was fill out a missing persons claim for her. When she left, I never gave her another passing thought. When the Graveyard Story broke a few weeks after, my captain called me into his office grilling me with questions about her."

Reitz shook his head. "There wasn't much to tell. Only that she was frightened and angry and wanted to find her kids. When I couldn't help her, she stormed out of the precinct. Just hope as the officer on record, being linked to her doesn't come back to bite me at some point."

Dick shook his head in astonishment. The similarities were mind-numbing. He was mindful that all families had been affected by a constant onslaught of tragedies, but he was so isolated that it took hearing it from the mouth of another man to realize he wasn't alone in this regard.

Officer Reitz stretched his arms above his head and shrieked in pain. What required so little effort before the quake had become such a tedious task since. No matter what position he put his body in, he never felt lasting comfort. "When my wife and son were killed, my first thought that day was I wished I was killed with them. It only increased during the months I spent in a hospital bed fighting for my life. But had I died, I wouldn't be where they are now..." His voice trailed off.

Dick gulped hard. His comment had hit too close to home. "What do you mean by that? I'm failing to connect the dots..."

"Like you, I was raised a Catholic." Reitz knew this from his profile stored on the police database. "But unlike you, I never went to mass or read the Bible or anything like that. Yet, if anyone asked me, I told them I identified as a Catholic, and fully believed I would end up in Heaven because of it, when my life came to an end. Imagine that...

"When my wife and son 'got saved'", Reitz said, using his fingers in quotations, "I thought they had been brainwashed."

Dick brushed off another shiver. *Not again!*

"As it turns out, I was the one who was being brainwashed, not them. I didn't have God's eternal assurance. Had I perished that day, they would be with Jesus, and I would be in hell, eternally separated from them...

"I became a believer for real after I was released from the hospital. Guess you could say I'm a newbie. Spending so much time on the couch gave me plenty of time to think things through for a change, without my world going a million miles an hour.

"One of the things I couldn't stop thinking about was my wife's Bible up in what was left of our bedroom. One day I crawled on my hands and knees up the stairs in agony. It took a while, but I was determined not to go back downstairs until I found it. It was beneath a pillow. It was as if God had perfectly preserved it just for me. It was amazing...

"Been reading it every day since. Now that I'm finally saved, I praise God for keeping me alive long enough to have his eternal assurance. I'm sure my wife and son will be shocked to see me. How could they not, when I all but cursed them when they converted to Christianity?"

John got all choked up. Showing vulnerability toward others wasn't one of his stronger features, especially those he met on the job. He paused a moment to collect himself. "My wife and I were in mid-argument when the quake struck. It was the first night we shared the same bed in weeks. I never got to apologize to her for being a jerk..."

"Hmm..." Dick tried piecing it all together. It was like he was looking in a mirror. He frowned. "It's impossible to fathom what has become of our world since the disappearances..."

"I used to think the same thing until just recently." John Reitz took another sip of water. It could wait no longer. "I need to ask, Dick, are you a true believer? I mean, should I even be here?"

Dick stared at the police officer quizzically. *Really? Him too?* "Yes, as you've rightly said, I've been a Catholic all my life..."

"I understand that. But are you born again? I'm asking because of your comment earlier about pleading with 'Mary'. It concerns me."

Dick sighed. Instead of being offended or trying to defend his position, he confessed, "I'm not sure what I am anymore..."

John nodded at him. "That's precisely how I felt before my conversion to Christianity..."

Dick paused. "Not sure I should be telling you this or not, officer, but I'll be going to..."

"Let me guess, Pennsylvania, right?"

Fear pulsated through Dick's body. "How'd you know?"

John raised a hand. "Cell phone and GPS records show that you were in southeastern Pennsylvania a while back." He paused. "I also know the GPS was disabled when you were there. It's in the police database."

Dick's eyes widened. A cold shiver quickly spread all throughout his body. "What?" He thought to himself, *Tony Pearsall?*

199

Reitz could tell he was caught completely off guard by the comment. "Well, now you know…"

"It'll only be a day trip this time." Even though they seemed to be at odds from a religious standpoint, Dick nevertheless felt comfortable enough to ask, "I was wondering if you could do me a favor while I'm gone?"

"What is it?"

"Locate Tamika Moseley's husband here in the city. His name's Isaac. He's someone else I was asked to contact here in New York. But after I left the precinct, I was so afraid that I went straight home."

Dick reached for the piece of paper on the coffee table with Isaac's address on it, and handed it to John. "Here's his address. Not sure if he still lives there. But if you could verify it for me, I'd appreciate it."

"I'll see what I can do. As of yet, no one at the precinct is mindful of my recent conversion. Just hope Ling doesn't change all that."

John saw another name scribbled on the paper. "Who's Nila Mirano."

"Far as I know, she's an old friend of Tamika's. She's had dreams about her too. She's the head nurse at Presbyterian Hospital."

"That's where I was taken for my injuries. My next appointment's next week. But I'll do a little sniffing around in the morning and see what I can find."

"I'd appreciate that, officer."

John stood to leave. It was late and both men were exhausted. "For the record, whoever disabled the GPS on your car did you a huge favor. But as an added precaution, I wouldn't use your phone in PA. They may not be able to track you with your car, but your phone is more than enough to leave a digital footprint, which would no doubt be revealed to the wrong people someday."

"Thanks for the advice…"

"In the meantime, I'll cruise by Isaac's house on my way to work in the morning to see what I can discover."

"I would appreciate that…" Dick extended his right hand.

Officer Reitz did the same. After shaking hands, he pulled his new friend in and held him tightly. It had been an emotional few years. Both men were lonely and desperate for fellowship. "Thanks for the hug, John, I needed it."

"You and me both."

Dick opened the front door and helped his friend down the five steps until John reached the pavement. He remained outside watching him limping ever so slowly to his squad car.

The reason he drove the squad car was that his personal car was crushed, when a house across the street collapsed on top of it. His wife's car was also destroyed.

It took him twice as long to lower himself into it than when he got shot on duty 15 years ago, but he was doing his best to adjust to his new reality.

Officer Reitz slid behind the wheel and turned the engine on. As much as he wanted to help the man, his biggest concern was Dick's relying on Mother Mary to help him. If he was truly saved, he would know better than to pray to her!

John looked skyward out of his front windshield. "I'm trusting in you, Lord…"

At that, he left for home…

41

LATER THAT EVENING

AMOS NYARWARTA ARRIVED IN Chadds Ford, Pennsylvania for this covert mission of sorts, at just after 3 a.m. What made it so covert was that the Mulrooneys were completely unaware that he was even there.

Amos was taken through the back entrance of the property, where two guards out patrolling on the inside of the wall escorted him straight to the hospital, in total silence, wearing a black parka coat, with a gray hoodie underneath covering his head.

Tamika greeted him with a warm embrace. "Good to see you again!"

"Likewise, my dear sister!" Amos said, yawning into his right fist.

"If there's one good thing about arriving so late, it's that the Mulrooneys are asleep…"

"That was my hope," Amos said, with another hearty yawn.

"So, what do you think about the new safe house number one hospital?"

Amos surveyed the room. "Looks like you're making good progress."

Tamika put her hands on her hips. "It's still in the process of being sectioned off. Just hope it survives the next round of judgments!"

Nyarwarta was exhausted and nodded his reply. Not only did the drive take twice as long as he had hoped it would, part of the 800-mile trip included being stuffed inside a coffin at times, in the back of a cargo van.

Nurse Moseley was mindful of this and checked his vitals. She wasn't surprised that her patient was a little dehydrated. Other than that, aside from the fact that he was totally exhausted from the long and grueling trip, he seemed fine. "Did you spend much time in the casket?"

Nyarwarta nodded yes. "At each checkpoint. There were several along the way. As a big man, it wasn't easy getting in and out of the coffin, especially since I injured my left hip and shoulder in the quake. They haven't been right since. But by the grace of God, I managed.

"Thankfully, none of the checkpoints were being guarded, so I was never in there long enough to need the oxygen mask. But you should have seen the disguise my driver wore. He's one of our guards in Georgia. He's thirty-seven, but they made him look sixty-seven! It was quite impressive."

Tamika could only shake her head. "I don't know how you did it…"

"It wasn't easy. When Travis first told me about the mode of transportation I would be taking, I wasn't happy. Soon that'll be the only way for any of us to travel about the country. And even that'll be risky once all the scanners have been reset and reprogrammed...

"Before I left Georgia, Clayton confessed that he would rather be tortured in Romanero's prisons than travel in a coffin. He's extremely claustrophobic. Just the thought of it fills him with panic."

Tamika snorted sarcasm. "I'm with him! Here's some water. I need to check on another patient. After that, I'll bring you food."

"Thank you, Tamika."

When Nurse Moseley returned, she handed Amos two peanut butter and jelly sandwiches. He removed a sandwich from the plastic baggie, thanked God for the food, then took a big bite out of it.

Tamika sat on the chair across from him. "Have you seen anything else in your dream since we last spoke?"

Amos took another bite of the sandwich and shook his head. "Aside from seeing your husband in danger, after renouncing his faith in Islam, and even feeling more convinced that God wants me to go there, I saw nothing else. Wish I could tell you more, but that's all I saw. We need to remain patient and see what happens..."

Tamika sighed. "Are you sure you still wanna do this?"

Nyarwarta swallowed the food in his mouth. The tone in her voice and expression on her face led him to believe she had serious reservations about this trip. "Why do you ask?"

"I dreamt last night that me and Isaac were trying to reconcile, but some invisible force kept blocking it from happening. We kept trying to reach out to each other, but it was impossible. I woke early this morning thinking either Satan was invading my dreams, or I had the dream because you were going to New York to meet him."

"That could be a good thing, seeing how God has already connected us through dreams," Amos said, in reply.

Wow! "I admit the not knowing's driving me crazy..."

Amos raised his hands, as if signaling for Tamika to calm her spirit. "Relax, my sister. Soon we'll know."

Tamika glanced at her patient. A chill shot through her just thinking about the many potential grim possibilities. "How do you do it, Amos?"

Nyarwarta yawned into his fist again. "Do what, my sister?"

"You always seem so calm when everyone else is falling apart. I mean, don't get me wrong, I'm grateful for the eternal assurance I have in Christ Jesus, but other than that, I'm scared out of my wits most days!"

Amos smiled wearily. "I get scared too, Tamika. When I was awakened by the earthquake and thrown from my bed and slammed into a wall, in total darkness, I was frightened for my life. I was reminded of just how powerless I really was. My left hip and shoulder haven't been the same since. But I kept telling myself in the darkness that God works all things for good. After a while, the fear was gone."

Tamika grinned, brief as it was. "You're right! It really does come down to perspective."

"Indeed! The key for me is not to let my human side rise above my spirit side. The instant I let my guard down, like I did in the quake, I get just as scared as everyone else."

"Hmm, don't you think it's easier said than done?"

Amos nodded at him. "That's why I find myself praying to our Lord, day and night, without ceasing." He became more reflective. "If you only knew the hatred I once harbored in my heart toward Jews and Christians, you might understand my position a little better. Had God not saved me and removed all hatred from my heart, I would still be that way."

He shook his head sadly. "The anger I saw on the faces of the Muslim men in my dream was a stark reminder of who I used to be. If God can perform such a radical change in my life, how can I ever doubt Him going forward?"

Amos took another bite of his sandwich and took his time chewing, before swallowing. "When I get to New York, I hope to share the Gospel with them. How awesome that our Lord made it possible for me to love those who may want to kill me!"

Wow! Tamika was dumbfounded.

Amos licked the upper inside of his mouth to remove the peanut butter that was stuck there, then took a sip of water. "So long as I'm alive, I will keep doing the will of our Father in Heaven. When the day comes and I'm no longer here, just knowing I'll be spared from the eternal judgment I deserve fills me with a gratitude I've never known before. Despite the ongoing chaos, I feel protected from above, which explains the great joy I have inside. How cool is that?"

"Cool indeed..." Tamika became teary-eyed and shook her head in amazement.

Amos yawned into his fist again. "What is it?"

"I don't even know where to begin. I mean, how can I possibly thank you for what you're doing? We hardly know each other!"

Amos took the final bite of the first PB&J sandwich. "True, but we'll have an eternity for that, when we're no longer trapped inside these sin-stained bodies."

A smile curled onto Tamika's lips. "Your words truly inspire me! I could listen to you all night..."

Amos laughed. "Thanks, but would it be okay if we continue this in the morning? I need sleep. I'll save the other sandwich for the trip to New York in the morning."

"Sure. There's a cot and space heater set up for you in the back room. Should be nice and quiet in there. I'll bring you food in the morning."

Amos nodded his thanks at her.

Tamika leaned in and hugged Amos. In her mind, he was right up there with Brian and Charles. Sleep well, my brother. I love you."

"Love you too, Tamika..."

PATRICK HIGGINS
42

AT 6:30 A.M., MEERA Singh peeked her head in to find Amos snoring away. As much as she didn't want to wake him, it was time to get a move on. She whisper shouted, "Amos?"

When he didn't reply, she whispered his name again, only louder this time. It was enough to rouse him from his deep slumber.

Amos rolled onto his side. Seeing Doctor Singh, he smiled. "Good morning, my dear sister! So nice to see you again…"

"Likewise, Amos. As much as I hate disturbing you, I just got word that Brian's father is already in the vicinity looking for you…"

Amos slowly sat up on the cot and stretched his arms above his head. "I understand. I wanted to meet Jakob before I go."

Meera nodded thoughtfully. "I'm sure he's already out winning souls. Hopefully, you can meet him when you get back from New York."

Amos still felt groggy from the long trip. His mouth was twisted in a wide yawn. "Hopefully, I'll get to win souls in New York myself! That's the plan!"

"Amen to that!" came the reply with a weary grin. "I've brought you breakfast. If you want to take a shower before leaving, there's a makeshift shower in the restroom. But I must warn that the water gets cold fast."

"Understood…"

Meera smiled wearily again. The dark circles beneath her eyes were humungous. Having so many new and expectant mothers at the safe house, as the only doctor for now, she felt as exhausted as Amos looked.

She needed an extended break, but didn't see that happening anytime soon. "I'll leave you now. Please be careful out there, Amos. You're going straight into the snake pit."

Amos rubbed his forehead. "Whatever happens, God will be with me."

"Amen!" Meera smiled wearily again. "We'll all be praying for you."

"Thank you, my dear sister." Amos ate his breakfast and took a quick shower, before two guards escorted him to the rear of the property.

Joaquim Guzman was seated on a 4-wheeler waiting to take Amos to a small open field just off U.S. 202, which led straight back to the woods, in case Guzman had to make a quick getaway.

206

Nyarwarta couldn't help but wonder if he was too big to get on the back of that thing as the second passenger. He shrugged his shoulders and mumbled to himself, "Beats being transported in a casket any day!"

The two guards heard him and chuckled. When Amos was mounted on the 4-wheeler, one of the guards said, "Godspeed, Amos!"

Amos saluted them, and Joaquim left at once. Upon reaching the end of the underground tunnel, two more guards already had the iron gate open so they wouldn't have to stop. This was where new members were smuggled in at night.

"Be back soon!" Joaquim shouted as loudly as he could.

The guards shot him thumbs-up gestures, and quickly closed the hatch.

"Hold on tight!" Joaquim said to Amos, switching gears and speeding off. The young man skillfully navigated the 4-wheeler through the uneven hilly terrain before coming to an open field.

Guzman was careful not to go anywhere near the extensive quake damage. After so many months of driving these backwoods, he pretty much knew where to go and which areas to avoid.

Nyarwarta held on for dear life each time the 4-wheeler raced uphill at full speed. At one point, he thought for certain that he would fall off.

A few moments later, they made it to the river. Joaquim slowed his vehicle and gently guided it across the shallow riverbed that was dry in some places and still slippery in others.

One of his daily chores was filling 25-gallon buckets with water, then bringing it back to the safe house to be used for growing crops hydroponically, and for the fish tanks. The rest was boiled and used mostly for cleaning and washing clothing.

Though safe house number one residents were grateful the water hadn't been contaminated, not yet anyway, since there hadn't been any rain since the last snowfall, they feared there would soon be no water to collect at all.

Ten minutes later, they reached U.S. 202, and the 4-wheeler came to a stop. Amos wasted no time jumping off the back of the vehicle.

"Just keep walking down that way until Brian's father spots you. Godspeed, brother," Joaquim said, quickly getting out of Dodge.

Amos felt dizzy from the short ride. He took a moment to stretch his legs, then walked on U.S. 202 northbound, carrying a bag full of water, snacks, and the PB&J sandwich Tamika gave him the night before.

Meanwhile, Dick Mulrooney made a U-turn on U.S. 202, and headed north for the fourth time, looking for a man from Africa wearing a black parka coat, with a gray hoodie underneath covering his head.

He was never given an exact time or meeting location, only that he was to keep driving on U.S. 202 until he spotted him, before taking him to New York, as part of Tamika Moseley's dream, whatever that dream was!

When Dick left the police precinct the other day, without being detained, he became extremely valuable to them. If he was ever pulled over by the police, aside from the fact that he was Brian Mulrooney's father, he was still in good standing, and not involved with any rogue groups.

This made him the perfect gopher for now, even if he didn't know it.

Roughly a mile and a half up the road, Dick spotted the man he was there to fetch. He pulled his car to the side of the road.

Nyarwarta wasn't the only hitchhiker on route 202 with his thumb out hoping for a ride—there were many others—but the fact that he was so tall, and husky, made him rather easy to identify.

Dick rolled down the passenger side window. As he had been instructed, Amos was quite animated, pointing his right hand in the direction he needed to go, just in case someone, aside from the scores of cameras, was watching them with any particular interest.

Dick nodded as he listened then waved the man inside his car.

Amos climbed inside and Dick held his pointer finger against his lips. Amos nodded that he understood the gesture. He was just thankful to be taking a regular mode of transportation this time.

At that, the two men left for the *Big Apple*. The excitement Amos had always had about seeing New York City up close and personal was gone.

When they were out of Pennsylvania, headed for the New Jersey turnpike, Dick breathed a sigh of relief. His heart was also filled with a deeper measure of sadness. Once again, he didn't get to see Sarah.

He felt trapped in loneliness purgatory.

To avoid possible detection from police, Dick left his cell phone at home. If New York City police knew about his last trip to the Keystone State, he felt certain that Pennsylvania law enforcement also knew, especially with Megan McCallister and Rachel Stein constantly updating them on everything.

No doubt the two women felt betrayed by him, for leaving them high and dry without giving the money he had promised them. Dick knew the reason Megan was trying to seduce him in the first place, using the sexiest body language she could muster, was partly financially induced.

What he didn't know was that it had caused Megan to spiral into a deep depression. With their money running out, and with no job possibilities, she felt like she wasn't earning her keep, as the saying went. Brian's father was her job, and she had failed to collect the $500 or his sperm donation from him.

Megan became severely depressed in the days following Dick's departure, and saw no reason to keep living this crazy life. She was all out of hope. The only way out of her ongoing dilemma was by ingesting enough bleach to kill herself.

Rachel got her to the hospital just in time to have the destructive chemicals pumped from her stomach. Once convinced her best friend would survive the ordeal, she took a knee right there in the hospital room and proposed to Megan, hoping that it might prevent her from finding another way to follow in her late sister's footsteps, once she was discharged.

Whereas Rachel had always preferred women over men, Megan preferred men. In that regard, she only accepted her proposal for the security her best friend could offer her simply by being a mother.

In the end, they needed each other. Megan wanted the security and Rachel didn't want to be alone, making their union a solid one.

WHEN DICK AND AMOS arrived at the Mulrooney residence, seven hours later, both men were exhausted. Dick yawned into his left fist. "Nice meeting you, Amos. First time in New York?"

Amos nodded that it was. "I've always wanted to come here…"

"Sorry you never got to see it in its heyday. With so many of our iconic buildings lying in massive heaps of rubble, the *Big Apple* more resembles a mostly eaten apple with its 'rotten-to-the-core' insides now exposed for the whole world to see. Used to be quite the place though."

Amos nodded. "It's only going to get worse."

Dick powered on his phone. He had a voice message from Officer Reitz. "Hey Dick, it's John. Hope you had a safe trip. I prayed for you all day. I plan on stopping by your house in the morning, at around eight a.m., to update you on what I've discovered…"

Dick texted his reply. "Just got back. It was a long drive, but relatively hassle free. Thanks for the prayers. I look forward to seeing you in the morning. The door will be open. Let yourself in."

Dick placed his cell phone on the coffee table. "That was Officer Reitz. He'll be here in the morning."

209

"Tamika told me about him," said Amos. "I am eager to meet him."

Dick yawned again. After a full day of driving, he was beat. But just knowing he would have something to do in the morning, and that it would bring him one step closer to being with Sarah—at least he hoped—his energy level was much higher than in past weeks. That was a good thing.

"We may be out most of the day searching for Isaac, so I'd suggest we get a good night sleep."

Amos said, "Lord knows I need it. Where shall I sleep?"

"I'd offer you one of the three upstairs bedrooms, but my roof collapsed during the quake, so they're pretty much uninhabitable."

Dick pointed to the living room couch. "That's been my bed since Sarah left. I'd offer it to you, but the sheets haven't been washed in many weeks. I don't think the love seat will be comfy for you. If you don't mind sleeping on the floor, I have plenty of pillows and blankets."

Amos smiled. "That would be just perfect." Compared to the cargo van and the small cot he slept on the night before, it was like having a king size bed to sleep on.

Amos dropped to his knees to thank God for guiding them safely to New York. When he was finished, he asked Dick, "Would it be possible to try New York City pizza while I'm here? All my life I've wanted to try it."

Dick looked up at the ceiling, as if deep in thought. "Not sure which places are still open, if any, but we can certainly look for one tomorrow, after we meet with Officer Reitz."

A smile crossed Amos' face. "Thank you, Dick."

43

JOHN REITZ PARKED HIS squad car down the street from the Mulrooney residence, then limped the short distance to his house. He let himself in without knocking first.

Dick was in the kitchen preparing hot tea. "Is that you, John?"

"Yes, it is!" he said, through labored breathing.

Dick hurried to the living room to greet his new friend. "Welcome back, John! I'd like you to meet Amos Nyarwarta."

"Pleasure meeting you, Amos."

Amos got up off the love seat and shook hands with the New York City police officer. "Likewise, my brother!"

Dick raised a curious eyebrow. "We're about to have green tea. Would you like some?"

"Sounds perfect..."

"Be back in a jiffy. Have a seat..."

John removed his coat. "By the way, Dick, I drove by Isaac Moseley's apartment building the past two days..."

Dick already sensed that much, from John's voice message the night before. "And?

Reitz shifted his focus onto Amos. "Let's just say I'm eager to hear more about the dream Amos had!"

"Not much to tell, actually," Amos said, in his deep gravelly voice.

John grinned awkwardly. "Tell me, anyway! I wanna know..."

"Me too. Just give me a minute." Dick returned from the kitchen, carrying a small tray with three steaming teacups on it. He placed the tray on the coffee table and took a seat on the couch.

John said to Amos, "So, as you were saying..."

"Okay, so in my dream, Isaac was pleading with them to stop calling him by his Muslim name, Abdul Mohammed. When he told them he no longer identified by that name, or as a Muslim for that matter, they were furious, and felt completely betrayed by him."

Officer Reitz asked, "Could your dream be connected to the group of Muslim men I saw loitering outside Moseley's apartment building yesterday morning and today?"

211

Amos leaned up in his chair. "Really? You saw them?"

Reitz reached for one of the teacups and blew into it, before venturing a sip. "What gave their Islamic faith away wasn't the clothing they wore—all were casually dressed in blue jeans and coats—but that they were all facing to the east, praying on their knees, on throw rugs.

"If they were trying to conceal their loyalty to Allah from the public, they were doing a lousy job. I seriously doubt they were residents. If so, why would they risk praying out in the open, when they could do it in the confines of their homes? If they weren't residents, why were they there in the first place?"

Amos said, "If they are the men I saw in my dream, they were there because they feel betrayed by Isaac. These men are radicals. Nothing will stop them from worshiping Allah, especially Salvador Romanero!"

Officer Reitz scratched his chin, not at all surprised to hear Amos say that. "What really sparked my interest was when they finished praying, they kept glancing up at an apartment window on the eighth floor, apparently looking for someone.

"When I got to work, I did a little poking around online to see who lived in the apartment on the eighth floor that they were so interested in. Sure enough, it was Moseley's apartment, which meant they were waiting for him, either to leave or return home…"

Dick took a small sip from his teacup. "Okay, so, where do we go from here. What's the plan of attack?"

Amos raised his hands in confusion. "Not much of a plan, really. All I can say is I'm just being obedient to the One I'm convinced sent the dream. I confess that Isaac made no mention about forsaking Islam to convert to Christianity in the dream. But I believe our Lord's calling him to salvation."

Nyarwarta sighed. "Otherwise, why would I be having dreams about a man I never knew? And why would I be in New York City?"

Officer Reitz shrugged his right shoulder. "Let's just hope you're right."

Amos nodded agreement with him.

Dick asked, "So, what happens if we bump into him?"

Amos grimaced, realizing he hadn't thought it all the way through. "Not sure, but I was thinking after we rescue Isaac from those men, if it's okay with you, we can bring him back here and question him to see if he had similar dreams, before sharing our true identities with him."

The question caught Dick off guard. The last thing he wanted was another media circus, if they ever caught wind of what they were plotting. He took another small sip of tea. "I guess that would be fine…"

Amos smiled his thanks to Dick. "Once we pull Isaac away from his captors, the goal will be to share the Word of God with him, hoping he'll become a Christ follower as a result. *You too, Dick,* he thought, keeping it to himself...

John adjusted his weight on the chair. "How do you know you'll see him?" He answered his own question. "I know, the dream, right?"

"Yes!" Amos declared, convincingly.

"Well then," John said, reaching for his coat, "what are we waiting for? Let's get going! Just hope today's the day we get to put the rest of the puzzle together before I start my shift three hours from now."

The three men finished their tea and they left the house.

Dick helped John down the concrete steps. "By the way, Nila Mirano no longer works at Presbyterian Hospital. No one on staff knows why she suddenly resigned or where she went from there. It's like she disappeared."

Dick didn't reply. In this age of nonstop lunacy, it only figured...

Since John knew the city like the back of his hand, he sat in the front seat of Dick's car, so his view wouldn't be obstructed.

After a while, Amos leaned up in the backseat. "How long have you been saved, John?"

"Truth be told, I'm a newbie. It took nearly being killed in the quake for God to finally get my attention. Not sure if Dick told you but I lost my wife and son, John junior, in the quake."

"He told me earlier before you arrived. Sorry for your loss, officer."

"Thanks. Both were killed when the roof collapsed on them. My lungs took the brunt of the damage. I was placed on a ventilator for three weeks until I could finally breathe again on my own, shallow as it was..."

John stared out the front window, sad expression on his face. "Everyone knows how much of a family man I was. I was so devastated by their deaths, had I not been rushed to the ER that night, I surely would have killed myself!

"Part of my grief came from how I treated them both after they were radically changed in the name of religion, especially after my wife removed the three statues of Mary from the house...

"I wasn't a strong Catholic or anything like that, but I was still offended. And concerned for my wife's well-being. Valerie used to pray to Mary all the time. When she suddenly stopped doing that, I thought she was a little cuckoo.

213

"How could I not, when all she wanted to do was read her Bible all day and night. My son, too! It was the craziest thing. Now that I'm a true convert, I understand completely. I rejoice knowing they're with Jesus now."

Nyarwarta's face lit up. "Hallelujah!"

Dick gulped hard, then winced. The similarities were undeniable.

John noticed, and went on, "The family downfall started the day of the Rapture, when my four-year-old granddaughter, Deidre, vanished before my very eyes. My son and grandkids came over to the house that day, as our wives went Christmas shopping. As the kids played with their phones on the living room floor, John junior and I watched the Griffin brothers vanish into thin air on the TV screen."

Amos asked, "Griffin brothers?"

"That's right, you're not from here. They were college football players who vanished on live TV with millions watching…"

"I see," came the reply. "I've always been more of a soccer fan myself, which, of course, is the true 'football'. In your game, the players use their hands. We don't!"

Officer Reitz laughed out loud, before sadness covered his face again. "Deidre was the light of my life. When she suddenly disappeared into thin air, I thought my heart would stop beating. My grandson, Jeremy, who was nine at the time, was unaffected by it.

"When it became known as a 'Christian' thing, my daughter-in-law, Ling, became angry and swore off anything related to Jesus or Christianity. That's why when my son got saved, she kicked him out of the house.

"Ling never stopped me from seeing my grandson, but she wouldn't let my wife or son anywhere near him.

"Since they were dissidents, there was nothing they could do about it. She warned them both that if they asked her one more time, she would call the cops on them. That was the last time John junior talked to his wife…

"When I was hospitalized following the quake, Ling visited me every day without fail. I could tell she was mourning their deaths, but she looked more relieved than anything else…

"Probably because she no longer had to fear going to prison for her husband's faith." He sighed. "Anyway, the day I became a Christian for real, Ling stopped visiting me. And she refused to let me speak to my grandson. My heart breaks for them. They need Jesus."

John choked back tears. "My greatest fear now is that she'll become an informant against me, like she threatened to do with my wife and son. Truth be told, that was my greatest fear with going back to work. I half expected to be questioned about my religious status when I went back yesterday...'

Dick remained silent but was listening to the conversation very carefully. As far as he was concerned, his main interest in all this was getting his wife back. But if that miraculously happened, where would they reside?

Certainly not at home! His focus shifted when he noticed John stiffen in the passenger front seat.

The New York City police officer stared out the window. "Pull the car over now, Dick!"

44

IN WHAT COULD ONLY be described as God's providence, when they arrived at Isaac's apartment, Officer Reitz noticed the increased activity outside the building. "Isaac's here!"

"How do you know?" Dick asked, almost nonchalantly.

The New York City cop pointed up at Moseley's apartment window. "That's his apartment. Look at how they keep gazing up at it. They're waiting to ambush him the instant he leaves the building."

When Amos' eyes settled on the group of men standing outside the building, he silently gasped. Chills raced up and down his spine. "The men in my dream!" Now that it was materializing before his very eyes, he had all the confirmation he needed that he was supposed to be in New York City, rescuing Isaac from these men.

He just hoped the Lord was calling Isaac to salvation. If he and Dick rejected the true Gospel message and died still in their sins, as a result, it would be the most tragic of outcomes. It would also force him to question why his Maker had sent him to New York City in the first place.

They weren't parked across the street for even ten minutes, when Isaac suddenly sprang out of the building at full speed, carrying a bag full of personal items.

The two men closest to the exit door raised the thick rope they were holding a few inches off the sidewalk, tripping Isaac. He fell flat on his face, breaking his nose and costing him his two front teeth.

In a flurry of activity, Moseley was surrounded by a dozen men, all of whom he recognized. It wasn't a happy reunion. The anger on their faces and in their voices, as they shouted at him in Arabic, was rather alarming.

As the seconds passed, they became more and more enraged, as if holding court over Isaac.

With the car window down, Amos easily understood every word they spoke. He knew he had to do something quick before they killed Isaac right in front of his apartment building, for his ultimate betrayal.

With a sinking feeling inside that it wouldn't end the way he had hoped it would, Amos said to Dick, "When you get home, I want you to read John fifteen, thirteen. Think about it whenever you think of me."

Dick looked at Amos in the rearview mirror. "Don't you mean when *we* get home?"

"I'm starting to think God may have other plans for me," Amos said, without taking his eyes or ears off the commotion going on 50 feet away from where they were parked.

Dick panicked. "What do you mean by that, Amos?"

With the most sincere eyes Dick Mulrooney had ever seen, Amos said, "Don't forget to read that scripture when you get home. I pray it applies to you someday…"

Dick looked confused. "Again I ask, what do you mean?"

Amos patted him on the right shoulder. "That's for you to figure out!"

Dick was blown away by this man's courage. In this potential life or death situation, it was awe-inspiring, especially since he couldn't have looked or felt any more fearful!

Amos turned on his Sat-phone and sent a voice text message to Meera Singh. "Just spotted Isaac. He's in serious trouble, just like I saw in my dream. Will do my best to help him escape. Not sure how it will turn out, but it doesn't look good. Pray for us, my dear sister." He then sent a similar message to Travis Hartings, before powering off his phone.

Sensing what the man in the backseat was about to do, Officer Reitz craned his neck back. "Regardless of how it turns out, I'm glad I met you, Amos. Truly, you are a mighty man of God!"

"You too, Officer…If I don't see you again on this side, brother, we'll surely see each other on the other side."

John nodded his sincere appreciation for what he was about to do.

With his body trembling, Amos opened the door and got out of the car. "If anything happens to me, Dick, do your best to escape."

Dick lowered his head and nodded.

Amos then said to John, "My phone has all the numbers you'll need to contact those who can help you, if you escape from New York. Under no circumstances should you use it for any other reason."

"Got it." John Reitz scratched his head. *Am I a mighty man of God like him? I feel nothing like that.*

Amos slowly approached the agitators and greeted them in Arabic, hoping to stop them in their tracks or, at the very least, slow them down.

The man with the knife in his hand gave him a good looking over. "This doesn't concern you, now get out of here!" he shouted at Amos, positioning the knife to stab Abdul in the chest.

217

"Actually, it does concern me."

The man stopped, sensing that Amos was a fellow Muslim. After all, he spoke Arabic. "This man is a defector of the faith! He deserves death!"

Amos calmly asked, "To which faith are you referring?"

Isaac looked up at Amos. His eyes pleaded with him for help. He was frozen on the sidewalk.

"The only legitimate faith—Islam!" the agitator yelled.

Amos nodded, then said, "The one thing we all have in common is our shared hatred of Salvador Romanero." Everyone who heard him nodded agreement. "But where we differ, aside from your greatly flawed views of who Christ really is, is that I now support Israel..."

The man glared at Amos angrily, as the others shouted at him in Arabic.

Amos understood every word they spoke, which meant he also knew the end was near for him, and he wouldn't live in the Millennial Kingdom, not in human form anyway, not after what he was about to tell them. *So, this is why I saw nothing in my dream after traveling to New York? I'll never leave this place! Thy will be done, Lord!*

He glanced down at Isaac. "Greater love has no one than this, that a person will lay down his life for his friends." Pointing in the direction of Dick's car, he hollered, "Run Isaac, to that car over there. Escape while you can. You're still married! Go and have a child with your wife."

Shock filled Isaac's face. His eyes grew wide in befuddlement. *He knows Tamika? Is that why I keep dreaming that we're trying to reconcile?*

"Now, Isaac!" Amos barked, breaking Moseley from his near paralyzed condition. "Run straight that way. Do not fear for me. If you knew what I knew, you would be petrified for yourself, not me. The Jesus these men believe in is nothing more than a false prophet."

Amos kept an eye on the man with the knife in his hand, and kept going. "The only hope you have is to believe in Jesus for your salvation! There is no other way to God but through Him!"

The man repositioned his knife from Abdul Mohammad—a.k.a Isaac Moseley, onto Amos. "Run! Isaac now!"

The man became even more enraged and shouted, "Allahu Akbar!"

Amos held out his hands. "Before you kill me, can I pray for you?"

The man growled angrily, shouted "Allahu Akbar!" even louder, then jammed the knife into Amos Nyarwarta's belly region. He groaned in agony.

Isaac wanted to help this man who apparently knew Tamika, but it was now or never. When he turned and pivoted, two men tried grabbing him. Like a wide receiver breaking free from two defensive backs, his arms

218

flailed wildly, slapping the two men in the face and chest, stunning them enough to start his getaway.

If they had guns, they could have easily ended his life. But they didn't. All they had were knives…

Even buckled over in pain, instead of trying to fistfight his way out of it, Amos glanced up at them. In pained grunts, he said in Arabic, "Don't fear for me, I'm going to Paradise. Fear for yourselves. Repent and trust in Christ Jesus. He is your only hope. Without Him, you will all perish!"

Eyes aflame with vengeful hatred, the group of angry Muslims surrounded Amos, as two men stabbed him repeatedly in the chest and upper back.

Nyarwarta fell to his knees. He tried stretching his hands toward Heaven, but it hurt too much. Blood spewing from his mouth, he raised his eyes instead, and prayed, "Thank you, Lord Jesus, for Your kindness to me, and for Your mercy and grace, and for rescuing me from the false religion of Islam. You alone are the King of all kings and the One and only true God. Into Thy hands I commend my spirit…"

Amos lost all strength and fell hard onto the pavement. He was already dead when they beheaded him on the streets of Manhattan, as if carving a turkey. Holding his bloody head with both hands, they all shouted, "Allahu Akbar!" over and over.

Before Isaac could reach the getaway car, two other men tackled him in the middle of the street. Normally, he would have little trouble outrunning his pursuers, but the serious head blow he had suffered left him feeling concussed. He posed no challenge to his captors whatsoever.

Dick Mulrooney watched in horror. His hands trembled so much he was forced to clasp them together. He started hyperventilating, fearing for his own safety.

John Reitz was just as frightened himself, but he was also angry. *Not in my city!* As a New York City cop, having just witnessed a brutal murder, with one more possibly looming, his first instinct would be to call for back up, then do his best to neutralize the situation until they arrived.

But this was a whole new world. It was spiritual warfare.

John glanced over at Dick. "Here's the plan, when I get out of the car, start honking your horn and don't stop. Hopefully, it'll alert more citizens to the situation. I'll wave Isaac over to you. Once he gets inside the car, I'll do my best to fend off his chasers, as the two of you drive off to safety. Don't hesitate for even a second! Do you hear me?"

219

Dick's trembling increased. He nodded. "I understand..."

"Good, because it's go time!" He eyeballed Dick. "This is how much I trust in my salvation. I'm willing to lay down my life for another. My only hope is that you and Isaac will come to faith in God, through Christ Jesus as a result. Me and Amos have nothing to worry about. Our futures couldn't be brighter. But if you and Isaac escape this danger only to die in your sins, it'll end up being a failed mission for us.

"I just hope this huge sacrifice we're making will lead you both into the arms of Jesus. Either He will be your Savior or your judge. And don't forget what I told you about the virgin Mary. My wife was right. Anyone who thinks she has the power to answer prayers or save souls has no true understanding of the Gospel message. Only God can answer prayers and save souls, through Christ Jesus. No one else."

Reitz saw one man pulling a switchblade out of his pocket to stab Isaac with. "Once you redirect all your prayers to the Father, in Jesus' name, and His name alone, that's when the Gospel message will finally make perfect sense to you."

Dick lowered his head. It was Tom Dunleavey all over again. He felt no need to challenge him; there wasn't time to. Besides, when he spoke those words, it felt like something had shifted inside him. But what was it?

John reached into his pocket and retrieved his prescription meds. "Give this to Isaac. It's Percocet. His nose looks broken. I'm sure he's in a great deal of pain. And don't worry about the squad car parked up the street from your house. When I don't show up for work later today, someone will eventually pick it up."

Dick pleaded with his friend, "Please don't get out of the car, John! They'll kill you too."

John gazed deep into Dick's eyes. "I wouldn't recommend driving straight home. You may want to park your car far from your residence." Reitz gulped hard, hearing their voices at fever pitch now. It was now or never. "God's grace and peace be with you."

Officer John Reitz got out of the vehicle and opened the rear door for Isaac. Easily 50 pounds overweight, the stocky man swung his cane wildly at Isaac's chasers, but in his declining condition, he had no chance of overpowering these men, when he could barely raise his fists in combat, let alone anything else. But it was enough for Isaac to make his getaway...

When the first knife entered John's rib section, the pain was excruciating. As the two men took turns viciously stabbing him to death, he thought to himself, *Guess I really am brave after all*...

220

Officer John Reitz, 38-year veteran of the New York City police department, fell to the street face first with a hard thump. The last words out of his mouth before his head was severed from his body were, "I'm coming, Valerie! See you soon, my love. You too, son…"

Isaac dove into the backseat and glanced out the window of this stranger's car, sickened by what he had just witnessed, especially knowing that it should have been him instead. He started bawling his eyes out

He glanced over at the driver, who was paralyzed with fear. "Who are you guys?" he asked, gasping for each breath.

"Later, Isaac," Dick said, ever so fearfully.

"You're right! Let's get out of here, before they kill us too!"

Dick put the car in drive and sped off, knocking one man to the ground. Watching him rolling on the asphalt, he shouted, "I've just committed a hit and run! What should I do?"

"Keep driving," pleaded Isaac, "If not, they'll kill us too! Believe me, I know…"

Dick silently prayed they wouldn't follow them home in another car. *I'm a criminal now, just like my son!*

Ninety minutes later, after driving up and down a few passable streets, Dick was finally convinced no one was following them. He parked his car a few blocks away from his house, silently wondering if it would be the last time that he would ever drive it.

He grabbed Amos' Sat-phone and Officer Reitz's pain killers for Isaac.

When they reached his block, Dick pointed toward his house. "That's my house over there. Once I'm inside, make your move. The door will be unlocked for you."

Isaac nodded that he understood.

Dick hurried in silence, looking over his shoulder with every step he took, until he reached his residence. His legs were so wobbly, he was mildly surprised he had made it.

221

45

WHEN ISAAC ARRIVED A few minutes later, Dick was waiting at the front door with a dish towel full of ice for his injuries. His hands shook so much, he nearly dropped it when handing it to Isaac.

Isaac's hands shook just as badly. "Did that just happen?"

Dick glanced up and down the block, fully expecting the police to arrive any minute now to arrest him, for the hit-and-run incident from which he'd just fled. He knew he didn't kill the man, but fleeing the scene of an accident was a serious crime.

At least it used to be. Who knew anymore? He brushed off a shiver. "This is for your pain. Have a seat. I'll be right back with water."

Isaac took a few deep breaths. "Thanks. I appreciate it."

Dick returned from the kitchen with two glasses of filtered water. Isaac popped the Percocet in his mouth and swallowed it with one large gulp. "Who are you, and who were the two men who were just killed?"

Dick sighed. "I'm Brian Mulrooney's father. Do you know him?"

"Yeah. Had it not been for him, my wife might not be alive now. You know how hated she was in this city. It seemed everyone wanted her head on a platter. I'm convinced that had she gone to prison, one of her cellmates might have killed her before she could ever be released."

Not knowing what to say in reply, Dick sighed somberly. "The reason we were outside your apartment in the first place, was because of the first man who gave his life for you. I didn't know him all that well. In fact, we just met yesterday. All I can tell you is he's a former Muslim from Africa."

Isaac cleaned more blood off his face with the towel. "I'm failing to connect the dots. What does all this have to do with me?"

"Believe it or not, Amos had dreams about you. That's why he called Tamika asking about you. He's part of the Christian group our wives are involved with." Dick shook his head sadly. "Least he used to be…"

Isaac couldn't conceal the shock on his face. "Tamika's a Christian? Never thought I'd see the day! Her mother, Ruth, was a God-fearing woman in every sense of the word, but Tamika was agnostic at best."

Dick's mouth felt dry like cotton. He took a few gulps of water. "She's been living in hiding ever since my son helped her escape the city."

Isaac gulped hard. "You know where she is?"

"Not exactly. All I know for sure is it's somewhere in Pennsylvania."

Isaac was trying hard to process it all. "Why would that man be having dreams about me. It's not like we knew each other…"

Dick shrugged his shoulders. "All I can say is their group is big on dreams." He paused, then added, "The second man who died for us in true heroic fashion, I might add, was a New York City cop."

Isaac's mind was blown. "Seriously? I can't believe what I'm hearing."

Dick cupped his head with both hands, as if trying to keep his throbbing brain from escaping his head. "When the three of us left here earlier today, I never thought I'd be the only one coming back. They willingly died for us…"

The gravity of the situation fully kicked in and both men started sobbing.

After a while, Isaac said, "In case you're wondering, the men outside my apartment building were leaders of the mosque I attended the past six years. When I told them I no longer identified as a Muslim, the very men who had aided me in my conversion, and had affectionately embraced me as one of their own accused me of being an enemy of Islam.

"With more than a billion Muslims now gone at the hands of Salvador Romanero, they viewed my willingness to leave the only true faith as the ultimate betrayal on my part, something that was worthy of death."

Dick was blown away by how much it lined up with Amos' dream, vague as it had been. *So, that's why they rely on dreams so much…*

Isaac sighed. "It started three months ago. I glanced out my apartment window one morning to find some of my former Muslim brethren loitering outside, waiting for me to leave so they could exact revenge on me.

"When they kept coming back, day after day, I was so frightened I left in the middle of the night fearing for my life, without a penny to my name. The only place I could think to go was the restaurant I'd worked at before the quake all but leveled it. I set up a cot I found in the storage closet in the kitchen and have been sleeping in the walk-in freezer ever since…"

Dick shot Isaac a sideways look. "Walk-in freezer?"

Isaac nodded. "If you saw the building, you'd understand why. If it shifts again, even slightly, the rest of the roof will come crashing down on me. I jimmied a few small branches in the door hinge, so the freezer door wouldn't suddenly close and trap me inside.

"Another fear I had by staying there—aside from being bitten by the dozens of rats and mice sharing the space with me—was that the dishwasher

223

who had first introduced me to the Quran would find me there and report his discovery to everyone else."

Isaac shook his head in disbelief. "Never thought I'd be there this long. The reason I went back home earlier was I was out of food, clean clothes, toothpaste, deodorant, and a few other things. I left the few spare dollars I kept in my sock drawer behind. What would be the point? It's not like I can spend it, right?"

Dick nodded agreement.

"I knew they'd be there when I went there this morning, they always are, but I was so hungry I hid behind a burned-out vehicle across the street, waiting for someone to leave the building before making my move.

"When I saw Terrel, my friend on the fifth floor leaving, I knew I only had a few seconds before the door closed. Had that happened, I would've had to use my key, and it would be game over for me. I ran across the street as fast as I could and made it in the nick of time.

"They would have killed me on the way in, but I caught them off guard. Now that they had me cornered, I knew they'd be ready for me on the way out. Had I managed to escape, I would have gone back to the restaurant until I could plan my next move, whatever that would be..."

Isaac sighed. "In truth, I wasn't afraid of being killed by them. What pushed me into hiding had more to do with my wish to reconcile with Tamika, after having dreams about her. It's like we both wanted to reconcile, but something kept keeping us apart, like some invisible force."

Dick couldn't believe what he was hearing, especially since he was having similar dreams himself about Sarah. "After so much time apart, do you think reconciliation is possible?" He asked the question more to himself than to his new houseguest.

Isaac shrugged his shoulder. "I hope so, because that's the only thing keeping me alive." Sadness covered his face. "It's funny, the men I thought always had my back were the ones who tried killing me. Yet, two complete strangers representing a religion I hated just gave their lives for mine..."

Isaac wiped a tear from his eye with the dish towel. "After what just happened, my soul's even more on fire for the Truth." *Tamika's a Christian?*

The way Isaac said it touched Dick deeply in his soul as well. It forced him to question his own assurance. It didn't take long to conclude that it was shaky at best. He never would have offered his life for anyone other than Sarah. He barely knew Amos or John, yet they did just that for him.

Dick sniffled. "Before coming to your rescue, Amos told me to read John fifteen-thirteen when I got home. As a lifelong Catholic, you'd think I'd know what it said without having to reference it in the Bible..."

"Let's see what it says." Isaac opened the Bible that Amos had brought with him, then fingered back and forth a few pages until he found it. His eyes grew wide as he read it aloud. "'Greater love has no one than this, that a person will lay down his life for his friends.'"

Isaac lowered his head and slowly shook it side to side in awe. "That's what Amos said to me before pointing me in your direction..."

Dick started weeping again. It was too much to take in all at once.

It was at that precise moment that God changed their hearts, and everything made perfect sense to them. They wanted to know more of what God's Word taught.

Dick wiped his eyes with the sleeve of his sweater. "Okay, so what do we do now?"

Isaac eyeballed Dick. "Let's get on our knees seeking the One True God, through Christ Jesus."

After crying out to the King of majesty on their knees in the living room, and openly confessing their sins, and trusting in Christ alone for their salvation, both men felt a heavy weight lifted off their shoulders.

Even in a house that was barely standing, everything felt different. But in a good way for a change.

Dick had a sudden urge to read the Word of God from beginning to end, in search of answers to his many soul-stirring questions. He grabbed the Book off the table that was left behind by the man who just became a martyr for them both. "Shall we?"

Isaac nodded yes. "Since Amos quoted from the Gospel of John, let's start there. I'll read the first chapter, and you can read the second, and on and on, okay?"

Dick shot him a thumb's up. Suddenly, the Book he had once shredded to bits and pieces in front of his wife and late daughter, was the most precious commodity on earth to him. It was an amazing transformation.

In the process of receiving Christ as Lord and Savior, a bond was formed between Dick and Isaac that Brian and Tamika had enjoyed all this time.

Now, much like the two of them, they were plotting for the best way to escape their captors. "We need to get out of New York City," Isaac said, looking at the front door. "I don't think they'll ever stop looking for me!"

"I agree on both counts..." Dick grabbed Amos' Sat-phone off the coffee table and powered it on. "Time to start making calls..."

Dick searched the contact list. Seeing Charles C., he could only assume it was Charles Calloway. He kept scrolling looking for Sarah's name. He saw Clayton Holmes and Travis Hartings.

Dick had no clue who these people were. He scrolled down a little further and saw Brian M. stored on the phone. He had no doubt it was his son's phone number. Tempted as he was to call him to share the good news of his conversion, he wasn't ready yet.

He didn't see Sarah's name or number stored on it, but now that he believed like she did, he sensed he was getting closer to not only finding his wife, but also being reconciled to her.

For whatever reason, when he found Doctor Singh, someone he didn't know, he decided to take his chances with her.

A female voice said, "Hi Amos. I was just praying for you. How'd it go? Did you find Isaac?" It was Tamika. Meera was taking a much-needed break, after performing five deliveries into the wee hours of the morning.

Tamika was also sleep deprived, but knowing Amos was in New York for the sole purpose of meeting her husband, she was determined not to sleep until she heard from him.

Dick asked, "Doctor Singh?"

It wasn't Amos. Tamika's heart raced, as her mind ran wild playing out many different scenarios, none of them good.

Once again, the voice on the other end of the phone asked, "Hello? Is this Doctor Singh?"

Tamika went into defensive mode. "Who is this, and how did you get this number?" she demanded to know, feeling a full panic attack brewing beneath the surface.

"This is Dick Mulrooney," he said, not knowing it was her. "Not sure if you know who I am..."

Tamika gulped hard. *Brian's father?* Another dose of fear shot through the safe house number one head nurse. "Where's brother Amos? And why do you have his phone? He left a message earlier saying he was in trouble and that it didn't look good. Is he okay?"

Isaac had his ear as close to the phone as he could get. His heart raced just hearing her voice, which hadn't changed a bit. "Tamika?"

Dick shot a flustered look at Isaac. "Are you sure it's her?" he whispered, cupping the phone.

Tamika's shock knew no bounds. "Isaac?"

226

"It's me, baby…" With his two front teeth missing, Isaac slurred and whistled at times when he spoke.

Baby? Not knowing what had happened in her hometown, not to mention Isaac's spiritual condition, Tamika remained on edge. "What's going on, Isaac? Where's Amos?"

Isaac sighed deeply. "I'm afraid he didn't make it. Neither did Officer Reitz."

"What do you mean they didn't make it? Make what?"

"They're dead, Tamika," Isaac said softly. "They died rescuing us…"

Tamika gasped, then burst out in tears. "What happened to them?"

Isaac became quite animated, "You should have seen it, baby. The men I embraced as my brothers the past six years would have surely killed me, had it not been for Amos and Officer Reitz. They even had knives in their hands to finish me off."

Isaac lowered his head and started weeping. After a long pause, he said, "I can't believe two strangers willingly died for me today…My former brothers in Islam might die *with* me, but never *for* me…"

Tamika lost all strength and lowered herself onto a chair. Tears streamed out of her eyes one after the next, quickly falling to the floor.

Isaac said, "I know you're sad hearing this news, Tamika, but I want you to know their deaths weren't in vain…"

Tamika flinched. "Why do you say that?" She still couldn't fathom how she was talking to Isaac on the phone. She didn't know how to feel.

Isaac wiped tears from his eyes, and sniffled. "I know you're a Christian. I just found out today. I want you to know that I believe like you now. Brian's father and I both received Christ as Lord and Savior, and are forever indebted to them for what they did for us…"

Dick added, "Both were great men. I can't wait to meet John and Amos in Heaven someday, to personally thank them for saving my life until I was saved for real."

"You and me both!" Isaac said in reply, before asking Tamika, "Wanna know the last thing Amos said to me before they stabbed him to death?"

Tamika looked up at the ceiling and took a few deep breaths. Now that he was dead, she felt guilty. *He went there for me!* "Tell me…," came the reply, amid soft sniffling.

"He told me to go back to my wife and have a child. It blew my mind."

Tamika gasped loudly. It was too much to take in all at once. With a deep sadness in her voice, she said, "I gotta go and share the news about Amos with everyone else. Take care of yourself, Isaac."

Before the call ended, Dick said, "By the way, Officer Reitz told me to tell you he couldn't find Nila Mirano..."

"I see. Thank you, Mr. Mulrooney for the update."

At that, the call ended. The two men stared at each other, both silently wondering what might become of it all.

Isaac was the first to break the silence. "Would it be okay if I sleep here tonight?"

"Consider it your home Isaac for as long as you need it..."

Isaac became teary-eyed again. "How can I ever thank you for all you're doing for me?"

"Help me get Sarah back..."

"Let's both get our wives back!"

"Sounds good to me. I'm exhausted, Isaac. Hope you don't mind if I take a nap."

"Not at all. Could use a nap myself."

"I'm afraid the only place I can offer you is the living room floor. The entire upstairs was destroyed in the quake. But at least we can share the space heater."

"Beats sleeping in a walk-in freezer any day!"

"Well then, please make yourself at home, my friend. My house is your house."

Isaac gazed at Dick sincerely. "Thank you, kind sir..."

Dick winced at Isaac's words. *Kind sir? I've been nothing like that to my family since the Rapture!* He kept this dreadful thought to himself.

Both men went to sleep having dreams about their wives. Only this time, the invisible force accompanying their dreams was gone!

46

LATER THAT NIGHT

SINCE THERE HAD NEVER been a time in recorded history when women were faced with such a daunting challenge, female residents at all *ETSM* safe houses often gathered for fellowship and Bible study.

These meetings were special because they were able to comfort one another. Mothers who attended left their kids at home or at the nursery, for this much-needed time of fellowship during these difficult times. The chief topic of discussion was marriage and motherhood.

On some levels, they more resembled grief-counseling sessions than Bible studies. The women enjoyed this cherished time with their sisters in Christ as much as they valued sleep.

But this gathering at safe house number one was unscheduled. Even more telling, neither Jacquelyn nor Sarah knew anything about it.

Brian was mindful that Amos had had dreams about Isaac. But with so much turmoil in his family—raising a special needs child, his worsening lungs, to name a few—he had purposely been kept out of the loop ever since.

With so many dreams going in so many different directions, it was hard to keep up with it all, let alone know where it might all lead.

It was best to keep everything hush-hush for now, until things came more into focus, in God's perfect timing, whenever that would be.

After everything Sarah had already endured, why get her hopes up for nothing? They feared one more negative blow might cause her to completely shut down.

Tamika was the last to arrive. She still had a noticeable limp from her past injuries. But what stood out most was the deep sadness on her face.

Lila Choharjo asked, "Are you okay, Tamika?"

Tamika lowered her head, amid soft sniffling. "We lost one of our leaders today…"

Meera was mindful of what happened in New York City. She offered to tell them, but Tamika was insistent that she be the one to do it.

Lila's first thought was either Clayton or Travis. "Oh, my. Who?"

"Amos Nyarwarta."

229

Mary Johnson covered her mouth with her right hand, and stiffened in her chair. "The man from Africa?"

"I'm afraid so..." Tamika lowered her head. "He was killed doing something for me...Sort of, anyway..."

Seeing the confusion on everyone's faces, she backtracked, "Let me start at the beginning. Amos called me a few months ago, saying he had dreams about Isaac..."

Marta Gonzales' eyes grew wide with surprise. "As in your husband?" Her husband, Julio, was watching their daughter, Ruth, and grandson, so his wife and daughter could attend this emergency meeting of sorts.

Tamika nodded sadly. "I know, strange, right? Especially since they didn't even know each other. Anyway, in his dream, Isaac was in great danger; after telling his Muslim brothers he was leaving the faith. Amos said he felt led to travel to New York City, to hopefully rescue him." Tamika sniffled. "Turns out his dream materialized earlier today..."

Marta said, "Wait, I'm confused. How did Amos even know where to find Isaac?" She understood the supernatural dreams part—all of them did— but his exact location?

Tamika wiped her eyes with the sleeve of her jacket. "Isaac came to my apartment the day after the Rapture. After hearing on the radio that all young children were gone, he stopped by to check on us."

It didn't escape anyone's notice that she didn't say, "ex-husband" like all other times. "Believe me when I say, after so many years of no contact, he was the last person I expected to see through the peephole that day.

"Before he left, he slipped his restaurant business card under the door with his address written on the back of it. I already knew where he worked, but I had no clue where he lived until then."

Tamika rubbed her left wrist that was badly injured in the quake. Even after all this time, she still felt pain. "Anyway, as Amos kept dreaming about Isaac, I was having dreams about a New York City cop I met the day after the Rapture, when I went to file a missing person's report for my two boys.

"Long story short, Officer Reitz joined brother Amos earlier today to rescue Isaac. Brian's father was also there. Both men gave their lives so Dick and Isaac could escape capture."

There were more astonished looks on all their faces.

Lila asked, "If brother Amos was killed, how'd you find out?"

"I spoke to Isaac earlier on the phone. Actually, Brian's father called Meera's phone using Amos' Sat-phone. I just happened to answer it."

Marta Gonzales' eyes grew wide with surprise. "What?"

Lila looked at Tamika. "So, what happened next?"

"Amos secretly came here two nights ago. After spending the night, Brian's father fetched him and drove him to Manhattan..."

Mary Johnson became fearful. "Dick Mulrooney came to our safe house?"

"Of course not! Joaquim dropped Amos off on 202, posing as a hitchhiker. Since Dick isn't saved, we knew we were taking a huge risk by involving him in this secret mission. If Sarah wasn't living with us, we would have never considered using him.

"But none of this happened until after Dick went to the police precinct on my behalf, looking for Officer Reitz. When he wasn't detained, we knew he could be a valuable tool for us, but only because he wants his wife back."

Mary stretched her arms behind her back. "There's no way Braxton would have let us proceed, if he was still alive."

Tamika shook her head. "True that! Anyway, Amos spent the night at Dick's residence, before they went in search of Isaac earlier today..."

Lila's mouth was agape. "How remarkable! Reminds me of my former industry. What a movie it would make!"

Marta nodded agreement.

Tamika paused, then added, "I haven't told you the best part yet. Potentially, anyway..."

"Tell us!" Mary Johnson shouted.

"Isaac and Dick both claim to be saved!"

"There goes the Hollywood ending!" Lila said, trying to joke.

Marta asked, "Did they have dreams?"

Tamika pursed her lips. "Only about us reconciling. Crazily enough, I started having the same dream myself the night before Amos arrived. And like Isaac, something invisible kept blocking it from happening."

Tamika didn't need to elaborate on this point. Everyone in the room knew it was God's Holy Spirit.

Mary Johnson's face became crumpled in a shroud of concern. "The last thing I'd ever want is to rob you of the joy you have, Tamika, but how can you know for sure they're saved for real if they didn't have dreams?'"

Tamika sighed. "I don't. Part of me wishes I never knew about this secret mission, just like Brian's mother. I'd hate to travel down this path with Isaac, and get my hopes up, only to have it end in disaster again."

Meera sat to the left of Tamika, and rubbed her right shoulder. "The last thing Amos told me was that he wanted to win souls in New York. Perhaps

231

God answered his prayer in this regard. Mine too. I prayed all day and night that God would use our brother mightily on his trip."

Silence filled the cottage as everyone considered what Meera had said. Lila was the first to speak. "Okay, let's say Isaac's truly been saved. Are you willing to take him back?"

Tamika looked up at the ceiling. "I don't know how to answer that, Lila, I really don't. Had you asked me that question a week ago, you already know what my answer would be. Now, after finally working him out of my heart, I'm having dreams about reconciling with him?"

Tamika shook her head at the notion. "After all this time, lonely as I feel most nights, I couldn't imagine sharing a bed with him again. Too many years have passed for me and Isaac to simply pick up the pieces of our broken lives, as if nothing happened, and do our best to move on..."

Meera nodded agreement. "That's understandable, Tamika, but we're living in unprecedented times. The clock keeps ticking. The fact that we're so blessed to have Jakob residing here with us, all but guarantees that any child born here will be protected and will live to see Christ's return."

Tamika grimaced. "I know, you're right..."

Meera rubbed Tamika's shoulder again. "God knows how much you want to get pregnant again. I still see it in your eyes every time we deliver babies together. Perhaps one of the reasons Amos dreamt about Isaac is that God's opening this door for you..."

Tamika was dumbfounded by her words. "I don't know, Meera. I'm frightened just thinking about it."

Mary Johnson interjected, "How about you, Doctor? Have you considered getting pregnant?"

Meera sighed, then shook her head. "Prior to the Rapture, it was always my dream to be a wife and mother someday. But as the only doctor here, I can't be bogged down with a pregnancy of my own. Besides, in case you've forgotten, I'm in my fifties now. And even if I was willing to try, I don't have a husband, let alone the prospect of one."

The way she said it made everyone laugh.

Tamika folded her arms over her chest. "That's another thing. I'd like to think I'm also needed here."

Meera felt bad for her comment. "You're extremely valuable, Tamika. I don't know what I'd do without you. But as a still-married woman, if you have the chance to bring a child into the world, who will get to live in the Millennial period, it must supersede your own personal aspirations.

232

"If you do reconcile with Isaac and decide to get pregnant, don't think for a second that I'll let you off the hook! As badly needed as you are now, it will only increase in time, as more expectant mothers are moved onto the property."

Mary Johnson gulped back fear, and squirmed in her seat. "Not to be the Debbie Downer in the group, Tamika, but with so many dreams going in so many different directions, how can you be sure Satan isn't using your dreams to deceive you, which could potentially endanger us all?"

Tamika sighed. "All I can say is he sounded like a genuine believer on the phone. They both did, in fact. I know they've been through a traumatic experience, and that it could be fueled by loneliness and his need for reconciliation. That's why I won't get too excited, in case it's all an act..."

Mary sighed relief.

As the meeting came to a close, they prayed for all pregnant mothers on the planet, and for all women considering getting pregnant—saved and unsaved—but especially for those who truly belonged to God.

After that, they laid hands on Tamika and prayed that God would give her a supernatural clarity of thinking, one way or the other.

But mostly they prayed that Dick's and Isaac's conversions were genuine. If not, there could be no happy reunion between them...

47

SALVADOR ROMANERO DAY EVE

SALVADOR ROMANERO HAD A very bad feeling inside. On the eve of the second anniversary of his new celebrated birthday, he dreaded to think what the two lunatics at the Wailing Wall would unleash this time, to make him look foolish again the way they did on Universal Children's Day, and the Day of New Beginnings.

What had further exasperated the situation was knowing his leadership team, not to mention the rest of the world, were having similar thoughts.

How could they not? When the *Miracle Maker* first decreed Universal Children's Day, the Day of New Beginnings, and Salvador Romanero Day as international holidays—they were full of turmoil.

Universal Children's Day ended with countless millions of casualties. The Day of New Beginnings celebration had led to global humiliation for Romanero, when Yogesh Patel rebuked him in his very presence.

On the second anniversary of Universal Children's Day, earlier in the year, the decree made by the Two Witnesses that no rain would fall on Israel was extended to the entire planet. Not a drop of rain had fallen anywhere since, causing severe drought conditions everywhere.

Then on the second anniversary of the Day of New Beginnings, God's Two Lampstands called down a plague from Heaven. A meteor that was nearing the earth's atmosphere disintegrated at the last possible moment before impact could be made. But millions of bits of toxic pieces of it was scattered all over the globe, killing many, destroying homes, hospitals, transportation vehicles, and everything else in their destructive pathways.

Worse, one-third of the rivers and springs that had been struck were poisoned by them. Much like the oceans after the first meteor strike, they were turned blood red and made bitter, causing many who drank from them to die. This had since led to even more widespread sickness and disease…

At this point, having endured so much mind-bending tragedy, not even the top minds on the planet dared try explaining the remarkable powers that those Two Men exuded, in mass quantities.

Still mindful of the mighty miracles that Romanero had performed at the outset, which earned him the name *Miracle Maker*, it now seemed that those Two Men harnessed even greater powers than their leader did.

How could they think otherwise when Salvador the Great hadn't performed a single miracle in more than three years, yet it seemed they had the power to strike the earth with every kind of plague, as often as they wanted to, with remarkable clarity?

It didn't take a rocket scientist to conclude that the powers they had at their full disposal could no longer be chalked up as mere coincidences.

Another thing that couldn't be denied was that while the Two Men in Jerusalem were obviously judging everyone on the planet, these latest plagues had been directed mostly at their so-called leader.

The fact that they were sent on the first two holidays that Romanero himself had spoken into existence, was all the argument they needed.

One story that had received zero press coverage was, in addition to the plagues God's Two Lampstands had sent on Universal Children's Day and the Day of New Beginnings, they also sent a plague of frogs to New Babylon on both of those days.

Frogs blanketed the entire city! Most notably, Romanero's triangular-shaped palace was completely surrounded by these unclean amphibians.

The tens of thousands of construction workers who had been sent to New Babylon, to replace the tens of thousands who had perished in the quake, were knee deep in frogs, in various locations throughout the city! It took three days to remove them in both instances.

All had been warned by their bosses to keep their mouths shut or suffer the consequences. No one had to ask what that meant.

Jurgen Staat and Li Ping were both in New Babylon during the global quake. They were also there both times the plague of frogs were sent there. The former secretaries-general to NATO and the UN couldn't fathom how Romanero kept allowing the two lunatics at the Wailing Wall, to humiliate him the way they did on his three international holidays?

What sense did that make? The only logical answer was that he had no power over them…

They weren't the only two individuals thinking these debilitating thoughts. There were many others. Romanero could see it on the faces of everyone on his leadership team. Their eyes pleaded with him, "Why don't you do something?" It was almost treasonous!

As it was, many world leaders were still enraged with him for sparing Israel as their countries still suffered greatly.

Mindful of what everyone was thinking, on the eve of Salvador Romanero Day, everyone fearfully braced themselves for *Round Three*.

Much like how Adam and Eve had disobeyed God in the Garden of Eden, for the first time since being chosen by Satan to be his human agent, the *Miracle Maker* was about to willfully disobey his master.

Romanero knew the day would eventually come when he would finally silence the Two Ancients for good. But until then, he would remain powerless at their hands.

All efforts to silence them thus far had been fruitless. Anyone who tried killing them experienced their own deaths by incineration. Even the special forces teams that Romanero had sent in the middle of the night, on several occasions, to deal with them had all met their demise that way.

After constant pleadings with Satan to grant him that same power, his requests always went unanswered. Despite that the devil had warned his underling not to mess with them, that it wasn't time yet—fueled by rage and jealousy—Romanero couldn't overcome those human feelings.

It was time to take things into his own hands, and try to outwit those two deranged psychos and make *them* look foolish for a change. He just hoped his master would overlook this transgression and grant him the power to let it happen.

The problem for him was, whereas God the Father, Jesus the Christ and the Holy Spirit were one and the same, always working together in perfect accord, in no way were Salvador Romanero and the Pope co-equal to Satan.

There was no true love among them, no loyalty, no synergy…It was pure disloyalty, deception, and chaos.

Since Romanero had nothing else promising to share with his followers, instead of addressing them on television, he sent a brief, two sentence statement to be published by the global media, declaring in his own name that rain would fall in the Holy Land on his birthday.

The instant it was published, the world watched and waited expectantly to see what would happen.

The press in Jerusalem peppered Romanero's two staunch enemies at the Wailing Wall all day with questions regarding their leader's bold prediction.

But God's Two Olive Trees remained silent, like two lions who had just finished eating and were now at rest.

On December 25th, at 11:59 p.m., to the amazement of most, the Two Men at the Wailing Wall hadn't called down fire from Heaven, or sent another plague of frogs to Romanero's palace—which had just recently been completed in time for his new birthday celebration. Nor did they poison more lakes and rivers.

236

Fully expecting something to happen at their hands, mouths, rather it never came. They decided to let the Antichrist of the Bible call down judgment on himself, by using his own words against him.

When the clock struck midnight, not only did no rain fall in Israel, not a single drop had registered on any doppler radar screen anywhere in the world.

In that regard, nothing had changed...

At 12:01 a.m., on December 26th, many Jews who had waited patiently for the skies to pour rain down on them, cried out in the streets of Jerusalem. "Where's the rain, Mister Miracle Maker?! We're sick and tired of your empty promises!"

Instead of providing everyone with a viable explanation, or better yet, apologizing for falsely prophesying to the world, Romanero was so humiliated that he ordered everyone out of his palace, claiming that he wanted to be left alone. This caused even more people—Jew and Gentile alike—to further question his leadership capabilities.

Many Jews who had wholeheartedly believed that Salvador the Great had spared their nation from the global quake, were forced to rethink things through. After racking their brains senseless, they kept coming to the same conclusion. Perhaps the Two Men at the Wailing Wall that they had mocked and ridiculed all along, were responsible for sparing their country after all?

Did this mean the man they had signed a peace treaty with couldn't control natural disasters, as they had originally believed he could?

Until now, with exception to the plagues Yahweh's Two Witnesses had sent on the days of Romanero's new global holidays, many of his followers didn't blame their leader for the many other catastrophes bombarding the planet on which he was in charge.

But after standing toe to toe with the Two Ancients, by trying to reverse the drought that everyone knew they had called down from Heaven, when no rain fell anywhere on the planet, what were they to think?

It was becoming more and more apparent to most that the Two Servants of the Most High God of Israel had the ability to outmaneuver and out-prophesy the *Miracle Maker* seemingly in every instance.

This debilitating thinking wasn't without foundation. First, it was the great quake which cost many of Romanero's followers incalculable losses, not to mention that even his own palace had been destroyed.

Then, there were the many plagues being prophesied by the Two Witnesses, only to have the 144,000 rogue preachers double-down the

237

instant their prophecies came to pass, as coming from the very Book the so-called *Man of Peace* had recently outlawed as being evil.

The more these stories spread, the more it caused many who had staunchly supported him since the very beginning to wonder if the Two Men in Jerusalem were the true miracle makers, and not Salvador Romanero?

As if the blinders had suddenly been removed, many were coming to realize since Romanero's dizzying rise to power that there had been no growth to speak of, only regression—destruction would be a better description—which explained his reasoning for always addressing the world in private of late.

If he really was who he proclaimed to be, why were the two troublemakers still drawing breath in their lungs?

It was a question for which they still had no logical answer…

But one thing was certain, it was a dreadful time for everyone living on Planet Earth. Just knowing those Two Men were responsible for it, caused the unconverted to hate them even more!

48

THREE WEEKS BEFORE THE 5-MONTH PLAGUE

AFTER OPENING THE MEETING in prayer, Meera Singh said, "I'm sure you're as excited as I am to have our dear brother, Charles Calloway, here with us tonight..."

Calloway waved at everyone and smiled wearily. It was evident to him that they were as glad, relieved even, to see him again as he was to see them.

Ideally, the newly reconstructed sanctuary would have been the better place to have this meeting. But since the Mulrooneys were still being kept out of the loop, this place was the better choice of the two, as it was farther away from the main house. Tom Dunleavey remained at home with them, just in case.

"Charles is here to share potentially promising news with us. But I'll let him tell you all about it."

Charles smiled wearily again. The high energy he was known for was gone. He looked older, and more frail. "It's so nice to see you all again. It's been a while. Like Meera said, I've come bearing potentially promising news. But first, there's something I need to ask you all..."

Leticia Guzman, the first to give birth at safe house number one when she was only 12, became fidgety in her chair. "What is it?"

"Some of you are aware that the safe house I was staying at was destroyed in the global quake. It ended up burning to the ground. I was the only survivor..." Calloway became teary-eyed. "Miss Evelyn and Deacon Stone both perished in the quake, along with Santana Jiles..."

Mary Johnson gasped, and glanced over at Joaquim and Leticia. Miss Evelyn and Deacon Stone were part of their "trio" wedding last Christmas Eve. "They were such a lovely couple..." she said sadly.

"Yes, they were," Calloway said somberly. "I still miss them every day. Dylan and Purnima, the waiter and hotel desk clerk I met before joining the ETSM, also perished that day. They just got married a few weeks before the quake, and were working on getting pregnant. I believe they were already dead before the house caught on fire. At least I hope they were."

239

Calloway's voice trailed off… "If I wasn't out reading a blistering email from the owner of the company I represented before the Rapture, chances are good I'd be a goner too. It happened so quickly."

Tamika lowered her head and shook it sadly…

Charles sighed. "I was resigned to remain there with them until the very end, but now that they're gone, my question to you all is would you mind if I moved here with y'all?"

Tamika looked up at Charles with tears in her eyes. "Really?"

Charles grinned at her. "Since I already know so many of you, I figured this would be the best place for me. That is, if y'all will have me…"

Everyone clapped their hands enthusiastically, thrilled at the prospect of having him living among them. Tamika was the most excited. Since the Rapture, Brian and Charles had become her two human anchors.

Her beloved brothers in Christ couldn't stop what was coming, but just having them both with her comforted her greatly.

Charles looked at Meera, who smiled in anticipation. "Now for the potentially good news. Once communications were restored after the global quake, we started receiving numerous emails from members who left spouses to join the ETSM.

"Much like Isaac and Tamika, they all claimed to have had similar dreams about wanting to reconcile, yet there was some invisible force driving them apart. Now, I know what you're thinking, how can we know for sure who are truly saved or not?"

Heads nodded up and down, as Tamika squirmed nervously on her chair, wondering where Charles was going with all this.

"I'm sure you're all mindful of the plague of locusts God's about to unleash upon the world, to torment unbelievers for five months. Revelation nine, verse four states, and I quote, 'They were told not to harm the grass of the earth or any plant or tree, but only those people who did not have the seal of God on their foreheads.'"

Charles interjected, "Truth be told, Clayton wasn't sure if it referred only to the one hundred and forty four thousand, or to all true believers? That's why he seldom spoke about it. After everything we've already endured, he didn't want to give any of us false hope."

Everyone stiffened in their seats, greatly anticipating what would come out of his mouth next.

Calloway clasped his hands together. "After expressing his doubt to Moishe, I rejoice in saying that he confirmed to Clayton and Travis that we would also be spared the unspeakable torment unbelievers will suffer for five months."

There were many loud sighs and gasps, as relief flooded their souls.

"Ephesians one, thirteen states, 'And you also were included in Christ when you heard the message of truth, the gospel of your salvation. When you believed, you were marked in him with a seal, the promised Holy Spirit.'

"In short," Calloway added, "what this means is that these demonic beings won't have permission to touch anyone sealed by the blood of Jesus! Don't you just love our compassionate Savior?"

"Yes, I do!" Lila shouted, victoriously. Having been delivered from her wretched sinful past, she couldn't keep her declarations quiet.

Charles smiled at her, then continued, "Since we can now know for sure we won't be afflicted by the demons that will be loosed from the bottomless pit, praise God, these five-months will give us ample time to replenish our dwindling supplies. More importantly, we'll use that time to know for sure who is saved and who isn't."

Titus' ears perked up even more. "How, Charles?"

Calloway glanced over at Dr. Singh. "I'll let Meera explain that part to you."

Meera cleared her throat. "With so many spouses now having similar dreams, like Isaac and Brian's father, the only way we'll be able to know for sure whether they're truly saved or not, will be to examine them from head to toe, looking for welts and sting marks.

"I'm told they will be nasty-looking!" the *ETSM* doctor added, with a cringe. "If no marks or abrasions are found on their bodies, this will grant them another examination after the five-month period has passed. If they are still welt and abrasion free at that time, that's when we can know for sure that they are saved for real, and can be reunited with their loved ones."

"Amen!" shouted Donald Johnson, seated next to his wife, gently bouncing their son, Luke, on his lap to keep him occupied.

Julio Gonzalez stiffened in his chair. "What if marks or abrasions are found on them, Doctor?"

"Good question, Julio. Anyone found with sting marks on their bodies will be told to leave. No exceptions…"

Everyone nodded agreement. It was for their own safety.

Tamika twitched, then asked, "Will it be possible for someone to fail the first exam, then get saved for real later?"

241

Calloway answered the question for Meera. "Up until the Mark of the Beast has been received, there's still hope for anyone to genuinely repent and get saved. After that time, that window will close...Even praying for them will be a waste of time," he added somberly.

"But for us, as the unconverted world suffers unspeakable agony from these locusts, we can be out and about without ever being stung. We need to start planning now, so we can take full advantage of the situation once it happens."

Lila shifted her weight on the bench she was seated on. "Okay, so where do we begin?"

Meera nodded thoughtfully at her. "We're still praying and fasting about it and ironing out the details. Doctor Lee Kim is already setting up temporary VPNs for spouses having dreams to reach out to their unsaved spouses.

"The VPN he created for Hana Patel to chat with Brian and Jacquelyn went smoothly from start to finish, with no eavesdroppers. We must keep praying that it stays that way."

"How will these people get to us?" asked Tamika.

"Good question. In short, it'll be up to them to travel to the locations we send them to, before being blindfolded and taken to the examination rooms, which will be set up at some of the locations where we used to have items shipped to us, before the global quake.

"Once these temporary locations are operational, our hope is that hundreds will be examined every day at each place, by residents who've been trained on what spots or abrasions to look for on the body, as *ETSM* doctors remain at safe houses treating their many patients."

Meera paused, then added, "Only those claiming to be born again, like Isaac and Brian's father, will be invited to these places. After filling out questionnaires explaining how Christ saved them, they'll have to wait in observation rooms for an hour or so, as we go over their answers, plus monitor them to see if they show any discomforting signs of being stung by the locusts. If they were, they won't be able to hide it for long."

Tamika's face lit up. She had difficulty reaching for her next breath.

"Once the world discovers Christians are immune to those monsters, we must assume that many will do or say anything to stop the pain and mental torture, including falsely professing faith in Christ. Which is why I must reiterate that anyone found writhing in agony will be taken back to their vehicles without ever being examined. No exceptions!"

Calloway opined, "Imagine being tormented for five months by these hordes of demonic beings. The pain will be so terrible they'll want to die, but God won't allow it. No one among the unconverted will be spared this torment, including Romanero himself.

"With that in mind, once the examination begins, if questions ever arise regarding a particular spot or abrasion on the body, the person being examined will then be taken to a real *ETSM* nurse or doctor for a closer look."

Charles let his eyes settle on Tamika. "So, as you can see, this is promising news for many of us..."

Now that Tamika could see light at the end of the tunnel regarding the possibly of reconciling with Isaac, she lowered her head and wept softly.

Before everyone dispersed, Meera cautioned everyone, "We've successfully kept the Mulrooneys out of it all this time. I know it will be difficult, especially since we're all stuck here on the same property, but if Sarah's husband turns out to be a true Christ follower, what a blessed reunion it'll be! So let's not ruin it."

At that, they held hands as Charles led them all in prayer, thus bringing the meeting to a close...

49

THREE WEEKS LATER

THE INSTANT THESE DEMONIC beings were released from the pits, like heat-seeking missiles locked onto their targets, they wasted no time invading the planet, feasting on a smorgasbord of humanity, but only those not belonging to the Most High God.

This supernatural, demonic army from the abyss was so numerous, the clouds they created further darkened the skies in so many places. But these weren't ordinary rain-producing clouds—although that hadn't happened in many months—these clouds produced human blood!

They moved rapidly like flocks of angry demons, fully determined to wreak havoc on all for whom they had permission to attack, by way of gouging the unconverted with their tails.

Having been bound in darkness for so long, now that they had been freed from that wretched place, they had five months to torment multitudes, by inflicting unbearable pain on all who didn't belong to the Most High God.

Just one glance was all it took for everyone to run for cover indoors. Some were so overcome by fear they fainted trying to make it to safety, only to come to writhing in severe pain with welts and abrasions all over their bodies—some the size of golf balls.

Much to their dismay, even if their houses were still intact or had been repaired since the global quake and meteor strike, these demonic beings had little trouble getting inside those man-made structures...

Nothing could stop them from preying on all unconverted human flesh, not even brick and mortar. They would soon learn there was no safe place to hide! Anyone whose names weren't written in the Lamb's Book of Life would be tormented by them, some more than others.

What these beings had in common with locusts was their five-month life cycle. Only instead of feasting on crops, they feasted on humans!

Another area in which they differed was, whereas Proverbs 30:27 stated that locusts have no king, yet they advance together in ranks, these locust-like creatures were completely subjected to the commands of Satan.

He was their ruler, their king. The darkened skies and cold temperatures didn't affect them in the least.

These swarms of restless demons flitted this way and that, looking for humans to torture. Whenever one was located, they would eyeball that individual, up close and extremely personal, as if scanning their faces, awaiting permission from Satan himself whether to attack or flee.

For all who were stung by them, the pain was so intense that they wanted to die, just as the scripture had warned.

Even those who were saved and were being supernaturally protected from their aggressive advances, were terrified by their very presence. Being anywhere near them was the most frightening encounter.

Countless multitudes prayed to God asking to be saved, but only from the torment, not from their sinful lifestyles.

In short, with their hearts far away from the One who made them, God wasn't listening to their emotional pleas for help.

Whereas Jesus was the exact representation of the invisible God, in human form, the faces on these hideous beings resembled Satan's representative in human form, Salvador Romanero.

TWO WEEKS INTO THEIR global campaign, after being stung three times inside his new palace, unable to heal himself, the *Miracle Maker* was forced underground for the full five months, to hopefully prevent his followers from seeing the otherworldly welts and abrasions on his body.

The pain he suffered was excruciating!

The same was true with the Pope, and everyone else on his leadership team. By being enemies of the Creator of the universe, not even they could hide from these monstrous beings. All retreated underground as well.

What made Romanero's pain even more unbearable was when word got out on global news stations everywhere, that the vermin being detained in his newly constructed death camps were all being spared the same pain and anguish everyone else was forced to suffer, himself included!

No one was surprised in the least that the Two Witnesses and the 144,000 young Jewish males were being supernaturally protected from their stings. But once the story broke that all who trusted in Jesus were apparently unaffected as well, it caused hatred toward Christians to further intensify.

Until now, with Christ followers living in hiding, the Global Community had no way of knowing they were being protected from the locusts.

Initially, when prison guards working at Romanero's internment camps started complaining that they were being stung, but their captives weren't, most chalked it up as coincidental. But after hearing that the same thing was happening at all prisons detaining Christians, it became apparent that even they were immune to their stings.

As workers suffered unceasing torment from these beings, the vermin under their control weren't being attacked by the locusts.

Even wearing full protective gear, the demonic creatures easily tore through each layer, stinging the guards, causing them unspeakable anguish.

Some guards, after being stung numerous times, tried electrocuting themselves by grabbing hold of the electrical fences caging them in.

But God wouldn't let them die…

They became so infuriated by this that they took out their frustrations on their detainees by beating them senseless.

Some were so badly injured that they had to be dragged back inside to their wooden beds, with no mattresses on them, but without a single sting mark anywhere on their bodies…

Ever since Ajit Laghari was beheaded in one of his death camps, with a smile on his face, no less, those places had brought more grief to the *Miracle Maker* than joy, because it always made him question the level of loyalty of his many followers, including his top leaders.

The one thought that tortured him more than anything else was, even after losing all worldly possessions and being tortured daily for their faith, Christ followers were still willing to die for their King.

What added insult to injury, was when he received word that Hana Patel had left her new life to follow Jesus. The first words out of his mouth were, "After everything I did for her, she converts to Christianity?!"

Romanero was equally incensed that Yasamin Dabiri had also betrayed him, by choosing Jesus over him, especially knowing the ultimate connection between the two women—their late husbands' faith in Christ.

He couldn't accept how both had willingly abandoned the good life he had blessed them with, to worship the God of their dead husbands!

What made it worse was that the whole world knew about it. It made him look ridiculous, in that every promise of protection he had made to the two women wasn't enough to earn their unconditional loyalty. *They no longer deserve to live!*

This latest incident gave him another mountain of reasons to question the loyalty of his many followers.

For the first time since rising to power, he knew he needed to do something huge to reinstate the faith of the masses.

But what? He was still awaiting confirmation from below…

Romanero stared at his image in a floor to ceiling mirror. "Jesus hasn't lost any of His followers, yet I can't keep mine!" He hurled the half full glass of a vegetable smoothie at the mirror, shattering it where the image of his face was. "They will not get away with it!" he hissed.

It was becoming more and more apparent that the only chance Salvador the Great had of raising up an entire generation of individuals, who would believe every word he spoke and trust in him as king of kings and lord of lords, would be to start at the beginning of human life, namely the children.

Instead of trying to reprogram those who didn't agree with everything he said, he was willing to part way with them, by way of guillotine, if need be, then focus his full attention on a future generation of true worshipers...

AS THE *ETSM* USED this time to replenish their dwindling stocks, and relocate children to the 1000 locations at which the 144,000 were residing, God's sealed servants were also sending people their way, to include expectant mothers of special needs children.

Many pregnant women who were diagnosed in utero as having children with various mental and/or physical disabilities, started having dreams that Romanero would order their child killed, once it was born, which led many to the places at which the 144,000 were preaching.

Seeing how they were being supernaturally protected by their God, many flocked to these remarkable men in droves, to listen to everything they had to say.

Once true conversion took place, knowing their children would ultimately be silenced in Romanero's care, they were given directions to the closest remote locations to be checked for GPS locators in their bodies.

If one was found, they were sent to other remote locations—namely in pop-up tents—to have them removed from their bodies. This way, once the enemy tracked their last transmissions, they would be long gone before anyone showed up to arrest them.

Everyone that the 144,000 sent to *ETSM* safe houses were told to repeat the words, 'Keep fighting the Good fight. Pray for me as I pray for you. Yahweh is with us.'" The fact that they would say "Yahweh" instead of "God" would signal to the guards who had sent them their way.

That would be all the vetting that *ETSM* guards would do on them.

Whether they were sent to *ETSM* safehouses, or to any other safe havens on the planet, since God's sealed servants had sent them there, all were warmly welcomed...

247

With Bibles outlawed and all things Christian removed from libraries, schools, universities, and bookstores, and scrubbed from the Internet, Yahweh was using His beloved servants to open the spiritual eyes and ears of many who were raised in churches, synagogues, mosques, and temples, but had never been saved.

Until now, that is…People from all nations, tribes, and tongues were listening to the Gospel message being preached by them, and being saved by it, before being sent to various safehouses globally of Yahweh's choosing.

Suddenly, in the midst of endless tragedy and despair, the blind could see and the deaf could hear!

It was a miraculous transformation to behold…

50

TWO MONTHS INTO THE 5-MONTH PLAGUE

ISAAC MOSELEY ACCOMPANIED DICK Mulrooney on this, his third trip to Southeastern Pennsylvania since the global quake. The only thing they knew for certain was that they were being summoned to meet with someone from the organization that their wives belonged to. Nothing more.

Both men knew the potential dangers they might encounter driving there, but if it ultimately brought them back to the women they loved, they were more than willing to take the risk. Thankfully, they arrived without incident.

Tony Pearsall met the two at the appointed meeting place. Joaquim scanned Dick's car for hidden tracking devices, then parked it behind the building, quickly covering it with a tarp.

Once the two men were seated in the back of the cargo van, Pearsall blindfolded them both, then left for the next location less than a mile away, which was one of the places they had packages shipped to before the quake, roughly four miles away from safe house number one.

Even before the blindfold was removed, Dick sensed it wasn't the same location he was taken to last time. For one thing, this place, while musty, smelled nothing like a farm. And it was much quieter.

After filling out questionnaires and waiting for an hour in a makeshift observation room, Dick was led by hand, to another drafty room, as Isaac remained behind. Joaquim Guzman helped lower him into a chair.

Normally, with so many patients to deal with at safe house number one, Meera wouldn't have time to leave the premises. But because she was so emotionally involved, she wanted to be the one to examine Dick and Isaac. It was the least she could do for Tamika and Sarah, even if Sarah still had no clue about what was going on.

Tamika remained at the safe house. If Meera found welts, rashes, or any otherworldly abrasions on Isaac's body, she didn't want to be there. If his conversion wasn't real, it would be too difficult to see him again, only to know they would be forever separated.

When the blindfold was removed, the woman standing before Dick was someone he did not know. He rubbed his fingers through his hair. "Who are you and where am I?"

"My name is Doctor Singh. You recently called my phone."

Dick's eyes narrowed. "Are you my wife's doctor?"

"Sorry, but that's all I can tell you for now." In a professional tone, she explained, "The reason you're here today is so I can examine you to see if you have sting marks on your body, from the locusts which have invaded the planet. Did you know this was all prophesied in the Bible?"

Dick nodded at her. "Been reading about it with Isaac. It's so confusing to the both of us. Most of it sounds metaphorical to me..."

Meera nodded agreement. "So, you know that according to the Book of Revelation, those hideous creatures will torment all who don't believe in God for five-months. But those of us who are truly saved are immune to their stings. We'll soon be nearing the midway point."

Dr. Singh eyeballed her patient. "It's with that in mind that I need to ask, were you stung by them at any point during the past two and a half months? It's vitally important that you're honest with me..."

Dick shrugged his shoulders. "No. Unless it happened in my sleep..."

Meera half-smiled relief. "I assure you, if you were stung by them, even once, you'd know it, whether you were awake or sleeping. What about Isaac?"

"If he was, he never told me. We see them in the house on occasion. They fly from room to room before hovering over us for a few frightening seconds, as if trying to read our thoughts or something, before eventually leaving the house. This may sound strange to you, Doctor, but their faces sort of resemble Salvador Romanero's. It's freaky."

"Doesn't sound strange at all," she said. "I agree with you. We see them on our properties all the time. They're hideous looking! Even though I'm immune to them, praise God, they still frighten me to no end!" Meera reached for his right arm and rolled up his sleeve as far as it would go. "May I?"

Dick nodded yes, already sensing she wouldn't be denied. The determination on her face indicated that much.

Since there was no electricity at this place, the *ETSM* doctor turned on the portable generator she brought with her, and powered on the MoleMap camera, which was used to detect skin cancer, and began her careful inspection for welts or sting marks on his right arm.

Meera confessed, "Truth be told, after seeing the images online from those who have been stung by them, I really don't need to use this device on you. Some of the welts I saw are the size of golf balls, tennis balls even! Never saw anything like it before. If you were stung by them, I assure you it would be impossible to cover it up with makeup."

Dick shot her a sideways look. "Why use it then?"

"I'd rather be safe than sorry, as the expression goes." Seeing nothing out of the ordinary, she examined his left arm, then sighed relief. "Now I need to examine the rest of your body."

"Is this necessary, Doctor? Like you said, if I was stung, I'd know it."

"Not only is it necessary, Mister Mulrooney, it's vital that I finish the examination." She paused, then added, "That's how we'll know for sure if your conversion was genuine or not. At least preliminarily..."

Dick flinched. "Preliminarily?"

Meera nodded. "Once the five-months have passed, you'll have to be examined again, just to make sure. But for now, I need to continue my examination. Here's a gown for you. You can change over there."

Dick went behind a dresser in the corner and disrobed, then put the blue and white gown on.

Doctor Singh took her time examining him. The longer it took, the more anxious her patient became. He found himself constantly squirming on the wooden picnic table that was brought inside. Perspiration formed on his palms and forehead.

After a careful and thorough examination from head to toe, Meera removed her eyewear. "So far, so good," she said, with a sigh of relief, reaching for her clipboard. "You can get dressed now."

"So, what happens next, Doctor?"

Meera was taking notes and answered his question without looking up at him. "After I finish examining Isaac, Tony will take the two of you back to your vehicle. Sorry you had to drive so far for such a quick exam, but I would suggest you go straight back home and hunker down until this judgment passes. At that time, you will be invited back."

Dick's eyes pleaded with her that he was truly saved.

Meera wanted to hug the man. "I'm not saying I don't believe you, Mister Mulrooney, only God knows the heart. But none of our residents anywhere in the world has been stung by them. If someone ever was, we'd be faced with a whole new set of problems."

251

"There's too much at stake to take shortcuts. Once you've been reexamined after the five months have passed, that's when we'll know for sure. That's all we can do for now. Please try to understand my position."

"I understand, Doctor." Dick sighed. "Does Sarah know I'm here?"

"Not yet," came the reply evenly, "but hopefully soon, right?"

Dick nodded yes. "Shall I tell Isaac you're ready for him now?"

"Please do. Thanks."

When Isaac entered the room, Meera Singh introduced herself, then handed him a gown to change into before examining him.

Both rejoiced when he, too, had passed the first examination.

Before leaving, Meera prayed for their safe passage home. "Lord willing, I'll see you both three months from now…Until then, God's grace, peace and protection be multiplied to you both."

"You too, Doctor," they said in unison, as Tony Pearsall blindfolded them before taking back to Dick's car.

Isaac said on the way out the door, "Tell Tamika I love and miss her!"

Meera shot him a comforting smile. "I'll be sure to do that, Isaac…"

As the two men drove back to New York, Meera went back to safe house number one to share the good news with Tamika.

The head nurse was so nervous she couldn't even look Meera in the eye. "Well?"

"We're halfway there!" Meera said with a slight shrug of the shoulder.

Tamika tipped her eyes up. "Really?"

Meera nodded at her.

Tamika looked skyward. "Thank you, Lord!"

"Amen!" Meera replied, ever so cautiously. "But we're not there yet."

"I know, you're right." She paused, then asked, "How did Isaac look?"

Meera stretched her arms above her head. "Well, he's a little worn out like the rest of us. He lost his two front teeth trying to escape his captors, on the day Amos rescued him. Other than that, I'd say he looks good. Oh, and the long beard you spoke of was shaved off." She gazed into Tamika's eyes. "He told me to tell you he loves and misses you."

Tamika's forehead furrowed. "Really? He said that?"

Meera smiled wearily, then nodded yes.

Tamika placed her hands on her hips, to hopefully stop them from shaking so much. "So, what now?"

"They're on their way back to New York until the five-month period passes, so they can be examined again. I must say, I have a good feeling about them. They feel like true believers. I hated to have to send them away, but I'm just following the rules."

Tamika nodded that she understood completely, which she did. "It's already been six years. I can wait another three months."

"Well said, Tamika. Now, let's get back to work. Shall we?"

51

ONE MONTH LATER

CLAYTON HOLMES' SAT-PHONE rang. It was Jefferson Danforth. "Good afternoon, sir! What can I do for you?"

"Hi Clayton. I've been praying about something ever since the quake, which may require your involvement."

"What is it, sir?" Holmes asked.

"I'm going to ask Amy to marry me."

Clayton paused. "Seriously?" The fact that the two had spent so much time together, he wasn't overly surprised to hear this.

Jefferson said, "Yes. I think she'll feel a little more secure if we share the same bed as husband and wife. I won't deny I feel guilty about having feelings for someone else when I'm still mourning Melissa's death. But I feel she needs me, and I need her."

"That's understandable, sir. Since your wife's gone, you're free to remarry with God's blessing. Question is, are your thoughts based on feelings of loneliness, or do you truly love her?"

Jefferson hesitated for a few seconds. "I love her, Clayton…"

"So, when would you like to be married?"

"As soon as possible," came the reply nervously.

"Don't you think you should propose to her first?"

"Yeah, that might be a good idea," he said, with a anxious chuckle.

Jefferson sat next to his former White House chef on the subterranean living room couch. "I need to ask you something."

Amy braced herself, already expecting more tragic news. "What is it?"

Jefferson searched her eyes then froze. In his time as President of what used to be the most powerful country on earth, he had made numerous decisions which had affected millions of citizens, either positively or negatively. He agonized over each decision. Yet, he couldn't remember his stomach feeling so twisted like now.

Finally, with Clayton listening, he said, "Will you marry me?"

Amy's eyes widened. She gasped for air. "Seriously?"

"Yes, but only if you love me too."

Tears filled Amy Wong's eyes. "I confess that I fell in love with you the day you dropped to your knees at Camp David, in praise of God. It touched

254

me so deeply. But since you were still married at that time, I kept my feelings for you buried deep inside. You know how fond I was of the First Lady. I'm still mourning her death."

Jefferson nodded thoughtfully. "That makes two of us. But we're living in unprecedented times. I don't want to go through it alone. I know you don't either. This isn't an emotional plea out of loneliness or desperation. My feelings for you are true. I love you, Amy. If you feel the same way about me, I would be honored if you became my wife...

"Besides, Agent Sullivan will be leaving for Washington D.C. in the morning. That would leave just you and me at this place. Since we're not married, we shouldn't be here alone. So, what do you say?"

Amy Wong covered her face with her hands and burst out in tears It was a good cry for a change. She nodded her head up and down.

"So, that's a yes?"

"Yes, Jefferson, I'll marry you!"

"If you're willing, Clayton can marry us right now..."

Amy gasped. "Look at me, I'm a mess!"

"No one can see you. It's just us. Besides, I think you look beautiful."

Clayton heard what Amy had said. "Normally, I like seeing the couples I marry, but in this case, I'll make an exception, meaning no phone cam."

Amy shook her head in disbelief. "Okay, let's do it then."

"I'm almost embarrassed to have to ask these questions, but before you can exchange vows, I need to read the standard declaration we've put together for anyone seeking to get married on our properties."

"By all means, Clayton," Danforth said.

Holmes cleared his throat. "Even in a world under constant siege, as Christians, marriage is still a lifelong commitment. Divorce can never be an option. God is still in control and His commands need to be honored and obeyed. Do you both agree?"

Jefferson and Amy stared at each other. "We do..."

Clayton took his time going down the list of additional requirements.

Hundreds of unceremonious weddings were being performed for *ETSM* members globally. Only none were registered in the states and countries in which they were being performed.

But all were recorded in Heaven...

Holmes and Hartings always stressed to their younger couples, especially, that they shouldn't consider getting married for the sole purpose of having sex.

255

Even before the Rapture, the vast majority of humanity rolled their eyes at such a ridiculous notion. One man, one woman only? No same sex? And they had to be married before sharing the same bed? What a joke!

That mindset was outdated, mean-spirited, and had no place in this advanced and enlightened culture. What sounded utterly ridiculous to the unconverted world, before the disappearances, had become infinitely more ridiculous since, with leaders the likes of the Pope himself urging females to get pregnant, regardless of age or relationship status.

But for those who were saved, it made perfect sense…

Clayton finished reading it. "Do the two of you agree to everything set forth in this declaration?"

Jefferson and Amy locked eyes. "We do…"

"Great! Let's proceed then…" After a quick marriage ceremony, the couple said their "I do's".

Clayton declared, "It is with great joy that I now pronounce you husband and wife! Mister President, you may kiss the bride…"

After kissing Amy rather impressively, she wiped tears from her eyes. "Thanks for marrying us, Clayton…"

"I should be thanking you! How many people can say they got to officiate the wedding of a former sitting President!"

"Not that it will get you too far…" Jefferson joked.

"Still, I consider it an honor and great privilege, sir! Now that you're officially married, where will you go for your honeymoon?" Clayton asked jokingly, trying to make light of the situation.

"Funny you should ask, Clayton. We're thinking about Chadds Ford, Pennsylvania."

Clayton laughed, before realizing he wasn't joking. "Seriously, as in safehouse number one?"

"Yes. Amy's tired of living underground. She's going stir crazy here. After everything that's already happened, knowing what's still coming, she wants to be surrounded by as many Christ followers as possible beforehand." Jefferson paused. "Since we're still within the five-month window, wouldn't this be the best time for us to travel?"

"Most definitely!" Clayton answered. "Even though it's clear across the country, we'll find a way to make it happen. But it may take a while…"

"Understood," Jefferson said, already expecting to hear that.

"Thanks, Clayton," Amy said, gratefully. "I don't know what we'd do without you or Travis."

"You're welcome, Mrs. Danforth. Hope the two of you enjoy your first day together as husband and wife."

"We will, thanks…" Amy said, ending the call. *Mrs. Danforth, wow!*

Jefferson couldn't ignore the glow on his wife's face. "Be right back, my love…"

Amy smiled at her husband then gulped at the notion of being his wife. Her last relationship had ended 17 years ago. Now here she was married to the former President of the United States of America, without having even five minutes to mull it over in her mind! On many levels, her new life was even more surreal than her husband's. "Where you going, my dear?"

"To prepare our special wedding feast."

Amy shot her husband a sideways look. "Wedding feast?"

Jefferson kissed his new bride again on the lips. "Be right back."

Two years ago, Jefferson Danforth was the most powerful man on the planet. Now he was living in hiding, married to his former chef, making peanut butter and jelly sandwiches for their wedding feast. *Go figure!*

Jefferson rejoined his wife, blessed the food, then asked God to bless their remaining time together on earth as husband and wife, however short it might be. "Hope you like your meal. I haven't made PB&Js in many decades."

Amy Danforth smiled cutely and took a bite of her sandwich. "M-m-m, yummy!" She took a sip of water. "I assure you, the last thing I ever thought when I woke today was that I'd be a married woman."

The way she said it made Jefferson laugh. He grew serious again. "Now for the big question…"

"Yes, my love?"

"Do you want children?" Before Amy could answer, he added, "This is your first marriage, so I'll leave the decision entirely up to you."

"Not for now," came the reply, without hesitation. "Besides, I'm already in my mid-forties. I feel I'm too old to give birth…"

Jefferson looked deep into her kind eyes, which now looked fearful at the thought of bringing a child into the world at this point in human history. "The reason I ask is with Jakob living there, any child we bring into the world will live to see Christ's return, even if we don't survive…"

Amy frowned. "I know. It's a wonderful promise to be sure. But everything's happening so quickly. I need a little time to let it all sink in. For now, I'm thrilled to be your wife and happy knowing that we will be

257

leaving this place soon. I'm tired of always feeling trapped underground. It will be nice to be surrounded by more of our brothers and sisters."

Amy kissed her husband on the forehead. "Who knows, perhaps after spending time with children again, God will change my thinking..."

"Like I said, I'll leave that decision to you..."

Amy paused to let her husband's words sink in. "Why don't we retire to our sleeping quarters, my love..."

"I thought you'd never ask..."

52

TWO WEEKS AFTER THE 5-MONTH PLAGUE ENDED

WHEN TONY PEARSALL AND Joaquim Guzman informed Tamika Moseley that they were leaving for New York City, she took a short break to pray for her two brothers in Christ.

This was the big day for Isaac and Tamika. It was equally huge for the Mulrooneys, even if they didn't know it yet, with exception to Dick.

Pearsall would be taking the same van that Braxton Rice had driven to New York, when he fetched Sarah Mulrooney and Mary Johnston—her name at the time—and brought them back to safe house number one, just days before America fell under attack more than two years ago.

Only the magnets on the side of the vehicle advertising a fictitious local charity last time, were replaced with magnets that read: *Tri-State Home Corpse Removal.*

In normal times, the full tank of gas would be more than enough for the round trip to New York City and back. But with many roads still under construction, they loaded a 36-gallon steel fuel tank full of gasoline into the back of the van, so they wouldn't have to stop to refuel along the way.

As much as they would have loved to bring one of their new electric cars, none were big enough to transport a casket or, in this case, a body bag. The one good thing about driving this older vehicle was that it had never had any sort of tracking devices on it.

When they arrived at the Mulrooney residence, two men entered the house to collect the body, dressed in work overalls and face masks.

A few moments later, three men came out, four including Brian's father, who was taken out of the house in a body bag.

A neighbor inquired, "Is that Dick Mulrooney?"

"I'm afraid so, ma'am..." Tony Pearsall said somberly through his facemask, hoping she didn't notice the extra person.

The woman lowered her head. She wasn't surprised to see activity at the Mulrooney household again. But like everyone else, she was still trying to come to grips with her own family tragedies. "Real shame what happened to them. They used to be the nicest family."

"I'm sure they were, ma'am..." Pearsall said, pretending not to know.

The woman grew silent, wondering who on the block would be the next to die. Not knowing what she was thinking, they paused so she could pay her final respects before placing the body bag in the back of the van.

Pearsall climbed behind the wheel and started the engine. Taking a moment to jot a few things down onto a pad of paper to make it look official, he drove off, thus commencing the arduous task of relocating Isaac Moseley and Dick Mulrooney to Southeastern Pennsylvania, but only if they were cleared by Meera Singh.

Dick was never afforded the opportunity to take one final look at the house where he and Sarah had become a family. He was perfectly okay with it. The thirty plus years of warm and endearing memories they had created there had been replaced with endless nightmares, suffocating all good memories, replacing them with doom and gloom.

They were the very last thoughts he wanted swimming through his mind, especially being stuffed inside a body bag.

Once they pulled off the block, Joaquim unzipped the bag. "Are you okay in there, Mister Mulrooney?"

Dick shot him a thumbs up gesture, then removed his oxygen mask.

Even though the global population had shrunken considerably, the recent volcanic eruptions and tsunamis had also shrunken the earth's landmass. With so many now flocking to areas they hoped would be safer places to live, some cities were becoming decently populated again.

Many of the major roadways in those areas were being reconstructed. Even so, it still took them five hours to arrive in Chadds Ford.

A mile away from the safe house, both men were blindfolded. The reason they were brought there, instead of to one of the local examination areas, was that Dr, Singh was overwhelmed with patients.

Mostly due to the colder temperatures, and frequent sun blockage, someone was always sick at safe house number one. The influenza bug kept circulating at all *ETSM* safehouses. Thankfully, the many plagues circling the globe, as a result of God's judgments, hadn't reached them yet. They kept praying around the clock that it would remain that way.

Meera knew she was breaking the rules, but her gut told her that after she examined the two men, they wouldn't be asked to leave.

Dick and Isaac were taken to two separate cottages and handed gowns to put on.

Tamika peeked in on Brian's father. "Hi Mister Mulrooney."

Even with shorter the hair, Dick knew who it was. Without a trace of anger or irritation in his voice, he said, "Nice to see you again, Tamika."

260

"You too…I'm here to check your vitals before Doctor Singh examines you." she said, looking increasingly anxious.

"Go right ahead," Dick said.

Tamika checked his blood pressure. "Today's the big day for you."

Dick sighed. "Finally, me and Isaac will be counted as equals among your group."

Tamika frowned. "It's not like that, Mister Mulrooney. We don't think we're better than anyone. We just need to be one hundred percent sure, that's all."

"I understand, Tamika. But me and Isaac know we're saved! Our faith keeps growing by leaps and bounds."

Soon we'll know too! Tamika became teary-eyed. "Your BP's a little high. Other than that, you seem fine. Meera will be with you shortly."

"Thanks, Nurse…"

"My pleasure…" Tamika left the room feeling even more confident that this would be the day she would reconcile with her husband. She was equally nervous. Her mind was trying to catch up to it all.

A few minutes later, Meera entered the small room.

Dick said, "Doctor Singh, what a surprise!"

Meera smiled, and tried joking with her patient, "I know you left your house in a body bag while still alive. Now it's time to see if you're spiritually dead or alive."

"Good one, Doc," came the reply, "but I already know the answer!"

Meera nodded hopefully. "Shall we?"

"By all means! I'm excited." Dick's voice sounded confident, which Meera took as a good sign.

After a careful and thorough examination, from head to toe, Meera removed her eyewear and shot Tamika a joyful glimpse.

She lowered her facemask and gazed deep into Dick's eyes. "You're one of God's all right. Welcome to the Family, my dear brother!"

Dick stuck his chest out. "Told you so! The day Amos and John died for us, was the day me and Isaac got saved!"

"Correction, only the blood of Jesus and His resurrection saved either of you! Us to, for that matter!"

Dick smiled gratefully. "I stand corrected. So, what happens next, Doc?"

The joy Dick saw on Meera's face was there just as much for Sarah as for her patient. "I'll need you to get dressed so I can blindfold you again."

261

Not again! "Then?" Dick's eyes pleaded with her for clarification.

Meera smiled. "The main reason you came to Pennsylvania in the first place—to see your wife again. Isn't that what you want?"

Tear's flooded Dick's eyes. He lowered his head. *It's really happening!* "Thank you, Lord!"

Meera's face became aglow. "In the meantime, let me be the first to welcome you to safe house number one."

Dick blinked hard. "Safe house what?"

Meera giggled under her breath. "I'll let your family explain it to you."

Meanwhile, Tamika grabbed Dr. Singh's Sat-phone and left the room to call Charles Calloway on his Sat-phone at the main house.

Charles was expecting her call. "Hope you're calling with good news."

Tamika smiled cautiously. "One down, one to go."

"Amen!" Charles shot a thumbs-up at Tom Dunleavey. Tears rushed to his eyes. "Brian and Jacquelyn are up in their room, so now would be a good time to bring him here."

"Perfect," said Tamika, suddenly energized. "I'll send him now."

"We'll be here waiting. Call me after Isaac's been examined."

"You know I will, Charles."

"I have a good feeling…"

A smile curled onto Tamika's lips. "Me too, Charles. I'll be in touch…"

As Joaquim Guzman walked a blindfolded Dick Mulrooney to the main residence, Charles went down to the basement and carefully arranged one chair on one side of the room and two others on the other side.

After a short five-minute walk, they reached the main residence.

Joaquim said, "Here we are."

Dick's breathing became more erratic knowing he was moments away from seeing Sarah again. Over the past six months, more times than not, he doubted it would ever happen.

Joaquim broke his train of thought. "Just to give you a head's up, we'll be climbing five steps before entering the house. Once we're inside, I'll lead you down to the basement. The stairs were damaged in the quake. But don't worry, I won't let go of your arm."

"Okay." The young man's voice comforted Dick. He had no idea it was the same voice that had barked out orders to him on the phone, on the day he met with Tom Dunleavey, not Sarah.

Joaquim led Dick through the living room past a smiling Tom Dunleavey and Charles Calloway, and was taken down a flight of rickety wooden steps, where the young man helped him get settled on a folding metal chair.

Tom went upstairs and lightly knocked on the door frame to Brian's and Jacquelyn's bedroom.

"Yes?" said Brian.

"It's Tom. Are you busy?"

"Jacquelyn's feeding the baby. Is everything okay?"

"I need you both to come downstairs when she's finished. It's important. If Sarah's awake, ask her to babysit for a few minutes…"

What in the world? "What is it, Tom?"

"You'll see. I'll be waiting downstairs…"

Brian scratched his head in confusion. "Be there as soon as we can…"

Tom went down to the living room. It felt good to be excited again. He rejoiced even more knowing he had a small part in it all. *Surely, this is why you kept me alive during the quake, Lord!*

Brian and Jacquelyn left the baby with Sarah and slowly descended the stairs leading to the living room. Both had suspicious expressions on their faces.

Tom and Charles were seated on the couch. One of its broken-off legs was replaced with three stacked *Yellow Pages* books that were left there by the previous owners, before the disappearances.

Jacquelyn shot them both curious looks. "What's going on, guys?"

Tom did all he could to not burst out in laughter or into tears of joy, whichever came first. If anyone needed something good to happen to them, it was this couple. "Can you join me down in the basement?"

Brian asked again, "What's going on you two?"

Jacquelyn was growing impatient. "Are you okay, Tom?"

Charles grinned. "I don't even know where to begin. Soon you'll know. For now, let's go downstairs. And please don't say a word…"

"What's down there, Tom?" Jacquelyn demanded to know.

"Let's just say your mind's about to be blown, but in a good way for a change, a very good way."

Jacquelyn looked at Brian again and shrugged her shoulders. Without saying another word, they followed Tom down to the basement…

53

DICK MULROONEY HEARD THE commotion upstairs, muffled as it was, followed by footsteps slowly descending the stairs.

Upon seeing her father-in-law, Jacquelyn covered her mouth with her right hand in shock, wondering if her eyes were playing tricks on her.

Dick heard a loud gasp followed by soft sniffling. He remained silent. His legs twitched nervously. After a while, he felt cold hands on the back of his head, untying the blindfold covering his eyes. *Sarah?*

Dick saw Brian seated on a wooden crate across from him, wearing a facemask. Instead of rage filling his face, he lost all strength. His shoulders slumped and he started weeping.

Brian wiped tears from his eyes. His father was the very last person he expected to see at this place. His two friends upstairs had a lot of explaining to do. But it could wait. The broken expression on his father's face told him he had crossed over from spiritual death to life.

Hallelujah! Brian was so overwhelmed he started trembling. "Nice to see you again, Dad."

Dick took a few seconds to collect himself, then got up out of his seat. Instead of strangling Brian, like he'd threatened to do more than once—he held his son in his arms as both men wept tears of joy.

After a while, Brian said to his father, "Remember Jacquelyn?"

Dick craned his neck back and saw his daughter-in-law. She looked nothing like she did on her wedding day. Then again, who did? "I hope you can forgive me for the way I acted at your wedding…"

"Think nothing of it, Mister Mulrooney. Or should I say, Grandpa?"

Dick's eyes widened. He took a few moments to process what he had just heard. "Really? I'm a grandfather?"

Brian nodded joyfully. "You have a beautiful granddaughter. Her name's Sarah Eleanor Mulrooney. She was born with Down Syndrome. Wait till you see her, Pop! She's the most amazing child!"

"Yes, she is!" Jacquelyn grimaced. "Yet had she been born in Romanero's care, she wouldn't be here now. Can you imagine that?"

Dick was confused. "I'm not sure I follow you, Jacquelyn…"

"One thing you'll never hear in the news is how Romanero's been murdering all special needs children. He claims they don't fit into the perfect utopia he's creating. He's nothing but a monster!"

Dick raised an eyebrow. Now that he had a special needs granddaughter of his own, it was cause for concern. "Are you certain about this?"

"Sadly, yes," said Jacquelyn. "Believe it or not, President Danforth is the one who informed us of it." Before Dick could inquire, Jacquelyn added, "Yes, he's still alive. In fact, he's a resident here."

Dick blinked hard, unable to keep up with it all. "Seriously?"

Brian said, "He joined us here a month ago with his new wife. Now that I assume you're here to stay, you'll meet him soon enough."

"What can I say? My mind is blown!"

Jacquelyn wiped a speck of dust from her left eye. "The best part about living here is that our precious daughter's perfectly safe, along with all the other special needs children," not knowing if her father-in-law knew about Jakob yet. If not, he would know soon enough.

"When Sarah was born, I often wondered if God would heal her when He returned, to begin His Millennial Kingdom. Truth be told, I like her just the way she is. I wouldn't want to change anything about her. She's the most amazing child. If I could have twenty like her, I would."

Dick closed his eyes and sighed deeply, regretfully. Clearly, Jacquelyn wasn't the monster he'd thought she was. He removed his eyeglasses and wiped them with a handkerchief. "Congratulations, to you both."

"Same to you, Pop!" said Brian glowingly.

Dick stared at his son the way he used to when he was a child. It was as if nothing bad had happened between them. "Is your mother here?"

Brian nodded yes. "We're in the basement of the house we live in."

Dick silently gasped. "Does she know I'm here?"

"No. Truth be told, we just found out ourselves, Dad. Apparently, we were being kept in the dark all this time. Which would explain the raw emotions. I never thought the day would come. When did you get saved?"

Dick grinned. "A little more than six months ago. I can't wait to tell you all about it. It's quite a story. But first I'd like to see your mother. It's been more than two years…"

Brian wiped his eyes with his shirt sleeve. "Sure. By all means! Once the initial shock wears off, she'll be thrilled to see you again." It dawned on Brian. "I have to ask, Dad, does your being here have anything to do with Tamika's dream?"

265

Dick nodded at his son. "In fact, her husband, Isaac, is being examined by Doctor Singh right now, looking for welts or sting marks from the locusts. Just like with me, she won't find anything on him. He's about to become the next resident. We both converted at the same time. He's become a good friend to me. Like I said, it's quite a story…"

Brian sighed more relief. "Can't wait to hear all about it!"

With so much tragedy, not to mention that he and Jacquelyn were so busy dealing with trying to help Hana Patel escape to safety, he had all but forgotten about the day Amos called him looking for Tamika, after having dreams about her husband. He could only praise God that it had led to Isaac's salvation, his father's too!

Jacquelyn wanted to ask her father-in-law a million questions, but the pain she saw in his eyes from missing Sarah so much was evident. She placed her right hand on his shoulder. "Shall we?"

Dick paused. "Wait, don't I need to be blindfolded again?"

Brian and Jacquelyn both cracked up. "Those days are over!"

"That's a relief!" Dick's trembling increased, knowing the moment was finally upon him. He gulped nervously, then nodded that he was ready to proceed.

Brian cautioned his father, "I must warn you, she's quite thin. And her hair's completely gray now."

Dick sighed. "Understood…" What else was there to say?

When they reached the living room, Charles and Tom were seated on the couch. "Good to see you again, Dick!" Tom said enthusiastically.

Dick wasn't the slightest bit surprised to see either man there. "You too, Father…I mean, Tom."

Tom smiled. *He really was paying attention last time!*

Charles said, "The reason you were asked to wear a facemask again was that we wanted the first person you saw to be a family member."

Just as Dick was about to reply, Jacquelyn said. "Shh! You don't want Sarah to hear your voice before you have the chance to surprise her."

Dick nodded agreement, then followed his son and daughter-in-law up the flight of stairs, stopping at the door leading to Sarah's bedroom. A brown curtain hung where the door used to be.

Brian whispered to his father, "She's in there with the baby. We'll leave you." Brian and Jacquelyn retreated to their room, and wasted no time pressing their ears up against the adjoining wall, hoping to hear something, anything...

With clammy hands and a sweaty forehead, Dick asked God to calm his nerves, then tapped lightly on the damaged door frame.

"Come in…" Sarah's voice was soft, tired, melancholy.

Dick pulled the curtain back and saw his wife sitting in a chair, slowly rocking back and forth, holding their granddaughter in her arms, open Bible on the table next to her, staring solemnly out the window.

He silently gasped; tears rushed to his eyes. Even being warned in advance, after seeing her every day for 36 years, and knowing her face perfectly well, she looked quite different to him.

He was taken aback at how ghastly thin and pale she was. And older. Much older, just as Brian had warned. With her dentures removed, her chin and cheeks looked like they had caved in on themselves. Since arriving at safe house number one, the only time Sarah wore her dentures was when she was eating. Other than that, she preferred being toothless.

Still, she was the most beautiful sight that Dick's eyes had seen in a very long time. Seeing her holding the baby forced his mind back to when Chelsea was born. Sarah often rocked her back and forth in the chair in their bedroom facing the window, much like now. He was certain that thought had crossed her mind a million times already.

When Dick remained silent—he couldn't speak, he didn't know where to begin—Sarah slowly craned her neck back, expecting to see one of the five people who visited her in her bedroom—Brian, Jacquelyn, Dr. Singh, Tamika, or Mary Johnson.

Sarah's eyes widened. She started gasping for air. If her arms weren't cradling the baby, they would be covering her mouth or clutching at her chest, hoping her heart wouldn't give out on her. She couldn't believe what her eyes were seeing. Who, rather!

"What are you doing here, Dick?" she asked in a panicked voice. "Where's Brian?" *Had they finally been linked to the Henriksens? Were local authorities down in the living room ready to take them all to prison?*

"It's okay, Sarah, relax," Dick said, softly, "I believe you now."

"What?" Sarah also had a new round of dreams that she and Dick were trying to reconcile, but some invisible force kept preventing it from happening. She knew it was the Holy Spirit. Even so, she never told Brian or Jacquelyn about it, because she thought Satan was messing with her mind, by attacking her dreams.

Besides, why would he want her back after the heartache she'd caused him, which ultimately led to the death of their precious daughter?

267

Dick slumped his shoulders. "Or should I say I believe like you now."

Sarah shot her husband a sideways look, then paused to let his words register. "Are you saying you're a born-again believer now?"

Dick hesitated, then stared down at his feet. "Yes."

Sarah burst out in tears. "Thank you, Jesus," she shouted, waking her granddaughter.

Dick stood motionless, not knowing what to do or say next.

As if on cue, Jacquelyn poked her head through the curtain. The look on her daughter-in-law's face told Sarah this was really happening. She smiled wearily and nodded her thanks. "Let me take Sarah off your hands."

Before leaving them, Jacquelyn paused so Dick could have a good look at his granddaughter. "Sarah, meet your grandfather."

With fresh tears in his eyes, Dick kissed baby Sarah on the forehead. "It's a pleasure meeting you, sweetheart! You're so beautiful! Now that I'm here to stay, I look forward to spending lots of time with you."

Sarah started sniffling. "Really? You're here to stay?"

Dick peered deep into her eyes. "Yes, my love."

Sarah very gingerly got up out of her chair. Eyes steadied on her husband every step of the way, she collapsed in his arms and buried her face in his chest, sobbing uncontrollably.

Even though she was much lighter than when she left him a little more than two years ago, Dick still struggled mightily to keep from toppling over. Thankfully, he was close enough to the door frame that it broke his fall. He hit it with an audible grunt. The pain in his right side from striking it had nothing to do with it. Sarah was back in his arms. That's all that mattered.

They clung to each other for dear life, amid loud sobbing.

Jacquelyn quietly left them alone, and rejoined Brian in their bedroom.

After a while, Sarah looked up at her husband through blurred vision from so many tears. Through soft sniffling, she said, "I prayed every day that we would be together again."

Dick kissed his wife on the forehead. "Well, after what can only be described as a remarkable turn of events, which I'm eager to tell you all about, I started having dreams that you were standing right in front of me. But try as I might, I couldn't touch you despite my best efforts. Something invisible kept blocking it..."

"What if I told you I had the same dream?"

"I'd say I believe you. The day I was saved, I had the very same dream again, only without the invisible force. It was a nice dream. We may not have long to live, but at least we're together again. Now that I got you back, I'll never let you out of my sight. Promise!"

Sarah shed a new batch of tears. After two years full of constant trials and tribulation, and longsuffering, now that Dick was back in her life, she felt like she had been born again all over again. He gave her the added strength she knew she would need to survive what was still headed their way.

Dick kissed his wife on the lips this time, trying to absorb it all. He went from being all alone in the world to suddenly having his wife and son back in his life. Even better, he was a grandfather now. He mumbled a soft, "Thank you, Lord" skyward.

Sarah heard it and smiled...

54

MEANWHILE, MEERA SINGH WIPED a new batch of tears from her eyes, after finding no marks or abrasions anywhere on Isaac's body.

When she shared the wonderful news with her head nurse, even though she was expecting it, Tamika burst out in tears of joy, as her arms flailed wildly in the air. Her body shook so much, she had difficulty walking to the examination room.

When Isaac and Tamika first locked eyes, there was a long pause, as they took a moment to adjust to how different they both looked.

The first thing Isaac noticed was that her hair was too short, her cheeks were too hollow, her body was too thin, and she had dark circles beneath her eyes. It looked like she hadn't had a good night's sleep in a very long time. *At least she still has her front teeth!*

"Wow! Look at you! A nurse!" he said, seeing her scrubs. "You did it! I'm so proud of you, baby."

Tamika beamed her reply. "It's good to see you again, Isaac."

The couple embraced and held each other for the longest time.

To watch it all unfolding after a six-year absence, caused Meera's heart to swell within her chest. "Thank you, Lord!" she said, under her breath, leaving them alone.

Isaac became teary-eyed. "I'm so sorry for the pain I caused you in the past. I should've never left you and the boys. It was wrong of me. I hope you can find it in your heart to forgive me."

Tamika looked down at her feet. She thought it amazing how after so many years of pain and heartache at his hands, it was like the embers still left from earlier fires were suddenly extinguished. God had just taken all those raw emotions away. "Of course, I forgive you, Isaac…"

"Thanks," he said, with a smile. Eyes surveying the room, he asked, "So, where exactly am I?"

The way he said it caused her to nearly burst out in laughter. "At a safe house in Chadds Ford, Pennsylvania."

"Is this where you've been living all this time?"

"Yes. Used to be quite the place when we first moved here. The quake did serious damage. We lost more than five hundred residents that night. Praise God, they're all with Jesus now."

"Amen to that!" Now that Isaac finally had eternal assurance, his reply was both heartfelt and joyous.

Tamika sighed. "I was in the cafeteria eating when it happened, and was thrown into the wall. Messed up my hip and my left wrist. Could've been a whole lot worse though. Brian's wife Jacquelyn went into labor during the quake. It was a crazy night."

"Sounds like it," said Isaac. "When was the last time you were back in New York?"

"Not since Brian and Charles helped me escape. I went to Michigan first, followed by Tennessee for a few days, before coming here. Been here ever since. This is home now. For how long, who knows…"

"Believe me, you wouldn't recognize the city. It's totally different. I think one out of every three buildings were destroyed. The United Nations building's gone. The NBC building at Rockefeller Plaza's gone. The Chrysler building's gone too. Even Madison Square Garden's gone."

Tamika could only shake her head. "Doesn't surprise me in the least. I think you and Dick got out of the city just in time. I wouldn't be surprised if God completely levels Manhattan next time…"

Isaac replied, "You're right about that! Just glad to be here with you now." A lone tear rode down his cheek. "Now that we're back together, I wanna be the husband to you that I never was before. You deserve it…"

Tamika smiled cutely. It was like music to her ears.

"Not gonna lie, ever since Amos told me to go back to my wife and have a child, before he died for me, I can't stop thinking about it. There's nothing I'd like more. How about you, Tamika?"

Tamika looked down at her feet again, and gulped at the thought. It's as if he was there at the Bible study the other night.

Isaac noticed her change of expression and backpedaled, "But I'm willing to take things as slowly as you want. What's most important is that we're together."

Finally, she said, "If it's God's will, nothing can stop it, right?"

"Amen to that!" A smile formed on Isaac's face that was warm and sincere. Even with his two front teeth missing, it still captivated her.

Tamika added, "But let's take it one day at a time. For now, I say we don't sleep together for a while? After so many years, it would feel like sleeping with a stranger. We'll both know when the time is right."

Isaac searched his wife's eyes. "I'm willing to wait as long as it takes. I want you to know I never had a girlfriend the entire time we were apart."

More tears rushed to Tamika's eyes. Try as she might, she couldn't believe it was happening. He was so much calmer now, and more sincere, no longer cocky or edgy. *Thank You, Lord!*

After a quick tour of the grounds, which included Isaac being introduced to Jefferson and Amy Danforth, the Moseleys joined the Mulrooneys, Meera Singh, Charles Calloway, and Tom Dunleavey in the main house living room.

After Dick had explained the bewildering turn of events which led to his being there, beginning with his meeting with Tom Dunleavey—a meeting Brian, Jacquelyn and Sarah knew nothing about—he further blew their minds by confessing that he had stayed with Megan McCallister and Rachel Stein on that trip.

Sarah raised an eyebrow. "Seriously?"

Dick reached for his wife's hand. "Remember when Megan found some of Brian's credit card statements in Renate's bedroom after her death, the ones she referenced on the suicide video?"

Sarah shook her head sadly at the memory. "How could I forget?"

Dick frowned. "Well, it eventually led them to Pennsylvania hoping to find Brian. They want blood! They spend much of their time driving by convenience stores and fast-food restaurants, hoping to see you so they can call the police. Now that Rachel gave birth, who knows if they still do that…"

Brian gulped hard. "Do they know where we are?"

"No, but they're determined to find you, son. In their minds, you are the vilest person on the planet." Dick paused. "Then again, I'm sure they hate me just as much now for not leaving the money I promised to give them."

Sarah shot Dick a sideways look. "Money?"

"Yeah. They had sponsors. Craig Rubin was one of them before his death. I think Brian's boss in Michigan also donated to the cause."

Brian flinched. "Susan Marlucci?"

Dick nodded at his son. "Before I came to Pennsylvania, I offered to give them five-hundred dollars. But when Tom told me during our meeting that being with them could endanger Sarah, I left the next morning without ever giving it to them. And I never contacted either of them again."

Tom looked at Brian sheepishly. "Sorry for not telling you about any of this, brother. I was ordered not to…"

Brian nodded that he understood. "So what happened next, Dad?"

After Dick brought everyone up to speed on his encounter with Amos Nyarwarta and John Reitz, Isaac then explained how the two men had died for him the day he and Dick both got saved.

Brian's eyes widened; they volleyed from Tom to Tamika then back to Tom. "Amos is dead? Why wasn't I told?"

Tamika said, "I'm sorry, Brian. The reason we didn't tell you or your mother was in case it turned out to be a dead end. You've all been through so much. We didn't want to give you false hope. So we decided to wait until we knew beyond a certainty they were saved. That was today..."

Sarah held her hands out. "Personally, I'm glad you didn't tell me. You're right, had I known up front only to have it end in failure, I don't think I would have been able to overcome it. Thanks for keeping me in the dark, Tamika."

"You're welcome, Sarah." Tamika then said to Brian. "I know you're upset, but just know they died as true heroes..."

Brian took a moment to think it all through, then let it go. At least they were together again. "What can I say, Dad, it's quite a story. Would you like to hear something even more bizarre?"

Dick said, "I'm not sure..." Then again, what could be more bizarre than having Jefferson Danforth living at their safe house? "Okay, what is it?"

Brian took a deep breath and exhaled. "We're the Henriksens."

Dick blinked hard a few times, as if he was hearing things. He folded his arms across his chest. "You're Brad and Joan Henriksen? Do you know there's an international manhunt going on for the both of you?"

Baby Sarah sat on Jacquelyn's lap, her eyes probing everywhere, drinking it all in, as only a child could. But the one thing she didn't observe was the astonished reaction on her grandfather's face. She was the only one.

Dick leaned forward on his chair. He still couldn't believe it. "I must say, of all the disparaging thoughts I had about you, prior to my conversion, this one never crossed my mind." He scratched his chin. "So, that was you mailing the package to baby Salvadora's father?"

Jacquelyn nodded at her father-in-law. "Guilty as charged! Only her name's Cristiana now. When Hana converted to Christianity, she changed her daughter's name. Yet another story you'll never hear about in the news. Truth be told, we've been trying to bring them here to Chadds Ford ever since. The meteor strike delayed everything. Who knows when it will happen now?"

273

Dick smacked his forehead with the palm of his head. *Chadds Ford?* "So, that's where we are!"

Brian smiled. "Welcome to safe house number one, Dad! And to think, I went from being a hotel manager to managing the first ETSM safe house on the planet. I'm moving up in the world..."

Dick snorted jokingly, sarcastically. "ETSM?"

Brian nodded. "You're now part of the End Times Salvation Movement. There are millions of us. For how much longer, it's hard to say. Sorry the house isn't up to par, but you should have seen it before the quake. It was like paradise."

Dick stretched his arms above his head. "Believe me, compared to our house in New York, it's still paradise. I'm amazed I was able to live there as long as I did after the quake."

"True that," said Isaac. "I lived there for three months. The man knows what he's saying! But since I got saved in that house, it'll always have a special place in my heart."

"That's one way to look at it, Isaac." Dick glanced at his wife. "Anyway, the state of New York can have it now for all I care. I'm home now..."

Tears filled Sarah's eyes. "Yes, you are!"

There was a moment of silence. Everyone knew the peace and calm they felt wouldn't last. They were a hunted people. And with Romanero about to greatly escalate his search for Christian dissidents, most of them wouldn't be alive when Christ returned.

For now, they were contented just being together again, and letting God slowly rebuild their broken relationships.

As Dick and Sarah prepared to sleep together for the first time in more than two years, the one thing the newly restored couple never discussed was Chelsea. It was too soon...

They would surely have that conversation, just not now. Not tonight, anyway. It had been too perfect of a day to delve into it now...

55

JERUSALEM, ISRAEL

SALVADOR ROMANERO CALLED A press conference from the Wailing Wall. The fact that he had actually left his sprawling palace for a change, instead of addressing his once adoring public from inside his palace walls, in New Babylon, in private—like he had done since making his false prediction that rain would fall on Israel—prompted the press to think he finally had good news to share with them for a change.

After suffering through constant doom and gloom for three and a half years, with crops continually failing, those who still thought he was worthy of following, even if just barely, hoped their leader finally had something good to share with them. Most had already grown skeptical of his promises.

How could they not? Romanero knew the unshakable faith that most had placed in him at the outset had been greatly tested. He also knew, as their leader, it would take something monumental on his behalf to recapture the trust and loyalty that had been lost among many of his followers.

After spending much time with the Master Deceiver and fasting and sincerely repenting before him for prematurely taking matters into his own hands, Romanero felt restored again. It was time to redirect the "Miracle Maker" spotlight back onto himself.

Finally, after putting up with the Two Witnesses for three and a half years, the moment had finally arrived. Hence, the press gathering…

With most of the ash cleared out of the earth's atmosphere, it was once again safe to fly. Romanero invited many of the world's elite to join him in Israel for the earth-shattering news…

After a long drought, the omniscient power he felt coursing through his body, touching him everywhere, was all the confirmation he needed that this would really happen. Everyone else felt it just as strongly as he did.

No one was more relieved by this than his top leadership team. Many whispered under their breath, "It's about time! Welcome back!"

Cameras steadied on him, Romanero began, "Greetings, global citizens! I come before you today bearing good news—sensational news in fact! For three and a half years, I've given the Two Men at the Wailing Wall in Jerusalem the freedom to speak all sorts of blasphemies against me. During

275

this time, many rumors had been falsely spread suggesting that I had no power to overcome them.

"It's no secret that they were being supernaturally protected by their God all this time. And their many predictions cannot be denied. I concede that the God they serve is quite powerful, even if His Lordship extends to one of the smallest nations ever to exist!

"But I must say, His track record with His chosen people has been anything but stellar! Think about it, while He has the power to perform mighty miracles, where have they led the Jews over the centuries? There can be no denying the dark and tumultuous history of the Jewish race.

"Even the Savior that Yahweh had promised, His own Son no less, was roundly rejected by His own chosen people, the Jews themselves!" Romanero shook his head in mock disgust and went on, "Not only did they reject Him as their Messiah, but they went so far as to crucify God's Son more than two-thousand years ago! If He was all-powerful, why couldn't He save His own Son from crucifixion?

"The obvious answer is that He wasn't the Messiah. So, where is this Messiah the God of Israel has been 'promising'", he said, using his fingers in quotations, "to His chosen people for thousands of years? Where has He been hiding all this time?"

Romanero gripped the lectern with both hands. "What the Jews want, need, and expect is both a global and military leader, someone who is capable of protecting them now and saving them on the other side. Only someone possessing those traits could ever be worthy of being called Israel's Savior.

"This false Messiah that many had foolishly worshiped for two thousand years, never commanded an army in the brief time He walked the planet. He never led the nation of Israel or had an opulent palace to call His own. He was a peasant, a nobody, a fraud! Which was why strong measures were taken last year to remove all things 'Jesus' from society.

"Yet, even after all this time, there are some on the planet who still choose to follow Him, if you can believe that, despite that faith in Him has been outlawed. It's mind-boggling, to say the least!

"The very myth of Jesus needs to remain buried in the past, so children, especially, if ever exposed to that dangerous mythical Figure in the future, would laugh at the notion of Him being Savior to anyone. If His own people rejected Him, why should anyone else accept Him?

"And speaking of those who still foolishly choose to follow Jesus, strong measures are being taken that will speed up the process of rooting out

276

and destroying all defiant Christ followers where they are hiding. But more on that at a later time...

"For now, I won't deny the past few years have been difficult for us. I'll even go so far to say there's never been a time quite like this. But when compared to six-thousand years of constant failure and doom and gloom, with Israel's God leading the way, I'm sure you'll agree the past three and a half years are like nothing.

"Despite the many setbacks, many definitive steps have been taken along the way to ensure the peace of Israel. What started with the peace treaty signing nearly three and a half years ago was only the beginning. The next big step was taken when I spared Israel from the global quake."

For the first time since they began tormenting him, Romanero glared at the Two Witnesses with a measure of hatred in his eyes that frightened his leaders, but he elicited no emotion whatsoever from the Two on the receiving end of it.

He addressed them directly, "The next big step will be taken today. The Two of you have profaned my name, and the name of Israel, for the very last time. It ends today! It's time to silence the both of you for good!"

Romanero craned his neck back and glanced at Israel's Prime Minister seated behind him. The expression on his face conveyed to the masses that he didn't know what to believe anymore. Who, rather. He couldn't help but think by coming into agreement with this man, had he made the mistake of a lifetime?

After a while, Romanero let his eyes settle back onto the camera. "Before I give the order, in the spirit of fairness and grace, I challenge the God of Israel with this question. Are You powerful enough to rescue Your two servants from death? If You truly are the Creator of the universe and everything in it, as they proclaim You to be—which You have never refuted—surely You can rescue them now and spare them both from imminent death!"

Romanero let his comment hang thick in the air for a few moments, then looked skyward, once again full of confidence. "And, so I ask, will You rescue them now, or will You leave them to die like when You let Your chosen people kill Your only begotten Son? Here's Your chance either to prove Your omniscience or disprove it once and for all."

The *Miracle Maker* paused and waited, as if deadlocked in a game of high stakes poker with the Creator of the universe.

277

The world watched and waited, with bated breath, to see which side was speaking truth and which side wasn't.

Finally, Romanero stared into the many cameras that were steadied on him. "That's what I thought. Once again, when it matters most, You cower! But fear not Israel!" he declared, his voice dripping with arrogance, "I *will* deliver on my promise of peace for all Israelis!"

That was the signal for the split screen to be shown on cell phones, and TV and computer screens, with Salvador the Great on one side and the Two Witnesses on the other. "And now, my beloved citizens," the *Miracle Maker* boldly declared, "let your eyes feast on this miraculous occasion!"

The whole world watched on pins and needles, as a firing squad consisting of 12 men and women appeared at the Wailing Wall, wearing uniforms that no one had ever before seen. They marched with determined strides until they were ten feet away from God's Two Witnesses.

The expressions on their faces indicated that they expected a favorable outcome, without being incinerated by fire, which would be a first for anyone challenging them. They steadied their rifles on the Two and awaited the command to fire.

Romanero asked the two enemies of his soul, "Any last words?"

Without a trace of fear on their wrinkled faces, they shouted in unison, "'Now when they have finished their testimony, the beast that comes up from the Abyss will attack them, and overpower and kill them. Their bodies will lie in the public square of the great city—which is figuratively called Sodom and Egypt—where also their Lord was crucified...'"

"Enough!" Romanero hissed, his insides being twisted like sponges being drained of water. He paused a moment so he could collect himself.

Then, with a simple nod of his head, the 12 assassins fired at will. Instead of fire protruding from their mouths, God's Two Olive Trees fell backwards after their bodies were riddled with bullets.

The world remained on edge, not sure if their minds were believing what their eyes had just witnessed.

As the Two Ancients lay motionless in the streets of Jerusalem, two of the sharpshooters checked their pulses. With cameras trained on them, they nodded at Romanero that they were indeed dead.

The *Miracle Maker* declared, "I guess Israel's God chose to remain silent, thus proving His limited power *again* with the whole world watching. Now that they've been silenced once and for all," he said joyously, "we are one giant step closer to achieving our objective, which is nothing short of peace on Earth and goodwill to all who are with me..."

Romanero pointed to the new Temple behind him. "Behold this majestic work of beauty! From the moment I granted the Jews permission to rebuild where the Dome of the Rock had once stood, nothing has ever hampered its progress. I will let nothing stop the Temple from being completed!

"Once that glorious day arrives, which will be very soon, I'll return to Israel to celebrate again! But until then, with those two troublemakers finally silenced for good, I hereby declare the next seven days to be a time of global celebration! So enjoy yourselves wherever you are, knowing we will never hear from them again! May all who are with me be blessed in my name..."

The reaction was immediate—sheer joy and ecstasy, not only for the many spectators crammed into the Wailing Wall vicinity—to include many world leaders who were prompted to go there in advance—but the entire planet erupted in celebration, as they rejoiced over the deaths of the Two troublemakers.

The many who were sent to Israel at Salvador Romanero's behest, just received the shot in the arm that was sorely needed. Many danced in the streets, high fiving one another, hugging and kissing, even exchanging gifts that the *Miracle Maker* had encouraged them to bring with them.

In a world under constant siege, had the Two Witnesses not been killed, many would have become even more skeptical of the *Miracle Maker's* flowery words of peace on earth and goodwill to all who were with him.

Now that he had delivered on this most awesome of promises, the whole world breathed a huge, collective sigh of relief, sensing this would provide the spark that would slowly turn things around.

It was the first time humanity felt the need to celebrate in too long to remember. They wanted to dream again—live again! Their leader just gave them a reason to do just that.

It wouldn't last...

Epilogue

How will Salvador Romanero and his leadership team react when God's Two Witnesses are resurrected, with the whole world watching?

How will his many followers react?

What role will the 144,000 have in it?

Now that Isaac and Tamika have been reconciled, will they have another child together?

Will Hana and Cristiana Patel, and Yasamin Dabiri ever make it to America, or will God's impending judgments prevent it from happening?

What happened to Pastor Jim Simonton? Was he killed in the quake?

Find answers to these questions and so much more as you continue in this prophetic series...

Thanks for taking the time to read the seventh installment of the CHAOS series. I would be most grateful if you shared your thoughts on Amazon. Even a short review would be appreciated. May God continue to bless and keep you.

To contact author for book signings, speaking engagements, or for bulk discounts, email @ patrick12272003@gmail.com.

"But after the three and a half days

the breath of life from God entered them,

and they stood on their feet,

and terror struck those who saw them.

Then they heard a loud voice

from heaven saying to them,

'Come up here.'

And they went up to heaven in a cloud,

while their enemies looked on"

(Revelation 11:7-9).

About the author

Patrick Higgins is an Amazon bestseller and award-winning author of the end times prophetic series, *Chaos In The Blink Of An Eye*. The "CHAOS" in our present world is well documented in this timely series, which won the Radiqx Press Spirit-Filled Fiction Award of Excellence, soon after the first installment was published.

To date, more than 15,000 positive ratings/reviews have been posted on Amazon, Book Bub, and Goodreads, on the first 9 installments...and counting! Once completed, there will be 10 installments.

He also wrote *I Never Knew You,* winner of the 2021 Readers' Favorite Gold Medal in Christian fiction, 2021 Independent Author Network (IAN) book of the year winner in Christian fiction, and Finalist in both the 2022 American Best Book Awards, and the 2021 International Book Awards, *The Unannounced Christmas Visitor*, which won both the International Publishers Awards (IPA) and the 2018 Readers' Favorite Gold Medal Awards in Christian fiction, *The Pelican Trees*, and *Coffee In Manila.*

While the stories he writes all have different themes and take place in different settings, the one thread that links them all together is his heart for Jesus and his yearning for the lost.

With that in mind, it is his wish that the message his stories convey will greatly impact each reader, by challenging you not only to contemplate life on this side of the grave, but on the other side as well. After all, each of us will spend eternity at one of two places, based solely upon a single decision which must be made on this side of the grave. That decision will be made crystal clear to each reader of these books.

Higgins is currently writing many other books, both fiction and non-fiction, including a sequel to *Coffee in Manila,* which will shine a bright, sobering spotlight on the diabolical human trafficking industry.

To contact author: patrick12272003@gmail.com
Like on Facebook: https://www.facebook.com/patrick12272003
https://www.facebook.com/TheUnannouncedChristmasVisitor
Follow on Twitter: https://twitter.com/patrick12272003
Follow on Instagram: @patrick12272003

Looking for an editor?
Contact Susan Axel Bedsaul, the Complete Editor
Excellent Results. Reasonable Rates – complete-editor@outlook.com

www.ingramcontent.com/pod-product-compliance
Lightning Source LLC
Chambersburg PA
CBHW070320260626
47160CB00003B/900